Novels by J.M. Rankin

Darkness Forbidden

Retribution Darkened

Dark Child

Retribution Darkened

J M RANKIN

SCORPIUS BOOKS

Copyright © 2016 by J. M. Rankin

The right of J.M. Rankin to be identified as the Author of the Work has been asserted by her in accordance with the Copyright, Designs and Patents Act 1988.

First Published in Great Britain in 2016 by
J.M. Rankin

This edition published in Great Britain 2020 by
Scorpius Books

Excerpt from *Dark Child* by J.M. Rankin
Copyright © 2016 by J M Rankin

All characters and events in this publication, other than those in the public domain, are fictitious and any resemblance to real persons, living or dead, is purely coincidental.

A catalogue record of this book is available from the British Library.

ISBN 978 1 8380711 2 7

All rights reserved.

No part of this publication may be reproduced, stored in a retrieval system, or transmitted, in any form or by any means, without the prior permission in writing of the publisher, nor be otherwise circulated in any form of binding or cover other than that in which it is published and without a similar condition including this condition being imposed on the subsequent purchaser.

Scorpius Books have made a commitment to reducing their environmental footprint and being good stewards of the planet.

Scorpius Books
www.scorpiusbooks.com

For my family, who put up with all the hours it takes to write and prepare a book...

especially when it takes two years longer than planned!

Then...

A Distant Memory...

Death may be the greatest of all human blessings.

That was Socrates' opinion anyway. No one ever looks at it like that, of course, apart from just a few of us perhaps.

Time can be a dangerous curse.

The darkness engulfs me, the silence overwhelming. I glance at the woman beside me, not even her gentle breathing breaking through the wall of stillness that surrounds us.

Her head rests against the pillow, black hair framing her pale face. I tried so hard to pretend she was another, but it seems my efforts were in vain, for this beauty's eyes are not *Her* eyes, and her face is not the same one I dream about night after night; it is not the one that haunts me.

It's your fault.

The words echo in my mind, tormenting me.

You let them take her from you. You did nothing to stop them.

I can remember her so clearly, her beauty statuesque and not marred by time at all. But that is the exquisiteness of time itself, is it not? Does it not preserve all things in its own way?

I have tried to live without her, God knows I've tried, and for reasons I never want to remember ever again. Yet my need for her draws me back time and time again. I cannot and *will* not let her go.

She is my lover, my life. I am bound to her, as she is to me.

I close my eyes, unable to escape the images that are with me always.

I can still hear her defiant screams as they dragged her away, their punishment for her actions severe and relentless. Her intense green gaze, so filled with hate and rage, fixed on me as I stood by and let them take her.

The memories haunt me still.

I fear they always will.

I do not deserve redemption...

Now...

Chapter I

'What are you doing?'

Aurelia Demeter stood in the doorway of the cellar, staring down the narrow stone staircase to where her daughter stood in the darkness, dutifully tidying boxes.

Nadia seemed oblivious to her elder's presence as she picked up a broom from the corner of the room, raising it above her head to dust away a large cobweb from the ceiling.

A slow, insidious smile crept across her red lips. 'What does it look like I'm doing?' she asked, irritated by the interruption.

She turned to her elder; the light from behind bathed Aurelia in a halo too pure for Nadia's tastes. 'I'm tidying up. There's nothing else to do in this Godforsaken hole,' she sneered, turning away.

Aurelia's gaze darkened as she watched her daughter move around the cellar, sweeping the ceiling and brushing dust from the wine bottles in the large rack that dominated one side of the room.

'It is rather late for a spring clean, don't you think?' Aurelia asked carefully, appraising her daughter's skimpy black dress and high heels; they looked as spotless as they had earlier that evening.

Nadia glared at her elder. 'Like I said, there's nothing else to do.'

Aurelia could feel Nadia's animosity thickening the air, her fears about her daughter's movements tonight growing; she was almost afraid to ask about the fate of the human her daughter had left the house earlier to meet.

'Did Jason get home okay?' she asked gently, her gaze not once leaving her daughter's statuesque face.

Nadia didn't look up as she picked a bottle from the shelf and studied the label. 'My evening was fine, Mother, thank you for asking,' she sneered, sarcasm dripping from every word.

Aurelia didn't rise to it. 'Did Jason get home okay?' she asked again calmly.

Nadia rolled her eyes as she quietly returned the bottle to its original position, brushing her hands free of dust. She glared at the woman at the top of the stairs.

'He's still in one piece,' she hissed, shaking her head, nonchalant. She continued organising the wine bottles that didn't need to be moved. 'Alex even tailed me just to make sure.'

Aurelia frowned, uneasy. 'He did?'

Nadia moved another bottle. 'Yes,' she answered

simply.

Aurelia's gaze narrowed. 'Where is he now?'

'I don't know,' Nadia shrugged. 'He took off and I haven't seen him since.' Still she refused to turn to her elder as she continued bustling around the room.

She remembered with satisfaction how Alex had followed her to the bar earlier, just as she knew he would. He constantly tried to deny his jealousy, but she knew better; she'd witnessed it for far too long. She'd suffered at his hand because of it.

Alex had watched her dance provocatively with Jason, the pathetic human who'd lived his life ruled by his dick rather than his head. Every sensual movement of her dance had been for Alex's benefit, yet Jason had been too stupid to see it.

Nadia's smile widened as her arousal writhed. Poor Jason; he'd been a lot of fun until the end.

Her smile vanished as she remembered how Alex had disappeared from the crowd during her dance, seemingly unaffected by her efforts. She'd assumed he'd returned home, but had been disappointed by his absence.

Her anger writhed; where *was* he?

'You just could not let him be, could you?' Aurelia said gently. There was no anger or accusation in her voice, only disappointment.

Finally, Nadia glanced up, meeting her mother's gaze with a glare filled with animosity. A slow smile crept across her lips.

'I'm sure I don't know what you mean, Mother,'

she whispered, her tone mocking.

Aurelia maintained her daughter's stare, unwilling to be drawn into Nadia's dark games.

'You could not leave Alex be,' she stated flatly.

Nadia sneered as she looked away. 'He came to me willingly,' she hissed, ignoring her mother.

Aurelia sighed wearily as her daughter approached the stone steps. 'No one comes to you willingly, child,' she pointed out sadly.

'Alex did,' Nadia spat angrily.

Aurelia leant against the doorframe, thinking back over so many years shrouded in darkness. 'How I wish I had done things differently,' she said, her words filled with desolation.

Nadia snorted, her emerald eyes dark. 'What would you have changed, Mother?' she asked sarcastically. 'Would you have refused Alex's request to have me released from that fetid pit of a prison? Would you have stopped the Others from locking me away in the first place?'

She stared at her elder, her gaze darkening.

Aurelia didn't answer.

Nadia sneered. 'I didn't think so.'

Aurelia shook her head. 'You dragged him into your games... into your delusions, over and over.'

Nadia laughed, the sound empty and cold; it matched the hostility in her eyes. 'I didn't drag him into anything,' she hissed. 'He was always more than willing to partake for his own ends, or have you forgotten that?'

RETRIBUTION DARKENED

She climbed up several of the old stone stairs towards her elder, her green eyes vindictive. 'Think back, Mother dearest. Was he so innocent in all that happened?' she asked, venom in her words. 'I think not. Alex's hands are just as tainted as mine, if not more so.'

Aurelia maintained her daughter's gaze, unwilling to back down. 'You both could have been so happy,' she murmured, defeated by memories of the past.

Nadia's gaze narrowed. 'We *are* happy, with *each other*,' she hissed, gripping her mother's arm viciously.

Aurelia tried to pull away, her efforts in vain; despite being nearly twice her daughter's age, Nadia's strength far surpassed her own, as did Alex's.

'Alex is *mine*,' Nadia spat, her green eyes blazing with rage. 'You'd do well to remember that, Mother dear,' she sneered.

Releasing her mother's arm, Nadia pushed Aurelia aside and walked away into the house.

Chapter 2

The silence filling the air around him was terrifying.

Alex Demeter sat on the ice-cold ground at the side of the narrow country road, his hands shaking as he gripped them in his lap.

The darkness felt all too consuming as the dense forest around him cast its eerie shadows over the horrifying scene before him.

Time seemed to stop as he stared at the lifeless body of Catrina Holmes, battered almost beyond recognition after the fatal accident. His gaze settled on the abandoned Range Rover further up the narrow country lane, his stomach wrenching as he thought of the pain the joyriders had inflicted with their stolen vehicle before cowardly running away, leaving Catrina to suffer horrendously.

No, that was your doing. His own thoughts mocked him as he stared at her; beneath the cuts and blood her skin was deathly pale, her blue eyes wide open and staring at nothing. Her pelvis was shattered, her left leg positioned at an unnatural angle.

RETRIBUTION DARKENED

You killed the one woman you've ever loved, his thoughts mocked once more, his gut churning. It was his fault she'd been hit by the car; he'd scared her with his telling of his kind, and she'd fled from him.

He hadn't intended it to end like this; she'd begged for his help after the accident, and the thought of losing her had driven him to offer it in the only form he had. He'd fed her his blood, and to what end?

He wiped a tear from his eye; he'd lost her, causing her unspeakable suffering before she'd drawn her last breath.

He gently closed her eyes with his trembling fingers, their tips brushing through the blood on her face; *his* blood, mixed with the blood she'd coughed up in her last choking breaths.

Forcing his gaze away from her lifeless body, the guilt overwhelmed him as he choked back a sob.

What in God's name had he done?

He could picture Nadia all too easily, her mocking smile and gleaming emerald eyes; she'd been waiting for this moment, for him to fail in her pathetic wager that would have seen him seduce this woman before killing her.

It had stopped being a game to him as he'd slowly fallen for Catrina, her kindness and gentle nature breaking through the darkness that had dominated him for far too long. Yet his love for this human had only made Nadia more determined to see him end Catrina's life, if only to sedate her own insane jealousy.

Nadia would be immensely proud to learn of the girl's demise.

Alex shuddered.

He glanced back to look at Catrina.

Even though she was gone, he couldn't bring himself to leave her side; he couldn't leave her here at the edge of the road like this, and his mind was too full of chaotic thoughts to consider how to deal with her body.

He tentatively touched his fingertips to her matted, bloodied blonde hair, his thumb stroking across her forehead. She still felt warm.

'I'm so sorry,' he whispered, emotion raw in his throat as he tried in vain to hold back the tears. 'I tried.'

He stroked her hair again.

Her eyes snapped open.

Chapter 3

'Fuck!'

Alex scrambled away from Catrina's side, his back hitting a nearby tree. Panic swept over him.

Catrina gasped loudly as if breathing for the first time. Her back arched on the ground as her body stretched upwards, a strange unnatural groan escaping her lips.

She held her position for several moments before her body collapsed back to the cold ground, still once more.

Alex stared at her in amazement, unable to comprehend what he'd just seen, yet unable to deny it nonetheless.

Taking a deep breath, he tried to steady his nerves as he half-crawled towards her, his hands shaking.

He'd thought she was dead; he thought he'd killed her.

He stared into her eyes as he knelt beside her, her ice-blue gaze seeking his.

She was shivering, her body becoming accustomed to its un-dead state. Her lips quivered and between them he could see her sharp incisors.

He cupped the top of her head in his hand, supporting her as she continued to stare at him.

Alex watched, enthralled, as the cuts and lacerations to her body slowly healed one by one, leaving only the smears of blood across her unblemished skin. The broken bones grotesquely snapped back into place as the immortal blood within her veins repaired the imperfections it found along its journey.

She groaned with discomfort, but not pain.

He took hold of her hand, threading his fingers through hers and squeezing gently, thankful to feel her renewed strength as she gripped his hand in return.

The icy wind howled down the narrow country road, the darkness of the night enveloping them both as Alex cradled Catrina's head in his hand.

He leaned forward, brushing a tender kiss against her forehead.

'Thank God,' he whispered against her skin, raw emotion breaking into his voice. His heart pounded. This felt like a dream; he was terrified he'd wake any second and find her still dead by the side of the road.

The gentle squeeze of her hand confirmed this was all real.

'I thought I'd lost you,' he breathed, staring into her eyes.

RETRIBUTION DARKENED

She managed a small smile, her sharp incisors glistening with the remains of his blood. 'I thought you had, too,' she whispered, her voice weak and rough. 'I was so scared.'

A tear escaped the corner of her eye and he tenderly wiped it away.

'I know,' he soothed.

She shuddered and tried to move, the effort miniscule but nonetheless difficult.

'Stay where you are, my love,' he whispered. 'Let your body recover.'

She stared at him hard. 'It hurt so much,' she admitted. 'I couldn't see. It all went so dark.'

'Your human body was dying,' he said gently. 'I wasn't sure I'd helped you in time. I thought I was too late.'

She stared up at the sky above for a few seconds before forcing herself to move, propping herself up on her forearms.

The ground was ice cold beneath her skin and yet strangely she felt none of the discomfort. Every movement felt odd, her muscles moving almost before she needed to think about it. She felt like her old self and yet completely new all at the same time.

She looked around her; every leaf and branch of every tree stood out sharply against the deep blue of the night sky; every wisp of cloud curled in the air; every star burned brightly; the breeze whispered to her like a gentle voice. She could hear every movement of every creature in the undergrowth. It was as if she were seeing the world for the first time and she felt nothing but awe at the visions before her.

As she gazed around in wonder, a strange, faint buzzing filled her ears. She shook her head, trying to dispel it.

Alex reached out, cupping her face in his hand. 'Are you okay?' he asked tenderly.

The sound faded slightly, but still it persisted like the gentle hum of a bee. She forced herself to ignore it, smiling up at him.

'I'm fine,' she confirmed, staring at him as if seeing him for the first time. His green eyes seemed more intense than ever, his gentle smile supported by his strong jaw. Every dark hair on his head looked like it had been painted with the blackest of ink. His muscular body, hunkered down next to her, was perfectly suited to his expensive leather jacket. She felt her arousal flare, the sensation more intense than it had ever been; it startled her.

Slowly, she attempted to stand. Alex grabbed her arms in support, knowing she had the strength to do it herself but wanting to help her nonetheless; he wanted to feel the power in her body.

As she found her feet, the world started spinning and she would have lost her footing were it not for Alex's hold.

'Careful,' he said with a smile, righting her. 'Your strength is still returning. It will take time.'

Catrina stared up at him, the buzzing still persisting in her ears. 'Will that buzzing noise go with it?' she asked, shaking her head to no avail.

A gentle smile played along Alex's lips as he brushed a strand of her hair from her face. 'It will,' he assured her, his fingers trailing down her cheek. 'It's your hunger, my love,' he said carefully, trying to gauge her response.

'Oh,' she said flatly, unable to find anything else to say. It was the most obvious part of her new nature, yet one that had not occurred to her until now. She wasn't sure how she felt about it, but was greatly aware the idea didn't repel her as much as she would have thought.

Alex cupped her chin in his hand, studying every part of her face, needing to know she truly was okay; he needed to know she really was here with him.

'I'm so glad you're okay,' he whispered, his voice filled with relief. He pulled her to him, holding her tightly.

She wrapped her arms around him, feeling his body against hers and wanting him with a severity that scared her. She'd been beyond terrified in those final moments before death had finally taken her. She'd woken from that death as if waking from sleep, yet the world was completely different to her now; it scared and excited her all at once.

She twitched against him as the buzzing persisted in her head, aggravating her more and more, like a mosquito that wouldn't desist in its assault.

He pulled her at arm's length and stared down

at her with that same tender look that had her feeling like the most important woman in the world. There was amusement in his smile and she couldn't help but laugh.

'Don't tease me,' she pouted playfully, knowing how aware he was of her hunger.

He stroked her cheek with his finger. 'I don't mean to,' he assured tenderly.

She shook her head, trying to get rid of the annoying noise. 'Is it always like this?' she asked, perturbed.

Alex smiled. 'No. It's only because your body is renewing itself. Your strength may have returned, but you still need to feast before that renewal is complete.'

Catrina noted how he didn't use the word "blood", though she knew that was exactly what he meant; her body needed blood to fully heal itself and she was grateful for his subtlety while she accustomed herself to her new nature.

She glanced around her, saddened by the scene of the abandoned car that had been the cause of all the events of the evening. Blood stained the ground beneath her feet and she stared at it, strangely detached.

Alex frowned, concerned. 'Are you okay?' he asked gently, aware of her distraction.

She continued to gaze at the ground, her mind a myriad of thoughts. 'I died tonight,' she said softly, the realisation hitting her suddenly through the haze of excitement and contentment of being close to Alex; she'd died, leaving those she loved in a world she could never truly be part of again.

With the slightest trepidation, he cupped her cheek in his hand, gently forcing her to look at him. Her eyes were filled with sadness; it scared him.

He wasn't sure he knew what to say.

She stood there, looking up at him, easily able to see the torment in his eyes. 'I died and you saved me,' she said softly, unwilling to see that lost look on his face any longer. Yes, she was scared, petrified even, but in those final throes of darkness and pain she'd been even more scared of dying. She'd felt her heart stop, her lungs unable to take in more air, her body broken and burning with unimaginable pain; yet after that, there had been nothing but peace and serenity. She'd been aware of being alive, yet unable to move, as if her body had no longer belonged to her and she was somewhere else.

Alex watched the varied emotions cross her face; they were subtle but there nonetheless. 'You are still you,' he assured, knowing that somewhere among her myriad of thoughts there would be the one that questioned if she was still the same person; if the Catrina Holmes who stood here now was the same one who had died only minutes before.

'Am I?' she asked quietly. She felt like herself, albeit far stronger, and yet... she'd died. Could she really be the same person?

He brushed a strand of bloody blonde hair

away from her face tenderly, anxious to quell her fears. 'You are no less who you were a few hours ago,' he whispered, brushing a kiss against her forehead. 'I know you are scared, even if you do try and hide it,' he smiled, 'but please trust me.'

'I do,' she said. 'But you said as much yourself when you were trying to talk me out of it... you said I wouldn't be the same.'

He remembered back to that almost unbelievable moment when the balance of her life had rested solely in his hands. He smiled down at her.

'Actually, I said you wouldn't be like me, which you are not. I can only venture into daylight because I was born the way I am. *You* are now restricted to the night hours. Your day has become night.'

'So I'm not me,' she said flatly, not seeing his point.

Alex sighed. 'My love, I need you to understand. Your nature has changed, yes, but *you*, in terms of your thoughts, your feelings, your kindness... everything about you that I fell in love with is still intact.' He took her hands in his, squeezing them gently. 'I promise.'

His assurance, along with his smile and tender gaze made her relax enough to think about what he'd said. Her thoughts were all over the place, but she knew they would settle with time. If she took a moment to really focus through the cacophony in her head, she could *feel* she was the same. Thoughts of her friends, the only real family she had were as warm as they ever had been; she couldn't wait to see them all.

Echoes of her past relationships still felt as disturbing as ever, though just as before the sting of their pain was dwindling thanks to Alex. Then there was the love and attraction she felt for Alex himself, which if anything felt stronger than it ever had before.

The incessant buzzing in her ears reminded her that, as Alex had said, her nature was one thing that *had* changed and the thought wasn't as disturbing as she may have feared.

When she'd first discovered Alex's true nature, she hadn't been able to process the information, something he'd later told her was purely natural considering the human race didn't believe in such things as vampires. He'd told her that many humans had literally gone mad after discovering the truth about the world around them and he'd feared the same would happen to her; she'd certainly felt like she was losing her mind.

She'd called him a monster and a murderer; now she would walk the earth, taking lives in order to sustain her own and that knowledge didn't disgust her at all. It scared her to the core, but that was only because it was all so new.

'I believe you,' she whispered with a smile. 'I'm sorry.'

'Don't be,' he said gently. 'Your head will be a little fuzzy and confused to begin with. Your new nature is overtaking your old one. It's natural to feel a little bit out of sync.'

The buzzing in her head flared again, louder

this time, demanding her attention and she winced; it didn't hurt, but took her by surprise with its severity.

Alex smiled down at her. 'It's getting worse,' he said, more as a statement than a question.

She nodded.

He chuckled as he held her close. 'Then maybe we should do something to satisfy that new-found hunger of yours,' he smiled, his words gentle.

The idea of actually satisfying her new thirst for blood filled her with a dread matched only by her excitement at the prospect. It was a divide within her own self which she found strangely compelling.

Knowing Alex was right, she took a deep breath to steady her nerves. 'Okay, let's go.'

Chapter 4

The longer they searched for an appropriate victim the more nervous Catrina felt. She began to grow agitated, restless.

Alex looked at her and squeezed her hand in support. 'You can feel it, can't you?' he asked, his voice rough and edgy. 'You can sense it.'

She nodded when she realised his words were true; she *could* sense it... the hunt. Every nerve in her body felt on edge, every muscle poised for the attack; her heart pounded in her chest so loud she was sure every potential victim would hear it.

'It's all right,' he soothed quietly, smiling at her. 'The nerves won't last. It's only because this is so new to you. Because it's your first time.'

She managed a small smile in return, the buzzing in her head persisting as her nerves grew.

He sensed her disquiet. 'Hey, you'll be all right,' he assured.

Catrina nodded. 'I know,' she whispered; she knew he'd guide her through this, making sure she was never uncomfortable at any time.

With another comforting smile, Alex led the way along the dark and empty streets of Wiltham.

She watched him as he gazed along gloomy roads and alleyways, making eye contact with strangers as they passed, trying to find an easy target for her first kill.

Minutes ticked by, each one feeling like an eternity in the cold darkness of the early hours. The main town of Wiltham was still relatively busy as the bars slowly emptied, giggling women and singing men wandering along the streets, making their wobbly way home.

Alex turned onto a quieter street and Catrina followed, the excitement within stirring; the scent of the hunt flooded over her and where Alex went she felt compelled to follow.

After a few hundred yards, he slowed his pace and she was able to see that he was following a couple of women, laughing as they chatted on their way home. They strolled along, not drunk but clearly not completely sober, either; the scent of alcohol travelled on the air behind them.

They were too occupied with their own jokes and laughter to notice the two people behind them. Even if they had spotted the pair, the women would have seen nothing more than a couple making their way home hand in hand.

The two women turned onto another street, leading Alex and Catrina down a dark and quiet lane that ran along the back of the large square where the Wiltham Market usually took place. The ground was littered with all sorts of rubbish left over from the Saturday Market day and boxes and crates were piled up, ready for the rubbish collection during the week.

At the end of the street, the two women stopped, continuing to giggle and joke about their evening.

Alex and Catrina paused, their presence masked by the shadows around them. They watched silently as the two women kissed each other on the cheek and headed their separate ways.

One woman turned onto the next street along, the busy main road with its numerous bars and takeaway shops eliminating her as an option.

The other young woman continued to the right, along another darkened road that narrowed as it headed towards the back of a nearby housing estate.

Alex squeezed Catrina's hand as he led her onwards.

She looked at him, mystified. 'How did you know they would separate?' she asked quietly, the thrill of the hunt burning in her veins, her senses heightened and every muscle in her body poised for the final attack. 'They might have been going to the same place,' she added.

He looked round at her and grinned. 'You'll learn to anticipate such things,' he coached gently. 'Call it a sixth sense if you like,' he added, his grin growing wider. 'But reading their thoughts always helps, too.' He laughed as she playfully slapped his arm.

They continued along the road behind the woman until the pavement narrowed and turned onto an open area surrounded by old garages, many of them disused and vandalised.

For the first time, the woman looked around her as if unnerved.

A strange yet powerful scent filled the air and it flooded Catrina's senses, the buzzing in her ears growing louder until she was unsure how much longer she could stand it. Somehow, something deep inside – an instinct almost – told her it was the scent of fear. It aroused her new unnatural appetite even further.

The shadows still concealed the two hunters; the woman, satisfied she was alone, continued on her way.

Alex stopped Catrina in her tracks and released her hand. He turned to her, his emerald eyes dark in the shadows yet filled with something she couldn't quite define; it might have been excitement, mischief, anticipation, or something completely different.

'Wait here,' he whispered.

Panic and worry suddenly engulfed her. 'You're not leaving me here?' she asked, staring at the woman over Alex's shoulder. 'What do I do?' She was aware that her voice, although quiet, was filled with panic.

He smiled, brushing her hair from her face tenderly. 'You'll know,' he said simply. 'Follow your instincts, my love.' He brushed a kiss against her lips before turning away, disappearing into the shadows beyond the garages.

Catrina took a deep breath as she pursued the woman slowly, keeping her in sight yet maintaining her distance, the shadows continuing to conceal her silent presence; she was surprised at her new ability to pass almost unnoticed by the world around her, as if the darkness itself encased her in a shroud.

The woman turned to glance behind her again and Catrina saw the disquiet etched on her face.

When the woman turned away, she crashed straight into Alex, and Catrina was reminded of the first time she'd met him in Wiltham Park; just like tonight, he'd seemingly come from nowhere, nearly knocking her over and catching her just in time.

Just like that day, Alex helped the woman to right herself.

'I'm so sorry, I didn't see you,' he said softly, his tone genuine and in no way intimidating or threatening.

The woman's insecurity sent Catrina's thirst to fever pitch as she watched on, the buzzing in her ears being met with a soft thumping noise she quickly realised was the woman's heartbeat.

'No harm done,' the woman said, her words slightly slurred as she adjusted her bag on her shoulder.

Catrina became oblivious to anything Alex said to the woman as she watched from the shadows. She heard nothing but the soft rhythm of the human heartbeat, instantly mystified by how sultry and tempting it was.

A new and intense thirst flooded through her body, making every inch of her skin tingle. Her hunger writhed as if she hadn't eaten in days and the buzzing in her head became almost deafening; it all became too much to bear.

Her gaze settled on the woman's throat and locked, like a wild cat with its prey.

Alex moved aside, giving her a silent invitation.

Driven by a force that seemed almost detached from her own body, Catrina left the sanctuary of the shadows and raced at the woman from behind, overpowered by her own need for blood. Nothing else registered.

With a strength that felt too natural to be new, she easily overpowered the woman. Holding her close and covering the woman's mouth with her hand, Catrina bit into the soft flesh of the stranger's throat; her muffled cries of pain and fear lasted merely seconds.

As the thick hot liquid filled her mouth, Catrina knew she should be reviled by what she was doing; she was drinking human blood, and enjoying it. Yet the exquisite taste as it filled her mouth and coated her tongue eradicated any other thought beyond the natural necessity to quench her thirst and hunger. If she'd felt stronger before the kill, she felt invincible now; every nerve in her body felt like it was firing up for the first time, every part of her being tingled with excitement, her senses heightened beyond the unnatural to their full potential.

Although Alex wasn't in her field of vision, she knew he was watching; she could sense the smile that ran across his lips. He was pleased with her, proud of her. He was also incredibly aroused by what he was witnessing and that knowledge only increased her own desire, with the blood of her first kill intensifying that basic of all instincts.

The woman went limp in Catrina's arms; within moments she would die. Catrina slowly lowered the body to the ground.

She stared at the woman's corpse for a moment, a multitude of feelings flooding through her, her mind a cacophony.

Alex was by her side in a moment. 'I'll hide her,' he said gently, picking the woman up in his arms.

Catrina watched him walk off into the darkness and waited several minutes before he returned from the shadows.

Smiling at her, he brushed a streak of blood from her lips with his thumb.

'That was pretty good,' he commended, feeling her tremble beneath his touch; he couldn't deny he'd found himself incredibly aroused watching her feed. 'Hardly a drop spilt.'

She chuckled, embarrassed. 'I didn't think I'd find it so easy,' she admitted.

'How do you feel?' he asked gently.

'Like I should hate myself for taking a life,' she

said quietly, looking down at the ground.

Alex's expression darkened with concern. 'Like you're a monster?' he asked, remembering the way she'd looked at him before her accident.

Catrina looked up at him then. 'I shouldn't have called you that,' she said firmly.

He smiled gently. 'Your instincts have changed, my love,' he said tenderly. 'What you would never have considered as a human is now a natural process. You won't feel guilt over taking a life like you would as a human.'

She smiled coyly. 'Like I said, I should never have called you a monster. I couldn't understand what you were trying to tell me.'

He brushed her hair from her face, ignoring the matted blood in its lengths. 'It doesn't matter now,' he said softly, trailing his fingers down her cheek. He felt her tremble beneath his touch, her blue eyes seeking his.

Her lips parted as if she were about to say something, but she remained silent.

He swallowed past the lump of emotion in his throat as he trailed his thumb across her lips.

Her intense gaze maintained his.

It was suddenly all he could think of; to have now what he'd wanted the night he'd taken her to dinner. He needed to see the want and need in her eyes once again, knowing that this time nothing could stop him from taking what he wanted. He didn't need to hold back for her own safety; he could finally show her just how much he wanted and needed her, too.

He took her face in his hands, covering her mouth with his in the deep kiss he'd been forced to hold back so many times.

She made a hungry sound deep in her throat and in seconds the kiss exploded in passion and heat.

She groaned as his hands trailed down her body, pulling her against him tighter.

She wrapped her arms around his neck, pulling him closer as his mouth ate at hers.

He blindly pushed her against the nearest wall, running his hands down her thighs as he lifted her, groaning into her mouth as she wrapped her legs around him.

'Wait.' He ripped his mouth from hers, struggling for breath. She was panting, too, and the sound made him want to rip her clothes off right here, right now.

But here was not the place; he wanted to take his time and pleasure her like he'd wanted to for so damn long. He didn't want their first time to be in the dirty backstreets of London.

He looked down at her, noting the uncertainty in her eyes. He brushed a kiss against her lips. 'Not here, not like this,' he breathed.

He let her legs slide back down his body, but she didn't drop her gaze from his, her need intense.

He stared at her, his heart racing. He ran his thumb over her lips once more, feeling her tremble, sending his arousal to fever pitch.

'Let's get the fuck out of here.'

Chapter 5

Just like the night of their dinner, they travelled back to Catrina's place in silence, every second taking the tension and heat between them higher.

Alex's hands shook as they gripped the steering wheel. He dared a glance across at her.

She stared at him, that same hunger in her eyes from before.

He forced himself to swallow past the lump that appeared in his throat, returning his gaze reluctantly to the road ahead.

He steered the car onto her street, sensing her shift in her seat; she was nervous and the scent caused his arousal to flare until he thought he'd lose it before they even reached the front door.

He pulled up outside her house, killing the engine.

Another beat of silence passed between them before Catrina, still staring at him, grabbed her bag from the footwell and opened the car door.

Breaking his gaze for the first time, she climbed

from the car, her hands shaking as she rummaged in her bag for her keys. She heard Alex slam his door closed and heard his footsteps as he approached behind her.

She found her keys and pulled them from her bag as Alex pressed his body against hers, his hands bracketing her hips. His breath was hot against her neck as he kissed her skin, making her tremble with anticipation.

He watched as she found the lock with shaking hands and managed to open the door. Her uncertainty only took his excitement higher; he'd practiced self-control for far too long.

Once inside, he pushed the door closed behind them and then turned her so she looked up at him.

His emerald eyes were intense, setting off tingles through her body as her arousal flared, stronger than she'd ever known it as a human. She dropped her bag and keys to the floor.

Catrina drew a ragged breath as his mouth covered hers. She wrapped her arms around his neck, giving in to the sensations of his body against hers. His hands slid down around her ribs, barely touching her breasts.

She was trembling and Alex pushed her back gently against the wall of the hallway, his body pressed against hers so she could feel how much he needed her.

He took her head in his hands, his fingers buried in her hair as he kissed her, a low groan that sounded like her name rumbling deep in his throat.

Pulling back, he stared at her with a carnal craving that made her tremble.

Still maintaining his gaze, she tugged at his shirt until she pulled it free from his waistband. With trembling fingers, she loosened the buttons up the front. Finally she had access to the body she'd imagined so many times in fantasies that had no comparison to having him in her arms now. She bit her lower lip with anticipation as she fanned her fingers across his skin, feeling every flex and muscle as he shivered beneath her touch.

He kissed her softly, groaning as she pushed her body against his, teasing him. His excitement heightened as her fingers dug into his shoulders.

He shrugged out of his shirt as Catrina pulled off her blue jumper, the woollen material ripped and heavily bloodied after her ordeal. She dropped it to the floor, ignoring her blood-stained skin.

He pushed her back against the wall, kissing her with desperate ferocity as he pulled her bra straps off her shoulders. He twisted and ripped at the material, finally freeing her breasts and filling his hands with them, his palms brushing her nipples.

She breathed his name as he trailed kisses across her throat, pushing her tattered jeans and knickers over her hips and kicking them away.

She stood before him, naked and perfect, despite the dried blood smearing her porcelain skin.

He stared at her with complete adoration, his

green eyes filled with an intensity that aroused her and frightened her all at the same time.

As he kissed her, she gripped his shoulders and pulled herself up, twining her legs around his waist.

His pulse rocketed and he yanked at his belt desperately, his knuckles caressing her hot wet warmth as he pulled and twisted, making her moan. He dropped his trousers, pushed her against the wall and thrust as hard as he could.

Finally, her body surrounded him, pulling him deeper into their shared passion, his need for her driving him insane.

She cried out with pleasured gasps as he thrust against her, her blue eyes filled with need as she stared at him intently.

She gripped his shoulders feverishly as he dug his fingers into her hips, pulling her against him again and again, giving in to the beast that roared inside his head.

Her body arched and she cried out once more as she came, gripping him harder and dragging him with her.

He plunged a final time, the pleasure like a rock to his head as he cried out her name. He slumped against her, pressing her into the wall. His lungs burned as he gasped for air, knowing he had to have her again, and again.

He pulled back to see her face. She was panting as she grinned playfully.

Gently, he released her and she slid back to her

feet. He passed his hand across the crown of her head and kissed her tenderly, thanking whatever God or fate had led him to this amazing woman.

His past didn't matter anymore; he could no longer imagine a future without her in it.

She now completely possessed him. She was in his blood. She *shared* his blood, and he silently vowed never to let her go.

Chapter 6

'Hi, it's Jason. I'm probably having way too much fun to answer right now, but if you leave a message...'

Lola Freeman cursed in the darkness of her bedroom as she ended the fifth attempted call to Jason's voicemail.

She knew it was the early hours and she had no right trying to disturb him after what had no doubt been a very good night with Nadia Demeter, but she needed to talk to someone; after the previous day's events she knew her partner, Matt, sure as hell wasn't prepared to listen.

She shivered as she sat huddled on her bed, pulling the sheets around her to stave off the cold. She ran her fingers through her auburn hair that was still damp with sweat.

It had been the same dream again tonight.

Tears fell unchecked down her face. Her hopelessness increased every night, every time she saw those glaring red eyes in her sleep. It had grown slowly out of control over the last few weeks, until it had consumed her. She feared sleep, knowing what she would see once her eyes were closed.

Over the last few nights, she'd even tried to stay awake for as long as possible, hoping to avoid what she knew would come; at the very least she hoped exhaustion would render her sleep dreamless.

Yet her optimism was wasted and she found herself deep in the same nightmare night after night, waking in cold sweats.

She was completely exhausted. The rest of her life was beginning to suffer as a result; she had no energy at work, her duties as a veterinary nurse being the main victim of her exhaustion, for which she'd already received a verbal warning. She found herself increasingly afraid of the dark, a phobia she ridiculed herself for, and she knew she was alienating her partner, Matt, more and more; she couldn't remember the last time they'd enjoyed any quality time together, her days filled with fear and anxiety.

She thought of phoning him now yet she couldn't bring herself to press the call button. She'd pushed him away too many times of late to be able to turn to him now; even yesterday she'd only wanted to speak to her cousin, Jason, after seeing those terrifying red eyes once more, glaring at her from the shadows of the local market. She'd refused to let Matt anywhere near her.

She knew he was angry at her rejection and deep down she couldn't blame him; she was angry with herself for not finding a way through this, if there was a way at all.

There was always the terrifying anxiety in the back of her thoughts that she was simply losing her mind and there was no help to be had.

A sob escaped her in the darkness as she rested her head on her knees.

When she'd confessed to Jason the previous day of being haunted by the same red eyes she'd seen thirteen years ago in the house which now belonged to the Demeter's, he'd looked at her like she was crazy, solidifying her fears.

Her confession had also featured the strange word she'd heard constantly in her dreams since seeing it in a book in the town library; Vrolok. He hadn't known what to say when she'd revealed it was a Slavic word for vampire.

Lola's stomach wrenched in knots as she recalled every experience and dream that had dragged her to this point, where she sat huddled in the darkness, cold and terrified.

She tried to call Jason once more, the call going straight to voicemail.

Ending the call, she sighed wearily.

The images from her dream flashed through her mind over and over, occasionally making her flinch with their severity. There was no way she'd be able to sleep now and she dreaded the onset of another day full of exhaustion and fear.

Dread seized her as she heard the gentle tap at her window, just like she heard every night after waking from the dream.

The sheer terror of knowing what she would see outside seemed to freeze her blood in her veins, her body refusing to move.

She'd sat many times hoping the sound would disappear; that if she ignored it, she could somehow break the terrifying repetition.

It never worked.

The tapping sounded once more, almost with impatience, demanding her attention.

With a deep breath, tears running down her cheeks, she gripped the edge of the curtain, pulling it back in a sharp jerk of her arm, refusing to look at the glass or the darkness outside.

The tap sounded again, louder, making her flinch.

'Go away,' she said to herself quietly, her eyes closed, pulling her knees to her chest and wrapping her arms around them. 'Go away, please.'

Her tears continued to flow, her body shaking through a combination of fear and cold. She rocked back and forth, the motion oddly comforting.

Huddled on the bed, the minutes ticked by.

No sound came from outside.

After what felt like forever, but could only have been several minutes in reality, she glanced up, tentatively looking towards the window.

There was nothing there.

Wiping the tears from her cheeks, she shuffled across the bed, peering at the glass.

RETRITUTION DARKENED

There was nothing on her windowsill, as there had been so many times after her dreams.

Releasing a breath of relief, she almost smiled, a small glimmer of hope rising within her that she had finally chased away her demons in whatever form they chose to take.

Standing from the bed, she leaned against the windowsill, staring out into the blackness of the night as if to prove to herself that she no longer needed to be afraid.

Her heart sank and she choked on a sob as she stared out into the night.

The large black crow stood on the doorstep of the Demeter household across the street, having left its perch on her windowsill. Half hidden in the shadows, it stood forebodingly as if on guard.

Lola's tears fell freely as she stared at the bird that tormented her night after night.

The crow glared at her, its gaze mocking as always.

Chapter 7

Catrina fell back on the pillow, her breath coming in sharp gasps.

She turned her head to look at Alex. He looked as exhausted as she felt, but the smile on his face was unmistakable; childishly, she felt proud of herself for putting it there.

Reaching over to the bedside cabinet, she flicked on the light.

Alex glanced over, his gaze tender. Reaching out, he pulled her close.

She rested her head against his shoulder, his arms cradling her against him. She felt incredibly content and filled with a peace she'd never really known.

Alex planted a kiss against her hair. 'Any regrets?' he asked, his words tentative.

'Not at all,' she grinned, stroking her fingers along the contours of his chest.

He chuckled lightly, but his voice was serious. 'You know what I mean,' he murmured. 'A lot has happened tonight.'

She looked up at him then, rolling onto her front. 'You saved my life,' she said firmly. 'Despite everything, you put your worries aside to save me. How can I regret that?'

He rolled onto his side, running his fingers from her shoulder, along the curve of her back to her hips, smiling as she pushed her body against his, needing him once more.

'I couldn't lose you,' he whispered, staring at her. When he spoke again, both his face and his voice filled with sadness. 'Five hundred years is a long time to be lonely.'

Catrina took his hand, threading her fingers through his. She thought on her own past; it was one she wished could be erased, yet knew it was nothing compared to what Alex must have seen over the centuries.

'At least you had your family,' she soothed. 'You and Nadia are lucky to be so close.'

Instantly uncomfortable, Alex stiffened, grateful when Catrina didn't seem to notice. 'Well, Nadia's not the easiest person to get on with,' he admitted, forcing a smile. 'We've gone for long periods of time without speaking,' he added, not comfortable talking about his sister on such an important night.

'What was the longest?' she asked, interested by a life that must have seen so much.

He knew her curiosity was natural; she had no conception of what she was really delving into. He hoped she'd never know.

'It's difficult to say, really,' he lied, unwilling to divulge the truth; it was a can of worms that needed to stay closed. 'She travelled the world once for nearly twenty years back in the eighteenth century. She wrote home, but I didn't see her in all that time.'

'And the other times?' she asked, unaware of his discomfort.

His example had been the only safe one he was willing to give; other times had been for very different and tragic reasons.

He cleared his throat. 'Varying reasons,' he murmured, trying to find a way to change the subject. 'As I said, Nadia can be difficult at the best of times. A few centuries together can make anyone a little temperamental.' He leaned in and kissed her gently, hating himself for using it as an attempt to turn Catrina's attentions away from Nadia. Tonight was a special occasion and he couldn't stand it to be defiled by talk or thoughts of his sister.

She smiled as Alex traced his fingers delicately along the curve of her spine, his gaze taking in every feature of her immaculate skin.

'Do you miss your home?' she asked carefully. 'You know... Romania, where you grew up.'

He nodded, still watching the trail of his fingers along her skin. 'It's hard not to,' he admitted. 'It is my true home. It's in my blood.' He looked at her with a soft smile. 'I will take you there one day. You will adore it.'

'What's it like?' she asked, curious.

'Transylvania? Even now it resembles in many ways a fairy-tale picture book, with medieval villages and vast forests. There are places there that have barely developed in centuries and still use horse and carts.' Alex thought on his homeland, missing it yet fearing it all at once; he adored his childhood home and yet so much had happened there over the years it was mired in tragedy and pain.

'What about the rest of your family?' she questioned softly, smiling as his fingers brushed her waist, tickling her skin.

Alex chuckled as he thought on his many relatives. 'I guess the downside to being immortal is that the list of relatives simply grows and grows.' He winked at her. 'My elders,' he shrugged, 'the Others, reside mainly within Vallakia in the Carpathian Mountains.'

'Vallakia?' she asked, aware she may not have said the word correctly, yet Alex simply smiled, offering no indication either way.

'It is an ancient castle, nestled deep in the mountains of Transylvania. Over the centuries, my family have extended it many times. It currently belongs to Vlad, the eldest of our bloodline. He looks after it, maintains it. Vallakia has always been a sanctuary for the Demeter family.'

'A sanctuary?' she queried with a frown, mystified by this new world she faced.

Alex nodded. 'Naturally my family travels, a lot.

Immortality is far too long to spend in one place for any real length of time, yet Vallakia is the one place we all return to eventually, whether it just be for family, companionship, guidance or solace. Vallakia has never been modernised, so it is completely removed from the outside world. It's comforting to know that it is always there.'

She was touched by how warmly he spoke of his family and their sanctuary; she found herself eager to visit. 'Do many live there?'

He shook his head. 'Not any longer. Vlad and Gabriella are the only two permanent residents.'

'Gabriella?'

'My ancient grandmother. She was married to Vlad's brother, Ladislas. He died, many centuries ago in a tragic fire. When Vlad became the head of the family, she agreed to remain in the home she had shared with her beloved to keep watch over the family. They very rarely leave the building for any length of time. My cousin Monika used to spend all her time there when we were younger, but she hasn't been back to visit for some time.'

That was an understatement, Alex thought. Monika had stopped visiting Vallakia very abruptly years ago and had never returned; he'd never discovered the reason behind her sudden absence from the home she'd loved all her life.

He pushed the thoughts to the back of his mind and cleared his throat. 'I have some very fond memories of that place.' *And some horrific ones*, he added silently to himself.

'It sounds wonderful,' Catrina offered, seeing the warmth in Alex's eyes that told her his family were close and meant a lot to him.

'I will take you to visit as soon as we can,' he promised with a smile. 'You will enjoy the carriage ride through the mountains.'

She frowned. 'Carriage?' she queried, unsure.

He grinned. 'Some habits never die,' he laughed. 'Vlad was adamant that we never got rid of the old horse-pulled carriage the family used in the past. Whenever we would agree to visit, he would send the carriage to collect us and take us up to Vallakia. I don't mind, of course. I travelled in them enough over my lifetime, but the old-fashioned novelty of it in this day and age is somewhat of a joke amongst many of us.'

She smiled at him. 'Sounds nice though,' she admitted. 'Not many people get to travel through the mountains in a horse-drawn carriage anymore.'

Alex shrugged. 'Maybe not, but I prefer to drive all the same,' he said, offering her a wink.

She studied him for a moment. 'You must have seen a lot in your time,' she said quietly, knowing she'd touched on the subject before the accident; it had led to the argument that had caused her to run off in the first place.

Alex's jovial expression vanished. 'I have,' he said simply. *Too damn much,* his own thoughts mocked him. 'Too much can happen in nearly five hundred years,' he sighed. 'Too many wars, too much unrest. You can see the world change before your eyes and you find you are powerless to stop it.'

Catrina could see him drifting in a world of his own, filled with more memories than she could ever imagine; maybe she would understand one day, maybe she wouldn't.

'I'm sorry,' she said gently. 'I shouldn't have said anything.'

He smiled at her then. 'Don't be sorry,' he whispered. 'I haven't seen half as much as others of my family, including my parents.'

'They must have supported you over the years,' she said.

Again, it was a direction in the conversation he wanted to steer away from. 'They did,' he said shortly. He leaned across and kissed her delicately on the shoulder, trying to distract her. His efforts proved fruitless.

'Will they support you over what's happened?' she asked, looking uncertain.

He brushed his fingers through her hair, wanting to push away her doubts. 'They will,' he assured.

'Aren't you worried about how they'll react? Aren't you supposed to discuss things like this? I'm not exactly perfect partner material for a lord,' she added, staring down at the pillow.

He hooked his finger under her chin, forcing her to look at him. 'My parents are nothing like that, my love,' he assured. 'And they will shower you with affection, you have my word on that,' he grinned. 'I will take you to them in good time. I just want you all to myself for tonight.'

He trailed his fingers along her spine once more, smiling as she trembled beneath his touch.

He leaned across to kiss her, pulling her against him, needing her once more.

He tried to push her concerns from his mind, but his efforts were in vain. He was almost certain his parents would be happy for him, albeit a little concerned.

His main worry was about his sister.

Nadia wouldn't be happy and he didn't dare think on the consequences of her anger.

He'd witnessed her destructive wrath once before, a long time ago, all too clearly.

Chapter 8

Alex squeezed Catrina's hand in support.

It was with great reluctance he'd returned to his family home tonight after spending the past twenty-four hours naked with her by his side. He wanted nothing more than to keep her all to himself for as long as possible. Images of Catrina lounging naked on her bed refused to leave his thoughts, and as he stared up at the looming house before him he instantly wished he could be anywhere but there. The old Tudor building seemed somehow unwelcoming in the dark of the night with its thick beams and leaded windows.

Still, he took a deep breath, steeling himself for what was to come. He looked at Catrina, who was clearly nervous.

He smiled. 'It will be okay,' he whispered soothingly.

'Will it?' she asked, scepticism in her expression as she stared up at him. 'They've never met me and now you're introducing me as one of them...' She trailed off, unsure where her thoughts were leading her. After learning of Alex's nobility, she was worried about how his parents would react. She'd tried to dress for the occasion in a smart black and white panelled dress with her blonde hair loose about her shoulders, but she was still feeling increasingly self-conscious.

'They will understand,' he assured her.

Catrina wasn't so sure.

Alex picked up on her uncertainty. 'They will,' he confirmed, trying hard to believe his own words. He brought her hand up to his lips, brushing a kiss against her fingers. 'Ready?' he asked.

She shook her head. 'No,' she sighed, staring at the door before them.

He chuckled, knowing they would go in regardless.

Catrina took a deep breath and gripped his hand as he opened the front door.

Alex led the way into the hall beyond, feeling the tension in the air immediately; Nadia was clearly home.

Somewhat reluctantly, he opened the door to the lounge, gripping Catrina's hand harder despite himself.

He walked into the brightly lit room, his sense of discomfort exacerbated by the sight of his sister.

Nadia sat in the leather armchair across the room, dressed in a low-cut top, short black skirt and black thigh-high boots; she'd clearly been out hunting.

She drummed her fingers monotonously on the soft leather of the chair as her dark-green gaze instantly fixed on her brother. There was the smallest of self-satisfied smiles on her glossed red lips.

Alex walked further into the room.

Nadia's smile disappeared, her emerald eyes narrowing as Catrina entered the room behind him.

'I see you're back... finally,' she sneered, glaring at him. 'Only took you two days.'

He stared at her, no emotion on his face. 'I didn't realise I was being timed,' he said flatly, aware of Catrina's discomfort as she stood next to him. 'Are Mother and Father here?' he asked, pulling Catrina closer.

Nadia glared at him. 'Maybe,' she taunted.

'We *are* here, Alex,' came his mother's reply.

Aurelia Demeter wandered into the room, offering her daughter a reprimanding glare, which was wasted.

As Aurelia turned her attentions back to her son, her gaze caught Catrina's.

Catrina stiffened nervously beside Alex and he wrapped his arm tighter around her waist, trying to calm her anxiety.

He offered his mother a smile as his father, Victor, entered the room behind his wife.

'I'm glad you're all here,' Alex said gently.

Nadia sneered. 'What's *she* doing here?' she asked, malice filling every word.

Alex glared at his sister. 'I asked her here,' he

said sternly, turning to his elders and ignoring her. 'Mother, Father, this is Catrina Holmes,' he said proudly, aware of the uneasy glance his parents shared.

Yet Aurelia conducted herself as she always had and she smiled at the newcomer to their home. 'It is nice to meet you at last, Catrina,' she said graciously.

Catrina smiled coyly, intimidated by these people she knew to be centuries older than herself. 'It's nice to meet you, too, your grace,' she said quietly, noting how Aurelia and Nadia shared many of the same features; the green eyes, long black hair and stunningly beautiful faces. Aurelia looked no older than thirty years of age, dressed in a stylish blouse and ankle-length skirt.

'There's no need for such formality, my dear,' Victor assured with a smile. 'Alex has told us a lot about you,' he added, wariness in his gaze as he glanced at his son.

Catrina picked up on the exchange. 'All good I hope,' she smiled, pleased to receive the same from Alex's father. Victor was tall and handsome like Alex, though his features were sterner, his demeanour more rigid. He looked no older than his wife, his grey suit expensive.

Alex looked at both his elders in turn; he knew they were uneasy that Catrina knew all about them after he'd confessed everything to her during their original and somewhat catastrophic date where he'd nearly killed her.

They would never suspect that she now shared their immortal blood.

Victor watched his son carefully. 'So to what do we owe the pleasure of this young lady's company, Alex?' he asked gently, his gaze momentarily catching Catrina's. 'Is there something wrong?'

Alex glanced at Catrina by his side and grinned, all too aware of Nadia's seething glare.

'Nothing's wrong,' he assured, turning back to his elders. 'Quite the opposite, in fact.'

Nadia's eyes narrowed as she stared at the pair before her.

Aurelia didn't look convinced. 'But something *has* happened,' she stated, concerned. She threw her hands in the air, agitated. 'You are worrying me now, my child,' she said.

Alex wasn't willing to see his mother agonize. 'Don't be worried, Mother,' he soothed. 'A terrible accident occurred yesterday,' he said soberly, the tragic event replaying itself in his mind. 'Catrina was involved. It was a fatal accident and she needed my help.' He looked at the woman by his side with a smile. 'And I realised I loved her too much to let her go.' He placed a tender kiss against Catrina's hair.

Aurelia gasped excitedly, her immaculate face breaking with a wide smile, revealing her sharp incisors. It warmed Alex through; it had been a long time since he'd witnessed his mother so happy. She gripped her husband's arm and beamed at him.

Victor grinned back at her, planting a tender

kiss to her forehead before gently pulling her along towards their son.

Aurelia reached out and took Catrina's hands tenderly in her own. 'Is it really true?' she asked, excitement filling her voice.

'It is,' Catrina said with a wide smile, relief washing over her; she'd been so nervous about their reaction.

Aurelia screeched again and hugged Catrina tightly, bouncing on the spot like a child.

Catrina laughed.

Victor embraced his son, his usually sombre expression transformed by a large smile. 'Congratulations, my son,' he said, genuine affection in his tone. 'It is truly wonderful news.'

Nadia stood from her seat where she'd been watching the fiasco unfold before her. She glared at her brother, her emerald eyes dark with suppressed rage.

Alex glowered straight back as his parents fussed over Catrina; he wasn't backing down from his sister this time.

'Game over, dearest.' He threw the thought at her, each word filled with sarcasm.

Nadia's eyes narrowed. *'Not until I say so,'* her thoughts spat back venomously.

'Nadia?' Victor's voice interrupted the pair's silent interaction as he stared between the twins. 'Will you not congratulate your brother?' he asked sternly.

She stared at her father, feeling her blood

boil. 'No, I will not,' she hissed viciously, scowling at Catrina before returning her gaze to her brother. 'You're a fool, Alex Demeter,' she sneered.

Pushing by him angrily, she left the room, the front door slamming soon after.

Alex cursed his sister's behaviour under his breath, unnerved by her words and equally frightened by her seemingly easy dismissal of the whole thing; he'd expected a much fiercer reaction from her.

Forcing the thoughts aside, he wrapped his arm around Catrina's waist and held her close. 'Ignore Nadia's little tantrums,' he whispered. 'She likes being the centre of attention. She'll come round.' He looked at both his elders with unease; they all knew from experience not to take Nadia's thunderous silence for granted.

Catrina rested her head against Alex's chest, wanting to believe his words; something about Nadia's dark glare had seriously unnerved her.

Alex looked at his elders. 'Thank you both for understanding,' he said with a grateful smile; their acceptance meant more to him than he was able to voice.

Aurelia approached him and took his face in her hands gently. 'There is no need for thanks, my darling,' she said tenderly, releasing him. 'You are our son. After everything, *despite* everything, you have found happiness at last.'

Her tone and her words struck Catrina as unusual and she felt uneasy about the meaning behind them, yet she pushed the thoughts away as Alex placed a tender kiss against her forehead.

'I couldn't let her go,' he admitted, memories of the accident flooding back like a very vivid nightmare. 'The bastards hit her with their car and ran off. I had no way of calling for help. She was dying, and I—'

'You do not need to explain, my child,' his mother whispered, placing her hand against his cheek. 'What you did, you did for love. It was an extremely selfless thing to do.' She smiled at him tenderly. 'We are very proud of you.'

'Your mother is right,' Victor agreed with a smile. 'Now let us all relax,' he added gently, inviting Catrina to take a seat on the sofa where Aurelia instantly joined her.

'It is time we got to know our newest member of the family,' he added warmly.

* * *

It had been so warm and inviting it hurt.

Catrina hadn't experienced such a close-knit family since she was a child and even then they were only fleeting memories, almost eradicated by the betrayal of her father's adultery and the messy divorce that followed soon after.

Both Aurelia and Victor had made her so welcome, inviting her into their lives without question or reservation; they were simply content in the knowledge that she had made their son the happiest he had ever been, which Aurelia insisted on telling her numerous times.

The four of them had spent the evening talking about everything and anything, and Catrina had been eager to learn more of the family history; she'd been totally engrossed in both Aurelia's and Victor's life stories that spanned over nine centuries. They'd witnessed things most people only dreamt of, or dreaded; they'd witnessed wars and peacetime, countries and people fall and prosper. They lived and breathed history.

The night had passed in no time. Nadia had dutifully made herself absent for the duration of the whole event, which had suited Catrina just fine; she always felt so inferior in Nadia's presence, like a frightened little child in a room full of grown-ups who were ignoring her.

There was something incredibly intimidating about Nadia Demeter; a feeling that hadn't diminished, despite Catrina's renewed existence.

The early hours of the morning crept along into a cold pre-dawn that promised a very frosty and grim day.

Alex led Catrina up the stairs to his room as his elders remained sitting in the lounge, quietly chatting.

Catrina followed him along the landing and waited as he opened the door to his room.

Just like all the other rooms in the Demeter household, Alex's bedroom was large with white walls, a beamed ceiling and large leaded windows. The wooden floor was highly varnished with a thick chocolate-coloured rug in the centre. His large, oak-framed double bed with cream linen dominated one wall and the oak furniture looked old and expensive. Thick mocha curtains hung at the windows and Alex pulled them across, dutifully making sure that no light could get through once the sun rose above the horizon.

She watched him carefully, something disturbing her thoughts. 'What did your mother mean?' she asked quietly. 'When she said that despite everything you found happiness?'

A wave of uneasiness passed over him as he looked at her. He could never explain what his mother had truly meant; it was far too painful to his own ears without divulging the twisted and sadistic events of his past.

He crossed the room to stand in front of her. He shrugged, forcing a smile.

'She meant just that,' he said, trying to put as much levity into his voice as possible. 'I've been around a long time, my love,' he whispered, rubbing his thumb gently across her lips. 'She's pleased I've found you.'

She smiled up at him, planting a delicate kiss against his lips. 'So am I,' she breathed.

Taking her hands, he pulled her close, staring down into those blue eyes of hers that always seemed to destroy any bad feelings or thoughts; she was his serenity incarnate.

He brushed a kiss against her lips, his gaze instantly serious. 'Marry me, Catrina,' he breathed, staring down at her, touched by the tears in her eyes.

Her hands trembled in his. 'What did you say?' she asked, her voice tiny.

Alex smiled, brushing her hair tenderly away from her face. He knew with every fibre of his being that he wanted nothing more.

'Will you marry me, Catrina Holmes?' he said again, wiping a tear from her cheek. 'I want you to be my wife for all eternity.'

She choked back a sob as her face broke with an enormous grin. 'Yes,' she said with a wobbly voice, throwing her arms around his neck. 'Yes, I will.'

He wrapped his arms around her waist and pulled her to him tightly, a sense of warmth invading him as he kissed her deeply, needing her embrace.

He would have given anything to remain like that forever, trapped in their own little bubble where nothing could touch them.

A movement outside the bedroom door caught his attention and he glanced up, his gaze meeting the cold green stare of his sister.

Unnerved by her silent return, he glared at her. Her arms were crossed angrily over her chest, her eyes dark and dangerous. Her lips curved into that insidious grin he knew so well. She winked at him and bit into her lower lip, blood beading on the skin.

Alex looked away, released Catrina and turned

to kick the door closed in a bid to eradicate the images of his sister from his mind.

His efforts were in vain, he knew all too well.

He'd tried and failed far too many times to escape the terrifying hold Nadia had over him.

Her vicious laughter echoed in his mind.

Chapter 9

'I thought you could do with this,' Nadia said gently, placing the large glass of brandy on the coffee table in front of Lola.

Lola glanced up at her neighbour, the smallest effort of a smile on her pale face. She took hold of the glass with a trembling hand.

She hated she was back in this house, the one she'd abhorred since childhood. She looked around her at the opulence of the lounge, remembering the same room when she'd been sixteen, the house abandoned; dust and cobwebs had been thick on every ledge and in every corner. The entire building had felt devoid of life. She still had nightmares about the place.

Now it was a warm and welcoming home, with expensive furniture and a roaring open fire, warming the room to a level that could have made Lola sleepy had she not felt the overwhelming need to speak to Nadia about Jason.

He hadn't been seen for three days now, ever

since his "big date" with Nadia on Saturday night, and he hadn't answered his phone once. Matt had received a text from him on Monday morning telling him "Won't be in work today *wink**wink*", but after that there'd been nothing but silence. Jason had never done anything like it before; no matter how wild his weekend, he'd never failed to make it into the office.

Lola couldn't shake the feeling that something was horribly wrong.

'Are you all right?'

Nadia's soft accented voice dragged Lola from her thoughts and she stared round at her friend who'd sat next to her on the opulent leather sofa.

Lola took a sip of the brandy, the liquid burning her throat as she swallowed. She grimaced, cupping the glass in both hands. She nodded.

'I tried calling him again,' she managed, her voice trembling. She'd lost count of the number of times she'd tried to call Jason's phone since Saturday, every time clinging to a vague hope that he'd answer; instead, she was constantly connected to his voicemail, the sound of his recorded voice making the sense of loss worse.

Nadia smiled grimly. 'So did I,' she confessed.

Lola stared down into her glass. 'I just want to know why,' she said quietly, looking up at the woman beside her. 'Why has he just disappeared? I've known him all my life and he's never done anything like this before.'

Nadia rested her hand on Lola's shoulder in support. 'I wish I knew what to say,' she soothed. 'I know how close you are.'

Lola felt the tears she'd fought all morning to suppress sting her eyes. She took another sip of brandy, hoping the burning heat of the liquid would keep the pain at bay. She was disappointed.

She turned back to Nadia. 'Are you sure he didn't say anything to you on Monday?' she asked for what felt like the millionth time. 'Anything at all?'

Nadia's expression was full of sympathy as she shook her head. 'He didn't say a word,' she murmured. 'We had a really great time,' she added, her voice breaking as her emerald eyes glittered with tears.

Lola didn't need to ask how much of a "great time" the pair had had; Jason and Nadia had been flirting heavily with each other for weeks and Jason had never been backward at coming forward.

She hated to ask the same question of Nadia again; the whole ordeal was upsetting her friend as much as it was her and Nadia had been really supportive over the last few days.

'I'm sorry,' Lola offered, sipping the brandy again. 'I shouldn't keep asking.'

'It's okay,' Nadia soothed. 'You have every right to want answers. Jason's family, it's important.'

Lola stared at the amber liquid in her glass, swirling it around gently. 'It feels as if you're the only one I can talk to,' she admitted, more to herself.

'Oh?' Nadia asked.

Lola had said too much and yet couldn't ignore the truth any longer. 'Matt and I haven't exactly been seeing eye to eye recently,' she mumbled, her gaze still fixed on the remainder of the brandy in the glass. 'He doesn't understand.'

'I thought he and Jason were close friends?' Nadia asked gently.

Lola glanced up at her friend, disliking the use of past tense. 'They are. Matt's worried too, he's just hiding it.'

Nadia frowned. 'Then why do you not feel able to talk to him about this? He is your partner. He should be there for you.'

How true Nadia's words were, yet they nonetheless reflected the grim reality that he hadn't been there for her... especially not since the incident in the market when Lola had turned to Jason instead.

The memory angered her; was Matt really *that* egotistical?

She looked back at Nadia. 'That's kind of why I'm here,' she said carefully. 'I wondered if you'd go with me to the police station. I want to report Jason as a missing person.'

Nadia's eyes softened with compassion and she placed a hand over Lola's. 'Of course,' she pressed. 'Finish your drink and we'll go straight away.'

A noise in the next room had Lola glancing towards the doorway.

Alex grabbed his jacket off a dining chair and

shrugged into it as he strolled through the door. His gaze caught Lola's.

'Lola,' he said, clearly surprised to see her. 'I'm sorry, I didn't realise you were here.'

She forced a small smile. 'I came for a chat,' she said quietly, holding up the brandy to indicate the nature of the conversation.

Alex's expression quickly sobered. 'Still no news from Jason?' he asked, concern filling his tone.

She shook her head. 'Not yet.'

'We're going to the police to report him missing,' Nadia chimed, concern in her voice.

Alex stared down at his sister. 'Good idea,' he murmured, his voice flat.

The two of them glared at each other. Alex's eyes were blank.

Lola glanced between the pair, uncomfortable with the atmosphere that had suddenly developed.

She cleared her throat. 'Are you off to see Cat?' she asked, trying to alleviate the disquiet between the twins. She knew it was a silly question; whatever had caused Catrina's reservations over Alex last week had clearly been resolved as the pair had been inseparable ever since.

Alex nodded with a gentle smile. 'She's been feeling better over the last few hours, so hopefully she'll be back on her feet soon.'

'Poor thing,' Lola said, feeling sorry for Catrina who'd text her to say she'd been housebound since the weekend with a severe stomach bug; having another of her friends out of the picture, albeit temporarily, didn't make Jason's disappearance any easier to deal with.

'Give her my best,' she offered.

Alex smiled, clearly grateful. 'I will. Good luck at the police station.' With a final glare at his sister, Alex left the room and the house.

Unable to hold back the obvious question, Lola asked, 'Everything okay?'

Nadia beamed at her friend, swiping a hand through the air in dismissal. 'Everything's fine,' she said cheerfully, completely at odds with the dark glare she'd given her brother seconds before. 'We simply had a disagreement. Alex likes to throw his toys out of the pram over the smallest of things.'

A grim smile tickled the corners of Lola's mouth. 'Whenever me and Matt had an argument I'd always turn to Jason,' she admitted, drinking from the glass again, squinting as the liquid burned once more. 'And now he's not here,' she added, her voice shaking with the threat of tears. She fought hard to suppress them and Nadia reached out, covering Lola's hand with her own.

'Well, I'm still here for you,' she offered kindly. 'And we're going to get him back.'

'Thank you,' Lola said, smiling through her pain.

Nadia's expression was warm, her green eyes gentle. 'You're most welcome,' she said. 'Anytime you want to talk, about any little thing, you know where

I am.'

It was a genuine, selfless offer and Lola couldn't find the words in that moment to thank her.

She thought on her friend, Camilla, who was always so judgemental. Lola was unable to comprehend the issues Camilla seemed to have with both Alex and Nadia. For weeks, Camilla had made her distaste for the twins clear and had tried desperately to keep Alex and Catrina apart for no real justified reason, as far as Lola could see. Now they were a couple, it seemed Camilla's attentions had swapped to Nadia.

Since Jason had disappeared, Camilla had bombarded Lola with phone calls and texts, practically accusing Nadia of being involved, without any real cause or decent explanation.

Lola pushed the thoughts aside and downed the last of her brandy.

'Shall we get going?' Nadia offered, taking the glass from Lola's hands and placing it on the coffee table. With a supportive grasp of Lola's hands, Nadia pulled her to her feet.

Lola took a deep breath and nodded, thinking about Camilla once more.

As Nadia handed Lola her coat and shrugged into her own, Lola knew Camilla was being completely unfair.

After everything that had happened over the last few days, there was no way Lola would ever believe Nadia capable of anything but kindness.

Chapter 10

He'd felt empty as he'd stared at his sister.

Alex hadn't spoken a word to her since her outburst on Sunday and she'd barely even looked at him.

He knew the tension between them wouldn't have gone unnoticed by Lola, who'd foolishly turned to his sister in her hour of need. He bared his sharp teeth in a silent snarl as he thought of his sister accompanying Lola to the police station.

Nadia was involved in Jason's mysterious disappearance; Alex knew that for certain, though some of the details confused him. He hadn't asked her about it outright and if he had he knew she'd only lie; he didn't want to think about what she'd done to Jason that night, but Alex's morbid curiosity conjured images nonetheless.

He'd begged Nadia to cancel their date on Saturday night and she'd refused, knowing what would happen. He blamed himself for not doing more to stop it all from getting to this point; he feared innocent blood had been spilt for nothing more than a bet.

Once again, their games had gone too far.

'Are you okay?' Catrina's voice disturbed him from his myriad of thoughts.

He turned away from the window in her bedroom, unwilling to burden her with his troubles.

'I'm fine,' he soothed, looking at her. She was fresh out of the bath, her blonde hair still wet about her shoulders and her body wrapped in a satin robe.

He crossed the small room in several strides, taking her in his arms. 'I missed you today,' he said softly, stroking her hair away from her perfect face. He ran his thumb over her lips, making her shiver.

She smiled up at him, her need for him plain in her eyes. 'I missed *you*,' she whispered, running her hands across his chest, her nails plucking at the buttons on his shirt. 'You left early this morning.' She pouted playfully.

He laughed. 'You're insatiable,' he breathed against her lips, teasing her, his hands slowly travelling over her hips.

She grinned at him. 'I think you should make it up to me,' she flirted, wrapping her arms around his neck.

With a hungry growl, he kissed her hard as she pushed her body against him, her need evident.

Alex smiled against her lips, her heavy breathing arousing him further. 'Patience, my love,' he whispered, noting the disappointment in her eyes.

'I have something to give you first.'

Catrina fanned her fingers across his chest, her gaze suggestive. 'I'm glad to hear it,' she teased with a wide smile.

Alex couldn't help but laugh, unable to deny his need for her body.

While he still had a logical thought in his head, he stepped back from her and reached into his pocket as she looked on curiously.

He smiled at her. 'Two nights ago I asked you a very important question,' he said, pulling a small blue box from his pocket. He presented it to her, opening it to show the large, solitaire diamond ring within, smiling as an unintentional gasp escaped Catrina's lips.

'Will you marry me, Catrina Holmes?' he asked once more, aware of the tears glittering in her sapphire eyes.

'Yes,' she said, her voice filled with emotion. She watched as he took the ring from the box and placed it on her finger tenderly.

She threw her arms around his neck and he held onto her tightly, a deep sense of joy running through his veins.

He buried his face in her damp hair, smelling that gentle essence of apples from her shampoo. He'd never felt so complete and he no longer cared how cliché that might have sounded to his own ears or anyone else's.

He kissed her tenderly.

She smiled up at him, her face full of excitement. 'I can't wait to tell Lola and the others,' she squealed. 'They'll be so surprised.'

Alex stiffened, instantly concerned. 'You can't see them,' he said without thinking.

Catrina frowned, not liking the insinuation of his words. 'Excuse me?' she asked as she stepped back, extremely piqued.

Alex shook his head gently. 'I'm sorry, I didn't mean it to sound that way.' He ran his hands over his face. 'I only meant that it's dangerous for you to see them right now.'

She didn't follow. 'They're my friends, Alex,' she said flatly.

He tried to explain as gently as he could. 'Yet you are not who you used to be, my love,' he said.

'I thought you said I was still the same person,' she countered, her frown increasing.

He closed his eyes, trying to be patient. 'You know what I mean,' he said, looking at her.

She shook her head, dumbfounded. 'I don't believe this,' she huffed, staring at him hard. 'I can't pretend to have a stomach bug for the rest of my life,' she pointed out, aware she was referring to herself as if she still had a life expectancy. 'I've already accepted that I'll have to give my notice at work. Given Jason's disappearance, everyone's going to want to know I'm okay. Camilla will be beating down the door if she can't make sure everything is all right. You know what she's like.'

Alex crossed the room back to the window, unsure what to say; she was right, of course, and he hated to even consider keeping her from those she loved. Yet he was trying to protect her, as well as them; how would she feel if she was unable to control herself and harmed one of those friends she held so dear? She'd never be able to forgive herself.

'Lola's heading to the police station with Nadia to report Jason missing,' he said, knowing he was changing the subject yet trying to get her to take his point; things could get out of hand far too quickly.

'Good,' he heard her say from behind him. 'It's not like him to just take off.'

Alex sighed. 'I know,' he murmured, hating himself even more; he'd known what would happen and he'd done nothing. 'If they investigate, I can't promise what they'll find,' he warned.

He heard her intake of breath. 'Do you know what happened to him?' she asked carefully, uncertainty in her eyes.

He shook his head. 'No,' he said shortly, knowing what her next question would be.

'Does Nadia?' she pushed.

She'd asked the question before; they'd discussed her worries over Jason's disappearance numerous times over the last few days as they'd lay in her bed.

'Not that she's told me,' he admitted. 'She's as worried as Lola from what I can see.'

'And you trust her?' she asked firmly.

No.

'She's my sister,' he shrugged. 'I have to trust that she'd tell me the truth.'

He heard her take a step towards him. 'But something *could* have happened,' she stated quietly.

Alex sighed, unable to deny the truth. 'Of course it could have,' he admitted, turning to look at her. 'Just as something *could* have happened between us the night of our first date. I could have killed you.'

He noted the sadness in her eyes; she'd been so happy a moment before. 'Remember how you felt that first night when we hunted that woman?' he asked carefully. 'Remember how you became instantly in-tune to her heartbeat, needing her blood? That wasn't a choice, my love,' he continued. 'It was your instinct and one that will take over if you are not careful.' He watched the uncertainty flash in her blue eyes. 'And trust me, it can so easily take over.'

Alex reached out to her and she crossed the room to join him. He took her face in his hands. 'I couldn't bear to watch you put yourself through such agony,' he said, hoping his words would make her understand.

Catrina looked up at him, warmed by how much he cared for her. She knew she was still naive about her new life and the powers she'd been given; it was all still so new and the abilities she knew she possessed scared her more than she was willing to admit. But the thought of hurting her friends, the only *real* family she'd ever really known, scared her more.

'I know what you're trying to say, Alex,' she said with a gentle smile, pulling his hands away. 'I know you're just trying to protect me and I love you for it,' she added, reaching up and placing her hand against his cheek tenderly. She stared at him for a moment. 'But I would never hurt those I love.'

Alex took a deep breath. 'You might not want to, but you might not be able to control yourself,' he argued.

'You don't trust me?' she countered, wary of his answer.

Worried he'd upset her, he took her hands in his. 'I trust you implicitly, my love,' he said, hoping his words and his gaze conveyed the truthfulness of his words. 'I simply need you to understand how deeply your nature has changed. You know as well as I do how easy it is to lose control,' he whispered. It still haunted him how close he'd come to killing her on the night of their first date, despite him convincing himself he could never harm her.

'I was so sure of my own self-control that night, so sure I could handle being close to you,' he said gently. 'But I still lost control, Catrina, and I'm nearly five hundred years old. You are still so new to this and I don't want to see you hurt yourself and those around you. I know you could never live with that.'

Catrina stared up at him as he continued to hold her hands. He was right, she knew, in regards to her naivety. She knew he was only trying to protect her from the worst. Yet she also knew she couldn't carry on with the masquerade of being ill and hiding herself away; Camilla, if no one else, would soon get suspicious and that in itself could be dangerous.

She smiled at him gently. 'You're right, I couldn't live with it,' she admitted, sadness in her tone. 'And I *do* understand what you're trying to say, honestly.'

Alex opened his mouth to speak, but she placed her fingers over his lips to stop him.

'But *you* need to understand that my friends mean the world to me and I couldn't even imagine harming them. Maybe that makes me naive and stupid, but I don't care. I *will not* hurt those I love. I don't care how painful it might be, I'll find a way around it. I can even leave early if I start to feel uncomfortable, but at least I would have shown my face and lessened some of their worries.'

Alex stared at her as she slowly removed her fingers from his lips. His instincts screamed at him that this was a very bad idea and yet he found himself unable to argue against her.

He'd known from the beginning that her friends were, in essence, her family, certainly more so than her real one had ever been; he couldn't ask her to simply turn her back on them, especially now with Jason missing. They all needed each other more than ever.

With a sigh, he pulled her close, hugging her.

'Okay, you win,' he whispered, beaten.

Chapter 11

Alex froze as he met his sister's smug gaze, her piercing green eyes full of amusement at his obvious discomfort.

Since agreeing to meet with the group of friends a couple of days ago, he'd felt an increasing sense of unease and now he found he'd be forced to share the evening with his sister, whom he had barely spoken to; he'd spent the last few days with Catrina, unwilling to share the same space as his twin.

'How nice of you to grace us with your presence,' Nadia purred, sliding up next to him as he stood at the far side of the room, waiting for the others.

It was the usual Friday night and Carri's bar was busy, the place filled with the sound of chatter and laughter. The air smelt of stale beer and perfume.

'What the hell are you doing here?' he asked, his voice a rough whisper as he kept his gaze on the group of friends at the bar.

He watched as Catrina chatted with Lola, Matt and Camilla, occasionally glancing over her shoulder to smile at him. He noticed the subtle distance between Lola and Matt, a void growing ever wider thanks to his sister's twisted games.

'Enjoying the ride, my love,' Nadia said smoothly. 'Just enjoying the ride.'

Alex smiled at Catrina as she glanced over at him again. She quickly turned back to face Camilla, who was chatting away. The barman was placing each drink on a tray on the bar as he prepared it.

Alex's smile disappeared as he thought on his sister's words. 'This is supposed to be an occasion for friends... for support,' he pointed out. 'Not really your scene now, is it?' he taunted flatly.

Nadia shrugged, unfazed as ever by his words. 'Lola invited me,' she said simply. 'She asked me here for "support", as you say, so I have every right to be here.'

He tried not to laugh. 'You have *no* right and you know it,' he growled. 'Your support is as farcical as your friendship.'

She rolled her eyes. 'Must we have this conversation *now*?' she asked dryly. 'Try and remember why we are here,' she added sarcastically, a friendly smile decorating her pink lips as Lola headed across to the pair with drinks in hand.

'Here we go,' she said, her smile warm though it failed to light the sadness in her brown eyes. She handed the twins their drinks, a gin and tonic for Nadia and a whiskey for Alex, which they took with gratitude.

'Thank you,' Alex said, unable to ignore the dark circles under Lola's eyes or the pallor of her skin. 'How are you holding up?' he asked gently.

Lola shrugged. 'I'm doing okay,' she said, little emotion in her voice. 'All things considered.'

She glanced over her shoulder towards the bar where Camilla, Matt and Catrina were beckoning the three of them to a table nearby.

Lola nodded and motioned for the twins to follow her, leading the way through the throng of people towards the back of the building, stopping at a circular table where Camilla, Matt and Catrina had already settled themselves.

Purposefully, Camilla had picked a table with seven chairs, the group agreeing to leave the last one empty for their missing friend.

Lola stared at it as she slid into the seat on Matt's left, the empty chair on her other side.

Alex seated himself between Catrina and Matt, realising he was unfortunately placed opposite his sister, her emerald gaze full of humour at his discomfort.

He also didn't fail to notice that she'd seated herself on the other side of the empty chair meant for Jason, like some grieving widow; she certainly looked the part in her black cashmere sweater and tight black jeans. He tried in vain to prevent a sneer.

He glanced around the table. The empty chair seemed to be the main focal point for them all; Lola's gaze was full of pain as she stared at it, her eyes glistening with tears.

To her right was Matt. Although the pair sat close together, the distance between them was evident; he showed her no support, either physically or emotionally, and seemed more content to keep hold of his pint glass.

On Alex's right was Catrina, who looked conflicted; she was happy to be spending time with her friends, especially after sharing the news of their engagement, yet she was also hurt and upset that her close friend and confidant wasn't here to share it with her.

Instinctively, he reached out and covered her hand with his, receiving a grateful smile in return.

Next to Catrina was Camilla, who had been evidently relieved to see Catrina out tonight after her "stomach bug" had lasted a little longer than these things usually did.

Alex studied Camilla for a moment; she looked somewhat uncomfortable and it took him a few moments to decipher that it was due to being seated next to Nadia.

His own discomfort increased as he tried to divert his attention; his gaze caught his sister's and she smiled at him.

He ignored her.

Camilla turned to Lola. 'Any news from the police?' she asked, her gaze darting to Nadia before she focused her attention back on her friend.

Lola looked uncomfortable as everyone looked

her way. She shook her head. 'Not yet,' she murmured. 'The forty-eight hours aren't up yet. It'll be reviewed after that, they said.'

Nadia took a sip from her drink. 'We gave them all the information they needed,' she added, sadness in her eyes. 'He's apparently classed as 'no apparent risk' because he's not ill or suffering with a mental illness.'

Matt nodded. 'And the fact he's got his phone and wallet with him,' he added, looking at Camilla. 'The investigating officer asked to search his room and the rest of the house. His bed was slept in and his keys, phone and wallet weren't where he usually leaves them. She told me that it's more likely he's gone off somewhere, but his passport was still in the drawer so at least he's still in the country.'

Alex watched Camilla's gaze flicker towards his sister once more.

He cleared his throat and looked at Lola. 'What else did they say?' he asked, trying to divert Camilla's attention.

Lola sighed. 'Sergeant Bell, the investigating officer, took some photos of Jason with her. She said they'd be distributed to hospitals and so on. They have his phone details and she said they'd try and contact him.'

Camilla stared at Nadia. 'Did you tell them about your date the night he went missing?' she asked, none too friendly.

Lola frowned as Nadia looked at Camilla,

shocked by the affront.

'He didn't go missing Saturday night, Cam,' Lola pressed, anger in her voice. 'We told them everything we could.'

Camilla realised everyone was staring at her and she lowered her gaze to her glass, saying no more.

Lola sighed as she fished around in her bag and pulled out a handful of small white business cards with the police logo on the front.

'Here,' she said, passing them around the table. 'These are the contact details for Sergeant Bell. I've written the reference number she gave me on the back. If we hear from Jason, or get any other information we have to contact her straight away. She said they'd be in touch with me after forty-eight hours.'

Catrina picked up her card from the table. 'What happens then?' she queried.

Lola shrugged. 'It gets reviewed by a detective.'

Catrina glanced down at her drink, still mindlessly fiddling with the card in her hands.

Alex stared at her. 'Are you okay?' he asked softly, referring to both her emotions over Jason as well as her hunger. He noted how she still sipped at her drink; she didn't need it, but he appreciated that some habits would be harder to break than others.

She smiled at him yet the sadness remained in her eyes. 'Sort of,' she said simply, understanding his concern. Her gaze flickered back to the empty chair, which sat opposite her own. She drew a deep breath. 'I guess I feel guilty,' she admitted quietly. 'Maybe we shouldn't have said anything about us just yet.'

'Yes, you should,' Camilla chimed in, clearly having overheard Catrina's worries. She smiled at her. 'Jason would be the first one to want to know about you getting engaged.'

Matt laughed. 'And the first one to want a party for it, too,' he joked, gaining a chuckle from all seated around the table.

'Cam's right,' Lola added, looking at Catrina. 'Don't feel guilty about it, Cat. We're all happy for you. Jason will be over the moon for you both.'

Matt lifted his pint glass. 'I'll second that,' he said, as the rest of the table lifted their glasses. 'Congratulations to you both,' he toasted with a smile, as the rest of the table repeated his sentiments.

Alex glared at his sister as she lifted her own glass, her face brightened by a cheerful smile; only her eyes betrayed the seething anger her jovial exterior masked.

He turned back to Catrina with a smile, noticing the tears in her eyes. He took her free hand in his, squeezing it supportively before lifting his glass, turning his attentions back to the group.

'And here's to Jason,' he said firmly, looking at each of them in turn as they raised their glasses once more. He stared hard at his sister as she continued to play her role as the grieving widow. 'Wherever he may be, let him return to us safely.'

His heartfelt toast was met with agreement from the group as they all clinked their glasses in the middle of the table.

Alex noticed Camilla's sour expression aimed at his sister and he tried to ignore Nadia's tearful act, turning his attention to Lola. She smiled at him, a deep sadness in her eyes.

'Thank you,' she said quietly across the table.

'You're welcome,' he mouthed with a supportive smile.

The chat amongst the group remained muted for a while, no one really knowing what to say other than make small talk, something that felt alien to them all.

The stern glances between the siblings at the table continued and Alex became aware of Lola's interest in their disquiet. He watched as Lola leant across the empty seat to her left so she could whisper to Nadia without the others overhearing; Alex, of course, heard every word.

'Are you two okay?' she asked, tilting her head in Alex's direction.

Nadia smiled gently, placing her cold hand over her friend's. 'We're fine,' she said, playing with the straw in her drink with her other hand.

'Are you sure?' Lola pressed. 'There seemed like there was some tension the other day and the two of you seem a bit at odds tonight?'

Nadia chuckled lightly. 'Nothing much gets past you, does it?' she teased.

Lola smiled.

Nadia shrugged. 'We're fine, honestly,' she

assured, glancing at Alex. 'Just silly sibling stuff. We fall out over the silliest of things all the time. The curse of being a twin.'

Nadia's jovial take on the situation had Lola relaxing and Nadia gently tapped her hand. 'You don't need to worry,' she said.

Her smile widened, a darkness in her eyes only her brother understood.

'After all,' she purred, knowing he could hear her. 'It always sorts itself out in end.'

Chapter 12

Nadia slumped on the sofa, gazing around the lounge at nothing in particular.

She was bored. Drumming her fingers on the soft leather of her seat, she gazed out of the window, the heavy silk curtains framing the leaded glass. The day had been overcast, leading into a dull evening with cloud that threatened rain before nightfall.

The small carriage clock on the mantle chimed six o'clock and she rolled her eyes; today had certainly seemed to drag. She spotted the small framed photo of Catrina that Alex had dutifully added to the mantle; she sneered with distaste.

Hearing the bathroom door open upstairs, Nadia grinned. She listened to Alex's footfalls along the landing above her as he reached his room.

With a renewed vigour, she pushed herself from the sofa, strolling through into the dining room and then into the large rear drawing room, pressing the piano keys randomly as she passed.

Sneering at the sound of Alex gently humming

to himself, she climbed the stairs, her hand gripping the handrail tighter than was necessary, her knuckles turning white.

As she rounded the top of the staircase, her gaze focused on the door to Alex's room, her green eyes narrowing.

She knocked on the door, hard.

'What?' came the hostile reply.

With a gentle push, Nadia opened the door, meeting her brother's gaze in the large mirror above his dresser.

She stood in silence, watching him shrug into a white shirt.

Alex glared at her. 'What do you want?' he asked, angry with her interruption.

She smiled sweetly. 'I thought you might like to join me for dinner,' she offered gently.

Her ability to act as if nothing had happened never failed to amaze him. 'I already have plans,' he said bluntly, buttoning up his shirt.

She sighed heavily, her smile dimming. 'Of course you do,' she said flatly, rolling her eyes.

He glared at her through the reflection. 'What is that supposed to mean?'

She leaned against the doorframe, eyeing him carefully. 'Nothing, dearest,' she said innocently with a shrug. 'You simply haven't been very... *available* recently.'

He snorted as he finished buttoning his shirt, still watching her in the mirror. 'It may have escaped your notice, but I have a life away from this house now.'

She glared at him, her eyes darkening. 'Nothing ever escapes my notice,' she said coldly, perversely amused to see the flash of discomfort in his emerald eyes.

He turned from the mirror then, pinning her with a hard stare before heading for the door. 'I don't have time for this,' he growled, pushing past her.

Nadia turned to watch him stalk along the landing.

She sighed heavily, throwing her hands in the air in frustration. 'Oh, come on, Alex, this is stupid,' she said, watching with satisfaction as he paused at the top of the stairs.

His delay didn't last long. 'I think you'll find you started it,' he called over his shoulder as he continued down the stairs.

Baring her sharp teeth in a silent snarl, she pushed herself from the doorframe and hurried after him.

Finding Alex standing in the lounge, she sighed. 'Well then let me put an end to it, please,' she said, almost pleading.

He stared at her for a moment, unsure what to make of her words or tone. 'You didn't need to react the way you did,' he pointed out sternly, unwilling to let the matter drop so easily. 'I asked for one thing which was your blessing,' he added sadly.

Nadia took a step closer, her face filled with

regret. 'I was in shock,' she admitted, her eyes sad. 'It was the last thing I expected to happen and I couldn't take it all in. I was angry.'

He watched her take another step closer. He could understand her shock over the matter and appreciated her honesty. Yet he wasn't willing to forgive it so easily; her words had, after all, been hurtful.

With a small nod of acknowledgment, he turned from her and headed for the lounge door.

In a few quick steps she crossed the room, grabbing at his arm, forcing him to stop and look at her; there was desperation on her face.

'Please, Alex,' she pleaded. 'I know how I acted was wrong and I'm sorry.'

He laughed scornfully. 'You've never been sorry for anything in your life,' he pointed out, trying to pull his arm from her grip.

She refused to let go.

'I mean it,' she said. 'I swear I'll apologise to Catrina when I next see her. I just can't bear to fight with you anymore.' Her eyes were desperate.

Against his better judgement, Alex found himself believing her. 'I don't want to fight you, either,' he said gently. 'But you have to apologise to Catrina and our elders,' he warned. 'And accept that Catrina is my life now.'

She smiled gently, looking almost relieved. 'I will,' she said simply, releasing his arm.

He smiled at his sister, grateful. 'Thank you,' he

whispered, pulling her close in a gentle hug.

She rested her head against his shoulder, slowly brushing her lips against his throat, her tongue licking at the skin.

With a snarl, he pushed her away angrily, disappointment raging through him.

He glared at her. 'And there I was thinking you really meant that apology,' he said, shaking his head, unable to believe he'd fallen for it all again. 'I really wanted to believe you,' he whispered sadly.

She laughed, maintaining his gaze. She licked her lips seductively, winking at him; if his anger or disappointment bothered her at all, she didn't show it.

'Come now, my love,' she purred, leaning against the wall provocatively. 'You know you can't resist,' she teased.

Alex stared at her hard for a long moment, his mind swamped with memories of their numerous games over the centuries, each one always ending with Nadia walking away the victor; devastation, pain and suffering left in her wake.

He stepped towards her slowly, his gaze not once leaving hers. Tentatively, he reached out, gently stroking her cheek with his fingers. He brushed her raven-black hair from her face, running his fingers through its lengths until he cupped the back of her head with his hand.

Staring into her eyes, he grabbed her hair hard, pulling her head back sharply. His eyes were dark with anger, finding himself repulsed by her very presence.

She snarled at him, trying to claw at him with her long nails, but he quickly moved behind her, pinning her arms to her sides with his own.

He growled against her ear, reviled by this creature he'd once envied, adored and loved; this creature who had once been his sister.

'I will not say this again, Nadia Demeter, so make sure it sinks into that thick skull of yours,' he whispered, his words dripping with menace. 'You can push and push as much as you like, but we are done. Do you understand me? Done.' He pushed her away harshly, not wanting to be near her any longer.

She snarled at him as she straightened herself, brushing her hair back from her face.

'Done?' she seethed, her eyes blazing. 'You can't exist without me and you know it,' she taunted.

He ignored the voice inside his head that told him she was right. He wasn't backing down this time.

'Stop playing games,' he growled. 'You don't hold any more cards.' He stepped back towards her, his gaze filled with rage as he looked her up and down; he was disgusted with what he saw.

He turned from her abruptly, leaving the room.

A few moments later, the front door slammed closed as he left the house.

A deep-seated growl rumbled through Nadia's chest as she stared after her brother, her green eyes narrow. She bared her sharp teeth in a silent snarl.

'Done?' she whispered, her voice edged with malice. 'You're done when *I* say so, brother dearest.' She squeezed her fists tighter until her nails bit into the delicate skin of her palms, making them bleed. 'You can't walk away from me,' she snarled.

A slow sadistic smile played across her lips as she continued to stare at the empty lounge doorway.

She still had one particularly devastating card left to play.

Chapter 13

Catrina shifted uncomfortably as she entered the Demeter's lounge.

Nadia managed the smallest of smiles in greeting as she sat herself in the armchair.

'Where's Alex?' Catrina asked, not quite able to meet Nadia's glare.

Nadia's smile widened. 'He must have forgotten you were coming,' she lied, no interest in her voice.

Tentatively, Catrina took a step further into the room, trying to ignore the hostility in Nadia's tone. 'Will he be long?' she asked quietly, glancing around her.

'As long as it takes,' came the flat answer.

Catrina didn't bother to argue as she sat herself down on the leather sofa; she could feel the intimidating woman watching her. There was an uncomfortable essence in the room. It made her skin crawl.

Nadia crossed her legs casually, the split in her black knee-length skirt falling open to her mid-thigh.

Her slender calves were covered with patent black knee-high boots with killer heels; her silver shirt was open down to her cleavage.

She stared at the girl, her contempt barely hidden below the surface; Catrina looked far too virtuous in her pale blue jeans and pink, soft-knit jumper.

Catrina cleared her throat. 'Are your parents here?' she asked, hope in her voice that their presence would improve the suffocating disquiet in the house.

Nadia sneered. 'They went into the city earlier. They've been gone for hours. You know what parents are like.'

It was a dig at Catrina's estranged family and she knew it. She didn't offer Nadia the satisfaction of a reaction.

Catrina shifted in her seat, unable to prevent herself glancing over at the woman seated across the room.

Nadia reclined in her seat, her green eyes dark in the dimness of the room; despite the growing darkness outside, there were barely any lights on within the house. The corners of Nadia's mouth were curved in the slightest of smiles, adding a vindictiveness to her glare that was altogether intimidating.

Unnerved by Nadia's very presence, Catrina looked away.

With a gentle sigh, Nadia finally broke the silence. 'Look,' she said flatly, 'I know Alex would have liked a fanfare to your news the other night and has been sulking ever since because he didn't receive one,' she sneered, rolling her eyes. 'However, perhaps the reaction he *did* receive was not completely fair.'

Nadia's tone sounded mocking, yet when Catrina glanced up, the expression on Nadia's face seemed genuine.

'Oh?' She found it hard to form coherent words under Nadia's hard emerald gaze; despite her genuine expression, there was still something threatening in her eyes.

A slow smile crept across Nadia's ruby-tinted lips. 'I'm afraid that was my attempt at an apology,' she said, her tone light. 'Feeble though it may be. Alex's news somewhat shocked me at the time. We've always been so close. I suppose I felt rather piqued that he left me out of such an important life decision.'

Catrina couldn't deny she was surprised at Nadia's sudden admission, but she was comforted by it; she didn't want to feel like she'd placed a rift between the twins.

'I'm sure he would have discussed it with you if he could,' she soothed with a smile.

'Quite,' Nadia offered flatly, with little in the way of a smile. 'But in any case, it wasn't fair of me to make you feel unwelcome in this house. I can see how much Alex cares for you and as his twin I shouldn't argue against any life choices he makes.' She paused briefly, never once altering her gaze. 'It's good to see Alex happy,' she said, little feeling to her words.

Catrina smiled. 'I'm glad I make him happy,' she said.

Nadia laughed. 'Indeed you do,' she purred. 'You make a lovely couple.' She clapped her hands together, making light of the whole conversation. 'Who would have thought such a happy ever after would come from a bet?' she said, her words light and jovial, yet with the added malice needed to secure Catrina's attention.

Catrina was confused. 'What do you mean by that?' she asked, frowning; she felt suddenly uneasy.

Nadia grinned, her expression cold and in no way comforting. 'Our silly bet?' she offered, almost helpfully as if trying to remind Catrina of some unimportant forgotten fact. 'Of course, it's irrelevant now, seeing as everything worked out nicely in the end,' she added with the smallest of sneers.

Catrina stared, her mind working overtime to try and comprehend what this woman was telling her. 'A bet?' she queried with a frown. 'What bet?'

Nadia overplayed her surprise, her eyes wide. 'You didn't know?' she asked, astonished. '*Really*? Oh, now I feel completely awful,' she groaned. 'He truly didn't confess anything to you?'

Catrina's stomach lurched and her chest felt tight; the room suddenly seemed far too small, the walls closing in inch by inch. 'Confess what?' she asked, her voice small. 'I've no idea what you're talking about.'

Nadia's eyes were full of malice. 'You were a bet, my sweet,' she sneered. 'Everything from the very moment you met to your first kiss and beyond was orchestrated by Alex.'

'Why?' It was the only word Catrina could form as she tried to find her voice.

Nadia's callous smile widened. 'We bet on how easy it would be to get you into bed,' she said cruelly. 'I bet him he couldn't do it before killing you... he doesn't have much self-control.'

'He wouldn't do something like that,' Catrina argued, trying to convince herself the words were true; Nadia's malevolent glare was telling her otherwise. 'I know him.'

'Yes, he would,' Nadia said softly. 'And after four centuries together, I know him so much better.'

Catrina shook her head, forcing herself to maintain eye contact. 'So *you* say,' she said, trying to copy Nadia's sneer; she failed miserably. 'Why would he? What would he get out of it?'

Nadia's grin was victorious. 'Me,' she said simply.

It took a moment for the word to sink into her head as Catrina stared at the woman across from her. It didn't make sense.

'What?' she asked, her voice wobbling with a weak excuse for a laugh as she attempted to shrug off Nadia's insinuation.

Nadia leaned forward, resting her elbows against her knees as she stared at her rival, hard. 'His prize was me,' she said slowly, making sure every word sunk in. '*All* of me,' she added, ensuring the enormity of her statement was understood.

Catrina shook her head, her stomach rolling. 'You're his sister,' she finally managed to say.

Nadia's eyes gleamed. 'And so much more besides,' she hissed venomously.

Catrina's entire body felt detached. 'I don't believe you,' she muttered, her voice shaking. 'You'd say anything to hurt me and him. You're just jealous.'

'Of you?' Nadia snorted.

Catrina tried hard to ignore the malice of Nadia's words but they still ate into her resolve. She swallowed past the lump of emotion in her throat.

'Jealous of Alex being happy,' she finally managed.

Nadia laughed. 'Alex has always been happy...' she purred. 'With me.' She stood from her seat, glaring down at the girl on the sofa. 'Perhaps I didn't make myself clear,' she growled, 'but you were a *bet*. Nothing more. You were something to keep him entertained. Don't try and convince yourself otherwise. You're nothing special, sweetie, you're just a new hobby.'

Catrina fought against the tears that brimmed in her eyes, her hands shaking as she battled for control of her emotions.

'You're wrong,' she stammered, the act of speaking making her tears fall. 'We're engaged. Alex loves me.' She tried clinging to the hope her words were true, but after what Nadia had told her, she was no longer sure; Nadia had, after all, just insinuated Alex was in a relationship with his own sister.

RETRITUTION DARKENED

In a swift move, Nadia crossed the room, grabbing Catrina's hair and dragging her from her seat, ignoring the girl's pained cries.

With a vicious push, Nadia forced Catrina to look in the large mirror above the mantle and grinned at the tears that ran down the girl's pale cheeks.

'Look at you,' she snarled at their reflections. 'Look at the state of you.' She squeezed her fingers as they tangled through Catrina's hair, pulling it at the roots. 'You're nothing,' she hissed. 'Why would Alex love *you*?' she asked, every word she spoke dripping with hate. 'You could *never* compete with me. I'm everything to him. I'm his life.'

Catrina choked on her tears as her mind processed Nadia's words. *You could never compete with me.* The words were vindictive and sick and yet they mocked her with the truth; Nadia's beauty was devastating, her sexuality overwhelming, her position in Alex's life unassailable. Her hope that all this was some misunderstanding on her part diminished.

'Alex wanted *me* in his life,' she managed.

'You're dead now, or had you forgotten that?' Nadia sneered, her lips brushing close to Catrina's ear so her words of menace wouldn't be misinterpreted. 'You're *diseased*. You're not supposed to be here anymore.'

Catrina shook her head, tears escaping down her cheeks. 'Alex wanted me here,' she said quietly, her voice feeble under the hateful glare of the dark woman beside her. 'He wanted to change me.'

Nadia laughed, the sound spiteful. 'He changed you to save your life, not because he actually *wanted* to,' she taunted. 'He's terribly soft in that respect. Guilt made him do it. You're something new... a novelty.' She drew a ragged breath. 'Fresh meat. But it won't last. He'll soon get bored.' Nadia brushed her lips against the skin of Catrina's throat. 'Men stray when they're bored.'

Catrina tried to get away but Nadia pressed her nails into her neck harder, watching with a sick satisfaction as tears fell freely down the girl's cheeks.

Nadia brushed her lips against Catrina's ear once more, her words vindictive. 'When Alex makes love to you it's *my* face he imagines before him.'

Catrina felt the bile rise in her throat, her stomach churning at the images flashing through her mind.

'It's my blood he craves,' Nadia whispered maliciously. 'My body he lusts after.' She traced the contour of Catrina's jaw with her finger. 'When you're sleeping do you think he spends the day alone? He comes to *me*.'

Anger ripped through the revulsion, burning in every vein. Despite her tears, hurt and humiliation, Catrina tore herself from Nadia's violent hold, lashing out with her hand to land a stinging blow across her rival's cheek, her nails catching the skin until blood beaded along the porcelain surface.

Nadia snarled at her, rushing at her and pinning her to the wall by her throat. 'You little bitch,' she hissed, her sharp teeth bared.

Catrina tried in vain to stop her hands from shaking but failed miserably under the hateful glare of those haunting green eyes. The room spun around her as her mind tried to process everything she'd heard, knowing from the gleam in Nadia's eyes that everything she'd told her had been the truth. Her stomach retched again.

'Does the truth hurt, *princess*?' Nadia growled, her lips inches from Catrina's face, making sure the girl felt every word. 'You're *nothing* to him, do you understand? I've been part of his life for over four centuries. I own him. He belongs to *me*.' She tightened her hold on Catrina's throat, leaving her unable to speak. 'The game ends here, my lovely,' she taunted. 'I *always* win.'

'What the hell is going on?' Alex stared at the pair of them, his eyes dark with concern as he stood in the lounge doorway.

Under her brother's harsh glare, Nadia released her hold on Catrina, who crumpled against the wall, defeated.

Her legs felt like jelly as her body trembled, sobs choking her. She stared at the floor beneath her feet, trying to calm her churning stomach.

Nadia glared at her brother as he stepped towards her, his green eyes blazing with the anger he was suppressing for everyone's sake.

'I asked you a damn question,' he snarled. 'What is going on?'

His sister shrugged and he angrily pushed her aside, hunkering down by Catrina's side.

'It's okay,' he whispered gently, reaching out to brush her hair from her face.

Nausea swept over her at his touch and she shied away, unable to look at him; her mind was still too full of images of depravity and the centuries of lies used to conceal it.

Alex drew a ragged breath. 'Princess, what has she done to you?'

The care and gentleness of his words reviled her and angered her all at once; how could he act so innocent when he'd done all that Nadia had revealed?

'As if you care,' she spat at him, looking at him finally. She saw the uncertainty flash in his green eyes, feeling any doubt in Nadia's words melt away.

Again he reached out for her as she attempted to get to her feet, but she pushed his hands away.

'Don't touch me,' she screamed. 'I don't want you anywhere near me.' She steadied herself against the wall, her legs weak as her stomach churned.

Alex glanced over his shoulder at his sister, who sat perched on the arm of the sofa, a self-satisfied smile on her face.

He turned back to Catrina. 'What has she said to you?' he asked carefully.

Catrina glared at him, her blue eyes seething. 'A lot more than you have,' she hissed. 'No wonder you kept it from me. You're sick,' she spat, finding the strength to push herself away from the wall and step past him; the need to get away from him and this house was suddenly overwhelming.

She wobbled across the room, ignoring Nadia's smug smile as she pushed herself towards the entrance hall.

She reached the front door before she felt Alex's grip on her arm, turning her so she was forced to face him. He looked extremely unnerved.

'Don't run away from me, Cat,' he said firmly. 'What has she said to you?'

Again she shook off his grip, unable to tolerate his touch. 'The truth,' she screamed, her sharp teeth bared in anger. 'You're twisted... sick.'

'Princess, let me explain–' he sputtered.

'What part?' she cut him off, unable to listen to his words. 'What part would you like to *explain*, Alex?' she sneered. 'The part where you kiss her? The part where you share her blood?' Tears fell down her cheeks unchecked as all the emotion and revulsion she'd tried to hold back rushed to the surface as she looked at this man she'd trusted. 'Or do you want to explain the part where you're fucking your sister?' she screamed again, spinning away from him, pulling the front door open and running through it.

Alex stood stock still, unable to move as he watched her run away from the house.

'Some people should really learn to be more open-minded,' Nadia teased behind him, the same self-satisfied smile etched on her face.

He turned to face her then, his green eyes

seething with rage. 'What in God's name have you done?' he asked quietly.

She shrugged, standing from her seat on the sofa. 'She had a right to know the truth,' she said flatly.

His restraint snapping, Alex flew at his sister, pinning her to the doorframe by her shoulders.

'The truth?' he shouted. 'How could you do that to her? To *me*?'

She glared at him, defiance in her eyes. 'I did what was right, my love,' she soothed.

But Alex shook his head firmly, detachment in his eyes. 'No, Nadia, you did what was right for *you*, as always,' he said angrily. 'Only this time you've gone too far.'

Gripping her arms, he threw her across the room violently, disgusted by the very sight of her.

I'll kill her, he thought, the intensity of the idea overwhelming him.

With an angry hiss, she brushed her black hair away from her face as she stared up at him, her gaze cold.

'She had a right to know, Alex,' she growled, her eyes narrowing.

'You had no right to say anything,' he shouted at her, crossing the room.

Nadia pushed herself to her feet, brushing her hands down her clothes calmly. 'She needed to know the truth,' she said, matter-of-factly.

Lashing out, Alex slapped his sister hard across

the face, her head snapping back from the blow.

'You bitch. You wouldn't know the truth if it hit you in the face,' he snapped. 'I bet you loved telling her every little twisted detail.' He shivered despite himself, unwilling to think of the things he knew she'd have taken great pleasure in disclosing.

'Don't take the moral high ground with me,' she warned. 'You're hardly innocent in all this.'

'It wasn't your place to tell her,' he argued. 'If it was to come from anyone, it should have been me.'

Nadia laughed. 'And you would have happily disclosed your *real* past, would you?' she taunted. 'You can't base a relationship or a marriage on lies.'

'What would you know?' he asked viciously, darkly satisfied to see the briefest flash of hurt in her emerald eyes.

In seconds it was gone, replaced by a darkness that unnerved him.

'I did this for *us*,' she soothed, taking a step towards him. 'Don't you realise that? All these lies are not healthy and now she knows the truth, you're free.' Another step closer to Alex and she reached out for him, placing her hands gently against his chest. 'Everything can go back to the way it was, just the two of us.'

Snatching her wrists in his hands, he glared down at her, revulsion washing over him. 'You're mad,' he seethed. 'I want nothing to do with you after what you've done.'

He released her wrists, turning to head for the

door.

'You *need* me,' she called after him, her tone cold and taunting.

Alex stopped in his tracks, turning to look at his sister. She smiled at him, that age-old hardness in her eyes. There was a satisfaction in that cold stare and his rage spiralled out of control; this madness had to stop, *now*.

Taking a step back towards her, he brutally forced her against the wall, squeezing her face in his hand, using all his willpower not to move that hand to her throat.

'I don't need you for *anything*,' he hissed. 'We're finished, do you understand me?' He squeezed harder until he could see the pain in her eyes, despite her defiance.

'I'll never forgive you for what you've done. Ever.'

Pushing her away, he stormed out of the house.

Chapter 14

'Here we go,' Matt smiled, lowering the two drinks onto the table.

He took a seat and stared across at Nadia, who'd begun absently playing with the straw in her glass.

'Thank you,' she said quietly, clearly upset.

Matt's watched her carefully. 'You sounded really upset on the phone,' he said, remembering how she'd called him out of the blue in tears; he couldn't deny he'd fantasised about her calling for weeks... among other things. Without another thought, he'd agreed to meet her for a drink, leaving the office half an hour early with a feigned migraine.

'I'm sorry,' she said quietly. 'I didn't mean to disturb you at work.' She dipped the straw in and out of her drink absently. 'I just didn't know who to call. Lola has so much on her plate already.'

Don't I know, he thought, then mentally reprimanded himself. He shook his head. 'Don't worry about it. They've had enough overtime out of me over the last few weeks,' he joked, trying to coax a smile from her.

His efforts reaped little reward.

Nadia continued to stir her drink, seemingly deep in thought.

Matt took a sip from his glass, his brow creasing in concern. 'So what's up?' he asked gently.

She met his gaze, her green eyes shining with fresh tears; it was a look that had him wanting to take her in his arms and hold on to her.

'I had a fight... with Alex,' she said softly, her voice delicately trembling with emotion she was clearly trying to hold on to. 'Quite a bad one,' she added.

He shifted in his seat. 'Oh?' he asked shortly. 'Can I ask what about?'

She shrugged. 'It doesn't really matter,' she said sadly, looking at the drink in front of her.

'Well it does if it's upset you like this,' he pressed, concern filling his voice as he stared at her.

'Really, it's not important,' she insisted, still not looking up at him. 'It's not like we've never argued before. We're twins, it happens. It's what we do.'

Matt wasn't convinced. 'So what made this time different?' he asked.

Nadia managed a small apologetic smile. 'I wasn't very nice to Catrina,' she confessed, glancing up at him to see his reaction.

His expression gave nothing away. 'In what way?' he asked carefully.

'I didn't mean it,' she said quickly.

'I didn't say you did,' he offered.

Nadia coyly played with the straw in her glass, poking at the rapidly melting ice cubes. Her smile was grim.

'I've not been dealing with things very well lately,' she admitted. 'I shouldn't have taken it out on Catrina. It wasn't fair.'

'I guess we're all suffering at the moment,' he said, hoping to lighten her mood. 'I wouldn't beat yourself up about it too much.'

She smiled as she stared into her drink. 'You're just being nice,' she chuckled.

Matt shook his head, his expression soft. 'Not at all. Catrina will understand. She's not one to hold a grudge, trust me. She's probably suffering just as much over Jason.'

Nadia looked up at him. 'Do you think so?' she asked, hope in her voice.

He nodded. 'I know so. She's not dealing with it well, either, according to Lola. She's close to Jason. He's like a surrogate brother.' He took a sip of his pint. 'I'm sure you and Alex will sort it out, and you and Catrina have more in common than you probably know. That's why we all met up the other night. We all need to stick together at a time like this.'

Nadia smiled warmly, clearly grateful for his words of advice. 'Thank you, Matt,' she said softly. 'I knew you would help.'

He chuckled. 'I guess it's the solicitor in me.'

'I hope I'm not being charged for your time?'

she asked playfully.

Matt shifted in his seat, unsure if she was flirting with him; he hoped she was. 'I wouldn't dream of it,' he said, trying to push away the thoughts of what he *would* dream of.

She grinned. 'You're such a gentleman,' she purred.

He smiled in order to hide his discomfort at her words; the thoughts he was having about her right now certainly weren't gentlemanly. He cleared his throat as he took another drink from his pint, watching her surreptitiously from over the rim of his glass. She looked amazing, as she always did, with her ink-black hair trailing down her back, her grey shirt and pencil skirt hugging her figure perfectly. Her boots were sexy as hell.

Nadia played with the straw in her drink once more, barely taking a sip as she glanced up at him. 'How's Lola?' she asked brightly. 'I haven't seen her since our drink the other night.'

Matt straightened in his chair, instantly uncomfortable. He suppressed the urge to roll his eyes, biting back a sarcastic retort.

Nadia watched him closely. 'Is everything okay?' she tested gently.

He wanted to lie, to avoid any mention of Lola and her ridiculous problems that had her fearing the dark and her own shadow; yet Nadia's gentle gaze and concerned expression made him want to confess every horrendous detail.

'She's been under a lot of pressure lately, work and stuff, you know?' he offered as a starting point, watching as Nadia simply sat and listened; he hadn't had anyone to talk to properly since Jason had disappeared. 'She's not been coping too well. Then when Jason did his disappearing act...' He couldn't find the words to finish the sentence.

With a warm smile, Nadia reached across the table and covered his hand supportively with her own. 'I'm sorry,' she said gently. 'I didn't realise. I knew she wasn't dealing with it all very well, but I didn't know quite how bad it was.'

Matt stared down at her hand covering his, feeling a load lift from his shoulders for what felt like the first time in a long while. There was once a time when this would have been himself and Lola, talking like this; he could tell her anything and she'd listen and advise. He was becoming more and more convinced that those times were all but gone.

'She hides it well,' he admitted. 'The pressure has really built up. I don't know how much longer she can carry on before she...' Once more he trailed off, unable to speak the words that hovered through his mind; she's crazy, she's mad, she's losing her grip on reality.

He considered telling Nadia the truth, about the red eyes, about the voices, everything; but he knew it wasn't his place to tell her. Lola thought highly of Nadia and counted her as a very close friend; if Lola wanted Nadia to know the truth of her problems then he was sure she would have confessed them before now.

'You poor thing,' she whispered. 'It must be hard for you, too, living with this burden.'

Once again, his gaze fell to her hand covering his and he forced himself to smile. 'Wasn't *I* supposed to be making *you* feel better?' he asked with a chuckle that lacked any humour.

Nadia smiled. 'I guess we both needed someone to listen to our problems,' she said softly with a shrug. 'I'll try and talk to Lola, see if I can do anything to help.'

Matt appreciated her help, feeling lighter than he had in a long time; it was a feeling he wanted to savour. 'Thanks, that would be great. Maybe she'll open up to you.'

She sure as hell won't to me anymore, he thought harshly.

'Well, I can try,' she offered, her smile widening. 'No promises.'

He tried to ignore his growing need to push this situation further, to see how far their seemingly innocent flirting could go. Yet he resisted, mentally pushing the urge away. Nadia was just being a friend; he was the one needing comfort and attention and he wasn't the type to take advantage of a friend's help.

'Anything you can do would be a help, however small,' he confirmed, glancing to her hand covering his once more. He found his imagination running away with him again, thinking of the many other things she could do with those perfectly manicured hands of hers.

'That goes for you, too,' she said warmly, pulling her hand away as if she'd known what he was thinking. She resumed playing with the straw in her glass, stirring the alcohol within. 'If you need a friend to talk to...' She left the invite unvoiced.

'Thanks,' he said, grateful. 'I might have to take you up on that at some point,' he added, his voice weary.

'Please do,' she urged with a smile, that slight edge of flirting filling her voice once more.

You're imagining things, he told himself, though decided he preferred his imagination if it resulted in the images that filled his mind. Taking a deep breath and asking himself what the hell he thought he was doing, he decided to test the water.

'Well, maybe next time I can treat you to something to eat, just as a thank you,' he offered, his grip tightening on the glass in his hand.

If she was surprised by his offer, she didn't show it. Her smile was filled with warmth. 'That would be nice, thank you,' she said softly.

Matt relaxed a little, grateful he hadn't forced the situation or made an innocent drink between friends too awkward.

'Great,' he breathed, his voice a little rougher than he'd expected and he cleared his throat, embarrassed.

'Thank you for listening to my problems,' Nadia

said, her gaze holding his.

He tried to ignore the burning need that flowed through him in that instant. He forced a smile. 'I think you listened to me more,' he pointed out.

She shrugged. 'Maybe, but you made time for me and my silly problems. That means a lot,' she soothed, glancing up at him from under her thick lashes.

He held her captivating gaze. 'No problem's silly if it bothers you,' he advised. 'But I'm sure you and Alex will sort this out. Trust me, Catrina is suffering as much as you right now. You probably both need a little space.'

Nadia nodded. 'I'm sure you're right,' she agreed softly. 'And I'm sure Lola just needs time, and a little TLC.'

Matt didn't agree but he nodded nonetheless. 'I'm sure you're right,' he lied.

'Of course I am,' she grinned playfully, lightening the mood. 'And you're just the right man to make her feel better,' she added.

'You think?' he asked, unable to prevent the scepticism in his voice.

'I *know*,' she confirmed, placing her hand on his once more, her cold fingers stroking his knuckles. 'You are a very good friend, Matt, and Lola is a very lucky woman to have you,' she purred. 'Very lucky.'

There was something in her eyes that Matt couldn't decipher, but whatever it was it had his heart rate increasing, making his need for this stunning woman ten times worse. Her words, seemingly innocent on her part, carried a faint need of her own.

His imagination ran wild again with images of what that need could be and he found himself wanting more than ever to find out.

He finally had to admit to himself that he wanted this woman, badly.

He shifted in his seat.

If her intense green gaze was any indication, he was damn sure she wanted him, too.

Chapter 15

Catrina closed her eyes, counting the seconds as her phone rang on the coffee table in front of her. She didn't want to see Alex's name flashing up on the screen or imagine what he'd say as he tried desperately to explain.

Finally, the ringing stopped, just it had the last twenty times.

She opened her eyes and stared at the phone, hugging her knees as she huddled on the armchair in the darkness of her lounge; she'd refused to switch on any lights on returning home.

She felt cold, numb, and incredibly alone.

After escaping from Alex's house, she'd found herself gravitating towards Lola's place out of habit, but had thought better of it before she'd reached the door; she could never hope to explain the reality of her problems.

Reluctantly, Catrina had wandered the streets for over an hour instead, her mind a cacophony of thoughts as she tried to make some sense from the events of the last few hours; it was impossible, but she tried in vain nonetheless.

Instinctively, she'd headed for the lake in Wiltham Park, her favourite thinking place, but the icy waters did nothing to help the desolation she felt and she knew it would be one of the first places Alex would look for her.

Now, hidden in her home, she watched as her phone began to buzz once more on the coffee table, the very sight of Alex's name almost too painful to endure.

A fresh wave of nausea washed over her as fresh images entered her head of the depraved things Nadia had insinuated.

The phone stopped ringing and Catrina grabbed it quickly, turning it off and burying it under a cushion on the sofa, tears filling her eyes; she'd given herself to Alex and he'd promised her the world.

Returning to the armchair, she pulled her knees to her chest, supressing a sob.

The world no longer made any sense.

An involuntary shiver ran the length of Catrina's spine as the doorbell rang.

She squeezed her eyes closed, silently begging Alex to leave her alone.

The doorbell sounded again.

'Please, go away,' she murmured to herself, the tears falling over her cheeks.

A gentle voice sounded on the other side of the door. 'Catrina, my dear, I know you're in there.'

Catrina sighed.

Aurelia Demeter's voice was stern. 'Alex told me what happened,' she murmured, sadness in her tone. 'He's been looking for you.'

Catrina shivered as she reluctantly moved from the armchair, stepping slowly from the lounge into the hallway.

She stared at the front door and the silhouette of the woman behind the glass.

'Did he send you to find me?' she asked quietly.

God, how she wished she would wake from all this to find she'd overslept for work, the harsh buzzing of her alarm rousing her from what she prayed was a horrendous nightmare; it was wasted optimism, she knew too well.

Aurelia sighed. 'No,' she admitted. 'I decided to conduct a search for myself. I thought perhaps we could have a little talk. Just the two of us?'

The tone of Aurelia's voice brought a fresh realisation crashing down; her tone was full of regret.

Fresh revulsion surged through Catrina's entire being. 'Oh, my God,' she breathed, her stomach churning. 'You knew, didn't you?'

Aurelia's voice was full of desperation. 'I know you are upset, my child, and you have every right to be. But can we not talk together to discuss things?'

Catrina snorted. 'I think I've heard more than enough,' she said loudly.

Aurelia sigh was weary. 'Can I at least come in?' she urged. 'I do not think the doorstep is the best place to discuss such matters.'

Catrina remained silent, unable to make sense of the myriad of thoughts rushing through her head.

'Please?' Aurelia pleaded. 'I ask only this one thing of you, my child.'

Catrina stared at the door in front of her for a long time. Was this some ploy to get her to speak to Alex? Was he waiting somewhere to try and beg her forgiveness?

The more she stared at Aurelia's silhouette through the glass, the more unlikely those thoughts seemed; Aurelia was not a devious or manipulative person. Catrina had learnt that much. Aurelia was simply a woman looking after her family; the very word had the nausea sweeping over Catrina again and she fought hard against it.

Feeling beaten by all the questions and uncertainties rushing through her mind, Catrina sighed in reluctant agreement, remaining silent as she slowly unlocked the door and pulled it open.

For a long moment she found herself unable to look at the dark-haired ancient standing on her doorstep, unwilling to meet those eyes which so closely resembled Alex's... and his sister's.

Outside, the evening was icy, frost clinging to the cars parked along the roadside. The air was crisp and should have invigorated every drop of blood in Catrina's body, yet it didn't; it made her feel so incredibly alone she had to fight back the tears.

She'd wanted so desperately to run to Lola earlier, the habit still strong within her. Yet her misery and loneliness had only intensified as she'd walked away from her friend's door.

Catrina glanced at Aurelia, still not meeting the woman's gaze. A grim reality seeped in; whether she liked it or not, right now this woman was the only person she had to confide in.

Unnerved, Catrina glanced along the street.

'Alex has not followed me, my child,' Aurelia soothed gently. 'I am completely alone, I assure you.'

So am I, Catrina thought sadly.

Her shoulders slumped as she turned away, leading the way into the house.

Aurelia followed, closing the front door behind her.

In the lounge, Catrina flicked on the lights as she went, unwilling to think of the nights and days spent with Alex within its walls; the thought of his hands and lips on her body made her sick.

'Have a seat,' she offered quietly.

She watched as Aurelia sat herself down on the sofa, while Catrina returned to her armchair opposite.

'Thank you, my child,' Aurelia offered softly. 'I know this is difficult for you,' she said.

'Difficult?' she choked. 'I think that's an understatement, don't you? I've discovered the man I'd given my life to, literally, is fucking his sister.'

Aurelia had never liked bad language, having lived throughout the centuries where gentleman never used such foul words in front of ladies, and she stiffened at Catrina's coarse reference to what she'd been told.

She sighed. 'I am unsure what has been described to you, my dear, but know that there is so much more about our history you do not understand.'

Catrina stared at her, unable to comprehend the calmness with which Aurelia spoke. 'You knew,' she repeated, tears filling her eyes. She stood from her seat, pacing the floor, shaking her head.

This wasn't happening. 'How can you know about such a thing and be so calm? Is this some sort of family tradition? Is Victor your father?' she snapped.

Aurelia watched her closely. 'My child, please try and calm yourself,' she said softly, watching as Catrina continued to pace the floor.

Catrina shook her head back and forth too quickly. 'Calm myself?' she choked, her voice several octaves higher than normal. 'The man I wanted to spend forever with is sleeping with his sister... and you *knew*,' she screeched, rubbing her hands together over and over. 'Do you all know? Of course you do.' She answered her own question, still pacing and barely glancing Aurelia's way. 'You're all as sick as each other.'

Aurelia clasped her hands together. 'My dear, I appreciate you have had a nasty shock, but I need you to sit down and listen. Allow me to explain what my daughter perhaps did not.'

Catrina stared at the woman before her for a moment, seeing Alex reflected in her emerald eyes. With a choked sob, her shoulders slumped, the fight leaving her; running away wasn't working this time.

She sat herself down in the armchair, pulling her knees to her chest in an upright foetal position.

Sensing Catrina's surrender, Aurelia took a slow breath. 'I understand you must be shocked and confused, and–'

'And sickened, and disgusted...' Catrina added with a sneer. 'And like my whole world has fallen apart... again.' She sobbed, unable to hold back her tears any longer.

She stared at Aurelia, desperate for an answer that would numb the pain. 'How could he do this to me?'

Aurelia sighed. 'I am not for one moment condoning what Alex has done. But there is much more to his past than you know. A darker side I'm sure he believed he was hiding for good reason.' She glanced down at her hands sadly. 'It doesn't do any of us any good to recall it, yet for obvious reasons I feel that now I must. Perhaps it is the only way to make you understand.'

Catrina stared at Aurelia, wariness in her eyes. 'I'm not sure I can take any more revelations at the moment,' she admitted cynically.

Aurelia stared at her. 'There are a great many things you do not know about our family... about its history.'

'Incest being one of the perks, is it?' Catrina mocked over the top of her knees, lowering her gaze under Aurelia's withering stare.

'We are not talking of a human past here, Catrina,' Aurelia continued, her tone serious. 'For Alex, we are dealing with a past spanning over four hundred years. However human your mind may still be, you *have* to appreciate the magnitude of a life so long. Humans believe immortality to be so fabulous and fun-filled. You have only begun to live, my child. Can you really imagine yourself in four hundred years' time? Do you want to, knowing you would have seen everyone you love die? Knowing you will watch humanity destroy itself with wars, wrecking entire continents? Living with the knowledge that you are yourself death incarnate? I was born to this nature, but in all worldly honesty, after nearly eight hundred years, I would not choose it should I have had a choice. You truly have my profound respect, my child, for being so brave and making the sacrifices you have.'

Catrina stared at the ancient woman across the room. She'd never heard Aurelia Demeter speak in such a way. For a moment she found herself unable to speak.

Finally, she found her voice. 'That doesn't make it okay,' she argued. 'What Nadia told me was—'

'Her own twisted words,' Aurelia interrupted. 'Born from anger and hatred. She wanted to hurt you.'

Catrina shook her head. 'So she was lying?' she asked, her tone cynical; Alex's devastated gaze had told her otherwise.

Aurelia sighed, her gaze full of sympathy. 'All I can do, my dear, is offer you the truth. Something perhaps Nadia's own words denied you.'

Catrina took a deep breath, her hands shaking as they gripped her legs tighter to her chest. She closed her eyes, composing herself.

'Okay,' she sighed, defeated. 'I'm listening.'

Chapter 16

The last few days had been nothing more than a blur.

Alex closed his eyes, running the images of Catrina through his mind; she'd looked at him with such disgust it had broken his heart. He was unsure what he could do to reverse the damage his sister had done.

He'd been immensely grateful to his mother for explaining the truth to Catrina, though the thoughts of what she'd needed to divulge sent a painful shiver through his entire body. Whether it had helped Catrina to understand or not, his past would still not have been easy for her to discover.

Afterwards, Catrina had told his elder that she needed time alone.

He hadn't seen or heard from her since.

Alex had barely left the house for fear of missing a visit from her and he constantly kept his cell phone by his side in case she called.

He'd avoided and ignored Nadia and had barely spoken to his elders as he tormented himself, scarcely sleeping as he imagined Catrina and the damage he'd caused. He'd convinced himself she hated him and would never forgive him for what he'd done.

He didn't deserve forgiveness.

As the daylight hours dwindled by, he sat on the sofa, listening to the monotonous ticking of the clock on the mantle. He thumbed through the newspaper, trying at least to focus on something other than the thoughts and images that were slowly driving him crazy; it was as if every moment of his past was reliving itself, tormenting him with memories of all the pain and suffering he'd ever caused.

He checked his cell phone again, though he knew he'd received no messages or calls.

'Is she *still* ignoring you?' Nadia pouted, teasing him from the lounge doorway.

He didn't know how long she'd been standing there and he didn't really care. He glanced up at her briefly, angered by her self-satisfied smile. He returned his attentions back to the newspaper in his hands.

Nadia watched him closely. She hated to admit it, but she was impressed by his self-control; she knew there had been many times he'd wanted to lash out at her over the last few days and yet he'd resisted.

She knew his mood wouldn't last; she could recall countless times over the years when he'd tried to distance himself from her. Every time, he'd come crawling back like a lost puppy.

'She won't forgive you, you know,' she said, her

words harsh.

Alex shifted in his seat, uncomfortable with her statement but unwilling to give in to her rouse.

'And ignoring *me* won't change that,' she added.

'Leave me be,' he growled, unwilling to look at her again. He focused all his attentions on the newspaper, though his thoughts were elsewhere.

Nadia took a step into the room, gauging his responses. 'You're tormenting yourself and it isn't helping.' She took another step. 'I'm your sister,' she whispered. 'I'm only looking out for you.'

He snorted, still refusing to look up from the pages in front of him. 'You're no sister of mine after what you did,' he said flatly, sensing her moving towards him; it was unnerving.

Nadia shook her head, the smallest of smiles on her face. 'Oh, Alex,' she sighed, amused. 'How many times have we played this little game?' she asked. 'Yet here we are.'

Her words were true, he knew; too many times he'd tried to ignore her, punish her and walk away, yet time and again he returned to her side, knowing the horrors she was capable of and forgiving her just the same.

Nadia perched herself on the arm of the sofa, facing him.

Briefly, Alex looked up at her, noting her knee-length skirt with the split that revealed her thigh as she sat down. She leant forward, her low-buttoned white blouse falling open and he returned his gaze to the newspaper, unwilling to be sucked into her games once more.

'You can't ignore me forever,' she said in a sing-song voice, amusement in her tone as she swung her legs back and forth, the split in her skirt opening further.

He sniffed with distaste. 'I'll have a damn good try,' he growled, though his words were not as solid as he would have liked.

Nadia laughed, entertained by the belief in his words. 'And try is all you'll do,' she teased, jumping up from her seat and heading for the window. She pulled back the curtain, looking out into the dull, overcast evening; spring was late this year and March had started off cold and miserable, which suited her perfectly.

She smiled as she spotted Lola crossing the street towards her home, Camilla in tow. Lola's face was void of any emotion, though she looked tired, Nadia mused.

Lola spotted her neighbour at the window and smiled her way, raising her hand in a friendly wave.

Nadia waved back, a friendly smile decorating her lips. She duly noted Camilla's hard glare.

'Lola's waving hello,' Nadia said cheerfully over her shoulder. She turned away from the window, dropping the curtain back in place.

Alex still refused to look at her. 'You're still tormenting her, aren't you?' he asked numbly, wishing she'd leave the poor girl alone; Lola didn't deserve what Nadia was doing to her.

Nadia shrugged as she perched once more on the arm of the sofa, looking at him. 'Not as much anymore,' she said flatly. 'She's pretty much doing it for me,' she laughed, thinking of the last time she'd really spooked Lola in the market before Jason had died.

That one act had been enough to destroy Lola's faith in Matt, plant seeds of doubt in the minds of her friends in terms of her sanity, and drive a hardened wedge between Lola and Matt as she turned to Jason instead of him.

The game was coming to an end and the anticipation of the final goal was becoming overwhelming.

'You're destroying that girl for no reason, you do know that?' he asked fiercely, crumpling the pages of the newspaper in his hands as he gripped them tighter.

She shrugged. 'I have *my* reasons... don't they count?' she pouted playfully, that same cruel smile playing across her lips. Her eyes sparkled with mischief.

Finally, he lowered the newspaper to his lap and met her gaze, his emerald glare dark. 'And what about Matt?' he asked, disgusted by her complete disregard for the lives she was playing with.

Nadia's smile grew and she bit her lower lip as she considered the possibilities. 'Well now, really that's all your own fault,' she said.

Alex stared at her, dumbfounded. '*My* fault?' he choked.

She nodded, licking her lips slowly as she continued to stare at him. 'You have a very short memory,' she teased.

He shifted in his seat, uncomfortable with her words; he hadn't forgotten anything and she knew it.

'*You* were the one who stopped me playing that night, remember?' she asked with a grin. 'I was enjoying myself, having a little play before the feast. Matt was enjoying it, too... even if he doesn't remember it,' she pointed out, crossing her legs so the split in her skirt fell wide open, revealing the lacy top of her black stockings.

Alex tried to ignore her, but her words commanded his attention and he was compelled to look up at her.

'He wanted me that night,' she whispered, her gaze intense.

Alex snorted. 'He was asleep. He didn't know what he wanted.'

'Oh, he knew,' Nadia sneered. 'His body made that painfully obvious. And he was denied me... by *you*.' She waved a finger at him, a smile playing on her lips. She leaned further forward, closing the gap between them. 'So I *will* have my playtime,' she said, her words hard. 'Without your jealous interfering.'

He didn't want to think on the implication of her words; dread seized him as he thought of her intentions towards Matt and the horror of the consequences.

Nadia grinned at him, a dangerous gleam in her emerald eyes. 'It *was* jealousy, wasn't it, Alex?' she purred gently. 'Admit it.' She dangled the challenge in front of him, willing him to say the words she knew were true.

He stared at her, remembering so much from their past; jealousy had a lot to answer for.

'I know you too well, my love,' she whispered with amusement. 'You can't hide it from me.'

He clenched his fists in his lap, crushing the newspaper below them.

'Alex,' she sang, swinging her legs back and forth like an excited child as she laughed.

Her mocking was the final straw.

He snapped, leaping from his chair. He pinned her to the sofa, his hands pressing hard against her shoulders as he glared into her green eyes, seeing himself reflected back.

'Okay, I was jealous,' he shouted at her, his sharp teeth bared in anger. 'I was jealous and I stopped you. Satisfied?'

She grinned up at him, refusing to back down. 'Not yet I'm not,' she said softly, her words tempting. 'But I will be, eventually.' The last word was a whisper against his lips and Alex pushed her away.

'You sicken me,' he growled, wiping his mouth with the back of his hand; even the taste of her breath was a poison he was fatally addicted to. 'Stop playing games with Matt,' he warned, glaring at her.

'You're jealous,' she sang at him again with a giggle, knowing she was pushing him to his limit; it was something she'd always found sickeningly amusing.

'Bullshit,' he shouted, punching the wall above her head; satisfaction flooded over him as he watched her flinch. 'Those people don't deserve what you're doing to them,' he snarled. 'You've dragged them into your sick games, fucking with their lives. Leave them *all* alone.' He straightened himself and turned angrily from her, leaving the room.

Nadia laughed after him as she pushed herself from the sofa, straightening her clothes. She stared after him, her eyes narrowed.

'You can't walk away from me, Alex,' she whispered, knowing he could hear her in the other room.

She stood from the sofa and headed back to the window, glancing out across the street to Lola's house.

'You've tried too many times and failed, brother dearest,' she hissed.

A cunning smile spread across her lips as she thought on Jason and the entertainment he'd supplied.

Her smile grew wider.

She still had one more pawn to add to her collection.

A frown creased her forehead as she watched the dark car drive slowly up the street, coming to a stop outside the house.

She watched, her eyes narrowing as she observed the two people step from the car. One was a tall, well-built man in his late forties, she would have guessed, and the other was a reasonably young woman; both were in suits and looked rather official.

She watched them approach the house, turning from the window as the heavy sound of the doorknocker vibrated through the hall.

Alex appeared in the doorway almost immediately, a hopeful expression on his face.

Nadia rolled her eyes. 'Don't get too excited,' she sneered. 'It's not your little princess.'

The loud knock sounded again and Alex made a move towards the hallway, his disappointment confirmed when he opened the front door.

Two strangers stood on the doorstep, one man and one woman. The man offered him the smallest of smiles as he held up his credentials for Alex to see.

'Good evening. I'm Detective Inspector Markham and this is Detective Sergeant Bell.'

Nadia approached behind her brother, offering the kindest of smiles.

The DI addressed the two twins. 'Alex and Nadia Demeter?'

Alex nodded solemnly.

The DI offered him a smile that was anything but friendly.

'Do you mind if I come in? I have a few questions regarding Jason Taggart.'

Chapter 17

'You did what?' Lola stared at Camilla, who simply shrugged.

'I called the police,' she stated flatly. 'That's why they're visiting them now.'

Lola couldn't believe what her friend had done; she stood against the window frame, staring out across the road as the two plain-clothed police officers disappeared into the Demeter household.

'Maybe now the witch will get what's coming to her,' Camilla mumbled, taking a sip of her steaming coffee before placing the mug back onto Lola's coffee table.

Lola turned away from the window and stared at her friend who refused to meet her gaze.

She shook her head, baffled. 'What have you done?' she whispered, falling into the armchair nearest the window, her own coffee forgotten on the table; any cheer to Camilla's visit had quickly vanished.

Camilla shrugged. 'You gave out the contact

cards,' she pointed out. 'I had further information for the case so I called them.'

'You had no right to do that, Cam,' Lola said, angry that Camilla could think so badly of Nadia. 'Nadia's been nothing but a good friend to me since she moved in and especially since Jason went missing.'

'Guilty conscience, if you ask me,' Camilla sneered, finally meeting Lola's accusing glare.

'Bullshit,' Lola blurted. 'She was really upset when I spoke to her after he disappeared. She really cared about Jason and she's supported me a lot these last few weeks. She's just as worried about him as I am.' There was a finality in her words, making it clear she wasn't prepared to listen to anything that called Nadia's actions into question.

Camilla shook her head, ignoring Lola's defence. 'You're just not willing to see what's right in front of you,' she stated plainly. 'I don't care how upset she *acts*,' she sneered. 'She was the last person to see him alive. In my book, that makes her the prime suspect.'

'Have you heard yourself?' Lola squeaked, completely dumbfounded by Camilla's inability to let anything go; first it was Catrina and Alex, now it was Nadia and Jason. 'Prime suspect for what? We don't know what's happened to Jason. You're on a witch hunt for God only knows what reason. You've never liked Nadia *or* Alex and all this crap is just making you sound paranoid. You have no proof, or even a motive. Why would she hurt Jason? They were on a date.' She spoke the last few words slowly, in the vain hope they'd sink in.

'You're completely blind,' Camilla huffed, frustrated. 'What is it with all of you?' she asked, mystified. 'You all think the sun shines out of that family's arses. Catrina's been following Alex like a love-sick puppy for weeks and Jason was practically biting off Nadia's knickers with his teeth–'

'What is your problem?' Lola asked angrily. 'Catrina's happy, can't you see that?' she spat. 'And Jason and Nadia were good together... why do you have to poke and poke away at people's lives? Is your own life so shit you can't handle others being happy?'

Camilla stared at Lola, clearly wounded by her words. 'How can you say that?'

Lola snorted. 'Quite easily given how you've been lately.'

'Oh, and you've been so perfect?' she bit back angrily. 'Anymore visits from those "red eyes" recently?' The moment the words left her lips, Camilla's eyes grew wide, realising what she'd said.

'Get the fuck out,' Lola screamed, unable to look at Camilla any longer; she fixed her gaze on the coffee table.

'Fine,' Camilla grunted, standing from her seat on the sofa. She snatched her bag from the floor and headed for the door. 'But I'd keep an eye on Matt if I were you,' she added as she opened the lounge door. 'He's in line to be her next biggest fan.'

Lola flinched as first the lounge room door

slammed, followed by the front door moments later.

Her anger was barely contained; who the hell did Camilla think she was? She had no right to doubt Nadia when she didn't even know her, or had never wanted to. Camilla had no right to continuously interfere in people's lives and she had absolutely no right to throw Lola's nightmares back in her face.

She ran her hands through her auburn hair, breathing steady in an effort to calm herself down; it didn't work.

Lola tried to push the thoughts of the red eyes away but they were with her day and night now, whether Camilla had brought them up or not. They haunted her dreams, terrorised her waking hours, always taunting her with that ancient word: Vrolok.

She knew what it meant, but why did she hear it constantly with every dream she woke from in a cold sweat?

She'd practically alienated Matt because of them; they'd not had sex in weeks and any other intimacy had also long since been rendered pointless when she could no longer relax, taunted by moving shadows and whispered voices in the wind.

Her thoughts on Matt, Lola pondered on Camilla's dig about his attentions; had he been getting closer to Nadia while she'd been wrapped up in her own nightmare?

Lola didn't think so.

Nadia was a good friend who'd supported her through a tough time. Matt was her partner, who she trusted. She had no reason to doubt him and she never had before. She wasn't that kind of woman; she went into a relationship with her trust intact... otherwise, what was the point?

But she and Matt *had* been distant lately.

She shook the thought away, telling herself she was being ridiculous; why was she letting Camilla's digs get to her?

Matt would never be unfaithful, she was certain of that.

She stood from her seat and turned back to the window, staring out at the unmarked police car parked across the road.

Camilla's doubts and accusations refused to go away.

Chapter 18

Alex sat at the dining table next to his sister.

DI Markham and the accompanying Detective Sergeant Bell sat opposite them, both of them with their notebooks at the ready.

Markham shifted in his seat before glancing up at the twins, settling his gaze on Alex. 'Mr Demeter, were you acquainted with Mr Taggart?'

Alex maintained the DI's stare, intent not to let his discomfort show. He had no doubt Jason had come to harm, though Nadia had never confirmed that fact; the mystery of his body's whereabouts concerned him even more.

He nodded. 'I am, yes,' he said, determined not to speak of Jason in the past tense.

Markham looked at his notepad briefly. 'And when did you first meet?' he asked, looking back up at Alex.

'I introduced them,' Nadia interrupted with a gentle smile, her words tinted with a sadness that had Alex glancing her way.

Markham looked at something on his notepad, making Alex uncomfortable.

'You introduced them, Miss Demeter?' he asked.

'Nadia, please,' she offered with the smallest of smiles, her eyes filled with sadness. 'And yes, I did. I met Jason through another friend. My neighbour, actually. Lola Freeman. She's his cousin. We all met for a drink and me and Jason hit it off. I organised a house party, kind of a house-warming, and that was where they all met Alex.'

'All of them?' Markham queried. 'Who is this "all"?'

Nadia glanced at her hands clasped on the table in front of her. 'Lola, as I've mentioned, and Jason. Then there was Lola's partner, Matt, and their friends Camilla and Catrina.' She withheld the sneer she felt at the mention of Catrina's name.

Again, Markham glanced at his pad. 'That would be Catrina Holmes?' he asked. 'I'm led to believe you are in a relationship with Miss Holmes, Mr Demeter?' There was a slight edge to his question, though Alex sensed this was purely Markham's style and had nothing to do with accusation.

Alex was curious as to how Markham and Bell seemed so informed, knowing they must have spoken to one of the human group to receive such information.

'We are engaged, yes,' he answered, unwilling to split hairs with details or divulge their problems.

Markham raised an eyebrow, accompanied with

the smallest of smiles. 'Congratulations,' he offered, the word devoid of any real cheer.

He turned his attentions back to Nadia. 'So, Nadia, you say you and Jason "hit it off" when you first met?'

Nadia smiled sadly, shifting in her chair; the split in her knee-length skirt opened further and the neckline of her satin blouse flapped open to a dangerous level.

'We did,' she confirmed. 'We talked and flirted and after the party he invited me for a drink.'

Markham nodded. 'And this took place on the last night he was seen? Which was with yourself?'

Nadia wiped a tear away from her cheek, her green eyes glittering. 'I'm sorry,' she sniffed. She took several breaths, composing herself. 'It did and it was, in answer to your questions,' she said softly, her voice still shaky.

Markham glanced at Bell before looking back to Nadia. 'Would you say there was anything unusual about his behaviour that night?' he asked. 'Anything that may explain his sudden disappearance?'

Nadia gently shook her head, wiping away more tears. 'No, nothing. We had a really good night. Jason is the kind of guy anyone could get along with and he was cheerful all night.'

Markham stared at Nadia for a moment, his gaze making Alex uncomfortable. He seemed to be thinking about something before he spoke again.

'I appreciate this is all very upsetting for you,'

he said, with no indication of any truth in his words. 'But I wonder if you would be able to divulge some information on that evening, given that you were the last person to see him. Where did you go, for example?'

Nadia took a deep breath in an effort to compose herself, her green eyes full of sadness.

Alex fought the urge to laugh at her pretence.

'We met in Carri's bar at around seven and had a few drinks. We danced a little later. The place was pretty crowded.'

Markham nodded slightly. 'We've confirmed your presence in the bar from the CCTV. You left just before eleven,' he pushed.

Nadia nodded.

'And where did you go?' Markham asked, his tone flat.

Alex glanced at Bell who was still scribbling in the notepad. Her silence during this whole process unnerved him.

Nadia looked down at her hands clasped on the table in front of her, clear embarrassment in her green eyes. 'We... um... you know,' she said quietly, looking up at Markham from under thick lashes.

Alex watched Bell glance up and even Markham seemed to shift in his chair; despite his evident years in the force, Markham seemed slightly discomforted by Nadia's stare and at the same time equally interested by the scenario she was painting for them.

Markham cleared his throat. 'You and Jason

Taggart had sexual intercourse?' he questioned, as if somehow misinterpreting what she'd insinuated.

Alex inwardly cringed, not needing to hear this yet having little choice.

Bell picked up on it. 'Are you okay, Mr Demeter?' she queried.

Alex cursed her as Markham switched his attentions to him. He offered Bell a small smile. 'I'm fine,' he said smoothly, gently. 'I don't often discuss such matters with my sister, I'm sure you can understand?'

Bell nodded with the slightest of understanding. 'Of course,' she said. 'Our apologies, but I'm sure you appreciate we're only doing our job.'

Alex smiled at her once more, his gaze holding hers briefly before she glanced back down at the notepad.

'Of course,' he said quietly.

Markham lost interest in the conversation and turned his attentions back to Nadia. 'Miss Demeter?'

Nadia wiped another tear from her eye. 'Yes, we did,' she said softly.

Markham scribbled something in his own pad before turning his attention back to her. 'Did this take place here or at Jason's home?' he asked.

Now Nadia looked completely embarrassed as she stared at him, almost ashamed.

The pretence made Alex feel sick; she'd never been ashamed of anything in her entire immortal life.

'Neither, at first,' she admitted, biting her lower

lip and lowering her gaze.

'Oh?' Markham seemed a little too interested in the line of questioning in Alex's opinion; an interest that went far beyond his line of duty.

Alex watched as Markham's gaze fell to the opening of Nadia's blouse before shifting back to her face as quickly as he could; it was a fast movement, but Alex still caught it.

Sly old bastard, he thought.

Bell seemed oblivious, though she caught Alex's gaze on several occasions before quickly glancing away again, which amused him.

Nadia cleared her throat, looking up at Markham. 'We... um, found somewhere quiet,' she said softly, thinking back to that night; it took a lot of effort to maintain the sad facade when really inside she was smiling.

Markham seemed equally interested as he did impatient. 'I have to ask you where, Miss Demeter,' he pushed, his tone making Alex wonder if the location would be subject to some form of forensic check if Jason wasn't found.

Nadia glanced at Alex, uneasy, before turning back to Markham, embarrassment clearly etched on her face.

'Miss Demeter?' Markham prompted.

She took a deep breath. 'We found an alley round the back of the bar,' she breathed, wiping more tears from her eyes, her hands shaking. 'I'm sorry,' she said shakily. 'We were just getting on so well and we really liked each other.' She sounded so ashamed as she tried to explain their actions.

Alex saw straight through her act.

Liar. He spat the word at her mentally, angry at how she could act so distraught when she knew damn well what had happened to Jason, even if she hadn't divulged the details to him.

Markham sighed as he jotted something down in his pad. 'I see,' he said. 'And was that the last time you saw him?' he asked.

She shook her head. 'No,' she said.

Markham and Bell looked up at her.

'We went back to his place,' she explained, still with that embarrassed tone to her voice.

'Where you spent the night?' Markham pushed.

She looked back down at her hands before giving Markham another glance from under her lashes, aware of the affect it had on him.

'Yes,' she admitted.

Markham shifted in his seat once more. 'I see,' he muttered again. 'And you left the following morning? Did anyone see you?'

Nadia leaned forward, her blouse opening further with the movement.

Markham's gaze dropped once more for a few seconds. His gaze snapped back to hers quickly.

Alex caught Bell's glance.

'His housemate, Matt, saw me leaving. He asked how our night went and I told him,' she added matter-of-factly.

Markham scribbled in his pad, glancing up at her. 'Matt has already given his statement so we'll check into it,' he stated. 'And was that the last time you saw Jason?'

Nadia shook her head. 'We arranged to spend the day together on Monday. He called in sick at work.'

Markham continued to scribble in his notepad. 'And where did you go?'

Nadia stared at him. 'Nowhere,' she admitted coyly. 'We spent the day in bed together, at Jason's place. I left Jason in his own bed, in his own house later that night.'

'But no one saw you?' he queried.

Nadia stared at him, aware of the uncertainty in Markham's tone.

She didn't like it.

She took a deep breath, leaning forward slightly, her blouse falling open subtly. 'I appreciate you have a job to do, Detective,' she said softly. 'And I *really* appreciate all you're doing to find Jason.' She held Markham's gaze intently. 'I'm devastated he's disappeared and I wish I had more to tell you, but I don't. He was perfectly fine and in a brilliant mood...' she winked at him, '...when I left him.'

Alex could have swung for her for being so stupid; what did she think she was doing?

He caught Bell glance his way once more. He smiled at her, his gaze holding hers; he had no choice but to follow Nadia's lead.

'Jason is a good friend to me,' he said softly, intimately. 'He's a great guy and I was happy to see him dating my sister,' he lied through his teeth, wishing more than ever he'd done more to secure Jason's safety. 'I really, *really* hope you can find him and solve this whole conundrum of his disappearance. We all miss him.'

Bell smiled at him as she jotted in her notepad, closing it once she'd finished the sentence. 'We'll do our best, Mr Demeter,' she said genuinely.

Alex relaxed; it had been too long since he'd influenced a human.

He didn't like doing it.

Markham still watched Nadia's cleavage as she shifted in her seat. When he did look up, he caught that seductive gaze of hers.

'Thank you so much for your help, Detective,' she purred, holding out a hand, which he took willingly. 'I miss Jason, so much. We had such a *wonderful* evening,' she stressed with a smile. 'It's hurtful for a girl to not hear anything afterwards.'

If Alex didn't know better, he would swear she was pouting.

Markham maintained his hold on her hand, clearly enjoying her touch. He smiled. 'I'm sure that would never be his intention,' he said gently, as if he'd known Jason personally.

'Thank you,' she said with appreciation, releasing his hand.

Markham smiled for a moment before picking

up his notepad and standing from his seat, followed by Bell.

He addressed them both as if nothing had happened. 'Well, thank you for your time. I appreciate this isn't a nice thing to have to discuss and I can only hope we find Mr Taggart safe and well.'

Alex held out a hand. 'Thank you, Detective. It means a great deal to us that you are taking this seriously.'

Markham shook Alex's outstretched hand before giving them both a slight nod. 'No need to show us out,' he said with a genuine smile.

Alex watched the two officers leave the room, waiting until he heard the front door close.

His paranoia getting the better of him, he strolled through to the living room, glancing out of the window carefully. He watched the two officers enter their vehicle before driving away.

His anger flared as he thought of what he'd just done; what he'd been dragged into.

He stormed back into the dining room, where his sister still sat at the table. She buttoned up her blouse casually.

'What the hell was all that about?' he asked, bemused. 'You really cannot help yourself, can you?'

She smiled that usual, irritating grin. 'I have no idea what you mean,' she said sarcastically.

'Yes, you damn well do,' he snapped, his anger bordering on the edge once again. 'Flirting with a damn detective? Have you lost your mind?'

Nadia laughed, the sound hollow. 'Come now, Alex, there's no harm done,' she purred, her gaze intense.

'No harm done?' he choked, still mystified by her stupidity. 'You could have destroyed everything back there.'

'You joined in with the lovely Sergeant Bell, I seem to recall,' she jibed.

'You hardly left me with a choice, did you?' he bit back, angry at himself for being played yet again. 'If they decide to come back and follow through on some of the information, we're fucked.'

Nadia rolled her eyes, bored. 'For God's sake, Alex, pull yourself together, will you? There's nothing to worry about. They bought every word we said.'

He snorted. 'Every word *you* said, you mean?' he spat. 'You've only diverted their attentions for a while, but they'll be back after they check Matt's statement. You shouldn't have lied,' he stressed, unwilling to think about it; her game was still very much in play and he dreaded to think of how it would end.

She grinned, a smug expression on her pale face. She shrugged as she stared up at him. 'I wasn't lying,' she said flatly. 'Matt *did* see me leave the house and we *did* chat.' She glared at him hard, that same smug smile curving her red lips. 'Jason just wasn't in the bedroom when I left,' she said, her voice carrying the slight undertone of a laugh. 'He was already dead.'

His restraint snapped at the words he'd feared.

He flew at his sister, pulling her from her chair violently to pin her against the wall behind.

'Damn you,' he hissed.

Nadia laughed, the sound almost victorious. 'As if you're really surprised,' she taunted.

He stared at her, his hand clenched around her throat. There was something in her eyes, something deep and dark, that had his blood running cold.

'He didn't have to die,' he stated, his stomach twisting with guilt. 'You could have walked away, let him live. But you killed him to prove a point. To hurt Catrina, and me.'

Her dark stare narrowed, her smile widening. 'That was the initial point, yes. But it also served other intents and purposes.'

He let her go then, turning away, reviled by this creature who stood before him. 'I hate you,' he whispered, almost able to feel Jason's blood on his hands as if he'd killed him himself.

'No, you don't,' came the soft, gentle voice behind him.

He turned to look at her. She remained against the wall, her green eyes soft yet filled with that age-old seduction so many had come to know and ultimately fear once they'd grown too close; the same gaze he'd always become so lost in.

Her smile widened. 'You want me,' she breathed.

He held his breath for a moment, that green gaze of hers intoxicating, reminding him of all that had once been.

RETRIBUTION DARKENED

He snarled at her, his repulsion and anger winning him over and he turned his back on her.

Grabbing his jacket, he left the house.

Nadia watched him go, her smile remaining.

'Give it time, Alex,' she whispered after him, menace in her tone.

'Just give it time.'

Chapter 19

Catrina drew a ragged breath of unease as Nadia opened the door.

Nadia rolled her eyes. 'Can I help you?' she asked, as if talking to a stranger.

'Is Alex here?' Catrina asked quietly, unable to maintain Nadia's dark gaze; she stared at the ground instead.

Nadia took a step across the threshold, eyeing her rival coldly. 'Didn't you take the hint?' she hissed. 'He doesn't *want* you...'

'Nadia.' Alex barked as he stood behind his sister, his gaze cold and full of warning.

She turned and glared at him for a moment before baring her teeth in a silent snarl. With another roll of her eyes, she pushed past Catrina and stormed away from the house.

Catrina finally looked up; if Alex expected to see any warmth in her topaz eyes, he was grimly disappointed.

He cleared his throat. 'Will you come in?' he

asked, moving aside from the door.

She stood there on the threshold for what felt an eternity, finally taking a step into the house.

Alex released a breath he'd been holding and dutifully closed the door behind her.

Catrina wandered through into the empty lounge of the Demeter household. 'Where is everyone?' she asked, her tone empty and cold. She didn't turn to face him.

Alex instantly felt uncomfortable. 'Out,' he said simply, suddenly unable to conjure any of the words he'd practiced over the last few days.

Silence passed between them for a long while as she continued to stand with her back to him. He could tell she was looking around the room, dreading to think of the thoughts going through her mind; he didn't want to think of the images he feared she was seeing.

Finally, she turned to stare at him.

Her eyes were cold like stone, making his awkwardness worse; there was nothing he could ever do to rectify the harm he'd caused.

'I'm glad you came,' he said softly.

She continued to stare at him, no emotion in her blue eyes. 'Are you?' she asked flatly.

He nodded. 'I was worried you wouldn't.'

'You're lucky I did,' she spat.

Alex had never seen her like this, cold and detached; now he had, it hurt. It made him even more terrified she'd turn her back on him for good; he'd only have himself to blame.

'I've missed you,' he offered.

But Catrina held up her hands, her gaze hardening even more. 'Don't, Alex,' she hissed. 'Just don't. I don't need to hear it, just like I didn't need to hear a lot of what I know.'

He held back the tears that threatened to fall. 'I never meant to hurt you,' he whispered.

A laugh erupted from her, the sound cynical. 'Really?' she seethed. She turned her back on him as she paced the room, clearly trying to make sense of it all. When she spoke, her voice was tinted with sadness. 'I gave myself to you, Alex... in every way.'

He tried to find the words to comfort her, yet there were none; Nadia had seen to that.

He swallowed past the lump of emotion in his throat. 'Do you think I'd really want to throw all that away?' he asked desperately. 'Everything I said to you I meant with all my heart.' He knew he sounded cliché and desperate, but at that particular moment he didn't care; he just needed her to trust him, to listen to him, to believe in him again.

'I'm begging you, Catrina, to forgive me. Just let me try and–'

'Shut up, Alex,' she hissed, turning back to face him, her eyes narrowed with anger.

'I know I've fucked up,' he continued regardless. 'But I'm begging you to forgive me. You know the truth now and–'

'I know the truth your mother told me, yes,' she

interrupted again, her gaze penetrating his. 'Now I want to hear it from you,' she added coldly.

Alex stared at her, dumbfounded, falling onto the sofa. He felt a wave of cold wash over him.

He couldn't... there was no way he could even dare to think of it all again, let alone discuss it.

He moved his head in the smallest of shakes, unable to form coherent words.

She glared at him from across the room. 'What's the matter, Alex? Truth hurts, does it?' she goaded coldly.

Somehow, he found his voice. 'Catrina, I... please, don't make me do this,' he pleaded. 'You don't understand.'

There was no emotion on her face. 'That's the problem, Alex, I do, which is why I need to hear it all from you, in your own words.' She took a step towards him, glaring at him.

'You once promised to never hurt me. You lied,' she said, her words harsh. 'After everything you've put me through, I think it's the least you can do, don't you?' Her words were edged with ice, every one hurting him in turn and pricking at his conscience.

He stared at her, the hurt and betrayal in her eyes destroying his ability to hold back his emotions. He felt the tears sting his eyes.

Beaten by her words, he knew he had no choice.

Chapter 20

Lola shifted awkwardly as she stared at Nadia on her doorstep, still plagued by Camilla's scathing comments from their argument two days before.

Nadia offered the smallest of smiles. 'I'm not disturbing you, am I?' she asked. 'I know it's getting late.'

Lola thought about telling her it *was* too late, that she was tired after a long day at work and another lost night's sleep to strange noises and dreams of red eyes that still plagued her relentlessly; anything to prevent herself from feeling awkward around this woman who'd been nothing but a good and supportive friend to her.

Nadia sniffed and Lola realised she was upset.

'I'm sorry,' Nadia said. 'I'm disturbing you. I'll go.' She turned away from the door.

'No,' Lola found herself saying before she had time to think. 'Don't go. Come in.' She stood back from the doorway, inviting her neighbour in.

Nadia turned back to face her, the smallest of

smiles on her pale face. 'Are you sure?' she asked tentatively, that same sorrowful tone to her usually cheerful voice.

Lola nodded, unwilling to turn her friend away when she was clearly upset. 'I was just about to open a bottle of wine,' she lied, gesturing towards the kitchen as Nadia strolled into the house.

Closing the front door behind her, Lola led the way along the hallway and into the kitchen.

'Do you want a glass?' she offered, heading straight to the fridge and opening the door, bathing her in light. 'I know I need one after the day I've had,' she added with a laugh, trying to lighten her own mood and thoughts; Camilla's damning words of Nadia had filled her head for the past few days and it angered her that she couldn't shift them.

Nadia chuckled dryly behind her. 'My sentiments exactly,' she said cynically.

'Oh?' Lola asked over her shoulder, pulling a bottle of rosé from the shelf and closing the fridge door. She turned to her friend, placing the bottle on the table.

Nadia shrugged, pulling a chair from the kitchen table. 'It's been a bad week,' she sighed, sitting down.

Lola busied herself with fetching two wine glasses from one of the cupboards, along with a corkscrew from one of the drawers, before returning to seat herself at the table opposite Nadia.

'It's been a bad few weeks,' she sighed in agreement, proceeding to open the bottle.

Nadia nodded sadly as she watched Lola pour the wine into each glass before passing one across.

Nadia took it with a smile. 'Thank you,' she said kindly. 'I'm sorry for disturbing you,' she said once more, swirling the wine around in the glass.

Lola shrugged. 'It's okay,' she said, taking a sip of her wine. She closed her eyes, savouring the flavour. She released a long sigh. 'I definitely needed that.'

'Hard day?' Nadia asked, placing her glass on the table, her fingernails gently stroking the stem.

Lola shook her head. 'Nothing more than usual,' she joked. She sobered as she remembered her night of terrifying dreams. 'I just didn't sleep well last night,' she admitted.

'That makes two of us,' Nadia said sadly. 'Me and Alex didn't have a very pleasant weekend,' she sighed, looking at her friend.

Lola shifted uncomfortably in her seat, taking another sip of wine to hide her discomfort. 'Oh?' she asked, her voice raspy; she cleared her throat quickly.

Nadia shrugged, a tear forming in her eye that she quickly wiped away.

Lola frowned, hating to see her friend upset. 'Hey, are you okay?' she asked, reaching out and placing a supportive hand over Nadia's on the table.

Nadia shook her head, her face downcast. 'The police visited me and Alex over the weekend,' she said, her voice breaking with emotion. 'They wanted to talk about Jason.'

Lola silently cursed Camilla for putting her in such an awkward position.

She took a deep breath. 'I'm sure it's just procedure,' she said, as steady as she could manage. 'I suppose they have to question us all at some point now he's officially listed as missing. I wouldn't worry about it too much–'

'They acted as if I was involved,' Nadia interrupted, her voice cracking and her eyes brimming with fresh tears. 'Their line of questioning was awful. I had to divulge everything... in front of Alex. It was horrific. I've never been so embarrassed.'

Lola felt awful. 'I'm so sorry,' she said softly, squeezing Nadia's hand supportively.

Nadia wiped the tears from her face. 'You don't need to apologise,' she said, her voice still wobbly with emotion. She straightened herself in the chair and took a deep breath, trying to compose herself.

'I appreciate they have a job to do and if they're out there looking for Jason then I'm eternally grateful. I just don't understand why they acted like we were guilty of something. It's really upset me.'

Lola finished the wine in her glass with one long gulp and re-filled her glass. 'I'm really sorry,' she said again.

Seeing how hurt Nadia was by all of this only made her anger at Camilla worse and she didn't see why she should keep such information from her friend; Nadia had, after all, been like a rock since Jason had disappeared, sometimes hiding her own hurt to comfort Lola. She'd been nothing but a true friend and Lola felt guilty for ever doubting her. After all, she needed all the friends she could get at the moment.

She took a deep breath to steady her nerves. 'It was Camilla,' she said eventually, watching Nadia's face closely.

Nadia stared at her blankly, wiping the remaining tears from her eyes, slightly smudging her mascara. 'What was Camilla?' she asked, confused.

Lola sighed, weary with Camilla's antics. 'She was the one who called the police and got them to pay you a visit.'

Nadia sucked in a ragged breath. She pulled her hand away from Lola's to grab the wine glass, taking a large sip as if to steady herself. She downed half the wine in one go and placed the glass back on the table, glancing at Lola. Her emerald eyes were full of hurt.

'You're sure?' she asked, clearly dumbfounded.

Lola nodded sadly. 'She told me when I spotted the police at your door,' she confessed. 'I couldn't believe what she'd done. I ended up throwing her out.' Technically, she knew, she had told Camilla to fuck off and she'd stormed out, but it essentially added up to the same thing.

Nadia shook her head, clearly unable to process the information. After a few minutes of silence, she began to weep again, holding her head in her hands as she rested her elbows on the table.

'I can't believe this,' she sobbed, her voice

muffled by her mass of black hair that covered her face. 'I knew she didn't really like me, but I never thought...' She tailed off with another sob.

'I'm really sorry,' Lola said again, finding she was suddenly unable to find any other words. In that moment Lola almost hated Camilla for putting her in this position; she'd caused all this upset and hurt for nothing.

Nadia brushed her hair from her face so she could look at Lola. Her eyes streamed with tears. 'Why did she call the police on me? Why would she do that?'

She stared at Lola, who genuinely had no answers to offer. 'Does she dislike me that much? Or does she really believe I could do anything to Jason?'

'I really don't know,' Lola admitted sadly.

'I was falling for him,' Nadia blurted out, her tears showing no sign of abating. 'Why would I hurt him?'

'You wouldn't,' Lola said simply, determination in her words. 'You wouldn't hurt him and I'm so sorry this has all happened.'

Nadia wiped some of the tears from her cheeks. 'Will you stop saying that?' she said gently. 'This isn't your fault. I just can't believe she'd do such a thing.'

Lola scoffed. 'Neither can I,' she mumbled. 'I don't know what she's playing at lately,' she added, shaking her head. 'First she was constantly on Catrina's back about Alex and now this.' She took a sip of her wine. 'You think you know someone...'

Nadia took another sip of wine, her hand shaking as she raised the glass to her lips.

Lola watched her closely, feeling completely guilty for judging Nadia for even a second. Camilla's words had been vindictive and cruel and Lola had been an idiot for even considering them. Nadia had been the only one to truly understand her worry and torment over Jason's disappearance; the only one who'd truly listened to her myriad of thoughts.

She hated herself for doubting such a true friend.

As Nadia replaced the glass on the kitchen table, Lola reached out and took her hand, squeezing it supportively.

'Thank you,' she said with a smile.

Nadia frowned. 'What for?' she asked, her voice still wobbly as her eyes glittered with tears.

'For being there for me,' Lola said simply. 'For understanding and listening, when no one else seems to want to.'

Nadia covered Lola's hand with her own and smiled. 'It is what friends are for,' she affirmed.

'Well, after all this I at least know who my true friends are,' Lola admitted, sadly and silently confirming to herself that Nadia was the only one she could truly count on.

'We'll get through this,' she added with a determined smile 'Together.'

Nadia squeezed her friend's hand. 'Just the two of us,' she confirmed with a smile.

Chapter 21

Alex watched Catrina pace the room in silence.

As he'd talked to her, he'd watched her slowly become more and more agitated in her seat, before she'd eventually risen to her feet to pace the room, her hands rubbing together over and over. She stared at nothing and had barely looked at him the entire time he'd been telling his story.

She'd remained silent, simply listening and trying to digest the information he'd given her; her mind was now a myriad of thoughts and images.

Alex could tell from the changing expressions on her face that she'd found some of his story sickening, some of it saddening and some of it completely disgusting, but she'd remained to listen to the entirety of his history, and for that he was grateful; he wouldn't have blamed her for walking away at any part of what he'd just told her.

Catrina continued pacing, unable to form any coherent thoughts in her mind; she couldn't contemplate what she'd just listened to. Hearing it the second time hadn't been any easier, and listening to it from Alex's own point of view had somehow made it worse. There had been parts of Alex's story that had intrigued her, parts that had reduced her to tears and parts that had her stomach churning. There had been parts that had her wanting to flee the house and never step foot in it again.

Alex continued to watch her until the silence became too much to take any longer.

'Cat?' he asked tentatively, his voice quiet as if he were frightened he'd scare her should he speak any louder. 'Please say something,' he begged.

She stared at him for a long moment, her blue eyes shining with the tears he knew she was holding back. Her fingers played nervously with the hem of her blue cashmere jumper.

'You lied to me,' she whispered. 'About Jason, about your past, about why we even met in the first place...'

'I didn't know you then,' he said softly, remembering with disgust how he'd enjoyed the game of seducing her; he'd enjoyed the idea of destroying an innocent life.

'And that makes it okay?' she asked, infuriated.

He shook his head. 'No. I can never make it okay now, I know that. There's so much I would change if I could. Jason is dead because of me.' He knew it was true; he may not have taken his life directly, but Jason's blood was on his hands nonetheless.

She stifled back a sob. 'Do you have any idea

how fucked up this all is?'

Alex sighed. 'There was never going to be a right time to tell you any of this.'

'Alex, I spilled out my entire life to you. I told you *everything* about my past, all the sordid, gritty details and not once did you give any indication that your own life had been so fucked up. Not once.'

'I didn't know how.'

'Didn't want to,' she spat.

'Can you blame me?' he asked. 'The hell that has been the four centuries of my life can't just be talked about over dinner, Catrina. I didn't want to lose you. I'd been encased in this nightmare for so, so long... I finally found someone who made me feel free from that. Was I so wrong to want to hang on to it?'

'Do you have any idea how much you've hurt me?' she asked, her voice breaking and her eyes glistening with the tears she'd fought so hard to restrain. 'I trusted you,' she sobbed. 'I trusted you with everything and you knew how hard that was for me to do...' Her words trailed off as she broke down in tears, wrapping her arms around herself at the pain that shot through her.

Seeing her hurt so much was more than he could stand, and Alex crossed the room. 'Please, my love, don't cry,' he whispered, wrapping his arms around her.

She struggled against him, which he'd anticipated, but he maintained his hold and she no longer had the fight within her to resist his comfort.

She gave into his embrace, crying against him as he held her close. He didn't speak, he simply offered her his solace, knowing he'd do anything to take away the hurt and pain he'd caused her.

They stood there together, the silence broken only by Catrina's heartfelt sobs as every emotion in her broke free, the knowledge she now possessed separating her forever from the human world she'd so recently relinquished.

Tentatively, he smoothed his hand over her hair, soothing her as much as he could. He held on to her, wishing he didn't have to let her go.

Slowly, her sobs began to subside, her body still shaking with the emotions she was trying to bring under control.

Alex continued to stroke her hair, cradling her head in his hand as his fingers combed into her golden tresses.

She looked up at him then, her glistening eyes searching his. Her face was stained with her tears as they continued to fall, her breathing still laboured as she fought against the sobs that still wracked her body.

Alex stared back at her, unable to understand the look in her eyes. He simply couldn't look away.

'If I could take it all away, I would,' he said quietly, feeling her breath against his lips as she continued to stare at him.

'But you can't,' she said simply, her voice still cracking with emotion, fresh tears falling over her cheeks.

With his thumb, he brushed away some of those tears, wishing he could see her smile once more; they'd been so happy.

His hand paused as it cupped her cheek. His mind screamed at him not to push things, yet staring into her eyes he was unable to think of anything other than kissing her in that moment.

Tentatively, he lowered his face to hers, her gaze maintaining his.

For a second she pulled back, ever so slightly, her hands placed on his chest as if to push him away. But the gesture had no real substance and she remained in his arms as his lips brushed hers.

For a moment, she didn't respond to his kiss, yet she didn't pull away and his need for her in that moment grew to an unbearable level. He missed her, wanted her and *needed* her so much more than she knew.

Catrina slowly yielded to his kiss, her hands moving to grip his shoulders, her body pressing against his.

His need overtook any other thought and Alex deepened the kiss, relaxing as she responded to his touch, his fingers combing through her hair. His hand travelled down her back to rest against her hip, pulling her body closer.

Her breathing remained heavy as tears continued to fall over her cheeks. She kissed him back, her need evident as she wrapped her arms around his neck.

Alex trailed kisses along her jaw line and down her throat, feeling her tremble beneath his touch. His sharp teeth caught her skin, making her gasp and the sound sent his need for her spiralling.

He bit into her neck, feeling her fingernails dig into his back. Her sweet blood coated his tongue and he drank from her, the sensation of her blood washing away the horrors of the day.

He stiffened as Catrina bit into his own throat, her kisses gentle.

Kissing the wound he'd made, he pulled her away from him so he could look into her eyes. They still shone with tears but they were full of longing and a need that matched his own.

He took her face in his hands, kissing her lips that tasted of his blood, his tongue seeking hers.

They fell back against the sofa and Alex loosened his belt, pulling at his buttons.

He lifted her skirt up until it was around her waist, his fingers travelling down to grasp her thigh.

For three hard beats of his heart he stared down at her, taking in every detail of her face, his hands trembling.

Slipping his arms beneath her back, he kissed her with a quiet authority. Her lips were intense as he entered her with a slow admiration that stole her breath.

He brushed his lips over her ear, making her shiver as pleasure rippled through her body.

Slowly, he began to rock harder against her

until her heart was racing; until her restraint began to slip. He wanted, *needed*, to see her lose control, to know she wanted him as much as she ever had.

Her hands teased him, pulling him harder against her as she welcomed him in with her legs that twined around him, her moans of pleasure shattering his own control as he carried her with him.

As she started to cry out, he bit into the curve of her neck, peaking her pleasure at the ultimate moment, her body quivering beneath him as she recovered from the intensity of her orgasm.

She forced his lips to hers, tasting her own blood on his tongue as she pushed against him, bringing him along to his own peak. His fingers buried in her hair as he kissed her deeply, her sharp teeth catching his lips and tongue as he drove into her, his pleasure cresting as his body went rigid. He pressed hard and deep, forcing another moan of ecstasy from her lips before his breath left him in a rush. He collapsed against her, his face buried against her hair, shuddering.

Catrina smoothed her hands across his back under his shirt, up across his shoulders.

He lifted his head to look down into her face, his breathing still laboured.

Neither of them spoke a word as they stared into each other's eyes, the pain and hurt of the past lingering between them; a darkness not even their shared ecstasy could destroy.

It simply ran too deep.

Chapter 22

The dark images of his past forced Alex from his sleep, his gaze darting around the room as if to reassure himself they were simply dreams; recounting his past hadn't done anything to soothe his already tortured soul.

He wiped his hands over his face in the hope of eradicating the images that had haunted his sleep, only then turning to look beside him.

Catrina wasn't there.

The bedclothes had been thrown back and on placing his hand on the vacated spot he found it to be cold; she'd left the room some time ago while he was lost in unwelcome dreams.

He swallowed past the lump of emotion in his throat, unwilling to contemplate what her absence meant. He certainly hadn't intended to spend the evening in the way they had, but in the pleasure of her body he'd at least found some form of peace from the nightmare he'd relived in order to show her the real truth.

Pushing himself from the cold and lonely bed, he grabbed his white bathrobe from the back of his bedroom door and shrugged into it, slowly opening the door, uncertain of his actions.

As he stepped out on to the landing, he noticed a faint light coming from the slightly ajar bathroom door.

Unnerved, he headed for the door, knocking quietly.

'Come in, Alex,' Catrina said softly from within.

Taking a deep breath, and filled with a sense of foreboding, he stepped into the room.

The lights were off, the room gently lit instead by a number of candles placed around the room, the subtle smell of wax making his discomfort worse.

Catrina lay in the large bath, the milk-white bubbly water up to her chin as the steam swirled around the room on the opening of the door.

He closed the door to its original position behind him before stepping further into the room, watching as she relaxed in the water, her eyes closed.

'How did you know it was me?' he asked gently, leaning against the wall. He wanted nothing more than to sit by her side and hold her as he had only hours ago, yet he was unwilling to do so without being invited; they were still on very delicate ground, after all.

She opened her eyes to look at him, the water

stirring around her as she moved her arms beneath the surface.

'I heard your parents downstairs,' she said simply, her gaze suddenly icy. 'I think your sister's out.'

He didn't want to think about his sister right now; his anger was still hiding just below the surface over what she'd done.

'When you weren't in bed, I thought...' He trailed off, grateful he'd been wrong, yet unable to rid himself of the uneasy feeling of why she was sitting in virtual darkness in the middle of the night; what myriad of thoughts were going through her head?

'I know,' she said gently. 'I just needed time to myself, to think,' she admitted.

He couldn't take it anymore. 'If you want to leave I understand,' he blurted out. 'I deserve nothing else after the way I've treated you.'

Catrina stared up at him, shifting in the bath so that she sat up, pulling her knees to her chest to cover herself, an action that seemed to speak a thousand words.

'Come here, Alex,' she whispered gently, no emotion on her face.

Pushing himself away from the wall, he hunkered down beside the bath, resting his arms on the edge.

Reaching out, she ran her wet fingers through his black hair, her fingers following the line of his jaw before cupping his cheek.

'I'm not leaving you,' she whispered gently. 'There are just so many thoughts going through my head at the moment... I'm confused,' she confessed.

Alex leaned into her hand, her touch and her words sending such a wave of relief through him he could have shouted it out to the world. He thought of the evening they'd spent together making love; the very thought of her body against his sent a welcome warmth through him, yet he was worried that had been a step too far, considering their earlier discussions.

'I didn't plan for this evening to happen,' he said, trying to be honest for once. He looked at her almost sheepishly.

She smiled at him, that wariness still in her eyes. 'I don't regret it, if that's what you're trying to ask me,' she said lightly.

Alex maintained her gaze. 'But you *are* having second thoughts about everything, aren't you?' he asked, hating to see that distance in her blue eyes; her knees were still against her chest, shielding her body from his view, which only added to the rejection he felt.

Slowly, she shook her head. 'No, I'm not,' she admitted. 'You were honest with me today, and I know how hard that was for you, given everything that has happened.'

He offered her a small smile. 'But?'

She sighed heavily. 'But I can't simply forget all about it,' she said sadly. 'Too much has been said and done, and despite the real truth behind it all, it doesn't excuse how you lied to me and betrayed me. I was a damn bet, Alex... some sick game between you and your sister, with her as the prize. I can't live like that. That isn't who I am.'

'It isn't who *I* am anymore. I swear that to you. I've changed since I met you.' He took her hand in his, holding it tightly. 'You taught me how to live, Catrina, not just exist, and I promise I will do everything within my power to put right the hurt I have caused you.'

She stared at him, a sadness filling her eyes that chased away the wariness. 'I'm not sure how easy that will be,' she admitted. 'I'm not sure if I can forgive you.'

He closed his eyes for a moment, her words hurting. He wasn't sure what he'd expected, or what he deserved.

She'd at least been honest with him, and that was a start.

* * *

Nadia closed the front door behind her, a self-satisfied smile on her face; Lola had believed every word she'd said and every tear she'd shed; Lola's faith in her troublemaker of a friend, Camilla, had completely disintegrated.

Which was just as well, Nadia mused, given the punishment she'd taken great pleasure in delivering after leaving Lola's home.

She thought on so many of Alex's warnings in the past about the dangerous games she was playing. She snorted; the game ended when she decided, never before.

Passing through the entrance hall into the lounge, she rolled her eyes; both her elders sat on the sofa, their eyes watching her closely. She offered them both in turn the most sarcastically happy smile she could manage, passing by them without a word.

She didn't need them here; they were only interfering, whispering to Alex and turning him against her. They were foolish enough to dare to try and control her; as twins, she and Alex were far more powerful than any of their elders dared to admit.

She didn't need any of them; they were all weak, undeserving of her respect. She'd discovered that a long time ago.

She made her way towards the staircase, her gaze momentarily falling to the cellar door beneath as a thought passed through her mind. She shook it away and began to climb the stairs.

The faint essence of Catrina's perfume lingered in the air and Nadia suppressed a snarl. The bitch had been upstairs; she didn't want to consider the implications of that.

As she reached the top of the stairs, the smell of candle wax was all too abundant, and her attention was drawn to the faint light emanating from the slightly ajar bathroom door.

She could hear soft voices, which was a shame; she'd at least expected a little shouting and smashing of crockery to some extent.

Quietly, she approached the door, leaning against the wall to better overhear her brother's conversation.

'I promise I will do everything within my power to put right the hurt I have caused you,' Alex said.

Pathetic Alex, she thought, *really pathetic. Your promises are not worth shit*, she sneered inwardly. She'd discovered that a long time ago, too.

The memory of that betrayal still stung deeply.

'I'm not sure how easy that will be,' Catrina said. 'I'm not sure if I can forgive you.'

This made Nadia smile, a glint of malice returning to her eyes. She wasn't done with this little scenario yet; Catrina had disclosed the truth, and now it would be so easy to pick away at it until Catrina turned her back on Alex for good.

Yet as she listened on, Nadia's smile dimmed, and then disappeared.

Her emerald eyes darkened.

Her fangs bared in a silent snarl.

She didn't like what she heard, at all.

* * *

'If I have to work for the rest of my immortal life, I'll show you I mean everything I say,' Alex said, still holding onto Catrina's hand against his face.

RETRIBUTION DARKENED

She stared at him, her knees still pulled to her chest in the milky water. 'Alex, I don't need constant confessions of how you'll make all this up to me,' she said gently. 'It's not that simple, and it's just words. This isn't going to be fixed overnight, no matter how much either of us want it to be.'

'I just want to see you happy again. To know you trust me as you did before,' he admitted, almost pleading; he wasn't sure what else he could say.

Gently, she pulled her hand away from his, wrapping her arms around her knees and resting her head on top, staring at him.

'I can't promise how long that will take. You hurt me, badly, and all that you told me and everything that happened tonight doesn't change that. You can never take that back.'

Alex held back his tears, unable and unwilling to imagine his life without her in it; he couldn't stand the idea of her turning her back on him.

He rested his forehead against his arms on the edge of the bath, staring at the floor. 'If I could, I would,' he said quietly.

'I know,' she whispered.

He looked up at her then.

She reached out her hand once more to cover his own, her skin wet. 'I do still love you, Alex,' she said softly, no emotion on her face. 'I'm just not sure that's enough anymore.'

He closed his eyes for a moment, thinking of the evening they'd spent together, unwilling to accept there had been no meaning behind it. There was love there still, passion and desire, and he wouldn't give that up. He wanted her with him forever.

He opened his eyes to look at her, reading that unmistakable hurt and betrayal within her eyes. He could tell, from the look in her eyes and the way she shielded her body from him, that his sister's words still echoed in her head; despite knowing the real truth, she was still haunted by his sister's words of malice... the words that taunted Catrina of Alex's real carnal desires, displacing Catrina's place in his bed with her own.

It was Nadia who haunted Catrina's thoughts, and he wouldn't allow it any longer.

He would no longer allow Nadia to control and destroy his life.

He stood from the side of the bath, his face suddenly hard and serious.

'Let's get the hell away from here,' he said.

She stared up at him, her eyes wide and questioning. 'What?'

He nodded, confirming she'd heard him correctly. 'Let's get away from here,' he repeated. 'You and me.'

She continued to stare at him, unsure. 'You want us to leave? Just like that?' she asked carefully.

Alex returned to kneeling beside the bath, grabbing both her hands in his. 'Just like that,' he confirmed. 'Why not? You once told me you'd always wanted to travel, so why don't we?'

'But your family... my friends...' She was trying to argue, without much success.

'I'm not saying leave forever, Catrina, just for us to go and live our lives together. You'll see Lola and your other friends again,' he reasoned.

She looked at him dubiously but he could tell she was considering it; he knew she loved her friends as more of a family than her own had ever been, but there would come a point when they'd start to notice she wasn't aging, and perhaps some distance now would make that transition a lot easier in the future.

'What are you thinking?' he asked her gently.

She shook her head slowly. 'I don't know,' she admitted. 'What are you asking me to do?'

He kissed her fingers tenderly. 'I'm asking you to come away with me, Catrina Holmes,' he said gently. 'I'm asking you to trust me enough to leave Wiltham, even England. We'll leave this whole Goddamned mess behind us.'

He stared at her hard, making sure she believed every word.

'And I promise you, we will never, *ever* set eyes on Nadia again.'

Chapter 23

Nadia rocked slowly back and forth in her chair at the dining table, the room dark around her in the early hours of the morning. She tapped her fingers on the table monotonously, staring at nothing in particular, her emerald eyes narrow and filled with malice.

We will never, ever set eyes on Nadia again.

Alex's words echoed through her mind, her rage building up silently.

Did he really think it was *that* simple? Did he not think there was a price to pay after all he'd done?

Catrina had agreed to his plan, obviously.

Nadia snarled in the darkness of the room; who did the little bitch think she was? Did Catrina really think Nadia would simply allow the pathetic wretch to take her twin away from her?

She *owned* Alex. He was hers, and always would be.

They were bound by blood, always.

Catrina was a passing whim. She'd tugged on Alex's conscience with her little girl lost act, but that wouldn't last. His conscience never persevered; Nadia had all but destroyed it over the centuries.

Alex's game had gotten out of hand. She'd bet him he couldn't get Catrina into bed before killing her, and technically she was right; he had, after all, bedded Catrina after turning her. She was dead, a wretch. He'd turned her to save her life, nothing more. If he'd had a moment to think about it logically, without the panic-stricken situation to sway his thoughts, he would have refused her.

But the game was over now, and Alex needed to pay the piper. Catrina had no place in their lives.

She should have stayed away, Nadia thought in the darkness. *She should have listened to what I'd told her, stayed away and removed herself from Alex's life.*

As it was, Nadia would now have to do what Alex had been too weak to do.

She wanted her twin back by her side, where he belonged.

Give it a century and he'll no longer remember who she was, she reasoned with herself. *Just like he seems to have forgotten so many other things*, she sneered.

Nadia sighed to herself, shifting in her seat. A strap of her long, burgundy satin nightdress slipped off her shoulder and she mechanically replaced it without breaking her stare with nothingness.

The gentle creak of the staircase jarred her from her vengeful thoughts. She turned her attentions to the doorway.

The scent of uneasiness filled the air and Nadia's anger and hate writhed; there was only one person in the house who would emanate such a stench.

Her eyes narrowed as Catrina appeared in the doorway, her face pale; there was a glint of fear in her topaz eyes.

'I didn't realise anyone was down here,' she said quietly, her voice uneasy.

'Trouble sleeping?' Nadia sneered with a cold grin.

Catrina looked uncomfortable as she shifted from foot to foot, pulling the belt of Alex's bathrobe tighter around her waist. 'I needed some time alone.'

Nadia's grin widened. 'Please, don't mind me,' she purred.

Catrina took a deep breath, letting it out slowly. 'I don't want another fight,' she said wearily.

'As you wish,' Nadia shrugged, her gaze never leaving that of the pitiful creature before her. 'I see you and Alex managed to sort everything out,' she said, by way of a statement rather than a question, her eyes darkening.

'I don't see how that is really your business,' Catrina said, the slight tremble in her voice betraying her discomfort.

'Everything involving my brother is my

business,' Nadia growled.

Catrina met Nadia's gaze. 'I don't think he'd see it like that,' she said impertinently.

Nadia's anger writhed like an angry snake as she glared at her rival. 'Is that right?' she countered, her voice merely a hiss. 'And you know him *so* well, don't you?' she added, a sneer to her words.

Catrina maintained her stand, defiance in her eyes. 'Yes, I do,' she said flatly. 'He spent this evening telling me everything.'

Nadia froze in place for a moment, searching Catrina's face for any sign that the pitiful girl was bluffing; it became all too clear that she wasn't.

'Everything?' she asked simply, her voice trailing off as she became lost in her thoughts once more; he'd promised to never speak of the past ever again.

His promises mean shit, she reminded herself. *He's betrayed me.*

Catrina nodded, the smallest of satisfied smiles on her pale lips. '*Everything*,' she sneered back. 'So all of your lies mean nothing now. You can twist it all any way you like, but I know the truth. Every little thing you've ever done.'

Nadia seethed as she stared at the table in front of her. How could Alex do that to her? How could he relive every little detail to this pathetic creature? He'd betrayed her, and Catrina had forced him to do it.

Nadia's fingernails bit into the grain of the wood. He needed saving from her before she destroyed him.

'And so you're going to ride off into the sunset now, are you? Just the two of you, all moonlight and roses,' she growled, her eyes narrowing as she stared at the girl before her.

Catrina's eyebrows creased in the smallest of frowns, confusion filling her face. 'How did you know that?' she asked indignantly.

Nadia's smile returned, the expression void of any warmth. 'There is nothing he can hide from me,' she said viciously. 'Remember that.'

'Is that a threat?' Catrina asked, the essence of unease returning to her voice.

Nadia's expression was instantly filled with innocence. 'Now what point would there be in threats?' she asked softly. 'You and Alex are unbreakable now. Nothing can tear you two apart.' She pushed herself from her seat, standing and taking a step away from the table. 'The pair of you can ride off into the sunset now and live happily ever after,' she sneered, heading for the kitchen.

Catrina stared after her. 'Why can't you just let him be happy?' she asked, genuine confusion in her voice. 'Why is that so hard for you to do?'

Nadia turned on her heels, her green eyes cold and filled with something Catrina was unsure of. 'You know everything now, *Princess*,' she hissed. 'So see if you can figure that one out for yourself.'

With a dismissive turn, Nadia disappeared into the kitchen, leaving Catrina alone with her thoughts.

She stared after Nadia for a moment before

slowly lowering herself into the same chair Nadia had vacated moments before.

The minutes ticked by, silence blanketing the house.

A chill filled the air.

In a flash of movement, Nadia was behind Catrina's chair, her icy hand clamping across her mouth, stifling any sound the pathetic creature could manage.

With a triumphant and maniacal laugh, Nadia increased her grip as Catrina's hands gripped desperately onto Nadia's arm, trying in vain to loosen the woman's hold.

The girl's blue eyes grew wide with a deep-set terror, her screams muffled by the crushing strength of Nadia's hand as she bit hard into Catrina's throat.

Catrina moaned in pain, struggling against her attacker, but Nadia was too strong.

As she drained the girl of blood, Catrina's efforts to fight slowly diminished until she was weak, but still lucid.

Sadistically kissing the weeping wound, Nadia smiled as she whispered into Catrina's ear. 'Did you think I'd *ever* let you take him from me?' she growled, every word filled with hatred. 'He belongs to *me*.'

With an unrelenting force, Nadia bit back into Catrina's throat, tearing the skin open viciously, preventing the girl from making any further sound.

With ease, Nadia picked the girl up in her arms and carried her through to the other room, towards the door under the stairs. Catrina found herself unable to resist in her weakened state; every limb was as light and limp as a ragdoll.

She could only watch as they passed through the doorway into the icy coldness of the cellar beyond, a room she knew none of the family used, other than for occasional storage.

The stone stairway was deathly cold, the walls and ceiling decorated with cobwebs and dust, and as Nadia reached the bottom step, she callously dropped Catrina to the ground, kicking her in the chest for good measure.

With a look of complete contempt, Nadia strolled across the small room towards the large wine racks that dominated the far wall.

With a glare over her shoulder towards the pitiful creature, she turned back to the racks, pulling the one on the end until it slowly started to give.

'I insisted on having these racks put in,' she said cheerfully, as she worked on pulling the rack further away from the others. 'Alex wasn't really interested. Said it was a waste of money considering we're not exactly wine connoisseurs,' she joked, giving the rack one last pull until it was distanced enough from the others, the gap between them filled with shadows, revealing nothing.

'But,' she sighed, content, 'I won the argument, as always,' she laughed jovially. 'An old house like this *has* to have a wine cellar. Alex left me to it, uninterested, so I made the most of it. We all need a place where we can... reflect,' she said, settling on the word.

She turned back to Catrina, who stared at her, unable to move, despite the fear in her eyes that betrayed the fact she would have fled if she could.

'Which is what you will be able to do... reflect... for a very long time.' Nadia knelt by Catrina's side, gently running her hand over the girl's blonde hair as if soothing her.

'You're going to stay here and think about all the reasons why you should have just walked away. This is all your fault, sweetie,' she purred. 'I told you the truth, and you, being so desperate to be loved, thought you could forgive him. But despite what he says, despite his pleas of innocence and his promises, he will still betray you over and over again... he simply cannot help himself.'

Nadia smiled as Catrina tried to move, but there was no strength in her body; she'd been drained to a dangerous point and she'd need to feed to restore her strength.

'He belongs to *me*,' Nadia snarled, her fingers raking through Catrina's hair viciously. 'And I will *never* let you take him away from me.'

She stood quickly, her fingers still entangled in Catrina's hair, tugging her up to her knees.

Catrina's feeble whimpers of pain were non-existent from her torn throat. She had no choice but to allow Nadia to drag her roughly across the cold stone floor of the cellar, the stone lacerating her skin.

Tears seeped over her cheeks, her cries for help only in her mind.

'So,' Nadia hissed, dragging the girl towards the wine racks and dropping her back to the floor in front of them. 'You will stay down here until he has forgotten all about you... which, trust me, won't take long,' she grinned, stepping around the racks into the shadows beyond.

She rummaged around in the dark, her hands grabbing the object she was looking for. With a sadistic smile, she pulled it towards the gap in the racks, taking pleasure in seeing the fear in Catrina's blue eyes as she spotted the crudely made wooden box meant to replicate a coffin.

With an icy look of disdain, Nadia grinned at Catrina as she released the clasps that had been nailed into the sides, allowing her to push the lid free of the casket.

Finally, Nadia turned her full attention towards Catrina, her smile widening as fear clearly gripped the girl; her body visibly shook, her eyes wide with shock and terror. Her bottom lip quivered with the need to scream, which was denied by the gaping wound in her throat. She was weak and unable to move; a terrorised puppet unable to escape her mistress' bidding.

'This could have been avoided so easily,' Nadia sighed, standing over Catrina and glaring down at her. 'But we all have to do what's necessary. I'm helping you really,' she said simply, reaching out for the pitiful girl on the floor.

Catrina tried to shy away but her efforts were in vain; Nadia gripped her upper arm, her sharp nails digging in through the material of the bathrobe.

'Of course, I won't enjoy watching Alex pine for you like some lost puppy,' she sneered, dragging the girl sharply across the rough stone floor, her bare legs lacerating against sharp rock. 'But trust me, it would be much worse for you, watching him pine for me for eternity if you ran off into the sunset together. He simply cannot function without me. He'd eventually raise the subject, and slowly, bit by bit, he'd convince you to return to the family fold, where he could see me once more.'

Upon reaching the box, Nadia released Catrina's arm in order to grip her bathrobe at the shoulders, roughly pulling it from her body. She then easily lifted Catrina and dropped her top half harshly into the box.

'So,' Nadia continued, as she lifted the girl's feet. 'We'll settle for the lesser of the two evils,' she smiled, almost sweetly, 'and let him pine for you for a very short while, instead of the eternal torment of living without me.' She swung Catrina's legs across the box, dropping them inside with a thud.

The smallest of noises came from the girl's torn throat, but it was hardly detectable. Her eyes were still wide with terror, her head moving slowly from side to side as she silently begged Nadia not to do this atrocious act of vengeance.

Nadia straightened herself and stared down at Catrina in the make-shift coffin, surveying her handiwork. Pleased with her efforts, she disappeared back into the shadows, returning moments later.

'This is for you,' she said venomously. Her gaze darkened once more as she glared at Catrina, holding up her hand that was covered in a tatty old cloth.

A pitiful sound which should have been a scream escaped Catrina's lips as she stared at the crudely-made crucifix Nadia held in her covered hand, shielding her from its burning effects.

Catrina had no such protection.

With a swift movement, Nadia ripped the girl's nightdress away from her chest, exposing the skin. With a sickened satisfaction, she placed the crucifix onto Catrina's chest, the metal instantly burning her skin.

Catrina tried to scream, but only the weakest sounds emerged, her drained body unable to remove the object that caused such excruciating pain.

Throwing the rag across the room, Nadia hunkered down beside the box, watching the suffering before her, her face emotionless.

'Don't fear that you will be lonely down here, my sweet,' she whispered, her gaze flickering to the shadows before returning to the girl. 'You'll have some familiar company all too soon,' she laughed, standing up and grabbing the lid to the box from the floor.

With little effort, she positioned it halfway

across the box, watching the desperation and fear peak in the girl's face, tears flowing freely as her skin burned.

'Goodbye, Princess.'

With a final victorious grin, Nadia slid the lid into place.

Chapter 24

His sleep had been sound after the long discussion he'd had with Catrina, both of them falling asleep in the early hours.

Alex awoke to the sounds of birds chirping outside the window, surprised to see how late in the morning it was; he'd not realised how mentally exhausted he'd become over the last few days.

He rolled onto his side, instantly aware that the other side of the bed was vacant, just as it had been last night.

His hand travelled across the sheets, finding the empty spot cold. Catrina had been up for a while.

His mind was instantly filled with doubts; each one he tried to reason away with the thoughts of their discussions, his promises to her, and their lovemaking.

Yet still the doubts persisted, and he was worried that her mistrust in him had simply proven to be too much.

I do still love you, Alex. I'm just not sure that's

enough anymore. Her words ran through his head; each one had hurt, and he couldn't help wondering what *would* be enough to repair the damage that had been done.

He climbed out of bed, unwilling to stare at the vacant spot beside him any longer. He crossed the room to the chair in the corner, frowning when he couldn't find his bathrobe.

Giving up the search, he proceeded to get dressed quickly, pulling on his jeans and shirt in record time, noting Catrina's clothes were gone.

He opened the door and left the room, heading along the landing until he reached the bathroom, reasoning to himself that maybe Catrina had simply needed some more time to herself to consider what they were planning to do.

He pushed open the bathroom door.

He was disappointed.

This time the bathroom was empty, and there was no sign of it having been used since last night.

With unease, he descended the stairs, the house seemingly silent. All the curtains had been drawn back, the overcast day bringing very little light into the house; it was a sign the house wasn't completely lifeless, but confirmed Catrina's absence.

At the bottom of the stairs, he crossed the room and passed through the doorway into the dining room, which was just as empty.

A noise from the kitchen finally disturbed the silence. He wandered through, his mood darkening when he saw his sister sitting on a stool by the breakfast bar, flicking idly through a magazine.

'Have you seen Catrina?' he asked, barely looking at her; he couldn't wait to get away from this house... away from *her*.

'Good morning to you, too,' Nadia said cheerfully, not looking up from the magazine.

He ignored her jibe and asked again: 'Have you seen Catrina?'

Nadia shrugged. 'What if I have?' she asked flatly, still not looking at him.

A low growl escaped him as he glared at her, unable to prevent the image of his hands tightening around her throat entering his mind. 'For fuck's sake,' he hissed.

'Ah, ah, language, Brother Dearest,' she teased, finally looking up at him. 'What would Mother say?'

'Have you seen her or not?' he asked once more, unwilling to rise to her taunts.

Again she shrugged, returning her attentions to the magazine. 'She left before dawn this morning,' she said simply.

With a savage snarl, his patience hanging by a thread, he glared at her. 'What did she say?' he asked, his tone demanding an answer.

Nadia looked up at him once more, her face unreadable. 'She didn't say a word.'

He frowned. 'What?'

'She simply came downstairs and left. She didn't say anything to me.' The corners of her mouth turned up into the smallest of grins. 'You didn't have another fight, did you?'

Alex glared at her for a moment before turning away, unable to look into those green eyes any longer; those eyes in which he saw himself reflected right back.

Heading through the lounge, he passed into the entrance hall, grabbing his leather jacket from the peg by the door.

'Where are you going?' Nadia called from the other room, her tone full of humour.

Unwilling to acknowledge her at all, he shrugged into his jacket, grabbed his car keys from the top of the bureau and headed out the door.

Chapter 25

Something was wrong.

Alex tried to call Catrina once more, her phone simply going to voicemail like it had every other time he'd tried it over the last week.

He'd spoken to Lola and Matt several times over the last few days, but they hadn't heard from her or had any luck in tracing where she may have gone; none of them had heard anything from Camilla, either, in over a week, and he was starting to suspect that Catrina may have turned to her steadfast friend in her hour of need.

It made as much sense as anything, given how protective Camilla was of Catrina.

Still, he couldn't shake the feeling that there was something devastatingly wrong. Catrina's disappearance so soon after Jason's now had them all extremely worried, and he was certain Camilla would be all too aware of that; it seemed unlikely that she'd want to create any further panic among the friends by going to ground with Catrina.

Alex tried to push Jason from his mind; after all, he knew the truth of his fate. The same couldn't be applied to Catrina.

He dropped his cell phone onto the dining table where he sat, running his hands over his face, hating every second of the day that passed with no news of where she was.

He felt like he was losing his mind. He'd barely left the house, and when he did it was only to drive to Catrina's house and back again. He'd look about him sadly, the world around him continuing on its little path, just as it always had, unaware of the horrors living parallel to it.

A horrid, cold and empty feeling flooded over him.

Not for the first time in over four hundred years, he felt very, very alone.

He'd barely feasted in days, his body aching and head pounding. His elders had commented on his paleness a number of times.

He glanced up as his mother hovered in the lounge doorway, her gaze sympathetic.

'Still no word?' she asked gently.

He shook his head. His mother had also voiced her concern at Catrina's silence, and the support of both his elders had been all that had kept his sanity intact.

Aurelia stared at his phone on the table for a moment, as if willing it to ring.

There was nothing more she could say, Alex

knew.

Sadly, she turned away and headed back into the lounge, where she'd been sitting with his father.

Every second of every moment he'd spent with Catrina flooded his mind, the images far too vivid, making him flinch. It was becoming too much tolerate.

He lowered his head to the table, resting against its cold surface, his eyes closed.

He allowed the thoughts to flood through him, each one painful and agonising.

He frowned when footsteps interrupted the silence that surrounded him.

The smell of his sister's perfume made him feel sick.

'Do you have any idea how pathetic you look?' she asked flatly, no malice to her words, only honesty.

With a heavy sigh, he sat himself up, refusing to look at her. 'I didn't ask for your opinion,' he growled, unwilling to get into another argument with her; he simply didn't have the strength.

'Just as well,' she scoffed. 'Because you wouldn't like it if you did.'

A sarcastic smile crept across his lips. 'And you're *always* the voice of reason and sympathy, aren't you?' he asked scathingly, still staring at the table in front of him.

She ignored the jibe. 'If you mean I don't tell you all you want to hear and attend to you with kitten gloves then no, I'm not,' she sneered. 'The softly, softly approach isn't doing you any favours,' she added.

'Your presence isn't doing me any favours,' he spat at her, finally glancing round at his sister who stood in the doorway, noting the washing basket she gripped in her hands. He stifled a laugh; she'd picked one hell of a time to go all "domestic goddess".

'You can be like that if you wish,' she said calmly, without any sourness. 'But taking it out on me won't change anything.'

A low growl rumbled through his chest as he stared at her. 'Perhaps,' he grumbled.

Nadia rolled her eyes.

Without another word, she walked away from her brother, crossing the dining room in a few strides as she headed for the kitchen.

Alex stared after her, suspicious of her actions; she never let the opportunity for an argument go so easily.

Against his better judgement, he pushed himself from the table and strolled into the kitchen, just as she dropped the wash basket in front of the washing machine.

'What's going on?' he asked flatly, watching as she stared up at him.

Nadia opened the wash basket as she continued to look at her brother, curiosity on her face. 'What do you mean?' she asked, opening the machine door.

Alex glared at her. 'You know what I mean,' he said sternly. 'You're trying to offer me advice, a couple of days ago you did yet another spring clean, today you're doing laundry... what's going on?'

She picked up a handful of washing from the basket and pushed it into the machine. 'Are you being serious?' she asked, laughing. 'It is not the first time I have ever cleaned or done laundry, Brother. I do it regularly, unlike some,' she said with a playful grin. 'You've just never noticed. You should make more of an effort yourself,' she shrugged. 'That piano of yours is disgraceful.'

He stood there as she continued to shovel washing into the machine, unable to rid himself of the idea that there was something a bit too nice about Nadia's behaviour lately; he couldn't believe she was being truly supportive over the Catrina situation.

Nadia slammed the machine door closed. Alex watched as she set the wash cycle.

He sighed, feeling defeated.

She turned and looked at him. 'Seriously, Alex, you need to pull yourself together,' she chastised, her gaze cold as she pushed past him. 'Wake up to the truth. Catrina's gone.' She headed for the door.

Alex stared after her for a moment. 'She didn't say *anything*?' he asked desperately as Victor appeared in the doorway, watching the pair closely.

With a sigh of frustration, Nadia stopped in her tracks, turning to stare at Alex, boredom etched on her face. 'No.'

His eyes narrowed as he stepped towards her. 'You're lying.'

A chuckle escaped her lips. 'Excuse me?' she

hissed.

'She said something to you, didn't she?'

Nadia threw her hands up in the air, frustrated. 'What difference does it make?' she asked.

Victor glared at his daughter. 'It makes a great difference, my child, if what you say is untrue.'

She stared at him, loathing in her eyes. She took a step towards the door, but Alex grabbed her arm fiercely.

'She *did* say something,' he stated, his words sharp. 'That's what all this niceness has been about.'

She glared at him with malice. 'I've tried to *support* you, and this is the thanks I get.'

He tightened his grip on her arm as he looked into her eyes; he didn't like what he saw.

'What did she say?' he asked again, disgusted.

With a struggle, Nadia managed to pull her arm free from his grip, her gaze withering. 'She said she was leaving you, okay?' she shouted at him, her words full of malice. 'She didn't say where she was going, and I didn't ask.' Without another word, she pushed past her elder in the doorway and stormed off through the dining room, heading for the drawing room and the stairs.

Alex stared after her for a moment, her words solidifying within him what he'd feared; he had lost the one person he'd ever truly loved.

He quickly followed his sister. 'Why didn't you stop her?' he asked, unable to disguise the hurt in his voice.

Nadia stopped by the side of the piano. She turned to look at him, her gaze ice cold. 'Why would *I* beg her to stay?'

'For my sake,' he said flatly, hoping to get through to her.

She laughed at his words. 'You were the reason she was leaving,' she sneered. 'You told her *everything*, Alex,' she hissed, her green eyes blazing with anger. 'After all that, why would she go away with you?'

His eyes narrowed. 'How did you know we were leaving?' he asked, accusation in his voice; a chill ran the length of his spine as he considered her words.

Nadia grinned, her green eyes full of malice. 'Walls have ears, Brother,' she spat, her anger all too evident. 'You of all people should know that.'

In that instant he knew she'd done something; she knew he'd planned to leave with Catrina and he knew there was no way his sister would allow that to happen. He'd seen Nadia's devastating wrath all too closely before.

'What did you do to her?' he asked firmly, taking a step closer to his sister.

'Nothing,' she said simply, matching his step.

'Stop lying,' he shouted, grabbing hold of her wrists as she struggled against him. 'You knew we wanted to leave. To get away from *you*,' he bellowed as he struggled with her.

'You think I would *let* you abandon me?' she screeched as she fought against him, her nails clawing at his wrists. 'She wasn't going to take you away from me.'

'She wasn't taking me away from you, Nadia,' Alex said harshly, pushing her back. 'You *drove* me away.'

As if his words had physically wounded her, she screamed at him, rushing at him with a snarl, her sharp nails slashing his hands as he held them up against her.

With a sharp push, Alex shoved her back, sending her crashing into the cellar door, the impact cracking the wood. He snarled back at her, all his anger and frustration venting.

'You drove me away, Nadia,' he repeated, aware of his elders in the doorway, alarmed by the chaos. 'You've done too much, pushed me too far. You've destroyed innocent lives for no reason. I would have been happy to never set eyes on you ever again. You disgust me,' he spat, turning his back on her.

In a flash of movement, Nadia sprang from the crumpled door and launched herself at her brother, grabbing him around the throat as she bit into his shoulder hard, ignoring his cries of pain.

Reaching round, he grabbed hold of her blouse and pulled her off him, ripping the material from her shoulder. He gripped her wrist, squeezing hard.

She struggled against him, finally pulling her arm free.

'What did you do?' he asked once more, his voice filled with aggression. 'Where is she?'

'She left you,' she screamed at him, victory in her eyes. With a vicious push, she threw him back against the cellar door as he'd done to her, the crumpled wood giving way completely and he crashed through it onto the stone steps beyond.

Aurelia stepped forward, concern etched deeply on her pale face. 'Enough of this,' she hissed at them.

Nadia ignored her. She approached Alex as he struggled to his feet, dust from the stone steps covering his clothes. With a callous thrust, she pushed him down the stairs, her green eyes gleaming as he hit the stone floor at the bottom.

'She left you, Alex, like I never have,' she stated flatly. 'No matter what befell us, I was *always* there.'

She turned on her heels, a finality in her action and her words.

In a burst of movement, Alex was on his feet and up the stairs, his anger spiralling out of control. He grabbed her hair, deriving pleasure from her cries of discomfort.

'Just like a disease,' he snarled, throwing her backwards and sending her down the stairs, her whimpers of pain satisfying him.

Alex followed her down, taking each step purposefully, determined she wasn't going to continue ruling his life. He'd let her have control for far too long, and all it had brought with it was misery for him and countless people around him; it needed to end, now.

He stared down at her coldly, his green eyes

burning with hatred. 'Where *is* she?' he growled. 'What have you done to her?'

Nadia glared up at him from the cellar floor, brushing her black hair from her face. She was aware of her elders hovering in the doorway at the top of the stairs. They were silhouetted against the light behind them, their faces cast in darkness, but she could easily imagine the disapproving expressions on their faces over their offspring's behaviour; brawling was hardly the behaviour of distinguished lords and ladies, after all.

Alex snarled, stooping to grab his sister by the tops of her arms, shaking her violently as he pulled her to her feet. 'Tell me, damn it,' he shouted, his voice echoing around the dark underground store.

She grinned, her gaze vindictive. 'Go to hell,' she hissed.

Anger raging, he lashed out, hitting her hard across the face before pushing her away violently, sending her crashing into the large wine racks that dominated the far wall. The impact dislodged one of them. Bottles rattled and smashed to the floor, sending glass and ruby liquid across Nadia and the stone beneath her. The sounds of the smashing bottles, splintering wood and scraped stone echoed loudly around the cavernous cellar.

Alex stepped forward as his sister grasped at the rack behind her, steadying herself as she tried to stand. Wine dripped from her clothes and her hair, and she glared up at him, a snarl on her lips.

He stared at her, seeing the madness he knew that dwelt within.

Alex's gaze flickered to the gap in the racks he'd never known was there.

Through the gloom between the wood, he could just make out a pile of what looked like large wooden crates.

He continued to stare at the gap in the wine racks, the sense of unease growing as his stomach churned.

Nadia's own gaze flickered between her brother and the rack next to her, uncertainty in her eyes.

'Alex—'

Without letting her finish, he pushed her aside as his elders crept down the stone stairs behind him.

His hands were trembling as he reached out for the thick wood of the rack before him. For a moment, he froze, every inch of his body screaming in protest.

It was this sense of dread that spurred him into action.

With a deep breath, he pulled on the damaged rack with all his strength, the dislodged wood grating loudly against the stone floor beneath his feet. More bottles fell, smashing against the floor, the ruby liquid pooling around his feet.

The crates he'd seen on the other side toppled, pressing against the damaged wood as he pulled it free.

Something gave, and the rack toppled out of his hands.

RETRIBUTION DARKENED

Alex stepped back, the wooden crates from behind crashing to the floor, three of the lids smashing open on impact.

The smell that instantly filled the room made him heave, but it was nothing compared to the sight before him.

Alex stared at the bodies that now littered the cellar floor, each one at various stages of decomposition.

The world around him seemed to stop as he stared at the ghastly sight before him, the air suddenly too thick to breath.

He thought he heard his mother gasp behind him as she caught sight of the atrocity before her, but he wasn't sure; nothing seemed to breach the cacophony in his head.

Two of the bodies were unrecognisable, such was the level of their decay. The skin was clinging to the bones where sinews of muscle were plainly visible, their limbs barely connected to the torso. One of them was missing his genitals.

Alex's gaze roamed over the sickening sight before him, the smell constantly making him retch; he'd seem some shit over the centuries, but never anything like this.

'You bitch,' he whispered venomously, staring at the carnage before him. 'You monstrous, evil bitch.'

His heart ached and his stomach twisted as his gaze fell upon the third body, the beginnings of decomposition failing to hide the identity of the unfortunate soul.

Alex felt tears sting his eyes as he stared at Jason Taggart's body. His skin was grey, the beginnings of rot and decay setting in, delayed only slightly by the coldness of the cellar.

'What the hell have you done?' he asked, his voice quiet and hoarse as he tried to get the words past the lump of emotion in his throat. Jason had been a friend, a decent human being who enjoyed life to its fullest with no regrets. He'd never hurt anyone, and he sure as hell never deserved anything like this.

Alex's gaze swiftly passed over the numerous other boxes stacked against the far wall, knowing instinctively that each one held the body of a man foolish enough to fall for Nadia's seductive charms.

He could feel his sister's gaze as he stood there in the gloom of the cellar. He swallowed the bile that rose into his throat before he felt able speak.

'You're keeping dead bodies in this house,' he said numbly, his voice still quiet and disbelieving. 'You're keeping someone who was a friend in our house.'

Nadia took a step forward. 'Alex—'

'His friends are beside themselves with worry,' he said, his voice finally rising above a whisper. 'They try and phone him every damn day in the vain hope he'll answer, and you've been keeping him in here, yards from their homes, like some fucking trophy?' he bellowed, flying towards her and pinning her to the wall, his hands around her throat.

His sharp teeth were bared, his fingers tightening around her neck. His hands trembled with his rage and shock, unwilling to release her. She needed to suffer, he told himself; she needed to pay for what she had done.

'He wanted me,' she managed, her voice raspy. 'Just like the rest. *All* the rest.' Even despite Alex's tightening hold on her throat, she still managed a smile, taunting him.

'And they pay for that by rotting in our cellar?' he asked, fresh tears filling his eyes. 'He was a friend, damn you,' he shouted in her face.

This is all your fault, the voice in his head taunted, *you created what she is. You could have stopped her long ago.*

'Alex,' Victor said, his voice stern and full of concern as he stared into the gloom before him.

Alex continued to glare at his sister, his hatred overwhelming him. 'Would you have me let her go, Father?' he roared. 'There are no words for what she has done.'

'Indeed, I would not,' Victor confirmed quietly, his gaze remaining on the shadows. 'But I fear it may be prudent to check these other crates,' he murmured, his voice filled with urgency.

Fresh bile rose as Alex's stomach churned, icy tendrils crawling over his skin as he stared at his sister. 'Please tell me you didn't do it again,' he pleaded, tears breaking his voice.

Nadia didn't answer him and he released her

quickly, unable to bear touching her for a moment longer.

With desperation, Alex stepped over the bodies on the floor and rushed behind the rack, pulling at each crate from the pile.

'Catrina?' he called, his mind filled with horrific images of what he was going to find; Nadia's rage would not have spared Catrina any mercy.

He moved across the floor, pushing past each box he came across, listening against the lids. The smell of putrefaction filled the air and he resisted the urge to retch each time, his only goal to find Catrina.

He glanced up at Victor as he joined him in the search. Alex's eyes filled with tears.

'You know what she did last time,' he said quietly, too many memories flooding back; each one physically hurt.

Victor nodded slowly, his gaze darkening with the memory. 'And I fear this will be worse, my son,' he soothed, glancing around him at the decomposing bodies that littered the floor.

The pair of them moved between the crates until Alex stiffened, staring down at a box on the floor before him.

Listening against the lid, he heard the faintest of whimpers, the sound only clear to his heightened hearing.

Dropping to his knees, he grasped the clasps that Nadia had dutifully added to the crudely-made coffin. He yanked at them, forcing them open.

RETRIBUTION DARKENED

Taking a deep breath to steady his nerves, Alex gripped the edges of the lid and threw it back, the sound of the wood hitting the floor echoing across the room.

He froze as he stared into the crate, his blood running cold.

He stared at the back of a woman with dark hair, who'd been placed in the box face down, her naked body badly lacerated by what looked like Nadia's nails.

His stomach twisted, instinctively knowing who the woman was. With trembling hands, he reached out and grasped her cold, rigor mortised shoulders as Victor took hold of her ankles.

Gently, they lifted the woman from the box.

Alex's entire being felt frozen with terror as he stared at the brutalised body of Camilla, her throat torn open. He felt bile rise into his throat; her tongue and eyes had been cut out, her mouth frozen open in what he assumed to have been a scream of terror.

Desperately, he turned back to the box.

Catrina lay there, still alive; the sight of her had Alex's heart breaking with the pain of the suffering and brutality she'd endured at the hands of his own sister.

Inside the makeshift coffin she sobbed silently, the sounds barely audible due to the large bloodied puncture wound to her throat, which had been viciously torn. Her arms and legs were lacerated. Her skin was so pale it was almost translucent, her body unable to heal itself due to major blood loss.

His gaze fell to her chest. Nadia had pulled the bathrobe from her naked body, callously revealing her breasts, and had placed a crudely-made crucifix on the skin between them. Completely weakened by the loss of blood, Catrina had been unable to remove it; over the time she'd been locked away it had severely burnt her skin, until it had eaten at her flesh, the surrounding skin blistered and oozing. The smell was gut-wrenching.

'What has she done to you?' Alex asked quietly, his gaze seeking hers. She was so weak she could barely open her eyes and he couldn't be sure if she even knew he was there; delirium would no doubt have set in with the starvation of blood and the severe pain she'd been forced to endure.

Tears fell down his cheeks unchecked as Alex looked down at her. He'd known what his sister was capable of and he should have done more to stop it; every offence she had ever committed was all down to him.

Victor lowered Camilla's body to the ground gently, affording her as much respect in death as he was able. He took a step forward; there was a deep sympathy in his ancient eyes.

'Come, my son,' he said quietly, his words filled with support. 'Let us give her some peace, such as it is.'

Alex could hear his mother sobbing behind them as she watched on.

Nadia simply glared at them from the corner of the room where he'd left her.

He turned back to his father, lost and unable to consider what had to be done.

Victor turned away for a moment, searching for something. When he spotted the item in the shadows, he picked it up and handed it to Alex.

'Use this,' he advised, as he passed the dirty cloth to Alex. 'Protect yourself.'

Alex stared at the cloth in his hands, disgusted by it; no doubt it was the same one Nadia had used to protect herself when she'd placed the crucifix on Catrina's chest in the first place.

Mechanically, he wrapped the dirty material around his hand, making sure every finger was covered, along with the palm of his hand.

He glanced again at his father, uncertain.

'You must be strong, my son,' he soothed, placing his hand supportively on Alex's shoulder. 'For Catrina's sake.'

With a deep breath, Alex grabbed the crucifix and tugged on it gently, his stomach rolling as Catrina attempted to scream, the sound virtually muted by her weakened state and wounded throat, but nonetheless chilling.

He pulled his hand back, unable to cause her more agony than she'd already suffered.

'You need to remove it, Alex,' Victor guided gently, his voice still maintaining its urgency. 'It will cause her pain, however gently you try.'

His stomach churning and heart pounding, Alex closed his eyes, unable to watch as he again tightened his grip on the crucifix and pulled as hard and as quickly as he could, the unmistakable and sickening sound of flesh tearing making him retch. Tears fell down his cheeks as the horrifying sounds of Catrina's gargled screams ripped at his resolve.

He threw the cross away forcefully, disgusted by it.

It took all his will to open his eyes, knowing what he would see; his stomach roiled at the sight before him.

What has she done to you? The thought ran through his mind as he found himself unable to physically voice the words.

Catrina's skin, already translucent due to the massive blood loss and starvation, was excessively burnt across her chest where Nadia had so cruelly placed the cross. The skin was blistered and charred, the muscles, cartilage and bone of her sternum grotesquely visible. Her entire body shook with the shock of her ordeal.

Victor turned to his son, his own hurt and pain evident in his eyes. 'She needs to be moved from here, Alex. She needs blood.'

His father's words snapping him back to the here and now, Alex jumped to his feet.

'I'll carry her,' he said through his tears.

Victor shook his head. 'She cannot be touched, my son. She is far too weak. You may cause her yet more suffering. We will have to take her in the crate.' He looked at Alex, regret etched across his ancient features.

'I know it is not a pleasant situation, but the less she is moved the better. Let's get her away from here and I will be able to better assess her condition. She needs to be fed, urgently. She has already been starved for too long.'

Alex read the unspoken words in his father's eyes; there was no telling how much damage, mentally, had been done, or whether it could ever be rectified.

With rage, Alex turned to look at Nadia, disgust filling every inch of his body; she was deranged, sick, and he should have done more to contain the vile creature that had once been his sister.

'How could you do this to her?' he snarled loudly, the outburst causing Catrina to sob once more. 'How could you do this to *me*?'

'You needed to forget her, Alex,' Nadia pleaded, losing her resolve as she moved away from the wall. 'You needed to move on from her.'

'No, Nadia,' he snapped, his voice breaking with the pain of the realisation that his sister had lost her mind. 'I need to move on from *you*.'

'Alex, we need to get Catrina out of here,' Victor said urgently, tugging on his son's arm.

'The Other's should have kept you locked away,' Alex hissed at her viciously. 'I should have let you *rot*.'

Without a second thought of this evil thing before him, he turned away.

Along with his father, he grabbed the end of the crate and lifted it from the ice-cold stone floor of the cellar. The two slowly manoeuvred through the other crates and bodies that still littered the floor, heading for the stone steps of the cellar.

Nadia stepped towards Alex, her arms reaching out.

Yet Aurelia's hardened grasp bore down on her daughter's wrist, tightening over the skin.

Nadia glanced round at her mother, matching the coldness in her gaze.

'Your damage is complete,' Aurelia condemned, her tone forceful.

Nadia stared after Alex, who refused to look at her as he mounted the steps.

She turned back to her elder, her expression filled with contempt.

Aurelia met her withering glare, her face set like stone.

'Forgiveness is beyond your reach now, child.'

Chapter 26

'She should be okay for a while,' Victor said quietly, eyeing the wound on his wrist.

He looked between Aurelia and Alex; they'd all taken it in turns to feed Catrina as much as they were able without weakening themselves.

They had brought Catrina upstairs to Alex's room, still within the coffin; it was the best place for her in terms of keeping her still and covered from the light.

She was resting slightly easier after feeding, though broken sobs would choke from her throat every so often.

'How could she do this?' Alex asked quietly, more to himself than either of his elders.

Victor glanced at Aurelia, uneasy, before pulling Alex to one side. 'Catrina's in the best place right now. Her wounds will heal faster if she is given complete rest. She is not out of danger yet.' He placed a supportive hand on Alex's shoulder, his expression grim. 'I would recommend keeping both this room and the coffin locked at all times when you are not with her.'

Aurelia looked at the pair, her gentle face hardened by the grief in her eyes; Alex knew all too well what she was thinking.

His sister had all but lost her mind, again.

He was still trying to process everything he'd witnessed down in the cellar; a room they had all passed numerous times, yet never contemplated what depravity had been hidden within. Alex's stomach churned at the memory of Camilla's mutilated corpse and Jason's body falling from his crude excuse for a coffin, his lifeless eyes and grey, decomposing skin haunting him. The stench had been horrific.

Aurelia offered Alex the smallest of smiles. 'You must be strong for Catrina now,' she murmured, taking his hand in hers in support.

Alex tried to hold back the tears that stung his eyes. 'I failed her, Mother,' he said, his voice breaking with emotion. 'In every way, I failed her. I created this. I made Nadia into what she is. It's all my fault. I failed Nadia and now I've failed Catrina,' he rambled, unable to keep his thoughts locked within any longer.

'Listen to me, my child,' Aurelia said sternly, taking Alex's face in her hands, forcing him to look her in the eye.

Staring back at him he saw his entire immortal life, with all its failings.

Aurelia stroked his cheek with her thumb. 'You have not failed Catrina, Alex, do you understand me?

Yes, you have done wrong, but are any of us without fault? Do you not think I feel I have failed *you*, as my child?' she asked sadly. 'Now is *your* time to protect *her*, care for her, and ensure she recovers from this. You are her lifeline now. She needs you, whether she dares admit it or not.'

She pulled Alex to her in an embrace that had him weeping. 'Now is your time to work for forgiveness, my child,' she whispered against his hair. 'For everything.'

'How can I protect her?' he asked, pushing himself away from his mother's embrace. He stared at her, lost. 'Nadia's lost her mind. She's capable of anything, we all know that.' He ran his fingers through his hair, trying to think past the cacophony of thoughts running through his head.

He glanced at Catrina's still body. He couldn't put her through this anymore.

'You need to take her away from here,' he said suddenly, turning back to look at both his parents in turn.

They stared blankly at him.

'We can't stay here now. Not after what we've witnessed in that cellar. You need to take Catrina back to Romania, away from Nadia.' His voice took on a tone of desperation. 'Take her to the Others. She'll heal with the aid of their blood.'

Victor took hold of his son's arm. 'Alex, Catrina has been drained of blood and left unable to feed. She is incredibly weak and fragile. Moving her at this point in time could be dangerous.'

Alex frowned. 'Leaving her *here* is dangerous,' he argued.

Aurelia stepped forward. 'Your father is not saying no, my child,' she said sternly. 'But Catrina needs rest and regular feeds.'

Alex shook off his father's hold. 'How long?' he asked angrily, glaring between his elders. He felt the binds tightening around him.

Victor sighed heavily. 'It is hard to tell,' he admitted. 'We will need to assess her overnight,' he said gently.

Alex stared at him before shifting his gaze to his mother, unsure. 'We can't stay here,' he repeated, feeling lost; they had already had the police knocking on their door and that was before he knew they had a cellar full of dead bodies. He shivered at the possible repercussions of Nadia's actions.

Aurelia glanced at first her husband and then back to her son. 'I know,' she admitted. 'But at this precise moment in time, there is nothing we can do. Catrina needs time to recover, even if only a little. She has been through enough trauma.'

Alex ran his fingers through his hair, his impatience building. 'I can't stand the thought of keeping her here in this house,' he sighed. 'We've got two of her closest friends dead in our cellar and the police skulking about. We all need to get out of here.'

Aurelia looked thoughtful. 'And what of your sister?' she asked.

The very thought of Nadia had Alex's rage flaring. 'Right now, she can rot for all I care. All I want is to get the hell away from here and keep Catrina safe.'

Victor nodded. 'I know, but for now we have no choice but to stay.' He glanced at his wife. 'We will guard Catrina for you over the next few hours and monitor her progress.'

Alex glanced between his elders. 'You'll guard her?'

Aurelia offered him a supportive smile. 'We will,' she confirmed. 'We will remain in this room with her, only leaving one at a time to feed, so she is never left alone.' She took her son's hand, squeezing it gently.

Victor nodded. 'We will keep the door locked, from the inside, and will only permit you to enter when you wish to spend time with her. We will protect her and feed her with our own blood in order to aid her healing.'

Alex stared between them. 'You would do that?'

Aurelia beamed as she pulled her son to her once more. 'Catrina is our daughter now,' she whispered against his hair. 'She needs protecting and we will guard her with our lives.'

Alex stepped back from his mother's embrace. 'Thank you,' he said, unable to find the words to truly express his gratitude at their sacrifice. 'Thank you both.'

Aurelia and Victor exchanged glances, their

smiles disguising a discomfort Alex knew all too well; they were happy to watch Catrina, but equally uneasy about leaving him to deal with his sister alone.

He wasn't greatly enthralled by the prospect either, yet given the circumstances knew there was no other choice. He took a deep breath; it wouldn't be the first time, and Catrina's recovery came first.

Victor glanced over his shoulder, watching Catrina rest for several seconds before turning back to his son.

'We will leave you alone with her now,' he said softly, his tone supportive.

Aurelia headed out of the door as Victor squeezed his son's shoulder, further conveying his support, before leaving the room and closing the door behind him.

Alex stood there in the silence of the room, staring at Catrina as she lay there. His hands shook by his sides with both rage and fear; she could have remained down in that cellar for weeks or months had he not found her. The damage she would have suffered in that instance, both mental and physical, may have been irreversible given her young age, despite it being he who had made her.

He swallowed past the lump of emotion that choked him, stepping tentatively towards the makeshift coffin that she would have to remain in until she healed. He hated seeing her in that crudely made box; she'd suffered enough within it, and now she would have to endure who knew how long suffering the nightmares it would impart on her.

He took another step towards her, the bare boards beneath his feet creaking in their ancient way.

Catrina's eyes slowly opened, her gaze meeting his almost instantly.

He wasn't sure what he'd expected to see in those topaz eyes, but he hadn't been prepared for the blankness within them; there was nothing there, no anger, no accusation, nothing... only a deep suffering that made his blood run cold.

'She... knew... ' she managed, her voice weak and barely audible. Her throat was still badly ripped and scarred, despite the healing effect of the blood she'd imbibed; although the three of them had fed her, it had barely scratched the surface in terms of repairing the damage.

Tears instantly stung his eyes as he stepped closer to her still, his entire body shaking with the coldness of his grief.

'She... knew... we wanted... leave... never see... her... again...' The torment in her weakened voice was evident, and it broke his heart.

He fell to his knees beside her, desperate to touch her and yet unwilling to, should he cause her more pain. The tears fell unchecked down his cheeks.

'I'm so sorry,' he wept, unable to form any other words through the grief that consumed him on seeing her like this.

'I... can't do... this... anymore...' she managed, tears falling unchecked down her cheeks.

Her words tore at his heart as he sat there. 'What do you mean?' he asked tentatively, petrified of her answer. He'd promised her she would never be hurt again, that he would never allow her to be hurt again, and yet here they were.

'I... can't fight... her,' she said quietly, her words sounding raspier as each word left her lips.

Despite her wounds, he reached out to take her hand, yet with what little strength she possessed she tugged her fingers away in the slightest of motions.

'You don't have to,' he said firmly, wiping the tears from his cheeks. 'We're done with her. She's no sister of mine,' he growled, his eyes narrowing. 'The Other's will punish her immensely for this.'

'They... let her... go,' she whispered.

'They won't this time,' he confirmed. 'I'll make sure of it.'

They remained silent for a few moments as she stared up at the ceiling.

Alex wasn't sure he wanted to know the thoughts that were flashing through her mind; the haunted look in her eyes was heart-breaking enough.

Eventually she spoke: 'Cam...' she breathed, pain in her eyes.

The memory of Camilla's mutilated body made him retch, her placement in the same box as Catrina the ultimate torment, forcing Catrina to stare endlessly into her friend's empty sockets.

'I'm so sorry,' he murmured, knowing it would never be enough.

'Why?' she asked quietly.

Alex sighed. 'I don't know,' he answered honestly. 'We all thought you'd gone to her and she was...' He trailed off; it didn't matter what he'd thought anymore.

'There were... bodies...' she said hoarsely, not looking at him.

He knew what she meant.

'Yes,' he said gravely, knowing she'd clearly heard everything that had transpired in the cellar before they'd found her.

'She was keeping them down there. Like trophies,' he cringed, forcing the bile that suddenly filled his throat back to where it came from as he thought on the horrifying sight in that cellar under his home.

'Jason,' she said simply.

Alex nodded, unwilling to divulge any further information than a simple confirmation; she didn't need to know the details now.

'I'm sorry. I had no idea,' he admitted, having wondered so many times what Nadia had done with Jason's body, considering it hadn't been found by the police or the public; Alex would never have even considered the horrifying truth.

'She's... evil,' Catrina managed, continuing to stare at the ceiling.

Alex stared at nothing. There was nothing he could say in answer to that; he'd known Nadia was evil for far too long and done nothing to stop her, giving in to his need for her blood over and over again.

That one weakness had destroyed too many innocent lives over the years.

Fresh tears began to fall down Catrina's cheeks as she finally looked at him, shame filling her eyes.

'You... can't love... me... now,' she said tearfully. 'I'm... monster.' She began gasping again as the struggle for words became too much.

Without missing a beat, Alex bit into his wrist, reaching across her and placing his torn skin to her lips, allowing the viscous liquid to drip into her mouth, knowing she was too weak to actually drink it herself.

Her tears continued to fall as she swallowed his blood.

He wished he could see some evidence it was beginning to repair the damage her ordeal had inflicted, but there was none to be seen; the wounds ran too deep to be healed so easily.

He took his wrist away after another minute, pressing his fingers to the wound until the skin healed. He'd already given her as much as he could, his weakness growing; he'd need to feed soon.

Alex reached over, placing his hand on the crown of her head.

He felt the minute twitch of her head that he knew was supposed to be a flinch, but without her strength she was unable to manifest the action into anything obvious.

RETRIBUTION DARKENED

He gently ran his fingers over her blonde hair, unwilling to say a word when strands of it came away from the scalp.

'I love you, Catrina,' he said firmly, wiping the tears from her cheeks tenderly. 'What's happened hasn't changed that.'

'She's... still... beautiful,' she managed, her voice stronger after imbibing his blood.

His gaze darkened. 'I need you to listen to me,' he said resolutely. 'She is *not* beautiful. After everything I've told you, you should know that. Her features hide a sick, deranged and twisted individual who enjoys seeing others suffer, and I will never forgive her for what she's done to you.' He looked down sadly. 'I underestimated her and I shouldn't have. I learnt a long time ago that doing so is a fatal thing to do.'

Despite his tears, he managed to smile at Catrina, taking her hand quickly before she could even think of moving it away. 'I know it's hard to see a way through this right now, but you'll recover from this. You are so strong and brave. Your wounds will heal in time.' The voice in his head told him that despite this, the mental scars would never disappear, and the prospect scared him; she'd suffer nightmares over this for a long, long time to come.

He leant over and planted a gentle kiss on her forehead, meeting her gaze once more. 'And once you're completely recovered, we'll leave here, just as I promised.'

'I... want... to believe... you,' she whispered sadly. 'But... she...'

Alex shook his head. 'She's dead to us. Dead to me,' he assured. 'We'll never even speak of her again. She doesn't exist, do you understand me?' He wanted her to believe him, for every word he spoke he knew was the absolute truth; Nadia was dead to him now as she should have been a long, long time ago.

Unable to nod her head, Catrina closed her eyes tightly, tears escaping down her temples. After a minute, she opened her eyes once more to look at him, the sadness running deeper than he could ever comprehend.

He managed a small smile, pushing past the heartache of seeing her like this, knowing that ultimately it was all his fault.

'You need to rest, my love,' he said softly, leaning over to kiss her gently on the forehead before preparing to stand from the floor.

'Stay...' she said simply, the one word all she was able to manage through her exhaustion.

Alex stared at her for a moment, unsure if he'd heard her correctly. When he saw the tears falling from her eyes, he knew he had.

He settled himself back beside her on the floor, smoothing his hand once more over her head as she closed her eyes.

Within minutes, she was asleep, and Alex was left alone with his thoughts and nightmares.

Just as he always had been.

Chapter 27

The darkness engulfed her as Lola's heart raced within her chest.

Icy tendrils crept up her spine, rendering her immobile as she stared into the shadows before her.

The streets around her were beyond dark, the faint light from the two streetlamps failing to penetrate the hideous shadows that blanketed the buildings around her.

She stared as the shadows seemed to mutate into shapes, stalking through the darkness before dissolving once more.

She wanted to call out, to cry for help, yet her voice seemed stolen from her throat as she stood there, frozen to the spot, feeling so alone it chilled her very blood.

Another shadow swirled before her and Lola felt that horrendous hot wave of absolute panic sweep over her body, the sensation that always rendered her helpless; it was the ultimate loss of hope. It was the fight or flight sensation that failed her on both counts.

The shadow seemed to grow, its essence more solidified.

Tears streamed down her cheeks as she shook her head in defiance of what she knew she was going to see.

The shadowy figure stared at her, its eyes glowing that all too familiar shade of red.

In a movement too quick for Lola to anticipate, the creature grabbed her with its unnatural strength, its long sharp fingers gripping her shoulders.

It hissed at her, no other features clear other than its sharp teeth and terrifying red eyes.

'Lola,' it snarled, the word spat from its mouth with disgust.

All at once, she found she could move and she struggled against this inhuman creature that tormented her every waking hour, as well as her sleep.

'Lola,' it hissed again, its breath hot against her face.

Through her fright and panic she summoned as much strength as she could, lashing out with her hand to strike the creature's invisible features.

'Fuck, Lola, wake up!'

As if plucked from a spell, she suddenly awoke, the bright light streaming in from the window hurting her eyes. She was disorientated and confused, and it took her several moments to realise she was in Matt's bed.

She rubbed her trembling hands over her face;

she didn't even remember closing her eyes.

'What the fuck is wrong with you?' Matt asked.

She turned to look at him as he sat on the edge of the bed, his hand cradling his left eye.

Another few moments of confusion passed before she realised she'd hit him.

Sitting up quickly, she continued to stare at him, not believing what she had done.

'Did I do that?' she asked, her voice raspy. She cleared her throat.

He glared at her, his temper evident. 'Yes, you fucking did,' he said, his voice filled with scorn as he felt around his eye socket with his fingers. 'What's wrong with you?'

'I'm sorry,' she said, reaching out for him. Complete rejection flooded over her when he pulled away sharply. 'I was having a dream. Something got hold of me, and—'

'That was me,' he shouted. 'Fuck sake, Lo, I was only trying to wake you. You were thrashing around and moaning. Next time I won't bother.'

Lola frowned. 'I said I'm sorry,' she managed as tears began to form. 'I didn't do it on purpose.'

Matt stared at her. 'All you say is sorry, Lo, and it's getting a bit boring.'

She stared straight at him. 'Excuse me?' she asked, her words forced from her throat as she tried to hold back the tears of hurt.

'You heard,' he snapped, standing from the bed. He stormed across the room, away from her.

'Why are you being like this?' she asked, tears falling down her cheeks.

She knew things had been strained lately; even more so since her "episode" in the market a few weeks ago when she'd only wanted to speak to Jason instead of Matt. Then Jason had disappeared and her already damaged attentions had been further stretched away from her time with Matt. Her lack of sleep, her nightmares and the anxiety caused by everything were ruining her life, and she was far too tired to fight it anymore.

Matt turned on his heels to face her, his expression clouded with pent-up anger.

'Because I'm tired, Lo,' he admitted, the tinge of desperation in his words. 'I'm tired because you wake me every damn night with these nightmares of yours. You freak out during the day at every little noise and shadow, and it's exhausting trying to second guess what mood you're going to be in every fucking day.'

'Do you think I like being like this?' she screamed at him, unable to hold back the hurt his words caused or the disgust she felt at herself; she couldn't explain what had happened to her, and she sure as hell couldn't explain why.

'I don't know anymore,' he countered. 'I don't know anything because you won't tell me anything.' His words were filled with desperation, needing to know.

She held her head in her hands. 'You wouldn't understand,' she said quietly.

RETRIBUTION DARKENED

'Oh, but Jason did?' he scoffed angrily.

She looked up at him then. 'I didn't mean to shut you out.'

'But you did all the same,' he gritted.

She shrugged her shoulders. 'I didn't mean to. I needed to talk to Jason.'

Matt's eyes narrowed. 'Why? Why couldn't you talk to me?'

Lola struggled to find the right words. 'I needed to talk to him about something that happened when we were kids.'

Matt took a few steps back towards her, finally perching himself back on the bed. He didn't say anything; he simply watched her, closely. There was something uncertain in his eyes.

She sat in silence for a moment, thinking over that day in the market. She thought of the conversation she'd had with Jason afterwards and the way he'd looked at her like she was crazy. Despite him knowing what had happened all those years ago, he still hadn't believed a word she'd said.

Lola stood from the bed and grabbed her clothes, using the process of dressing as a distraction from what she needed to say.

'Lo?' Matt pressed.

She sighed as she pulled on her top. 'When me and Jason were sixteen, we went exploring in the Demeter house.'

Matt looked surprised. 'You broke in?'

Lola frowned. 'Not really. It was empty, had

been for years as far as we knew. It was all overgrown and abandoned. You know about the rumours of it being haunted. It's a local thing. Jason had the grand idea that we should go and "ghost-hunt".' She found herself smiling at the memory, despite herself.

He nodded, no expression on his face. 'That sounds like Jas,' he said flatly. 'So what happened?'

'Jason went off exploring upstairs and I looked around downstairs. The place gave me the creeps,' she admitted. 'I eventually went down into the cellar.'

Matt looked confused. 'What has all this got to do with now?' he asked.

She stared at the floor, unwilling to think of his reaction when she told him the truth; he'd hardly been full of support since all this started.

'When I went in the cellar I saw... the eyes,' she finally managed to say.

Matt stiffened instantly. 'The eyes?' he asked, cynicism in his voice.

She nodded, still looking at the floor. 'I saw them and ran from the house. I never told Jason what I saw until I asked to talk him that day after the market.'

Matt remained silent.

'Then I saw them that night here with you, and I've been seeing them ever since. I hear whispered voices and a word over and over.'

'What word?' he asked carefully.

'Vrolok,' she said.

'What?'

'Vrolok. I had to look it up in the end. It's a

Slovak word.' She glanced up at him. 'It means vampire.'

Matt laughed. 'Vampire?' he asked.

She looked up at him, hurt by his reaction though knowing deep down that anyone else would have reacted the same way.

'You're telling me you're being hunted by a vampire?' he laughed, looking at her as if he expected her to reveal her joke.

When he saw the pained expression on her face, his laugh trailed off. 'You're being serious?'

'I don't know what's going on,' she admitted. 'I'm only telling you what I know. I saw the word the first time in a book in the library when Jason scared me. Ever since then, I see and hear it in my sleep, along with the eyes. I saw it that day in the market. That's why I ran.'

Matt stared at her, his eyes wide. 'Do you have any idea what you sound like?' he asked, his voice strained.

'I—'

'You sound like a mad woman,' he scathed, standing from the bed and pacing the room once more. 'You told Jason all this?'

Lola nodded, glancing up at him, feeling lost and alone at the sight of the rejection in his eyes.

'And what did he say?' he scoffed.

She didn't want to recall the look in Jason's eyes that day; it was the last time she ever saw him, and he left thinking she was losing her mind.

'He said...' She trailed off, unable to finish.

Matt shook his head with disbelief. 'He said the same as me, that you're completely mad,' he spat. 'Didn't he?'

Tears filled her eyes as she ran her hands over each other, panic flooding her body; why was all this happening to her? She shook her head as the tears fell.

'He didn't call me that,' she said loudly, too upset to shout.

'I bet he fucking thought it though,' he countered angrily.

'Why are you being like this?' she asked again, sobbing as the tears fell faster.

'Because you're talking shit, Lo,' he yelled at her. 'You're talking absolute shit, and I can't deal with this anymore.'

She stared at him, her stomach twisting with the pain of the hurt at his words. 'What are you saying?' she managed to say, her voice weak.

'I'm saying I'm done with this shit, Lo. I'm done trying to support you and—'

'What support?' she asked, choking on the words. 'You've given me fuck all support since this whole nightmare began.' She sobbed through her words, hating the hurt and anger that overwhelmed her. 'You called me a liar from the very beginning.'

'Can you blame me?' he bellowed. 'What would anyone say to someone who talks of red eyes and vampires? You're crazy.'

'Fuck you,' she screamed at him, all the hurt and pain boiling over.

'Get the fuck out, Lo,' he shouted, turning his back on her in a final act of rejection. 'I can't talk to you like this.'

Fresh tears streamed down her face as she stared at his back for a few moments, trying to think about the reasons why everything had gone so wrong.

Realising he wasn't going to say another word, she picked up her nightclothes and her bag from the end of the bed and stormed across the room.

Racing down the stairs, she didn't look back as she slammed the front door closed.

She got as far as the next house before she threw up.

Chapter 28

She *had* to be crazy.

The words tormented Matt over and over again as he sat on his sofa, staring at nothing. He'd spent the best part of his Saturday morning trying to make sense of the argument he'd had with Lola mere hours before.

The dreams, nervousness and anxiety had been bad enough, but now her dreams were making her violent; he truly couldn't see a way out of this.

His phone rang again for the twentieth time since he'd all but thrown her out. He turned his attention to the vibrating handset as it buzzed across the coffee table in front of him. Lola's name flashed on the screen.

So many times he'd been tempted to answer it, yet each time he was held back by the memory of what had happened earlier, the things he'd said to her and she to him.

Could he really believe she was crazy? How could she not be, speaking about vampires and red eyes? Even Jason, her own cousin, had all but questioned her sanity the last time Matt had seen him before his disappearance.

The phone screen stopped flashing and a message beeped, informing him of yet another voicemail added to the list of the many others she'd left him over the course of the morning.

He didn't pick up the phone to listen to it; just like he hadn't listened to any of the others.

His anger had subsided, yet he still couldn't bring himself to talk to her.

A little voice inside his head told him it was down to the guilt of his own message he'd sent only an hour ago; the one he'd sent to Nadia, telling her how his morning had been completely shit.

He hadn't received a reply.

He ran his hands over his face, his mind too chaotic to think clearly.

He missed Jason most in that moment; he missed the man-to-man advice, the stupid jokes that eased the strain, the bloke time in front of the football or console with a beer that instantly made him feel better, melting the stresses of the day away.

He groaned as his phone began to vibrate again, Lola's name flashing on the screen once more.

In frustration, he stood from his seat, grabbed the phone, hit the reject call button and turned the phone off, unwilling to deal with it all now; he needed time to think and get his head around the potential gravity of the situation.

He threw the phone back onto the table.

The doorbell rang and he cringed; *please*, he thought, *I don't need a big confrontation now.*

He stood there in the lounge for a moment, unsure whether to open the door or not; he really didn't want to face Lola right now.

He needed space.

The doorbell sounded again.

Still unsure whether to even answer, he took a tentative step towards the lounge door. Then another.

Telling himself he was being stupid, and somewhat of a coward, he headed for the front door, taking a deep breath before opening it.

He stared at the woman in front of him.

Nadia smiled sweetly, holding up a bottle of whiskey.

'I might be wrong, but reading between the lines of your text you sounded like you could do with this,' she said cheerfully, offering him the bottle, which he took willingly.

He laughed, surprising himself considering his foul mood moments before.

'You're definitely not wrong,' he said, stepping aside from the door. 'I might need help drinking it though,' he offered, by way of an invitation.

'Only if you're sure?' she asked carefully.

He nodded, waving an arm in an exaggerated "after you" movement. 'I'm not in the mood for drinking alone,' he added, watching her as she walked past.

RETRIBUTION DARKENED

He couldn't help his gaze travelling over her body, from her ink black hair that fell loose about her shoulders, to the low cut black jumper she wore, down to the red tartan skirt that just brushed her thighs and the black knee-high boots with killer heels.

He closed the door and followed her through to the lounge, watching as she turned to face him.

She was stunning.

He held out a hand towards the sofa, offering her a seat. She smiled at him and accepted his invitation, her skirt rising further up her thighs and he forced himself to avert his gaze.

He placed the bottle on the coffee table. 'I'll get some glasses,' he murmured, trying to push thoughts of what he could do with Nadia here and now out of his mind.

It didn't work.

He walked through to the kitchen, opened a cupboard and pulled out two glass tumblers. Closing the cupboard, he turned, his gaze falling to the table in the middle of the room. He couldn't help but remember the times he'd spent sat at that table with Lola and Jason, the fun times they'd shared, the laughs, the jokes.

He couldn't remember when he'd last seen Lola smile *or* laugh; it was a time that felt lost to him now.

Pushing the grim memories aside, he wandered back into the lounge with the glasses.

Nadia was perched on the edge of the sofa, the whiskey bottle cradled in her hands. She offered him a smile as he crossed the room and joined her, placing the two glasses together on the coffee table.

She unscrewed the lid of the bottle. 'Allow me to do the honours,' she said wistfully, pouring the amber liquid into each glass in double measures. She replaced the lid on the bottle and stood it back on the table. Then she picked up both glasses and handed one to Matt.

'Cheers,' he said, tapping her glass with his own before taking a large gulp, the liquid burning his throat. He cringed; he'd need a few more in order to make him feel even remotely better.

Nadia swirled the liquid around in her glass. 'So,' she said carefully. 'Why is today not a good time to be drinking alone?'

Oh, where to begin, Matt thought. He shrugged, unwilling to divulge all that had been said between him and Lola.

'Today's just been really shit so far,' he said with a sigh. 'The last few weeks have been really shit,' he added, taking another sip of whiskey.

Nadia nodded as if understanding what he was talking about. 'They've been pretty rough for us all,' she said softly, her gaze focusing on something he wasn't sure of.

'You okay?' he asked carefully, unwilling to upset her by mentioning anything to do with Jason; Lola had told him how badly Nadia had been dealing with everything, especially after Camilla had taken it upon herself to call the police on the Demeter twins.

None of them had heard from her since.

Nadia instantly snapped out of her private reverie. She offered an embarrassed smile.

'Ignore me,' she chuckled, shrugging off his concern.

No chance of that, he told himself, his gaze flickering to her short skirt once more. He took another sip of his drink in order to divert his own attentions.

'I'm supposed to be cheering *you* up,' she said cheerfully. 'I gathered that much from your text.'

Matt shrugged. 'I didn't mean to bother you. I just needed to vent, I guess.'

'Don't apologise,' she admonished with a smile. 'We all need someone to vent at sometimes.'

'Lola told me about Camilla and the police,' he said awkwardly, remembering Lola's anger over their friend's suspicions.

Nadia straightened her back as she sat on the sofa, her cleavage all too obvious above her low-cut jumper. 'I can't lie and say it wasn't a shock having two detectives show up on my doorstep.'

Matt tentatively reached out and placed his hand on hers, where it rested on her lap.

'I'm sure Cam's learnt her lesson. Lola hasn't heard from her since. I definitely think we all need some good things to happen for a change.' His gaze caught hers for a moment as he thought on what those "good things" could be; once more he diverted his attentions with a gulp of his drink, nearly emptying his glass.

'Here,' she said, putting down her glass. She removed her hand from his and grabbed the bottle of whiskey, quickly opening it and pouring another double measure into his glass.

'Thanks,' he said, watching as she placed the bottle back on the table and retrieved her own tumbler. 'You trying to get me drunk?' he asked with a laugh.

She playfully faked shock. 'Would I do such a thing?' she flirted gently, making him laugh.

Her gaze held his once more before she looked back down at her glass. 'How's Lola?' she asked, finally looking back up at him.

His joviality disappeared. 'She's... er... not too good,' he admitted, taking another sip of whiskey. 'We had a fight this morning.'

'Ah,' she said, revelation in her eyes. 'So that explains the text.'

'Like I said, I didn't mean to bother you.'

She waved a hand as if shooing away his apology. 'I told you not to apologise. You were there for me when I needed a shoulder to cry on a couple of weeks ago, and here I am for you,' she said softly, taking hold of his hand tenderly.

Her touch sent pulses through his skin, making his not-so-innocent thoughts of her worse. 'I guess I miss Jason at times like this. He was always the best at cheering me up.'

Nadia smiled. 'I know,' she said sadly, her eyes

downcast.

'Sorry, I didn't mean to upset you,' he said, noting the sadness in her eyes.

She shook her head, looking back up at him. 'It's fine,' she sighed, a small smile decorating her pink lips.

She took a sip of her drink. 'So, am I allowed to ask what this fight was about?' she tested.

Matt shrugged, not knowing where to start. 'She's been really stressed lately. It started a couple of months back, I guess. She doesn't sleep, barely eats. She's working herself into the ground and her moods are all over the place.' He took another gulp of his drink, the smooth liquid starting to have an effect. 'I don't know what to do anymore.'

Nadia sighed. 'I know things haven't been easy for her lately, but she didn't tell me how bad.'

'She barely tells *me* anything,' he admitted. 'It's like she's another person altogether.'

She squeezed his hand. 'Lola's been under a lot of stress,' she soothed. 'I'm sure she'll get through it eventually, with help.'

'She's been talking about red eyes and vampires, for fuck's sake,' he blurted, instantly regretting it.

Nadia's eyes grew wider. 'Oh?' she queried, concern filling her green eyes.

'I'm sorry, I shouldn't have said that,' he admitted, hating himself for breaking a confidence, yet at the same time considering that maybe Nadia would be able to help if she knew the full extent of the problem.

'Don't worry,' she said sweetly. 'I'm good at keeping secrets.'

There was something about her words that teased him to distraction.

Her gaze held his for several moments, sending his need for her higher. He tried to reason with himself over and over that this was Lola's best friend, who had supported her through a lot over these last few weeks.

Nadia was supporting him right now, yet he couldn't help but think there was something else between them; he was certain it wasn't simply wishful thinking on his part.

'Are you?' he asked, unable to stop the words escaping.

She didn't answer him. She simply stared at him as his hand held hers, brushing his thumb across her fingers.

He heard her sharp intake of breath and his arousal spiralled out of control. He wasn't sure if it was the drink, his mood, or simply his need for attention and relief; at that exact moment, he didn't care.

Her lips parted. 'Matt, I...' Her words trailed off as she continued to stare at him, something unreadable in her eyes.

Matt placed his glass on the coffee table and took hers from her hand, setting it down next to his own. He reached out and took her face in his hand, grateful when she leaned into his palm.

He leaned closer.

'I'm sorry, I can't do this,' she said quickly, pulling back. She brushed his hand away and stood from the sofa, his hand still holding hers.

He refused to let her go. 'Please, don't go,' he pleaded, worried he may have moved too quickly or read the signals wrong; though he was pretty sure he'd read them all too clearly.

Nadia stood next to him, staring at his hand holding hers.

Matt watched her face, the warmth of her body so close to him and so tempting it was unbearable. He tentatively placed his other hand on her waist, watching as she looked at him, her green eyes drawing him in further. He wanted everything this woman had to give, and more.

In a movement he wasn't anticipating, she leant over and brought her mouth to his, her lips gentle and so seductive it was maddening.

Her tongue sought his as he kissed her passionately. He released her hand and buried his fingers in her ink-black hair as her hands travelled up his chest, both palms cupping his face.

She groaned into his mouth, sending his arousal to fever pitch, and he fell back against the back of the sofa, pulling her with him.

She straddled him, pushing her short skirt to the top of her thighs, exposing the black lace underwear she wore beneath, tempting him even further.

He felt her body pushing against his, her gentle gyrating almost painful as his need increased. Her mouth ate at his as he pulled at her jumper.

She pulled back from him just long enough for him to pull the jumper over her head. She sat there on his lap, her perfect skin only covered by the enticing black lace bra she wore that covered her ample assets.

He couldn't imagine ever getting tired of looking at her body.

She kissed him again as he touched her naked torso, his fingers teasing every inch of her skin until she groaned, pushing her body against his even harder, making her own need all too obvious.

His hands travelled up her back, pausing when he felt the back of her bra.

She moved her mouth from his to kiss his jaw, her kisses soft and so, so tempting.

He shivered beneath her touch as he unclasped her bra, finally able to feel the skin of her back unhindered by anything.

She licked the line of his jaw until she came to his neck, her kisses gentle.

'Are you sure about this?' she asked, her breath hot against his throat.

He groaned as her hand slipped between his thighs, teasing him through his jeans.

He pulled her bra free, exposing her breasts.

The pair both jumped at the sharp knock at the door.

Nadia looked up, but Matt grabbed the base of

her skull and pulled her mouth back to his, unwilling to be interrupted.

'Ignore it,' he breathed.

The knock sounded again, more forceful this time, and Nadia pulled away, worry in her eyes.

Matt stroked her face with his fingers. 'They'll go away in a minute,' he whispered.

She smiled, the unmistakable twinkle of mischief in her emerald eyes as she kissed him hard, her fingers blindly pulling at the buttons on his shirt.

The knock sounded again, followed by a pounding on the door.

Matt forced the thought of Lola away, trying to convince himself it wasn't her standing on his doorstep.

The pounding sounded once more. 'Matt?'

Nadia sat up at the sound of Alex's voice, holding her arm instinctively across her chest.

Matt frowned, his breathing unsteady. 'What's your brother doing here?'

She looked down at him. 'I don't know.' She smiled as she brushed a kiss against his lips. 'I'm sure he'll go away if we ignore him.'

He smiled back at her as she gently bit his bottom lip, teasing him.

The pounding sounded again. 'Matt, answer the damn door,' Alex called, his voice filled with urgency.

Matt glanced up at Nadia, brushing her hair from her face. 'I'm not so sure he will,' he said with a disappointed grin.

She smiled back, brushing more soft kisses against his lips and jaw. 'I'm sure we can ignore him if we try really, *really* hard,' she grinned, pushing her body against his once more, making him moan in both pleasure and irritation.

Alex knocked on the door once more. 'Matt, I know my sister's in there,' he warned.

Matt sighed. 'Shit,' he breathed.

With a groan of frustration, Nadia sat up, reaching for her bra. 'Is he for real?' she asked. She pushed herself from Matt's lap, standing upright before grabbing her discarded jumper from the floor.

Matt grasped hold of her hand. 'How does he know you're here?' he asked.

She grinned at him, her eyes sparkling. She pulled her jumper over her head and rearranged her clothing. She leaned over and kissed him once more, running her tongue across his lips. 'Maybe he read my mind,' she teased.

He chuckled, hiding his discomfort at having to face Alex as he headed out into the hallway, seeing Alex's silhouette behind the glass. Nadia remained behind him.

With a deep breath, he opened the front door.

Alex glared at him.

Without a word, Alex pushed past Matt and stormed into the house, grasping his sister's arm firmly and pulling her towards the door.

'I want you out of here,' Alex hissed, ignoring Matt's protests.

Nadia made no fuss as she allowed her twin to drag her out of the house.

Alex stopped on the threshold and released her. 'Get out of here,' he warned, his gaze dark.

Matt frowned. 'Now, hang on—'

Alex turned to face him. 'This has nothing to do with you,' he snapped.

Her eyes downturned, Nadia looked beaten and Matt felt instantly sorry for her.

'It's okay,' she soothed quietly, turning away from the house.

'I'll call you,' Matt assured, looking back at Alex who eyed him with concern. 'Look, mate, we were just—'

'I know what you were just doing,' Alex stated.

'You didn't need to drag her out like that,' Matt argued. 'She was only here because I asked her.'

Alex's gaze remained resolute. 'Trust me, I'm here for your sake, not hers.'

Matt frowned. 'What the fuck's that supposed to mean?'

Alex pushed past Matt once more into the house without asking for an invitation. 'We need to talk.'

Matt sighed, staring at his friend hard. He wasn't impressed.

'This had better be fucking important.'

Chapter 29

'You're looking so much better already,' Alex soothed as he stared down at Catrina who sat in the backseat of his father's Bentley in the growing darkness of the evening.

After remaining under constant guard for the past twenty-four hours, some of her strength had returned; she'd begun to heal with the aid of his blood, as well as that of both his elders and animals they brought to her, though he knew it would still be a long road to recovery.

The deep slash to her throat had begun to repair itself, the skin now formed into a large grisly scar of purple and deep red, the tissue beneath the skin still severely damaged. She'd managed to hide it beneath a scarf his mother had kindly offered. The burns to her chest had paled overnight as the flesh started to heal, sinews beginning to form over the previously visible sternum. Her pallor was now much more radiant thanks to the feedings she'd received; now fully dressed in some of his mother's clothes, Catrina could at least pass for a healthy person on the long drive back to Romania.

'Do I?' she asked sadly, her voice extremely rough, yet at least much more fluid.

He sat himself on the seat next her, reaching across and placing his hand against the top of her head, noticing that her blonde hair had also started to thicken; it no longer came away from her scalp when he touched it.

'You do,' he confirmed, brushing her hair between his fingers.

'It feels like I've been like this forever,' she whispered, her voice lost somehow. She could move a little more now, though she was still weak and could only manage certain movements after she'd fed, the effect soon wearing off; Alex had carried her to the car.

'I know, my love,' he said gently. 'I wish things could be different. I'd take all the pain away if I could.'

She managed a small smile. 'I know.' She sighed. 'Your father said I'll need complete rest when we get to Romania. At least for another few weeks, until I have the strength to actually get up and move around, and even then...' She trailed off, unable to finish.

Alex watched the sadness fill her eyes. He wanted this nightmare to be over. He wanted to get away from this house and the suffocating presence of his sister. It was all getting too much to bear.

Catrina looked at him then. 'Is everything all

right?' she asked carefully, her gaze searching his.

He knew what she meant. 'It's as okay as it can be,' he said flatly, unwilling to bring his sister into the conversation. 'I think I got to Matt just in time.'

She visibly relaxed. 'Good,' she whispered, eyeing him carefully. 'You look tired,' she observed.

He smiled at her concern. 'I'm fine,' he said quietly. 'I'm just waiting for the day when this nightmare is over and we can be together again.'

'I know,' she said again softly.

Alex closed his eyes. 'I hate that I'm having to send you away on your own,' he gritted, angry at the idea of not being by her side during her suffering.

He opened his eyes and stared at her.

Catrina smiled. 'I won't be on my own,' she reminded him.

Her smile was infectious. 'You know what I mean,' he chastised. 'I should be with you. This is my—'

'This isn't your fault,' she interrupted, her gaze meaningful. 'And we can hardly all travel back to Romania together, can we?' She glanced down, sadness in her eyes. 'You can't leave Nadia here by herself,' she murmured. 'You know what she'll do.'

Alex growled. 'Destroy lives, likes she always does.'

Catrina looked up at him. 'Will you be okay here?' she asked carefully.

He sighed. 'It won't be for long. I'll only be a couple of days behind you.'

'How are you going to get Nadia to leave with you?' she asked.

Alex ran his hands over his face. 'Honestly?' he asked on a long breath, staring at his hands. 'I have no idea.'

They remained in silence for a moment, both of them lost in their own thoughts and nightmares.

'I miss you,' Catrina said finally.

He looked up at her. It was the first time she'd said anything like that to him since the whole nightmare had started.

'I miss you, too,' he said tenderly.

A tear entered her eye and he brushed it away as it trailed down her cheek.

Her gaze met his and they stared at each other, his hand hovering against her cheek. Alex brushed his thumb across her lips, knowing how it used to make her shiver with excitement. There was no such reaction now, but there was a softness in her eyes that told him she missed the sensation.

How he wanted in that moment to take her in his arms and hold her close, yet he didn't dare; her body was still frail and weak and she'd suffered enough when he'd lifted her to the car.

'I love you, Catrina,' he whispered.

She managed a small smile, despite the effort he knew that one small expression took. 'I love you, too,' she murmured.

Tears entered his eyes as he stared at her; he'd been worried he would never hear those words again.

Leaning over, he placed a gentle kiss against her lips, feeling the smallest of efforts on her part to kiss him back. He stared at her as he stroked her cheek with his finger.

'Rest now, my love,' he said softly.

She stared at him, something unreadable in her blue eyes. 'So should you,' she stated quietly.

His smile dimmed as he gazed into her eyes. There was no rest for him now; four centuries of tragedy and horror had seen to that.

Shaking the thoughts away, he forced a smile and stood from the car, watching as she closed her eyes.

As softly as he could, he closed the car door, a terrifying sense of finality to that single action.

Turning on the drive, he stared at his elders as they hovered outside the front door, watching him closely.

Victor's green eyes were filled with concern. 'Catrina is right, my son, you should rest. You do yourself or her no favours depriving yourself of sleep.'

Alex tried to shrug off his father's anxiety, yet his mother shook her head.

'Always the stubborn one, Alex Demeter,' she reprimanded, her gaze disapproving. 'You need to look after yourself.'

Alex opened his mouth to argue, yet Aurelia held up her hand to stop him.

'Do not tell me that you are doing so, my

child, because we all know that you are not,' she admonished. 'You barely sleep and have not feasted nearly enough given your care for Catrina. It will not do,' she sighed, frustration evident in her voice. 'I will not watch my son destroy himself with guilt.'

Alex stared at the ground beneath his feet. 'I fear it has already destroyed me,' he said softly.

Aurelia reached out and took his chin in her hand, forcing his head up so she could look at him.

'It has not,' she soothed with a tender smile, 'and it *will* not. Your guilt belongs to us all, my child. None of us are without fault. We all bear the wounds and scars of the past, as we always will, but it will not destroy *you*. You will live with your wrongs, as we must all do, but you have light in your life, Alex, and need not face the darkness alone.'

Alex felt the tears build as he stared at his mother. She had always been so tender towards her children, even when he knew they didn't deserve it; her ancient wisdom meant everything to him, as it always had. He found himself unable to speak.

Victor watched his wife and son closely. His concerned expression darkened.

'Your mother is right, my son,' he pressed, placing a hand on Alex's shoulder in support. 'Are we wrong to leave you here to manage your sister alone?'

Aurelia glanced at her husband, the same concern filling her emerald eyes. She looked back at Alex.

He felt somewhat scrutinised under their joint gaze. 'I need you to look after Catrina,' he said, his voice formal. 'She needs the protection and worry, not me.'

Aurelia maintained her hold on Alex's face. 'Are you certain, my child?' she asked softly.

Alex took hold of her hand, pulling it away from his face and planting a tender kiss against her fingers. 'I'm certain, Mother,' he assured, hoping his words were convincing; he tried to believe them himself, but failed miserably.

'I don't believe Nadia can be handled by anyone else other than me now,' he sighed sadly. 'This is the legacy I created, and I fear it must be me to contain it.'

Victor sighed in frustration. 'Alex, you need not be such a martyr,' he condemned.

Alex stared at his father. 'Perhaps not, but I will handle her all the same, if only for my own peace of mind and nothing more.'

Staring at both his elders with finality, Alex watched them shake their heads, neither of them happy with his decision.

'Please,' Alex begged, looking between them. 'Take care of Catrina.'

Aurelia smiled and pulled her son into a hard embrace. 'You have our solemn promise, my child,' she breathed against his hair. 'We will ensure her recovery until you return to us.'

She placed a gentle kiss against his forehead before releasing him.

Alex kissed her cheek before turning to his father.

Victor offered him a sad smile. 'Return to us soon, Alex,' he demanded, pulling his son to him in a tight embrace that conveyed his concern.

Alex nodded as he stepped back. 'I will, Father,' he assured.

Reluctantly, the ancient pair approached the car. Alex could plainly see the tears in his mother's eyes as she left her children behind to whatever horrors they were willing to subject themselves to.

Victor opened her door and allowed her to step into the vehicle, reminding Alex of himself the night he'd taken Catrina to dinner, a night that now seemed so long ago.

The slam of the car door jarred Alex from his reverie and he watched as his father climbed behind the wheel, starting the engine.

Alex wanted to stop them, to tell them not to leave and take Catrina away from his side; but he needed them to take her away from his sister and the danger Nadia posed.

He stared at his own car, the Jaguar parked on the drive, wanting more than anything to jump in and drive off with them right now. But he couldn't leave his sister alone, not now. She was far too dangerous and people's lives were still at risk; he needed to stop her path of destruction to ensure everyone's safety.

Alex watched as the car begun to pull away from the drive, catching Catrina's saddened gaze as his father drove away, making the most of the dark hours to get as far across Europe as possible before needing to shelter from the daylight.

With a profound sense of loss that had his stomach wrenching inside him, Alex stepped back into the silence of the house and closed the front door, staring at it for several minutes before reluctantly wandering into the lounge, the ticking of the mantle clock and the crackle of the fire in the grate the only sounds to disturb the stillness.

He strolled into the empty room, looking around him. His gaze flowed over the many pictures and portraits of himself and his family in happier times, saddened by the deep loss of those contented smiles; too much had happened to ever truly see happiness in the eyes of his family again.

He grasped the poker from the rack by the side of the fire, stabbing at the burning logs absently. In an instant, the flames rekindled an unwanted memory and he dropped the poker onto the hearth, a chill running through him.

He sat himself down in the armchair, thinking over his parents' words; he knew they were concerned about leaving him to deal with Nadia alone, and he wasn't exactly cherishing the situation either, yet what choice did he have? He could never make up for his past and he knew there was no point in trying. He just had to manage the situation the best he could.

He sneered as he stared at a picture of Nadia on the mantle.

RETRIBUTION DARKENED

The Others could deal with his sister; he no longer cared how brutal their punishments would be. She deserved nothing less.

He sat back in his seat. His elders had been right; he needed sleep. Every minute took his exhaustion higher.

He sat there, listening to the monotonous ticking of the clock as the minutes passed one by one, the silence bringing with it far too many unwelcome memories.

Alex's eyes drifted closed.

Then...

1739

'Alex!'

Nadia squealed like an excited child as she stepped out of the carriage, allowing the footman to take her gloved hand in order to help her down the step. Without thanking him, she ran across the snow-covered courtyard of her family home.

Alex beamed at her, his arms outstretched as he welcomed his sister into the circle of his embrace. He had missed her so much over the last twenty years during her travels; the letters he had received from her had been a joy to read, but had not quelled the loneliness that came from missing his dear twin.

He pulled her at arm's length so he could appraise her after so long an absence. She looked magnificent beneath her deep green travelling cape, dressed in a bright blue open gown, paired with a deep green petticoat and stomacher, which matched her eyes perfectly. White lace dripped from her elbow-length sleeves, yet there was an absence of any kerchief about her shoulders to conserve her modesty, her perfectly pale décolleté dangerously on show. A string of white pearls adorned her neck. Her raven hair, under her wide brimmed emerald bonnet that matched her cape, was pinned back from her face, with only a few delicate curls falling free of the pins.

Alex planted a tender kiss on her cheek. 'I have missed you, dearest,' he said gently, admiring her. 'How fine you look, sister.'

Nadia blushed with a coy smile, offering her brother a playful bow and curtsey. 'Thank you kindly, sir,' she laughed, her innocent flirt met with a wide smile.

'And don't you look quite the gentleman,' she teased, looking him over. His shoulder-length black hair was tied back with ribbon. His rich plum jacket, embroidered with gold thread, fitted over his dark waistcoat perfectly.

'Quite the fine lord they have turned you into during my absence, Brother,' she laughed.

Aurelia Demeter, who had been standing next to her husband, Victor, by the carriage Nadia had vacated, smiled at her daughter.

'That is a very daring dress, my child,' she said, without real judgement.

Nadia rolled her eyes playfully, turning to face her mother with a wide smile. 'Oh, Mother, really... it is all the fashion in Europe currently.' She turned to look at Alex over her shoulder with a smile. 'I dare not describe what they are wearing in Paris,' she whispered with a laugh, her tone playfully scandalous.

'Indeed, you better not,' he laughed, watching as she turned and walked towards their parents, greeting each of them in turn tenderly. She allowed them to fuss over her, their mother taking time to inspect her daughter's visible health and pallor, and Alex smiled with amusement.

Finally managing to untangle herself from their parents fussing, Nadia returned to her brother's side, where he took her gloved hand in his own.

'So what of your travels, dearest?' he asked, curious of the world she had seen since leaving his side twenty years before; all her letters had been filled with wonder and opportunity.

She beamed at him, squeezing his hand tighter. 'It is truly a world of wonder,' she said with excitement. 'The New World is so exciting, and Europe is magical. I do declare I could speak for hours on such small things.'

Victor chuckled as he approached his children. 'And indeed I'm sure Alex would welcome such stories,' he said with a smile, glancing at his son. 'He has been most lost without you these past years. But I'm sure your sister is tired after her travels. Perhaps we should allow her to freshen up. We can all enjoy her tales in the drawing room this evening.'

Alex looked disappointed, but Nadia smiled at him. 'I promise to regale you with tales of my travels, dearest.' She leaned in closer as her parents lead the way into the family home, her voice lowered and her smile widening. 'Though I may leave the more scandalous stories until we are alone, Brother,' she teased. 'I'm not sure Mother would appreciate some of the tales I could tell of the court in France.' She offered him a playful wink as she turned towards the family home, hurrying to catch up with their mother, the two women linking arms as they walked.

Alex chuckled to himself as he watched his sister stroll towards their home; her time spent travelling had certainly been eventful, and he envied her. While she had been away, he had spent many hours reading and re-reading her letters, imagining the fun and adventures she was having in strange lands and missing her greatly.

Since their birth in the year 1587, the pair had never been apart until the day Nadia had left on her travels. She was his little sister, born several minutes after himself, and he had prided himself on caring for her, protecting her. Nadia in turn had looked up to Alex, following him everywhere. As they grew older, they would hunt together, honing their powers and senses. It had been an innocent and joyous childhood, making Nadia's departure for foreign lands a heavy burden to bear.

Alex recalled their childhood with fondness. Born with the gift of immortality, as twins they were an extreme rarity, feared in part even by their own kin. Having shared blood in their mother's womb, their blood bond continued into their youth, sharing blood in small quantities from the wrist or hand.

RETRIBUTION DARKENED

Alex believed it was this blood bond that had solidified not only their closeness, but their abilities also. The powers he shared with Nadia were far beyond any of their kin's understanding. They could heal their own wounds in an instant, command animals and humans alike, and communicate mentally, much to the chagrin of their elders when they'd been children. As they'd grown into adulthood, those gifts had made them a formidable force.

They had both matured at the same time, considered another rare occurrence by their elders; the moment they stopped ageing and remained frozen in time forever at the age of thirty-two.

Over the following hundred years they had grown stronger still, feared for their name alone. Yet despite this, they had existed happily as any siblings should, surrounded by a supportive and loving family.

The year 1719 would be the saddest in Alex's opinion, for when Nadia had told him of her desire to travel, to see the world, taste other blood and hunt different continents, he had felt lost for the first time in his life. His sister had grown fiercely independent, like many of the women in their family, and insisted on travelling alone, a shocking concept to many of his elders. As a compromise, Nadia had agreed to take Margita, her maid, with her, but no one else.

From the letters she had written, Alex learnt of her travels around Europe, her name and title giving her access to the variety of royal courts. She would write home often, telling him of her journey, the people she had met, the parties she had enjoyed. She wrote of the conflicts within Europe, between France and Spain, and he would envy her such treats as seeing such things as the premiere of Handel's opera *Giulio Cesare* in London in 1724.

By 1731 she had travelled onto America to explore the New World and spent the next couple of years there before making her way back across Europe.

Alex had missed her dearly. After spending the first hundred years of their existence together, it had been unbearable being separated from his twin for so long, but he enjoyed receiving her letters. Each one was a joy to read and he had looked forward to the day when he would be able to travel as she had. Being the elder of the pair, Alex had spent his time in Romania learning the family history and the ways of their family traditions. He had inherited the title of lord, after all.

Alex smiled as he heard Nadia's melodic laughter flow from the open door to their family home, dragging him back from his reverie.

It was a sound he had missed desperately.

Finally, his sister was home.

* * *

Alex smiled to himself as he thrust the iron poker into the flames, stoking the fire in the large grate until the wood began to spit and crackle loudly once more.

The drawing room of his family home was encased in a mixture of light and dark, the glow of the fire and oil lamps not completely chasing away the shadows that hovered in the corners of the extravagant room. The white panelled walls were adorned with many portraits of family and Romanian scenery. Thick cream silk curtains hung at the windows.

He replaced the poker to its stand and turned to look at his family. His sister was sitting next to his mother on the Chesterfield, discussing many aspects of her travels. His father was seated in his usual chair by the fire, smoking his pipe, casually watching the two women with a gentle, contented smile; he was happy to have his family together once more.

Alex watched his sister gossip with their mother, the two of them laughing over silly little tales she had amassed from her travels.

He knew there were details she would not divulge to either of their parents; Nadia's love for the scandals of society was perhaps not a suitable undertaking for a young unmarried woman, and their mother especially was still very much fixed in a time when women did not discuss such things, let alone enjoy them.

He smiled to himself; he, on the other hand, looked forward to when she would divulge such information to him. He had always envied her ability to find joy in every small thing in life, no matter how dull or profane.

While she had been exploring the world around them, he had been back and forth between his family home and Vallakia, the ancient Demeter sanctuary in the Carpathian Mountains, spending countless hours with his elders who aimed to prepare him for the role and title he had inherited and would use across the world. It had been an agreeable education, yet a lonely one; with every passing day he had missed his sister dearly.

He had discussed her travels and absence on many occasions with his elders, welcoming their wisdom and guidance; they had tried their best to lessen the burden of her absence, yet he knew they would never truly understand. Nadia was his twin, his other half; it was difficult to be separated from her for any length of time.

Of course, his time at home had not been boring, by any standards; there had been plenty of parties and picnics, as well as family gatherings and important political meetings, yet these usually only made Nadia's absence more pronounced, for she was always the life and soul of any party.

'Are you troubled, Brother?' Nadia asked, jarring him from his meandering thoughts.

He looked at her, aware of his elders also watching him. They all looked amused by his obvious silent reverie.

He smiled at them, nodding to his sister. 'Indeed not, dearest,' he chuckled. 'I was just thinking.'

She giggled playfully. 'A dangerous pastime,'

she said, her words stirring a chuckle from their mother.

Alex laughed. 'You encourage her, Mother,' he said, no chastisement in his words.

Aurelia nodded with a smile. 'Perhaps I do, my child,' she said gently. 'But it is a joy to have my children back together once more. Our home is now complete.'

Victor nodded his head as he smoked on his pipe. 'That it is, my dearest,' he agreed warmly.

Nadia blushed, their praise and warm welcome clearly touching her heart, and Alex realised in that moment how much she had also missed them on her journeys.

She rested her head against her mother's shoulder, and Aurelia in turn wrapped her arm about Nadia's shoulders.

Alex watched the embrace between his mother and sister, warmth filling him as he treasured the moment of his family together, their gaiety filling him with a tenderness he knew he would carry with him always.

His family were his sanctuary and his life. He would do anything for any of them, and to have them all together once more filled his heart with joy.

He knew nothing would ever pull them apart.

'I do declare I am quite famished,' Nadia said cheerfully, rising from her seat and skipping to his side. 'Should you like to come hunting with me, Brother?' she asked, her tone playful as she looked at him with hopeful eyes.

Alex laughed, amused by her eagerness.

He nodded his assent. 'Of course, Sister.'

* * *

The evening around them grew colder, a delicate snow falling around them as they strolled through the rural village of Rășinari, just north of their family home in the Cindrel Mountains.

Nadia buried her hands deeper into her fur muff as she walked by Alex's side, her head and shoulders covered by her thick hooded, fur-trimmed cloak. Alex wore his tricorne hat, swinging his cane by his side as he walked.

People bustled around them, making their way home as the evening drew darker, the superstitions of old still very much in the minds of many within rural villages; the smell of fear enticed the twins further.

They walked side by side, appearing to those around them as a respectable couple of the aristocracy, villagers bowing or curtseying as they passed by, though many older people surveyed them with suspicion; the Demeter bloodline having been one of many suspected of vampirism over the years.

Alex was increasingly amused as Nadia bowed her head and smiled at every person who eyed them with suspicion, her actions exaggerated.

'You will only encourage their wariness, dearest,' he said with a chuckle.

Nadia glanced at him, mischief in her eyes. 'The world no longer values such ramblings, Brother mine,' she smiled. 'The suspicions of old no longer hold much sway.'

'I agree,' he said, as they continued walking the streets. 'The world has changed much.'

'Besides,' she continued, 'there is no sport to be had in scaring those who already fear,' she laughed.

He looked at her then. 'Sport?' he questioned, aware of the mischievous grin on her face.

She took a hand from her muff, gripping his arm tenderly. 'You have so much to learn, Brother dearest,' she teased. 'Twenty years spent away from home can teach you a few... strategies,' she said, settling for the word.

She giggled again, unlinking her arm from his. 'A lady on her own has to survive somehow, and an ambush isn't always possible, so I had to improvise. I then discovered it to be rather fun.' She took a step away, moving ahead of him.

'Trust me,' she called over her shoulder. 'And keep a respectable distance.'

He watched as she began to walk faster, glancing at him over her shoulder with feigned fear.

She headed towards the local inn as Alex continued to

follow her, making sure to keep his distance as she had instructed.

She rushed towards an elderly gentleman, who was strolling along the street towards his carriage.

'Please, sir, help me, I beg of you,' she called, gasping for breath as if she had run a long distance; a ruse Alex found impressive.

The gentleman turned to Nadia as she approached him, concern filling his face.

'My dear young lady, whatever troubles you?' he asked, welcoming her to his side. He was well dressed and clearly of means; he noted Nadia's expensive gowns and her well-spoken manner and welcomed her as one of his own circle.

Tears fell down Nadia's cheeks and the gentleman offered her his handkerchief so that she could wipe them away.

'Thank you kindly, sir. I beg you, forgive my public display. I am troubled by that man,' she said, pointing at Alex who still continued to move towards her.

Nadia looked up at the gentleman beside her. 'He has followed me as I try to make my way home, quite unashamedly.'

The gentleman glared at Alex, who was now much closer. 'You have no business here, sir,' he warned. 'I must insist you leave this young lady be.'

Nadia shied away from Alex, leaning in towards the gentleman, yet her gaze maintained her brother's.

'*Do as he says, Brother dear,*' she commanded mentally, amusement in her tone.

Alex stopped in his tracks, trying to disguise his own amusement over her deception. He offered a small bow of respect.

'I meant no offence,' he said flatly.

The gentleman turned his attentions back to Nadia. 'Miss, if I may be so bold, it would be my honour to escort you home in my carriage and ensure your safety,' he said gently, offering her his hand.

Nadia smiled sweetly at him, placing her hand in his. 'You are very kind, sir. Thank you.'

Alex watched as the gentleman led Nadia towards his carriage, still holding her hand.

She smiled at him warmly as he helped her up the step and into the carriage, while his footman held the door open for them both.

Alex watched them closely.

Nadia glanced his way as the gentleman climbed into the carriage after her.

'*Feel free to join me,*' she offered mentally, a laugh in her tone.

Alex realised what she had done and followed, approaching behind the footman as the gentleman settled into the carriage.

Alex heard the muffled sound resembling a cry from within the carriage as Nadia attacked the unfortunate gentleman, and Alex instantly grabbed hold of the footman before he had time to react.

Alex gripped his hand over the footman's mouth and forced him into the carriage quickly, people passing by not noticing anything out of the ordinary.

Inside the carriage, the gentleman who had been so kind as to assist his sister was slumped dead in his seat, as Nadia wiped the blood from her lips using his handkerchief, a satisfied smile on her face.

Alex held the footman tight against him as he bit into the man's throat, the hot blood instantly revitalising him as it filled his mouth. He was aware of Nadia watching him as he fed. His gaze met hers.

She smiled at him, clearly amused by her little ploy.

Alex lowered the body onto the opposite seat to the gentleman and took out his handkerchief to wipe his mouth. He laughed as he took in her expression.

'You have made a habit of such outings, haven't you, Sister?' he asked with a smile, replacing his handkerchief into his pocket.

She nodded her head. 'A lady on her own needs more than simple opportunity,' she pointed out. 'I had to make my own luck a number of times in my travels. It became somewhat of a delight.'

'Then I see all my worry regarding your travels was in vain, dearest,' he said with a chuckle. 'I feared for you whilst you were away, yet you were enjoying yourself more than I realised.' He laughed as he took her hand, helping her out of the carriage.

'I am more than capable of taking care of myself, Brother,' she smiled. 'It is far too easy to manipulate humans, such as my poor gentleman there,' she pointed out, linking her arm through Alex's as they strolled along the cobbled street, the darkness of the night enveloping them as they made their way home.

'So I see,' he chuckled. 'I promise not to underestimate you again, my dear,' he laughed.

RETRIBUTION DARKENED

He was overwhelmed with joy to have his twin back by his side, and could see that for all his worry while she had been away, she indeed was more than capable of looking after herself.

He found himself filled with pride as he glanced down at the woman beside him.

She wasn't his little sister any longer.

1749

'Nadia, the carriage is here. You need to make haste,' Alex called through the door to her bedchamber, impatiently checking his pocket watch.

'I will meet you in the courtyard, dearest,' she called back. 'Margita is just attending to my hair.'

He released a sigh of frustration. 'You said that a half hour ago. Mother and Father are growing impatient.'

He heard her chuckle behind the door. 'Then go and entertain them,' she called, the smile in her tone obvious. 'I will be with you presently.'

Alex couldn't prevent his smile; she never took anything seriously. Life was always so easy for her, so carefree. He envied her for that, as he did so many other things.

'Very well,' he conceded. 'Please do not be too long, Sister,' he pleaded gently, turning from the door and heading for the main staircase of his family home.

At the bottom of the staircase, he was met by

Claudiu, the butler.

'Your cape and hat, my lord?' he questioned, clearly noting the absence of Nadia.

With another brief chuckle, Alex nodded. 'Thank you, Claudiu,' he said gratefully, waiting as the butler brought him his black dress cape, his tricorne hat, and his cane.

'Thank you,' Alex said with a smile. 'That will be all.'

'Very good, my lord,' Claudiu said, bowing before walking away.

Alex checked his pocket watch once more, shaking his head. They were going to be late.

He knew he shouldn't be surprised; Nadia had always taken forever to dress for parties, and tonight clearly was no exception.

He slowly paced the large foyer of his family home, tapping his cane occasionally against the wooden floor, the sound echoing around the vast entrance hall.

He wandered around, trying to pass the time. He didn't want to join his parents in the carriage; they would only continually ask him where his sister was and complain about the length of time she was taking to get ready. Besides, he was happy to remain in the warmth of the house, rather than sitting in the cold carriage. It had started to snow outside; the journey into the mountains would be more treacherous.

He glanced up at the portrait that hung on the wall opposite the main entrance. The painting had been commissioned a couple of weeks after Nadia had returned from her travels. The artist had painted many of their family members in the past, and the depiction of both his parents, himself and his sister was exquisite. Alex smiled. Every detail was perfect in its rendition; a moment in time captured forever perfectly.

He took out his pocket watch once more, sighing with despair at his sister's appalling timekeeping. A small smile danced across his lips as he closed his watch once more; how many times had they been late to a party since Nadia's return ten years ago? He had lost count.

Nadia was a fascinating creature, but also a vain one; she would spend hours preparing herself for such events, and Alex often wondered whether it was her need for perfection or simply her desire for a grand entrance and attention that caused her delay.

Once more, he looked up at the portrait. Ten years had passed so very quickly since she had returned from her travels, and they had spent nearly every moment together since. It was as if she had never been away. The time had been filled with parties and afternoon tea, picnics and balls. They hunted and feasted side by side. They had enjoyed life together as one, as they had when they were children.

Alex stared at the painting of his sister closely, rubbing his wrist absently. Just like they had when they were children, they had been sharing blood, an act they had not practised since their childhood.

RETRIBUTION DARKENED

It had first happened one night three years ago while hunting, as a mark to celebrate their Maturity Day. Alex had offered Nadia his wrist after their kill in the ice-cold winter night, and she had taken it willingly.

It was something they had done many times as children, a simple extension of the blood bond they had shared in the womb. It was an innocent act that solidified the bond they shared as twins.

And so it had continued for the next three years, rarely at first, though as time passed they began to share blood more and more frequently, until it had become a habit they both enjoyed.

Alex looked down at his wrist, thinking of the last time, two nights ago, when his sister had last imbibed his blood; like most habits, it always took place away from the eyes of others.

It was their little secret, a quaint novelty they both enjoyed; it was an innocent game.

Yet there was a longing he felt growing within him, a need for the taste of her blood. He would never deny the taste of her blood was exquisite, a taste like no other. No human blood could ever compare. It filled him with ecstasy, the likes of which he had never known. It was addictive.

The sharing of their blood had brought them ever closer, if that were at all possible, and he frowned, momentarily confused by the feelings which had overwhelmed him far too many times of late.

In those moments of sharing blood, he felt

closer to Nadia than ever, his need for her growing, as he was sure her need was growing for him; he was certain it was not his imagination when she flirted with him, or looked at him for longer than she should have.

Her tenderness during their blood sharing had increased, and she would often hold him close, lovingly stroking his hair or cheek while he drew on her blood.

They now sustained one another, and it was a feeling he never wanted to relinquish.

Reaching into his pocket, Alex pulled out a small velvet box. Smiling, he opened it, looking at the emerald and diamond bracelet he intended to give to Nadia later at the ball. He had chosen it specifically because the colour of the stones matched her eyes perfectly.

He closed the box and hid it back in his pocket, pleased with himself. He knew she'd love it. It was the perfect Maturity Day present.

A sound on the staircase had him turning on the spot, and he gazed up at his sister who stood on the upper landing.

She smiled down at him, her hands held out, seeking his approval.

For a moment he was unable to speak. She looked completely striking.

Her hair was exquisitely styled, with delicate ringlets floating around her face. A sparkling tiara adorned her ink black locks. She wore a diamond necklace and matching earbobs.

Her face was pale, with her smiling lips set in a deep rouge.

Her dress was breath-taking. Specially commissioned for the ball at Vallakia, it had been created from the best black satin and silk. The stomacher and petticoat contrasted in a beautiful red taffeta. A saque of black silk fell from her shoulders and the mask she held in her white gloved hand was silver, with black feathers and red ribbon.

'Have I his lord's approval?' she asked playfully, curtseying.

Without another thought, Alex bounded up the stairs, taking her delicate gloved hand.

'You look exquisite, my lady,' he smiled, keeping hold of her fingers as he accompanied her down the staircase to where Claudiu had reappeared, holding out Nadia's fur-lined cape and muff.

'It is cold out there tonight, my lady,' he said.

Alex released his hold on Nadia's hand and strolled over to the butler, taking the cape from him. He then wrapped it around his sister's shoulders tenderly as she tied the ribbons to secure it.

Claudiu then handed her the muff.

Alex chuckled. 'Are we finally ready to leave, sister?' he asked playfully.

Nadia laughed, the sound light and joyful. 'I do believe we are, my lord.'

* * *

The journey into the mountains had indeed been a treacherous one. The snow had fallen heavier as the journey continued, and the mountain paths were slick and precarious. The horses had needed a lot of encouragement to continue.

Vallakia was settled deep within the Carpathians, and its windows, full of warmth and light, had been a welcome sight as they approached. On wintry nights such as this it was only the light from the windows that made it visible; the pale greyness of the stone and the swirling white of the snowstorm almost hid it from view, the building emerging like a giant towering ghost through the frost.

The carriage had continued through the large main gate and into the extensive inner courtyard, the ancient building looming around them.

Towers soared above them, ominous and threatening. The inner courtyard was extensive, overlooked by corridors and windows. The flagstone floor was ancient, and many bushes and shrubs brought colour in the summer months. An old stone well stood in the centre of the courtyard. Archways and steps led to the stables, kitchens, and extensive grounds.

It was an astounding building.

As they had many times over the years, Alex, Nadia and his parents exited the carriage and climbed the large stone steps to the main entrance, the heavy wooden door opening as they approached.

RETRIBUTION DARKENED

The steward of the castle, Demitri, smiled graciously at them.

'Good evening, my lords and ladies,' he said cheerfully.

Alex nodded his head in acknowledgement. 'Good evening, Demitri. I trust you are well?' he asked.

The steward bowed. 'Indeed, your grace,' he answered, stepping aside to allow them all entrance to the castle.

The main door entered into a tall hallway, with white walls, oak-carved arches and ceiling. A Persian-style hand-tied red carpet covered the wooden floor, one of four that Gabriella, his ancient grandmother, had had made in Bucharest.

A large stone crow stood on its pedestal by the main door, its ruby red eyes shining as it watched inanimately over those who entered its domain.

Large oak doors, over sixteen feet high, led into the great hall, which dominated the larger part of the centre of the castle, featuring the galleried landings where large portraits of family members decorated the walls, balconies, arcades and the grand staircase, all ornately carved. A number of people were standing around the hall, chatting and laughing amongst themselves. Music filled the hall from the open doors of the ballroom, one either side of the grand staircase at the far end of the hall. Men and women bowed their heads as the Demeters entered the hall.

The gothic splendour of the room was

overwhelming. Its magnificent hammer beam ceiling towered almost seventy feet above the ground. A large stain glass window featured the family emblem and crests, black crows interrupting the bright blues, red and greens.

The oak panelling was perfectly nourished and polished, and many small carved plaques decorated the walls, each one featuring family emblems and crests, offering memory to lost family members.

There was a false door on one side of the room, which had been placed to balance out the door to the library on the opposite wall.

A great stone fireplace dominated the far wall, a large fire burning in the grate. The light of the flames highlighted the features of the large wolves engraved into each side of the giant stone mantle.

Large wrought iron sconces lined the walls, the candles and flames burning brightly.

Two large torcheres stood on each side of the grand staircase, thousands of crystals hanging from them in delicate droplets, the glow of the candles framing the stairs in a soft glow. Another of Gabriella's red carpets ran the length of the staircase.

The grand staircase itself was made of solid oak, with carved crows on each of the newel posts.

Alex moved through the great hall, towards the open doors that led into the ballroom. The oak doors were also intricately carved with crows, wolves and forest scenes.

Inside the ancient room, the white plasterwork

RETRIBUTION DARKENED

of the ceiling and groins were intricately carved with roses and other patterns, and three large ornate chandeliers hung from along the centre of the room, hundreds of candles burning bright upon them, the crystals twinkling in the light.

The large marble fire surround had been created from the same quarries that had supplied ancient Rome, and had been carved with the family emblems on either side. A large fire burned in the grate, bathing the guests in warmth as the storm raged on outside.

Above the fireplace stood a large ornate mirror that reflected the large floor to ceiling windows that dominated the opposite wall, the thick, deep-blue velvet curtains pulled back to allow the night sky to backdrop the merriment. A large guilt clock ticked on the mantle.

The ballroom was filled with guests, all in striking dress and all wearing or holding masks of varying embellishments.

The orchestra, in the corner of the room, played gently as waiters and maids maintained full wine glasses where necessary, and offered their veins in private to those who required it.

The large room had been opulently decorated with garlands that framed the mirror and the windows and doors, several of them meeting with each chandelier as the focal point. Tables almost overflowed with food.

Alex strolled through the room, as men and women skipped to such dances as the Minuet and

Gavotte as the joyful music played, his mother and father included.

He smiled to himself; he never tired of watching his parents together. They truly enjoyed each other's company, forever laughing and smiling. They had fallen in love many centuries ago, in a time he could only imagine and read about. Theirs was a marriage built on a deep love and profound respect, and deep down he hoped that he would be able to find that sort of bond one day.

Alex scanned the crowd, searching for his sister, who had apparently disappeared.

He caught the eye of several young ladies as he glanced around the room. He bowed to them in turn with a smile, as they either giggled or hid behind their masks. One young woman, with sun-kissed blonde hair and dressed in a deep blue gown, curtseyed while still hiding behind her mask, her rouged lips curving into a smile.

He smiled back, drawn by her attentions. Straightening himself, he took a deep breath, prepared to approach her and ask her to dance.

'Are you enjoying yourself, young one?'

Alex turned to see his elder, Vlad, standing by his side. Like most of the Demeter bloodline, he was tall and dark-haired, though tonight his hair was powdered and tied back. He wore a long deep-blue dress jacket over a lighter waistcoat that matched his breeches.

He was the oldest surviving member of the

family and had once been human over three millennia ago. He had seen empires rise and fall, the world and its countries forge alliances and destroy one another. He had witnessed plague and famine. He had outlived many relatives, becoming the head of the family when his elder brother, Ladislas, had died in a tragic fire centuries before.

As the eldest family member, Vallakia was Vlad's property to oversee and protect. His age made him a formidable force to be reckoned with, and he commanded enormous respect from the rest of the family.

He had played a large part in Alex's education while Nadia had been away.

'Indeed,' Alex smiled. 'Another successful party.'

Vlad clapped a large hand on Alex's shoulder. 'As always the praise goes to your ancient grandmother. She never rests until every detail is perfected,' he chuckled.

Alex grinned. 'Well, I declare she has done herself proud once more,' he complimented.

'As has your sister,' Vlad commented with a warm smile. 'I have heard so many compliments offered to your parents tonight. She has indeed turned into a fine young lady.'

Alex agreed with a nod of his head, his gaze scanning the room for his sister, the lady in blue forgotten.

'Have you seen Nadia?' he asked curiously. 'I

seem to have misplaced her,' he added with a chuckle.

Vlad laughed. 'I saw her a few minutes ago, heading upstairs with Gabriella and Monika. They mentioned something about a dress,' he sighed, shrugging his shoulders. 'Only women know and care of such things,' he chuckled. 'I dare say you would find them all in Gabriella's chambers.'

With another pat on the back, Vlad took his leave, disappearing into the crowd.

Alex stared after him, his attentions returning to the dancing. He reached into his pocket, feeling the small velvet box and smiled to himself. He caught the eye of the young woman in blue once more and bowed with a smile, excusing himself as he made his way through the crowd towards the doors.

He stepped out into the grand hall of Vallakia, still filled with guests standing around talking and laughing. He greeted some of them as he passed by, heading for the grand staircase.

He bounded up the main staircase two steps as a time, turning left at the top and heading up the second staircase to the upper floor. As he walked along the galleried landing, he passed various portraits of family members, including one of himself and Nadia when they had been children, the innocence of youth captured forever.

At the end of the landing was a door, which he opened and stepped through. Beyond the door was a narrow stone staircase, which spiralled up. He followed it until he reached the top, the door opening out onto another, smaller landing, off which only three doors were positioned.

Hearing laughter and giggling coming from behind the second door, Gabriella's rooms, he smiled and knocked gently, listening as rustling and whispered voices continued, until eventually he heard Gabriella's voice:

'Come in.'

As he entered, he caught sight of Monika closing an old trunk quickly, her face filled with a warm smile.

Alex watched her for a moment, easily recognising the expression on his cousin's face; she was hiding something. The three women stood close together like three guilty children.

The room was simple in comparison to the ornate rooms below, though no less adorned. The white stone walls were warmed by another large fire burning in the grate of the stone fireplace on the far wall, the simple stone mantle decorated with various trinkets from Gabriella's life spent with her beloved Ladislas. Sconces burned on the walls that were covered with portraits and landscape paintings. The ceiling was beamed with solid oak and the leaded windows framed by red velvet curtains. A small door to the right led to her private bathroom.

The large, mahogany four-poster bed dominated one wall, the headboard intricately carved with crows. A dresser, cabinets, chairs and a small table, all of the same deep-red wood, completed the room.

Alex bowed. 'Good evening, my ladies,' he said softly, his gaze falling on each of them in turn. Monika simply looked awkward; Gabriella was unreadable as always, stood between the two younger women in her elegant silver and emerald gown; Nadia looked uncomfortable.

Monika's smile returned as she looked at him. She curtseyed.

'Good evening, Cousin,' she said cheerfully, crossing the room to embrace him.

'Dearest Monika,' he said with a smile, admiring her yellow satin gown which suited her pale skin perfectly. Her black hair fell in ringlets about her face. 'I trust you have been well?'

She nodded gently. 'Indeed,' she said, not quite meeting his gaze.

Alex glanced at both Gabriella and his sister. His smile widened.

'I do believe there is some conspiracy amongst you ladies,' he declared with a chuckle. 'Will you not share?'

Gabriella laughed gently as she stepped forward, taking Alex's hand in her ancient fingers. 'You look for conspiracies where there are none, my child,' she said softly, leaning in to plant a tender kiss against his cheek.

Alex softened at her touch, as he always had. Gabriella was his ancient grandmother by marriage, separated by generations and centuries. She was the second eldest surviving member of the Demeter family after Vlad, yet unlike him had been born with immortality. She had married Vlad's brother, Ladislas, centuries ago. Inconsolable after his untimely death, she had spent several centuries in a deep mourning. Eventually, in time, she had agreed to remain at Vallakia to assist Vlad in overseeing the Demeter family, effectively becoming his consort.

There she had remained, guiding the generations of Demeters with her wisdom and eternal love.

Gabriella studied Alex's face for a moment. 'You have clearly sought us out, my child. May I ask why?' Her voice was cautious, which puzzled him.

'I wished to speak to my sister,' he stated, glancing at Nadia. She still looked a little uncomfortable, and her silence throughout the last few minutes was proving to be unnerving.

He cleared his throat. 'If you ladies would excuse us for a moment?'

Gabriella and Monika smiled at him, no sign of discomfort on their faces. The two women nodded their assent.

Monika turned to Nadia, the flush of excitement on her face. 'We shall see you downstairs soon, Cousin,' she said, her voice tinged with a conspiratorial tone.

Alex watched as Gabriella and Monika left the room, closing the door behind them. He turned to look at his sister, who still remained motionless across the room, next to the trunk where Monika had clearly hidden something.

Nadia's pale face brightened as she laughed,

her eyes filled with humour. 'I do declare you look so serious, Brother,' she taunted playfully. 'What troubles you so?'

He was still slightly intrigued by the behaviour of the three women, but pushed his thoughts to one side; he did not wish to see his sister troubled.

'Nothing, dear Sister,' he soothed. 'Do not fret.' He took another step further into the room, glancing around.

He smiled. 'My apologies for interrupting your gossip,' he teased.

Nadia laughed lightly. 'Why do men presume we ladies spend all our time gossiping about them?' She winked at him playfully. 'Not all of our scandalous stories are about you,' she pointed out.

Alex laughed. He stepped further into the room, perching himself on the edge of an old chair that was positioned in the corner.

'So what were you ladies talking about, hidden away in here?' he asked, curious. 'It must have been important. Wild horses cannot normally tear you away from a party,' he pointed out.

Nadia shook her head, strolling about the room, her dress rustling around her. 'A lady must be entitled to some secrets,' she smiled.

Alex's expression softened. 'Indeed,' he agreed with a chuckle.

She studied him closely for a moment, scrutinising every aspect of his expression. 'You troubled yourself to follow me here, dearest,' she said quietly. 'Is something wrong?'

Alex glanced at the floor, aware he had been caught out; his sister was far too observant for her own good.

He glanced back up at her with a timid smile. 'Do I need a reason to spend time with my twin?' he asked.

'Indeed not, Brother,' she answered. 'But when you hunt me down during a party, I am inclined to believe there is some reasoning behind it.' There was a teasing tone to her voice and her eyes gleamed with mischief as she spoke.

Alex held up his hands in surrender. 'You are too wise, my dear,' he admitted with a laugh. He pushed himself from the chair, crossing the room to stand in front of his sister. He took her gloved hand and lifted it to his lips, tenderly kissing her satin-covered fingers.

'I confess I am not a very good liar,' he mused, looking up at her.

She chuckled. 'Then you are fortunate I do not require you to be,' she teased.

'Quite right you are,' he admitted. 'I have something for you,' he confessed.

A mischievous smile crossed her red lips. 'Do you indeed?' she asked playfully, her words innocent.

Alex chuckled, reaching into his pocket. He grasped hold of the small velvet box and pulled it out, presenting it to his sister.

Nadia stared at it for a moment, her eyes full of

questioning.

'Happy Maturity Day,' he said, his smile widening. He opened the box, watching intently as Nadia stared at the bracelet within, her eyes wide with wonder.

She eventually glanced up at him. 'For me?' she asked tentatively, as if expecting him to answer otherwise.

He removed the bracelet from the box. 'For you,' he confirmed, dropping the box to the floor as he took her hand once more in order to place the bracelet around her wrist.

Once fastened, Nadia stared at the glistening diamonds and emeralds now adorning her wrist.

She looked up at her brother. 'Alex, it is exquisite,' she said quietly, awestruck by his generosity.

'Then it matches its bearer,' he complimented softly, a seriousness in his eyes she was unsure of.

Her face instantly broke with a large smile as she leapt into his arms, ignoring the decorum expected of them; there was no one else to see their indiscretion.

'Thank you, so much,' she squealed. She wrapped her arms around his neck and held him close. 'You are the best brother any woman could ask for,' she praised against his ear, welcoming his embrace as he wrapped his arms around her tiny corseted waist.

'Then you like it, dearest?' he asked against her raven hair, the smell of her perfume endearing him as he continued to hold her close.

Nadia pulled back from him for a moment so she could look him in the eye. 'You are too generous, Brother,' she said with a smile. 'It is a stunning gift and I shall treasure it always.' She embraced him once more.

Alex could have stayed in that tower, in that embrace forever, having his sister close by, just as they always had been as children.

Their closeness had become more emphasised since they had started sharing blood; her absence almost feeling like a loss any time she was not close by.

It was an emotion that left him confused; did Nadia experience the same things? He felt unable to ask her, feeling like she may misunderstand him and poke fun.

'You are worthy of every jewel in the world and more, dearest Sister,' he whispered against her ear, the sound of her gentle breathing almost comforting.

The beat of her heart joined that of her breathing, and he recognised the faint pulse of her vein beneath the delicate skin of her throat. He thought of the times they had shared blood and the delicate pounding of the veins in her wrist before his teeth pierced the skin, spilling her sweet, addictive blood just for him.

It was a thought that had him craving that taste once more, and her proximity, paired with the sound of her heartbeat was as insatiable as any human he had ever killed.

The smell of her perfume was intoxicating.

Driven by an unknown force, Alex lowered his lips to her throat, his sharp teeth piercing her skin gently.

A sharp gasp escaped Nadia's lips as she stiffened in his arms.

All at once, she pushed him away, shock etched on her porcelain face.

They stood there, staring at each other in silence for a moment, one unsure what to say to the other.

It was the first time either one of them had tried to drink the others blood from anywhere other than the wrist. It was new and uncertain ground for both of them; an experience that felt all too intimate.

Alex tried desperately to ignore the exquisite taste of her blood on his tongue as he stared at her.

No thought that ran through his mind made any sense in that moment as he looked at this beauty before him, a woman who's exquisite blood tempted him like nothing else in the world ever had. Their bond had been solidified in their blood sharing, and now the barrier of intimacy had been broken; he had attempted to take her blood in a way a lover would his beloved.

Reason left him as he took her face swiftly in his hands and kissed her lips, hard.

Nadia's hands twisted into fists as she pushed them against his chest, forcing him away. She glared at him, disgust on her angelic face.

'What do you think you are doing, sir?' she demanded, her terms of endearment lost in anger.

Alex was instantly full of shame, and regret. 'Forgive me, Sister,' he said quickly, desperate to right the enormous wrong he had just committed. What had he done?

'You forget yourself, Brother,' she chastised angrily as she glared at him. 'I declare you are not yourself,' she added, clearly trying to justify his actions.

'Indeed, I fear not,' he agreed, looking down at the floor, ashamed.

'Is this the real reason for your gift?' she asked. 'Was it to be payment for stealing my blood?'

Her words hurt and he looked up at her. 'I swear to you, no, Sister,' he pleaded. 'I beg of you to forgive me. I did not intend for such actions to take place.'

She shook her head, staring at him with disbelief. She instinctively felt her neck with her gloved fingers; the wound had already healed.

'How could you do this, Alex?' she asked, exasperated. She paced the room, barely looking at him. 'Tonight was to be so special,' she mumbled, despair in her voice.

Alex frowned as he watched her pace the room. 'Why?' he asked, confused. 'What was to happen tonight?'

Nadia stopped and stared at him, regret in her eyes. 'Mother and Father were going to speak with you privately,' she said quietly. 'It was not my place to say.'

'Why?' he asked once more, his tone full of

impatience. 'What is to happen tonight?'

She sighed heavily, her eyes downcast to the wooden floor. 'There is to be an announcement tonight,' she admitted timidly, clearly uncomfortable that the duty to inform Alex of the news had fallen on her shoulders. 'They will announce my betrothal.'

Alex felt a cold chill run through him as he stared at his sister, trying to make sense of the words she had just spoken.

'Betrothal?' he asked, his voice hoarse. He cleared his throat as he continued to stare at her, feeling a deep-set betrayal fill his heart; his family had planned this without his knowledge. 'To whom?'

'Herr Walser,' she answered, staring him directly in the eye.

It took a few moments for her words to register in his mind. 'Lord Freiderick Walser? The fool from Germany?' he asked, his tone full of distaste.

Nadia frowned at him, angry at her brother's lack of support. 'Do not insult him, Alex,' she rebuked. 'You have always seemed to find him agreeable on his visits,' she pointed out.

He scoffed. 'It was my duty to be polite to him and his family while they visited our homeland,' he said. 'Had I known it was planned to marry you off to him then I would not have been so amiable.'

'I am not being married off, as you put it with such vulgarity. I accepted a genuine proposal of marriage from a good man, of whom I am very fond,' she stated, her anger rising at her brother's disregard.

Alex frowned at her. 'And when was all this decided upon?' he asked.

Nadia paled slightly as she stared at him, delaying her answer. 'He asked Father for my hand two days ago,' she said eventually.

His temper flared. 'Two days ago? And no one saw fit to inform me?' he snapped. '*You* hid it from me,' he added, hurt in his voice.

'Believe me, Brother, it was not my intention to deceive you,' she said quietly, her eyes downcast. 'He did not propose until this evening.'

Alex stared at her for a moment, his gaze momentarily flicking to the trunk that Monika had been so interested in concealing.

His gaze narrowed. 'What is in the trunk?' he asked carefully.

Nadia looked up at him, her eyes filled with apology. 'Gabriella offered me her wedding dress by way of tradition,' she said feebly.

Alex couldn't believe his ears. 'So practically everyone knows about this marriage except me? Your own twin is left out of the decision entirely?'

'It was not my place to say, Alex. Nothing was official until tonight. I did not intend to exclude you,' she said, exasperated.

'But you did nonetheless,' he shouted. 'You agreed to marry. One of the biggest decisions of your life and you hid it from me.'

'You make it sound like I have betrayed you, Brother,' she argued.

'In a way you have,' he spat back.

'How dare you. I made a decision for my own happiness, Alex Demeter. In what way is that wrong? I do not need your permission. You do not hold possession over me,' she growled. 'Would you have me stuck to your side for eternity? Would you have me bound to you in the way you insinuated only moments ago?' she asked angrily.

'You will not be happy, Nadia,' he argued, ignoring her jibe.

'That is not for you to determine,' she said.

'He is not for you, dearest,' he reasoned. 'There is no life within him. No real joy. He does not share your lust for life and fun.'

'And you do, of course?' she retorted.

'I understand you like no other, Nadia, and you know that. You are my twin, my sister. I love you. I do not wish to see you give your life to anything less than what you deserve.'

'And I love *you*, Brother, but you cannot understand everything about me, and are arrogant to assume you do. I am pleased with this match and I am happy with my decision, even if you are not. I will be happy in this marriage and I pray that you will be happy for me in time, even if you are not now.'

'And if I refuse to accept this match?' he challenged.

Nadia looked at him hard, a mixture of sadness and anger in her emerald eyes. 'Then you refuse it alone, dearest,' she said simply, pushing him aside and storming from the room, slamming the door behind her, the sound echoing off the ancient stone walls.

Alex had no choice but to stare at the door, his mind a myriad of chaotic thoughts.

Why did her decision feel like such a betrayal?

The question, along with the taste of her blood and the feeling of her lips against his tormented his mind as he continued to stare at the door, angry and confused.

Why did he suddenly feel so scared of losing his sister?

1750

Alex's fingers travelled effortlessly over the piano keys, the gentle melody soothing to his cacophony of thoughts.

As he sat at the grand piano in the drawing room, he stared out of the window next to him, numbly looking out across the lavish gardens of his family home, the gloom of the overcast day offering no joy.

He stopped playing for a moment, the silence around him only broken by the gentle ticking of the mantle clock and the occasional crackle of the fire in the grate. The ancestors in the portraits seemed to look down on him in judgement.

His thoughts were troubled, and he had not rested well.

He had not had a restful night's sleep for the past year, ever since the night of the masquerade ball at Vallakia; the night he had learnt of his sister's betrothal.

He thought back to that evening.

RETRIBUTION DARKENED

She had looked so happy as the announcement had been made and the engagement ring placed on her finger, and Alex had been numb to her emotions because he had had no knowledge of what was to happen. He had been blocked from the decisions and discussions regarding his twin sister's future, and it angered and hurt him.

The memories of what had happened in the north tower between them haunted him. Still, to this day, he did not understand his own thoughts and feelings.

Ever since they had first shared blood as adults, there had been a connection to his sister he could not break, and he felt a compulsion for both her blood and her presence, to the point where it had culminated in his actions in that tower.

The night at Vallakia had continued after their confrontation, and he had followed his sister back down into the throes of the party, full of anger at her revelation of an engagement. She was his sister, his twin, and he had been oblivious to the life-changing arrangements that had been agreed behind his back; they had always shared everything, every little secret, and her duplicity hurt immensely.

It still did, despite everything.

Throughout the remainder of that evening, including the announcement regarding Nadia's betrothal, he had been unable to take his eyes from her; she in turn had been unable to look away from him. She would cast furtive glances at first from behind her mask, yet as the evening wore on her gaze became more brazen, until they could barely keep their eyes off one another.

During the announcement, she had stood by her betrothed's side, her pale face a mask of happiness, and Alex had felt a stir of jealousy in that moment that had both confused and consumed him.

The chiming of the clock to introduce the changing of the hour distracted him from his reverie, and he released a long weary sigh, his fingers finding the keys once more as he continued playing the piano.

'I have not heard you play in a long time, Brother.'

Nadia's voice startled him and his fingers froze on the keys. He turned on the stool, his gaze meeting hers as she stood in the doorway in her riding coat and hat, her whip still held in her gloved hands.

He cleared his throat. 'I did not expect you back so early,' he said.

She straightened at his short tone. 'Shall I leave you alone with your thoughts?' she asked carefully, turning away from the door.

'No,' he said quickly. 'I fear they are too chaotic for seclusion,' he admitted, his gaze not quite meeting hers directly. 'You have finished your hunt?' he asked, changing the subject.

Nadia smiled. 'I made my excuses,' she admitted, stepping into the room. She placed her whip on the end table before perching on the nearest chair. 'All anyone can talk of is plans for the wedding, and I do declare I am sure even the horses had heard enough to tire of it.'

Alex stared at the floor, uncomfortable speaking of the wedding that was now only two days away.

'I would have thought you would be pleased of such interest in your special day,' he said, knowing that his sister's excitement for the forthcoming nuptials had been increasing as time had passed; he was also sure that her feelings for her betrothed had increased, though she had maintained her privacy on such matters.

A frustrated sigh escaped her pink lips. 'Naturally I am excited,' she said wearily, 'but it is all I have heard about for the past few months. No one seems to speak to me like a person any longer, with the exception of you,' she confided, her tone soft and soothing. 'Everywhere I go I am confronted by praise, congratulations, and mindless chatter about just one day of my life. It is so frustrating.'

Alex couldn't help but smile at her little outburst, knowing she would only ever trust him with her feelings; she would never dare disclose such frustrations to their parents or elders for fear of chastisement for being flighty.

It had been decided that she would return to Germany with her new husband once the marriage was solidified, and Alex had never quite been able to decipher how excited she was about the new possibilities her life was presenting to her.

He had tried to ignore the inane sense of loss he

felt every time he considered her leaving, yet it never quite went away. The thought of losing his sister, his twin, his equal, felt a burden too much to bear.

He smiled at her, hiding his torment. 'You have only to think, Sister, that in two days' time you will not be subject to such babble,' he chuckled.

Nadia grinned, her face filled with relief. 'Thank heavens,' she breathed. She stared at him for a moment as a delicate silence passed between them.

'Will you play for me, dearest?' she asked gently. 'It does soothe me so.'

Her request warmed him and he nodded his assent, turning on his stool to face the piano once more. He began to play a gentle melody, one that he knew to be one of her favourites, and it pleased him to see her delight.

His mind wandered as he played, the softness of the melody soothing as his fingers drifted effortlessly over the keys.

The last year had been filled with conflicting thoughts and emotions. Tensions had been high for a couple of days after the ball at Vallakia, and Nadia had barely spoken to him. His parents had naturally noticed the disquiet between the twins, yet both he and Nadia had upheld the belief that there was nothing wrong.

Eventually, they had confided in one another and made peace, knowing that their bond as twins was far too great to allow a silly argument to interfere.

Alex still had not been happy about Nadia's

RETRIBUTION DARKENED

betrothal, believing that her intended was not a good match; Herr Walser was too reserved, in Alex's opinion, and did not share Nadia's love of life and fun. Alex could see his sister becoming smothered and repressed once she was married, and he feared for her, especially since she was to move so far away.

The planning of such a grand event as the wedding had taken its toll, however, on Nadia's patience, and often she would come to Alex with her frustrations; she didn't like to feel "penned in" as she liked to put it, and she would rebel further when pushed, which amused him.

Only he truly understood how she felt, she would say to him, and he truly believed it; he believed only *she* truly understood *him* in return.

It had been one such conversation that had led to them sharing each other's blood once more, her delicate bite into the flesh of his wrist stirring in him a need far too great for him to express, yet he was certain she felt it, too.

As the months passed, their secretive act almost became a sanctuary for them both, an escape from the daily pressures they were finding placed upon their shoulders, and with it grew a dependency on each other; their blood sharing developed until it started to create other feelings and needs, their desire for each other's blood growing, until feeding from the wrist was no longer enough.

One night, after a particularly brutal day of planning, organising, dress fittings and endless chatter over the paleness of the bridesmaids dresses, Nadia found solace in Alex's company once more, the pair's closeness resulting in Nadia finally biting Alex's throat, as he had done to her that night in Vallakia. The surprise had been overruled by the euphoria of her sharp teeth piercing his skin, of her lips against his throat, of the feel of her drinking his blood so sensually.

She had then, in turn, allowed him to feed from her in the same manner, and his turmoil of emotions and feelings, along with the exquisite taste of her blood, all but drove him mad; it was simply too much ecstasy to withstand.

And so their closeness and intimacy had continued, infrequently at first, but increasing as time went on, their blood sharing becoming an addiction that neither of them could live without; their blood was simply too compelling to resist.

Although the blood sharing was a secret they maintained, their closeness did not go unnoticed. Their parents, elders and friends all noticed the dependency the twins had developed for each other, and if any of them guessed why, they never said.

Alex was aware on occasions of his mother and Gabriella watching them extremely closely when they were all in a room together, the two women almost scrutinising the pair's behaviour as they would laugh and giggle.

Further scrutinising seemed to come from Herr Freiderick Walser himself. As time passed,

RETRITUTION DARKENED

Alex became more and more suspicious that Nadia's betrothed did not like the twins spending so much time together, and he would often try and either involve himself in their conversations and activities, or simply try and pull Nadia from Alex's side using a variety of excuses.

Nadia, however, was not unwise to these tactics, and she would often counteract them with excuses and reprimands of her own, her rebellion clear for all to see.

It would amuse Alex to see Freiderick's discomfort and embarrassment, but equally made him concerned for the life his sister was to marry herself into; she was a free spirit, after all, and Alex was not convinced she would be given the freedom to be herself once she belonged to her new husband.

Alex's fingers drifted over the piano keys as his melody came to an end, his sister relaxed once more as she lounged on the chair, her riding bonnet removed and dropped onto the floor beside her.

He turned on the piano stool, his gaze meeting hers; she had been watching him the whole time.

He smiled at her tenderly.

'Are you relaxed now, dearest?' he asked softly.

A slow, lingering smile crept across her delicate pink lips, her green eyes filled with humour. 'Indeed, Brother. I dare say I could easily forget where I was,' she laughed playfully.

'I do not doubt it,' Alex chuckled, though his eyes were serious. 'I worry about you so,' he admitted.

She chortled as she straightened herself on the chair. 'You should know better than to trouble yourself, Brother Dearest,' she teased, her gaze faultless; her words were not filled with the same conviction. 'Worry is wasted on one such as me.'

Alex didn't bend to her teasing. 'As are rules and restrictions, my dear, yet I fear you will be subject to many once you are no longer of the Demeter name.'

Nadia's gaze flinched for a moment, yet her smile widened, hiding any discomfort he may have suspected she held.

'You really do think too much, Alex,' she laughed, brushing a stray strand of hair from her face. 'You must have far too much time on your hands.'

He couldn't help joining in her merriment. 'I wish it were so, my dear, yet all my time is taken worrying for you.'

She giggled playfully. 'Then I'm sure I must find you a new hobby,' she teased. 'Freiderick's cousin from Germany will be attending the wedding. She is most agreeable to the eye.' She pulled a face to indicate her words were false and she burst into peals of laughter, tears of merriment falling down her cheeks.

Alex shook his head as he also laughed, pleased to see her so happy and joyous; it had been sometime since he had truly seen her laugh like this. Yet equally, the notion that he should spend any time away from her side, especially in any romantic manner, repulsed him, and he found such reactions confusing.

Still, he joined in with her jests.

Their laughter and teasing continued as the doors to the parlour opened slowly, allowing entrance to Aurelia, Victor and Freiderick, returned from their ride.

The twins' laughter quietened as they glanced at the three in the doorway, and Nadia's smile vanished as she caught the reprimanding gaze of her fiancé.

Freiderick's chin lifted with reproach. 'I see your health has improved somewhat, my lady,' he said flatly.

Alex watched the pair intently, not liking the atmosphere that had instantly developed. He glanced at his parents, who also did not look overly pleased with Nadia's obvious duplicity.

Nadia seemed to regain her composure as she stared at him, using her charms as always.

'Indeed I do, sir, thank you,' she said softly.

Freiderick glanced at Alex, the same scolding gleam to his dark eyes.

Alex glared back, unwilling to be chastised by this fool whom he detested.

Freiderick turned his attentions back to Nadia, clearly unwilling or unable to maintain Alex's glare. 'I am glad you have made such a miraculous recovery, my dear,' he said scathingly. 'You indeed seemed quite out of sorts during our hunt.'

Nadia straightened at his remark, her gaze darkening with irritation; she clearly did not appreciate his tone, and Alex knew her too well to think she would allow herself to be spoken to in such a manner.

'Well, I am quite well now,' she insisted, her gaze unfaltering. 'I needed to rest.'

Freiderick was not backing down. 'So I believed, my dear,' he said, his words almost a sneer. 'Yet I find you in here with your brother, laughing and joking like a child.'

Alex's resolve snapped and he stood from his seat instantly, his gaze seething. 'How dare you speak to my sister in such a manner, sir,' he said angrily. 'I demand you apologise.'

Freiderick took a step back, clearly unnerved by Alex's outburst.

Victor ventured into the room. 'Come now, my son,' he said softly, eager to quieten the sudden intense mood. 'I am sure Herr Walser did not intend to offend you so.'

Alex had spent too long withholding his distaste for Nadia's intended, and he was not prepared to back down so easily. 'To hell with his intentions, Father. I will not accept him speaking to Nadia like that. He has no right.'

He turned back to Freiderick. 'Now apologise, sir,' he insisted.

Freiderick glared at the man in front of him. 'I will do no such thing,' he said adamantly.

Alex felt his anger overtaking him; it scared him. 'Apologise I say,' he gritted, his eyes blazing.

When Freiderick remained adamantly silent,

RETRITUTION DARKENED

Alex stepped across the room until he was toe to toe with the man. He was aware of Nadia watching both of them closely, worry etched on her porcelain face. His parents had no choice but to stand by and watch.

'I will not ask you again, sir,' Alex snarled. 'You owe my sister an apology.'

Still, Freiderick was stubborn. 'I will not apologise for being misled,' he insisted. 'I believed your sister to be unwell, yet when I return I find her very much in good spirits... with you,' he added, his eyes narrowing as he continued to stare at Alex indignantly.

A cynical smile played across Alex's lips. 'So that's the truth of it,' he said slowly. 'You are not angry that she was not ill, as you supposed, but more that she prefers to share her company with me.'

Freiderick could not hide his discontent at Alex's words, yet held his ground. 'I would prefer that my betrothed conduct herself like the lady she is, and not roll around like a child with her brother.'

Alex glanced at Nadia, who still sat in her chair, her expression grim; she silently pleaded for him to let the matter go, yet he had heard enough of her reservations and witnessed enough of Freiderick's almost dictator-like approach to their impending marriage to know that he had to intervene.

'Surely she is allowed some merriment?' he countered. 'I fail to see the wrong in such joy.' Once more, Alex glanced at his sister before looking back at Freiderick. 'My sister would not do well in a cage,' he hissed.

Freiderick straightened. 'How dare you, sir,' he stated flatly, his own anger clearly being riled. 'In case your memory fails you, my lord, Lady Demeter accepted my proposal of marriage. In no less than two days we are to be wed, and despite what you may or may not agree with, I will have her act and behave as a wife should.'

At this, Nadia finally stood up, her movement alone conveying her anger. 'I declare my ears must deceive me, gentleman,' she said, her voice filled with a combination of anger and disquiet.

She stared at each of them in turn, her gaze finally settling on Freiderick. 'Am I to be fought over like a bone by two rabid dogs?'

Her outburst took them both by surprise.

Alex tried to soothe the conversation. 'Dearest, I was only—'

'I do not wish to hear it,' she interrupted without even looking at him; her gaze remained fixed on Freiderick. 'I am appalled by you both. You talk of my behaviour, yet here you both are, arguing like children yourselves over some toy you both wish to possess.'

For the first time, Freiderick looked repentant. 'It was not my intention to offend you, my lady,' he said earnestly. 'I apologise if my words have done so.'

Alex scoffed. 'Your apologies mean nothing, sir,' he snapped.

Nadia glared at him. 'You would do well to

stand down, Alex,' she said firmly. 'You are both at fault.'

Alex's gaze narrowed as he stared at her. 'You would put me at fault for defending your honour?' he asked harshly, sending the rest of his thoughts to her directly.

'Do not torment me for protecting you,' he said silently.

Her expression softened as she continued to look at him. *'I do not wish to do so, dearest,'* she said, her voice tender in his mind. *'Trust me, I am protecting you.'*

Nadia turned to look at Freiderick; if he knew of the twin's silent exchange, he did not show it.

'Indeed, my good sir, it seems we have things to discuss, and I would speak with you alone,' she said firmly, her expression hard.

For the first time, Aurelia stepped forward, her expression clearly unsure. 'Nadia, I do not think—'

'Mother, I would speak with my future husband alone,' Nadia interrupted, knowing her mother was about to object to such a meeting without a chaperone. She offered her mother a playful glance. 'If it pleases you, I will leave the door ajar,' she said, teasing.

Aurelia looked exasperated, yet Victor took her hand as Nadia and Freiderick passed by, leaving the room.

Alex stared after them, uncomfortable with the scene that had just played out before him.

His gaze met with his mother's and he turned

away, his anger still spiralling.

'Do not turn from me, my child,' Aurelia said quietly, with no authority in her voice. 'I wish to know what was taking place in this room.'

Alex sighed, weary by the turn of events. 'It was nothing, Mother,' he said, still not turning to face her. 'As you saw, I only wished for his apology.'

Victor released his wife's hand, taking a step forward. His voice was stern when he spoke. 'Your mother was not referring to what transpired in the room while we were in it, my son,' he said carefully. 'She is asking what took place before we returned from our ride.'

His father's words worrying him, Alex turned to face his parents, determined to keep his expression unreadable.

'I do not know what you are asking, Father,' he said flatly. 'Nadia returned from your ride, feeling unwell and somewhat dismayed at the incessant discussions of her matrimony. She requested I play her something on the piano and I obliged. I was trying to cheer her mood, and believed I had done so when you all returned. Unfortunately, it appears my efforts were in vain,' he added, unwilling to back down.

Victor shook his head. 'We do not mean to say that you should not cheer your sister when she is in need of merriment, my son,' he said. 'But she has responsibilities now, and will have more so once she is married in two days' time. Her priority will no longer be to her family, but to her husband.'

Alex growled as he thought on the impending marriage and he turned away once more, standing by the window.

Victor continued to speak gently to his son. 'My child, naturally we know that you and Nadia are close, but—'

'But perhaps you are now a little too close?' Aurelia interrupted, no judgement in her voice, only questioning.

Alex once more turned to look at his mother, unsure of her meaning.

She smiled at him gently, sadness in her eyes. 'I am no fool, my child,' she pointed out. 'Your growing fondness for time spent with your sister has not gone unnoticed by anyone within our family, and especially recently it is hard to find the two of you apart.'

Alex shrugged. 'I am unsure why that should be a problem, Mother,' he said.

Aurelia would not back down. 'It will pose many problems, Alex, now that your sister is to be married. Her attentions should be on her husband, not on you,' she warned. 'There should be no dependency.'

Alex frowned. 'There is no dependency,' he argued.

'No? Then pray tell me why after many of your hunts together, Nadia covers her wrists and throat?' she asked firmly.

Alex froze; he felt completely stupid for being so naive in believing that his parents were not astute enough to notice the tell-tale signs of the blood sharing he and Nadia partook of.

He forced a smile. 'I'm afraid I cannot tell you, Mother. I am not one for women's fashion.'

Aurelia's forehead creased in the smallest of frowns, concern filling her gaze and her words. 'I do not want to believe that you would try and deceive me, my darling child,' she said sadly. 'But I fear I must ask. Are you and Nadia sharing blood and hiding it like some sordid secret that must be kept?'

Alex could not bear to lie to his mother, yet he had no choice; although he did not see anything wrong with his and Nadia's blood sharing, they had maintained its secrecy, which in itself conveyed something sordid.

He wasn't prepared to confess his feelings or how he believed his sister to be growing fonder of him. He could not bring himself to reveal the truth.

He was protecting Nadia as much as himself.

He forced a small smile, his expression filled with sadness. 'Mother, we have not done such a thing since we were children. It was a silly childish habit which we have long since outgrown.'

Aurelia cast her gaze to the floor, and Victor glanced at her.

Alex knew he had upset her; as she had said, she was no fool, and though she would not confront him, she knew he was not being truthful.

He hated himself in that moment for upsetting her so, and he took a step towards her. 'Mother, please do not be melancholy,' he soothed. 'Nadia is my sister, my twin. Our closeness is a result of our birth. I refuse to apologise for such. I will protect her, always, married or not.'

Aurelia glanced up at him, a softness in her eyes.

He crossed the room to stand before her and took her hands in his, kissing each one in turn tenderly.

'You need not worry, Mother,' he said softly.

He knew, from the look in his mother's eyes, that there was part of her that still doubted his words, but she remained silent and simply offered him the smallest of smiles.

Alex looked at each of his parents in turn. There was nothing more he could say, and with a small smile he brushed past them, determined to find his sister.

* * *

The scent of Nadia's cologne was easy to follow, the delicate aroma of flowers leading him through the house, until he came to his father's study.

The heavy oak door was ajar and the room beyond was flooded with light from the large leaded windows spanning the opposite wall.

Alex could hear his sister's voice from beyond the door and he crept up to the opening, able to see her standing in the room with Freiderick, his face set like stone; clearly he had been making his disappointment in her known once more, and Alex felt his anger rise.

Nadia had removed her riding coat, discarding it across their father's desk, and she stood there in her riding shirt and thickly striped brown skirt, her black hair cascading down her back where she had clearly removed the pins holding it in place.

As always, she looked stunning, and Alex couldn't help but assume that this was her intention; disappointment or not, she certainly had Freiderick's undivided attention.

Alex pressed himself against the doorframe, listening and watching intently.

Freiderick settled back against the desk, his face hard as he stared at Nadia. 'So, my dear, what do you have to say for yourself?' he asked flatly, his tone full of disappointment.

She sighed, looking at the wooden floor before glancing back up at him, her eyes full of sorrow. 'It was not my intention to mislead you,' she admitted.

Freiderick did not look appeased. 'Yet you spend the afternoon frolicking with your brother after feigning illness,' he admonished. 'An act for which neither of you seemed very repentant.'

Nadia took a step towards him, her hands held against her chest in plea. 'I realise my fault and will rightfully take all the blame, my dear, dear sir. Alex was blameless.'

Freiderick watched her for a moment, his expression softening somewhat. 'That is fair and true of you, my lady,' he said firmly. 'However, it does not excuse your brother's rudeness in the parlour,' he added.

Nadia shook her head. 'I am afraid I cannot answer for my brother's actions, only apologise for them. I do not wish for there to be bad feelings, especially so close to the wedding.'

For the first time, Freiderick smiled; Alex was surprised at how much it improved his demeanour.

'You are most gracious, my dear,' he said softly, her mention of their impending nuptials clearly lessening his irritation. 'I should hope that your brother appreciates such a virtue.'

Her smile was sweet. 'Indeed, I hope he does also,' she agreed, taking another step towards him.

Straightening himself, Freiderick removed his own riding coat, draping it across hers on the desk.

He sighed, almost wearily. 'Naturally, I appreciate your closeness to your brother. Yet I cannot help but notice how your behaviour changes when you are together. It is not acceptable for a lady to be seen acting like a child.'

Nadia's frown increased. 'You would have me sat like an old woman, then?' she asked harshly, taking him by surprise. 'Saying "yes, sir", "no, sir"? I will not be commanded, my lord,' she confirmed, her words demanding his attention; he watched her intently. 'I am to be your wife, not a slave or servant. I will conduct myself within my new position as I see fit, and not how it is expected.'

For a moment, Alex was certain Freiderick would storm from the room in a fit of rage, yet he simply stared at Nadia for a moment, clearly lost for words after her outburst.

Nadia ignored Freiderick's silence and continued, her gaze never leaving his. 'Did you not tell me when we met how you appreciated my uniqueness? You found me to be unlike other women, and that was what you found most intriguing.'

She took another step forward, until she was standing directly in front of him. 'Would you have me disappoint you by changing those very aspects of my nature you found so appealing?'

Alex shook his head with a smile, dumbfounded by her unique ability to switch an argument so easily with just a few clever words; men fell at her feet as she proved her point, while stroking their ego at the same time.

Freiderick continued staring at her for a moment, clearly processing her words. He took a deep breath, releasing it as a long sigh.

'Forgive me, my dear lady,' he said finally. 'It was not my intention to bring offense or distress you so.' He stood there for a moment, his gaze falling to floor. 'I declare I am a fool,' he said.

Nadia's expression softened. 'I would not taint yourself so, sir,' she said softly, her change in tone grasping his attention.

He looked up at her. 'I confess myself to have been jealous,' he admitted, his gaze filled with remorse.

She frowned. 'Jealous, sir?' she questioned.

Freiderick shook his head, clearly humiliated. 'You and your brother always seem to be so cheerful around one another,' he said. 'There is true happiness in your eyes when you are together.'

Nadia smiled at him, sympathy in her eyes. 'And is there not happiness in them when we spend our moments together, sir? Do you think me miserable?' she asked, taking his hand in hers.

He shook his head slowly and chuckled to himself. 'As I say, my dear, I am a fool. He is your twin, after all.' He paused for a moment. 'Such a rarity,' he said on the end of another sigh. 'No one can truly understand it, can they?'

She glanced at the floor, sadness in her expression. 'No, indeed they cannot.'

Gently, Freiderick hooked a finger under her chin, lifting her face so that she looked at him.

'I am sorry, my dear. I did not mean to make you so melancholy,' he said softly with another smile. 'I appreciate your closeness, though I may not understand it.'

Nadia smiled, her gaze fixed on his. 'You are too gracious, my dear sir,' she said quietly, her words soft and inviting. 'I confess I have not been as attentive as I should have, and can only apologise for my lack of thought to your needs. In my defence, I can only disclose my feelings for you have grown and waiting for our marriage has been quite difficult.' She stared at him, the smallest of coy smiles on her lips. 'It was not my intention to distress you with my avoidance. I only sought to disguise my own... sinful needs.'

Alex couldn't believe what he was hearing. He stared at his sister through the gap in the door, trying to fathom what she meant by her words; was she playing her games now, or truly speaking of her feelings? She was too convincing to be sure.

The strange jealousy he had been experiencing more and more of late flared within him.

Freiderick smiled at Nadia, her words clearly breaking down his unbending demeanour.

'My dear lady,' he breathed as she leaned towards him. 'You truly are a wonder. You captured my heart the first day we met and will have it for always.' He raised her hand to his lips, kissing her fingers gently.

She glanced over her shoulder, taking in the room around her; if she spotted Alex outside the door, she showed no evidence of it. She turned back to Freiderick.

'There is no one to witness, my lord, should you wish to kiss me,' she said gently, her words too inviting to resist.

She lifted her hand to his cheek, stroking it tenderly, and he leaned into her touch.

Freiderick looked into her eyes, and whatever he saw there seemed to melt all of his self-consciousness.

Slowly, he placed his hands about her waist and drew her closer to him, their lips finally meeting in what seemed a tentative kiss at first, only for it to grow into a more passionate embrace as they both seemed to release their hidden emotions for one another.

Alex glared at the pair of them, his anger and jealousy running unchecked through his body, his palms gripped into fists as he watched the pair, their embrace lasting longer and longer, until Freiderick began kissing Nadia's neck with unchecked enthusiasm, her arms holding him close as her breathing betrayed her excitement.

Alex felt unable to turn away as he continued to watch Nadia seduce her intended, the pair of them falling back against the desk.

He knew what he was about to witness, and despite his unwillingness to become such a voyeur, he could not tear his gaze away, still unsure of his sister's intentions.

She certainly appeared to relish in Freiderick's attentions as he lifted her skirts, revealing her stockings and garters, their passionate kisses continuing as she welcomed his lovemaking.

Alex snarled silently, his gaze now fixed directly on Freiderick as he continued to defile his sister.

Alex ignored Nadia's moans of pleasure that betrayed her rapture; he cared only about this stranger who had forced his way into their lives, and who intended to take Nadia away, no doubt to treat her in such a manner day after day until she was infected with his children, her care-free existence destroyed.

Alex wasn't prepared to stand back and watch Freiderick steal his sister away, and as Alex continued to watch the pair of them, Nadia's back arching with pleasure and Freiderick groaning with his release, Alex swore to himself he would do whatever it took in order to keep his sister by his side.

A growl rumbled through his chest as Alex watched the pair in their heated glow.

Whatever it took.

* * *

Without knocking, Alex pushed open the door to Nadia's bedchamber, greeted by gasps from both his sister and her maid as she attended Nadia in dressing for another evening of unwelcome company.

Nadia attempted to cover herself, unsuccessfully, by pulling her arms across her chest, barely concealing the chemise she wore.

Margita, her maid, quickly grabbed a robe and draped it about Nadia's shoulders.

'You should not be here, Master Demeter,' she said quietly.

Nadia touched her maid's hand delicately. 'It is fine, Margita. Please give me and my brother a moment. I will call for you directly.'

'Yes, Miss,' Margita said, curtseying before turning and leaving the room, pulling the door closed behind her.

Nadia pulled the robe about herself as she stared at her brother. 'We are expected downstairs, dearest,' she said, her tone devoid of any emotion.

Alex glared at her, unable to make sense of the

feelings that washed over him. 'I am sure they can wait,' he said shortly.

Her gaze became unsure and she turned from him to face the mirror on her dresser. She picked up two emerald earbobs, fixing them to her lobes before glancing at Alex once more.

'Something is troubling you, dearest?' she queried quietly. 'Please do share,' she smiled, teasing him.

Still, his face remained stony, his gaze dark. 'I would like an explanation,' he growled, ignoring her innocent expression. 'I would like you to explain to me what I witnessed this afternoon in Father's study.'

She froze, staring at him, her face instantly paling. She opened her mouth, yet no words emerged.

Alex took a step towards her, his gaze narrowing. 'What have you done?' he asked quietly, unable to prevent the essence of malice that tinged his words.

She was unable to meet his gaze as shame washed over her. 'I did what I had to do,' she said simply.

'You gave your maidenhead,' he hissed.

'To the man who is to be my husband,' she argued back, a frown creasing her forehead. 'Do not tell me you are judging me, Brother?'

Alex struggled with his rage. 'How could you do such a thing?' he asked, dumbfounded. 'I heard what you said. You allowed him to kiss you, to touch you. You—'

'I did what I *had* to do,' she repeated, her

tone more forceful. 'If you were listening then you witnessed Freiderick's reservations. I was not prepared to have him question my closeness to you.' She turned from Alex, her gaze downcast. 'I had to protect you,' she added quietly.

Alex softened as he watched her, yet could not push away the memories of seeing her in Freiderick's arms, or watching as she had allowed him to use her body.

'I could not bear to see you in his arms,' he admitted, knowing that what he said was foolish and completely immoral; yet the truth had been hidden within him for far too long, and after what he had witnessed that afternoon, he could no longer withhold it from her.

Nadia looked round at him. 'I did not intend for you to witness such a thing,' she said sadly.

'Yet I did nonetheless,' he countered. 'And I dare admit that I was jealous,' he gritted. 'Damn it, I cannot stand to see you with him, or think of you marrying such a man. He is stealing you away from me and removing you from your family. So help me the very thought disgusts me.' He paused to catch his breath, his gaze locked with his sister's. He took a deep breath to calm himself.

'There, it is said,' he said softly. 'Let all be forgiven.'

Nadia stared at him, trying to comprehend what he had just told her. Her own thoughts and feelings were a cacophony and she found she no longer had the strength to fight against them.

'I do not know what to say,' she said quietly. 'I do not know what you expect of me, Brother.'

He took a step towards her, finally close enough so he could reach out and take both her hands in his; he noticed she was trembling.

They stood there in silence, the ticking of the clock on Nadia's mantle the only thing breaking the peace around them.

Alex stared at her, hard. 'I cannot bear the thought of you leaving, dearest,' he confessed softly, his words filled with the emotion he could no longer withhold. 'You are my twin, my other half. I do not think I can survive without you close to me, by my side.'

Not wishing to see her brother in distress, Nadia pulled her fingers from his and cupped his face in her hands, a soft smile on her face.

'I will always be a part of you, Alex,' she soothed softly. 'You are the other half of me. We will never truly be parted. Distance cannot divide us.'

He frowned at her then, taking hold of her hands and pulling them from his face, keeping hold of them firmly.

'Then you have every intention to leave?' he asked, his words filled with hurt. 'You are willing to become his wife? To allow him to use your body like some wild beast in rut?'

Nadia's eyes narrowed as she pulled her hands from his forcefully.

'How dare you,' she hissed, glaring at him.

Alex didn't back down. 'You meant the words you spoke to him this very afternoon, did you not?' he accused firmly, unable to bear the feeling of loss that swept over him. 'Such genuine words could not have been a lie.'

Her gaze darkened as she continued to glare at him, her own hurt shining through. 'Is that what you truly believe, Brother?' she asked, exasperated. 'After everything I have confessed to you and discussed with you, you would believe that my words were genuine?' She turned from him, infuriated.

'My words had to be convincing,' she said eventually, her tone calmer yet still full of hurt that he would think such things of his own sister. 'I could no longer bear to hear him talk of you so, and his petty jealousy over my own flesh and blood appalled me. I did not have time to think, I simply did what I had to do and say what I had to say in order to divert his attentions from you. From *us*.'

She turned back to look at her brother, tears in her emerald eyes. 'I *had* to be convincing, dearest, for him to believe me, and in that moment I saw no other way than to give myself to him like a wife and whore.'

She stifled back a sob, and instinctively Alex went to her, drawing her close into an embrace, comforting her.

Nadia held onto him tightly, unwilling to admit her feelings as his body pressed against hers through her thin chemise.

'I am a wretch,' she said sadly, her head rested against his shoulder. 'A wretch and a whore.'

Alex soothed her, stroking her loose ink-black hair tenderly with his hand. 'You are no such thing, dearest,' he said softly, angered with himself for upsetting her so.

'No?' she questioned, unconvinced. 'I gave myself to a man, out of wedlock, not for love but for something else in return. Does that act not constitute a whore?'

Alex planted a tender kiss on her forehead. 'You judge yourself too harshly,' he whispered against her hair.

She looked up at him then. 'Or not harshly enough, Brother,' she warned, pushing herself away from him yet maintaining his gaze. 'My own feelings are a sin, yet I welcome them still, and I finally understand your own torment,' she admitted, aware of her brother's curious expression. 'Yours is a closeness I find myself craving more each day, as if you are more a part of me now than you have ever been, and I realise it is because of the clandestine bond we share.'

He watched her closely, her words sending a thrill through him that twisted his stomach in anticipation. 'What are you saying, dearest?' he asked cautiously.

She wiped fresh tears from her cheeks, her gaze still holding his with growing intensity. 'I confess, Brother, that since the first day we began sharing our blood, I have felt a closeness to you which I have been unable to ignore. I think of you always, and I declare you are even a part of my dreams almost every night.'

Alex took a step closer, unable to hide his delight. 'Why have you not said these things before?' he asked.

Nadia stared at him. 'Because I did not *want* to feel such things,' she confirmed. 'It is sinful to even think such things, without *feeling* them, and yet here I stand confessing such corrupt thoughts.' She held her face in her hands for a moment. 'I am such a wretch,' she mumbled into her fingers.

He took hold of her wrists, gently pulling her hands from her face. 'You are no such thing, my love,' he whispered, trying to soothe the anxiety he saw in her eyes as she looked at him. 'Do not torture yourself so.'

'Why, indeed?' she asked sadly. 'My purity is lost to me now, sold like some bargaining tool to protect my brother, for whom my thoughts are anything but pure, and I dare still call myself a lady. I am wretched and spoiled for anyone else now. I have no choice but to marry Herr Walser.'

Alex frowned at her. 'Nadia, you always have a choice. You do not need to do anything that will make you unhappy, and matrimony with Freiderick will be such. You know that as well as I. You will be contaminated with his offspring, bound to him and his own miserable wretchedness for eternity.' His expression softened as he stroked a finger down her cheek tenderly. 'I worry, dearest sister, that your own light, that which shines so brightly through all our darkness, will burn out once that cold ring is on your finger, and that is something I could not endure to watch.'

Once more she turned away, staring at nothing; she also feared his words were true. 'Then please pray tell me what I am to do, Brother?' she asked, an unusual helplessness to her voice.

Before he could open his mouth to speak, she interrupted him.

'You think life so simple, dearest. Yet despite our nature, you still see the world through the eyes of a man. You can never understand. We are of noble birth, and I am a woman. My choices and expectations are never easy, yet they are what they are.'

Without looking at him, she sat herself down at her dresser, taking a large silver brush and running it slowly through her long raven hair as she looked at her reflection in the mirror before her; her eyes brimmed with tears and she fought to hold them back, not willing to let Alex see her so disturbed.

She replaced the brush on her dresser, taking a deep breath as she continued to stare at herself, suddenly not recognising the woman in the mirror; it certainly looked like her, but the thoughts and feelings, and indeed actions, that ran through her mind were surely that of another.

She glanced down at her hands clasped in her lap. How she wished she could wake from this nightmare she found herself in, and find that she was once more a child, full of excitement and life, her closeness to her twin innocent and entertaining, their mischief nothing more than that of youth.

Alex watched her closely, his heart breaking at the sight of her anguished face.

'I cannot bear to see you so tormented, dearest,' he said, desperately wishing he could free her from her suffering.

'I have been so since that first moment we shared blood, my love. My need for you has grown to that which I can no longer bear to be without. You are my all,' she confessed, looking at him finally. 'My love for you is everything to me, and I despair at the knowledge that I am to be taken from your side.'

He watched a tear fall down her cheek and he rushed to her side, hunkering down beside her chair and wiping her tears away.

They sat in silence as the minutes ticked by, both of them lost in their own tangled web of thoughts.

Nadia cleared her throat, turning her attentions reluctantly back to the mirror. 'I need to dress for this evening,' she said sadly.

Alex watched her closely, the thought of having to sit through another evening with Freiderick simply too much to abide.

'Damn it, Nadia,' he hissed, standing from her side and staring down at her.

She looked up at him, unsure of the look in his eyes.

'Come away with me, Sister,' he said eagerly.

His suggestion surprised her, and she stared at him, perplexed.

'I do not understand,' she said softly.

Alex smiled down at her, taking her hand in his. 'Come away with me,' he repeated. 'Let us leave this place and all its obligations and travel the world, as you have done. You have always said you should love to travel once more, and your stories of all you witnessed have always delighted me. I have told you so many times.' He squeezed her hand in support. 'Let me rescue you from the fate you so dread.'

For an insane moment, the idea appealed to her. But then she remembered their parents and the rest of the family; despite her desperation to rectify the wrong turn her life had taken, she was unwilling to put them through such anguish.

'Your suggestion is absurd, Brother,' she said sadly. 'How can we go and leave Mother and Father, or any of the Others?' she asked, looking up at him. 'Mother especially would be heartbroken, and think of the shame of such an action. We would be leaving them to all that,' she advised.

Alex snorted. 'To hell with shame, Nadia,' he admonished. 'You are entitled to change your mind about the wedding. The ring is not yet on your finger, the vows not yet made.'

He pulled her to her feet, pulling her close so that she had no choice but to look at him. His gaze was intense as he stared down at her.

'Do not forget who we are, dearest,' he advised, his tone serious. 'We may not exploit our uniqueness, but it is there nonetheless, and all those around us are aware of such.'

Nadia tried to step away from his grip, yet he refused to let her go.

'We are power incarnate, Sister,' he continued. 'You know that, as well do the Others. They would not, *will* not, argue against our wishes.'

She stared at him, knowing his words were true; they never had used their power for their own ends, never abused the position they knew they held, albeit unspoken. They had power beyond that of their elders, even Vlad; they had strength and abilities above those hundreds of years older than themselves. Only they had the ability to communicate mentally, as they had discovered while playing as children. They had also found they could control certain animals, the crow being the main creature to obey their will; the crow, after all, was their family's emblem.

'You cannot be sure of such,' she argued, worried for her parents and the scandal their actions would cause. She lowered her gaze.

'Then what are you to do?' he asked her sternly. 'Are you willing to enter into a loveless marriage with a man who will no doubt make you miserable? Are you willing to leave your family?' He hooked a finger under her chin, forcing her to look up at him. 'Are you willing to leave me?' he asked softly, hurt in his voice.

Tears filled her eyes once again as she looked at him, the very thought of being without him tearing her apart. Yet, looking into his eyes and seeing the hurt there, she instantly realised the strength of her brother's feelings for her, and no longer did that thought disgust or scare her.

Gently, she shook her head as he released his hold on her chin. 'I am wretched at the thought of leaving you, Brother,' she confessed. 'To think of my fate as a poor, contaminated bride, forcefully torn from your side...' She trailed off, unable to continue through her tears.

Alex brushed his hands over her raven hair, cupping her head. He placed a tender kiss against her forehead.

'Do not despair, my love,' he whispered. 'We are one, you and I, and I will not allow such a cruel severance to befall us.' His words were forceful and heartfelt, and commanded her attention.

Nadia stared into his emerald eyes that so mocked her own; within them she saw herself reflected back, and with it all the hurt, desperation and longing she had concealed for so long.

'Then what is your solution, Brother Mine?' she asked quietly, her fingers gripping his arms as if frightened he would vanish from her embrace.

He gently wiped the tears from her cheek with his thumb, his gaze intensely serious.

'We walk away,' he said slowly, his voice filled with authority as he sought to exploit the power they possessed, finally done with hiding it for the sake of others around them; they were power incarnate, and he no longer saw any reason to withdraw from such knowledge.

'We walk away from this masquerade of a matrimony, from those who would argue against such an action, and from those who would suppress us from who we truly are,' he said seriously.

Nadia shook her head wearily. 'You make it sound so easy, my love,' she whispered sadly.

With a deep breath, he took her hands in his securely, staring into her eyes to make sure she listened to every word he was about to utter.

'You are stronger than you have allowed yourself to think,' he said firmly. 'You are more than capable of such an action, and I promise you, here and now, that if you will do this with me, if you will have the courage to walk away from all this, then I promise you I will never leave your side for as long as we live, no matter what.'

She stared at him, the strength of his words surprising her. She had not anticipated such a promise, and the thought of having him by her side forever, no matter what, melted away the coldness that had settled in her heart of late.

'Do you mean that, Alex?' she asked quietly, a smile brightening her pink lips.

'I swear it, my love,' he breathed. 'With every fibre of my being.'

Nadia released a breath of relief, pulling him

close, her arms wrapped around his neck.

Alex nuzzled his face against her hair, the smell of her cologne drawing him in further like a moth to the flame, and he knew he needed that sweet and over-powering taste of her blood once more.

Brushing her hair from her shoulders, he breathed in the scent of her skin, the excitement building within him as it did every time he took her blood; it was a taste like no other, and a taste he knew he could never live without.

He felt her shiver in his arms, as she always did when his lips were close to her flesh, and he knew she was anticipating his kiss.

With the greatest care, he bit into the soft flesh of her neck, her gasp of intense pleasure only sending his own excitement higher as her blood coated his tongue, the taste exquisite and delicate, the sweetness almost more than he felt he could endure. It was an ecstasy no human blood had ever raised within him, and as he drank he pulled her closer, the feel of her body against his arousing him all the more.

Tenderly, he kissed the wound to her neck, her breathing ragged. He stepped back from her, watching as she held her hand to the injury, waiting as her blood instantly healed the damaged flesh; it was another ability that separated them from the others around them.

Releasing her hold on her neck, she licked the blood from her fingers, an act that always had his arousal peaking.

In silence, she approached him, untying his cravat and pulling it from his shirt, allowing him to unbutton it along with his waistcoat, giving her access to his throat.

Entering into the sanctuary of his embrace, she kissed his throat before biting into the skin, savouring his blood as if it were to be the last time she would ever taste it; it had become a dependency, and she could no longer imagine her life without it.

She held onto Alex, his strong body pressing against hers in his obvious need. No longer did she fear the intensity of his feelings for her; she welcomed them, and with it felt free for the first time since she was a little girl.

She kissed the wound until it healed, licking away the last smears of blood.

She straightened, looking up at him. There was something unreadable in his eyes that sent a shiver down her spine; one she wholly enjoyed.

As the pair stared at each other in silence, knowing what they each desired, Alex cupped her cheek in his hand, his thumb tenderly stroking her perfect skin.

Nadia trembled as he pulled her to him, his lips slowly touching hers in the gentlest of kisses.

All at once, they both released a sigh of relief that the other had not pulled away, and they both relaxed against one another as their sinful kiss deepened, any thought of the indecent act they were committing pushed from their minds by the overwhelming power of their blood sharing.

Together, they felt as if a large weight had been lifted from their shoulders as they embraced, the promise made between them solidified; they would be together forever, no matter what. Nothing else mattered.

Alex hugged Nadia close to him tightly, a desperate need in his action.

In that moment, she realised that she now held complete and absolute power over him.

* * *

'I missed you this evening, my lady,' Freiderick said softly, as he and Nadia walked arm in arm along the terrace outside the parlour, the night air cold and uninviting.

She smiled coyly. 'I was a little tired after our talk this afternoon,' she confessed, a blush covering her pale cheeks. 'I decided to rest for a while. When I woke, I had already missed the better part of it, and dressing caused further delay.'

'And very elegant you look,' he offered, appraising her open gold gown embroidered with red. He smiled down at her, clearly pleased with himself. 'I hope I did not tire you too much,' he asked with a chuckle.

Nadia laughed at his insinuation in order to cover her distaste for his remark. 'You tease me so, sir,' she murmured, glancing around her. 'Though I am not too tired to enjoy the remainder of the evening with you,' she soothed, glancing around her.

'Are you quite well, my lady?' Freiderick asked gently, noticing her troubled expression. 'You have seemed most distracted this evening.'

Nadia stared at the ground as they walked, unable to find the words to answer; her mind was a cacophony of thoughts and needs, and she found herself lost amongst them with no guidance to be had.

'Should we return to the house?' Freiderick queried, concern in his voice.

She glanced up at him, desperate to find the strength to do what had to be done. 'I should wish to continue our walk, sir,' she said quietly, unable to bear the tenderness she saw in his blue eyes.

Freiderick nodded his agreement, though looked uncertain at the change in her demeanour. 'As her lady wishes,' he allowed, stepping with her down the terrace steps and onto the gravelled pathway that wound through the extensive gardens of her family's opulent home.

They strolled in silence for a time as Nadia struggled with the words she knew she must speak. Alex had given her the strength to see past her fear and restrictions, yet now, without him standing by her side, she felt alone and deserted; her strength failed her and she cursed her own weakness.

As they wandered further along the path, the night around them grew darker, the warm lights of the house growing dimmer as their distance increased. In no time, they were encased in pure blackness, their supernatural eyesight their only salvage in the dark.

Freiderick chuckled knowingly. 'I believe our privacy is more than covered, my lady,' he murmured, clearly mistaking her intentions.

Nadia pulled her arm free from his, unwilling to mislead him any further.

'I wished to speak to you in private, my lord,' she said quietly, continuing to walk along the path until it branched off towards the hedges and trees.

Once she knew they were completely sheltered from view of the house, she turned to face him, hating herself more for what she knew had to be said.

Freiderick's brow creased with concern. 'Something troubles you,' he observed, reaching out a hand to her.

Nadia stepped back, unwilling to take his offer of comfort. She found herself unable to look into his expectant eyes and instead focused her attentions on his blue silk cravat.

'My dearest sir,' she murmured, uncertain of her next words. 'I...' She cursed her own cowardice, her thoughts still so chaotic after the afternoon's events, both with Freiderick himself and with Alex.

A gentle chuckle escaped Freiderick's lips. 'My lady, I admit I have never known you to be so speechless.'

His amusement at her discomfort only served to solidify her determination.

She met his gaze. 'You do not know me at all,

sir,' she pressed, her chin raised in defiance. 'You only assume to, for which reason I fear I cannot continue with our union.'

Freiderick's gaze darkened with uncertainty. 'I do not appreciate such jest, my lady,' he stated firmly. 'What is this folly?'

Now the words had left her lips, Nadia felt unable to speak.

'I demand to know,' he snapped, making her flinch.

Yet she quickly found her resolve, disliking his tone. 'What *I* demand, sir, is that you listen to what I have to say.'

Freiderick sneered. 'You do not make demands of me, my lady,' he said harshly.

'My sister does as she pleases,' Alex sneered as he stepped from behind a nearby tree. 'Something which in all the time you have held her betrothal you have failed to realise, or nurture.'

Nadia stared at her bother, unsure of what he expected of her now; with no waistcoat, jacket or cravat, Alex looked primed for a fight. By her own admission to herself, she was now nervous.

Freiderick growled. 'Damn you, sir, this is none of your business.'

Alex's gaze narrowed. 'My sister's welfare is, and will always be my business, sir,' he snarled, pushing himself away from the tree. He took a step forward. 'I declare you a fool if you think otherwise.'

Freiderick stood his ground. 'I will not remain

here to be insulted so,' he said, looking once more to Nadia. 'I am finished with such childish games. Are we to forget such words spoken and return to the house, my lady?' he asked, his tone almost commanding her accord.

She remained silent, glancing intermittently between the two men.

Freiderick growled with impatience. 'I require that you answer me,' he pushed.

Nadia frowned at him. 'And I require my *freedom*, though I do believe I am left wanting in that regard, sir,' she spat, an unusual anger building within, giving her a renewed strength of will.

Freiderick chuckled lightly. 'Your freedom?' he asked, a sneer to his tone. 'And what, pray tell, would you use this freedom for? Playing like a child with your brother, who seems intent on controlling you much more than I?'

A snarl played on her lips. 'You may mock, sir, if you will, but it will not change what is truth. I am rebuked by yourself for laughing too loudly, for dancing too much or spending too much time with my very own twin, as if you feel challenged by his very presence. It is yourself, sir, who treats me as a child, and none so suffocated was there such as I.'

She glanced at Alex, something she determined to be pride in his eyes. The memory of their kiss was still all too vivid in her mind, the shame wiped away by the promise of having him by her side for eternity; the one man who would never judge her, never suffocate her. The one person in the entire world who understood her like no other ever could, bonded by blood as they were. In that one moment when their lips had touched, they had united beyond any earthly words or union; they were forever one.

She glanced back at Freiderick, his gaze fixed on Alex.

'Can you not see, my lady, how your brother is jealous of his own sister's happiness? He fears the abyss of the world without her and so seeks to poison her very thoughts.'

Nadia growled, determined to put an end to the conversation; she had already made her thoughts and feelings clear. 'You speak to my brother, sir, in a most disagreeable manner. He is your lord on this land, and you should show him the proper respect,' she said harshly, drawing Freiderick's gaze back to her, his surprise evident. 'You forget to whom you speak.'

Freiderick stared at her, unsure of her expression. He released a low sigh. 'My dear, in two days we are to be wed. I am willing to forget such words spoken here if you will relinquish your childish obsession with your brother.'

She looked at him, unable to think past the cacophony of thoughts that flooded her mind. Had she felt this indifferent to him before she had given herself to Alex? Had the blood she shared with her twin been the downfall of her feelings for Freiderick?

She could no longer be sure. There was only one thing she *was* certain of, and that was the unbreakable bond she shared with Alex; she would never allow anyone to come between that, ever. If she did, she would truly have nothing.

'No, sir, I will not,' she said simply, her words forcefully final. 'If you will not abandon your quarrel against my brother, sir, then I cannot see a way forward. You do not truly understand the nature of our bond, nor have you tried. It goes far beyond that of anyone's imagining.' She tilted her chin, a challenge in her eyes. 'Our power goes beyond that of our elders, who are millennia older than ourselves. You would do well to remember such things, and not provoke a quarrel which you are not suited to win.'

Frederick stared at her, his expression instantly betraying his discomfort at her words. 'I will not be threatened thus,' he stated firmly.

Alex took another step closer to his rival, his dark gaze unforgiving. 'My sister does not threaten, sir,' he said flatly. 'If you believe she does so, then you know nothing of her.'

Frederick focused entirely on Alex, his chin raised in challenge. 'I know much of her, my lord, as any man should know his wife,' he said sharply, his confession forcing a gasp from Nadia.

She stared at him, shocked at how easy he would divulge such information; it was irrelevant that Alex already knew the truth.

Alex snarled at him, his sharp teeth bared in aggression. 'How dare you, sir,' he spat.

Frederick did not back down. 'Do you doubt

my words, my lord? I can assure you they are true.'

Nadia stared at the ground, mortified; here was a man she had agreed to marry, to honour and obey, yet there was no honour in his behaviour now. He was willing to divulge the details of their intimacy at will to win an argument, destroying her reputation in the process. With his easy confession, she was a lady no more, but a mere wretch and a whore.

Alex took several steps forward, placing himself between his sister and Freiderick; his gaze never left that of his rival.

'Whether you tell the truth or not is not material, sir,' he growled. 'You dare to make such a mockery of my sister's honour while she stands in your presence?'

Freiderick's gaze was dark and scathing; there was disgust written all over his face. 'She has no honour, my lord. She gave herself freely to me, out of wedlock, and then dares to relinquish our betrothal.'

Nadia found herself unable to speak, her hands shaking by her side; her entire world had suddenly become tainted and mired in filth; she would be an outcast, loathed by society and shunned by all those she held dear.

Freiderick sneered. 'I see now that you have indeed done me a great service in refusing my betrothal, my lady. I cannot be certain of your knowledge of a man before I, and I should not wish to marry such a diseased specimen.'

Alex snarled, his anger raging. 'How dare you,' he bellowed. 'That is my sister you address, sir, and you will show her the necessary respect.'

'Respect?' Freiderick choked with a laugh. 'Respect? Am I to respect a woman who makes free with gentleman and cavorts with her own brother?' he asked, disgust filling every word.

'You are to respect a lady in her own household,' Alex said vehemently.

Freiderick squared his shoulders. 'I see no lady, my lord,' he sneered. 'I only see a conniving little whore.' He glared at Nadia, his gaze dark.

'I warn you, sir,' Alex growled, stepping towards the man who dared to insult his sister so; he was not about to let this man cause her any undue pain or embarrassment. 'You will apologise for such insults,' he said between clenched teeth.

Freiderick glanced at Nadia and sneered. 'I will not, sir. She has no honour, other than that of a whore who wallows in the filth. Be damned to you.'

Alex saw red. He was not prepared to allow this man to destroy his sister's reputation, or to have her name dragged through the mud to satisfy his damaged ego. In a flash of movement, he reached out and grabbed Freiderick's arm.

Freiderick struggled, spinning on his heels and landing a punch against Alex's cheek.

Alex reeled for a moment from the unexpected blow, aware of Nadia's gasp as the blow was struck.

Alex straightened himself, snarling with a ferocity he had never used against another of his kind, his anger overriding everything; his only desire was to see his rival destroyed and his sister set free.

Freiderick's face paled, his breath forced from his lungs as Alex took hold of Freiderick's throat, squeezing it until the man began to choke.

Alex struck out whilst still holding him by the throat, landing a powerful punch to Freiderick's face, the blow drawing blood from the man's cheek.

With disgust, Alex dropped the injured man to the ground as if he were tainted with disease, snarling his authority.

Freiderick looked up at Alex, shock and fear in his soulless eyes. He wiped the blood from his cheek, his hands shaking.

Alex hunkered down in front of him casually, his expression like stone. 'You dared to threaten my sister's honour in her own home,' he snarled, his face drawing close to Freiderick's; every word he spoke was filled with venom. 'Your life, such as it is, will not be missed.'

Freiderick's body shook with fear as the enormity of Alex's words sunk in, yet he was frozen to the spot.

Alex lunged at Freiderick, pinning him to the ground. The man tried to raise his arm against his assailant, but he was no match for the strength of the twins.

Alex bit into the flesh of Freiderick's forearm.

The man cried out in pain as Alex ripped the flesh from his arm, blood flowing from the wounds onto the man's jacket and the grass beneath him.

RETRIBUTION DARKENED

Freiderick tried in vain to beat Alex off, yet he was powerless against the strength of a Demeter.

Alex grabbed hold of Freiderick's injured arm, squeezing the wound hard, maximising the pain.

Freiderick screamed, desperate to pull away. 'Please, my lord, I beg of you let me be,' he wept, his voice shaking.

Alex glared at him, a victorious gleam to his haunting green eyes. 'You defiled my sister,' he whispered close to the man's face. 'And neither I nor my sister will mourn your passing beyond that of our respectable duty.'

With one last look into Freiderick's fear-filled eyes, Alex lunged, grasping his shoulders and biting hard into his throat, ripping the skin from one side to the other.

As Freiderick gasped and choked from his wounds, Alex pushed him against the blood-soaked ground.

Placing his hands either side of Freiderick's face, he snarled as he snapped his neck sharply to one side, breaking the man's spine.

Alex sat there for a moment, his mind racing. Then, in a final move to destroy the body, he punched hard into the man's chest, breaking his ribs and grasping his heart, ripping the bloody muscle from the cavity.

Alex dropped the organ to the ground as he stood away from the body, his clothes and skin soaked in blood.

He stared at the body numbly, studying it for a moment. His heart was pounding ferociously as he considered what he had done.

He wasn't sorry the man was dead.

He could still taste the blood in his mouth; it made him feel sick.

The chilling scream from behind him had him turning to see Nadia staring at the body by Alex's feet, the blood saturating the grass.

He took a step towards her. 'Nadia—'

'What have you done?' she asked, her voice quivering and her gaze still fixed on the body.

Alex took another step towards her, noticing how she flinched at his movement. 'I did what was necessary, my love,' he said calmly. 'He dishonoured you to satisfy his own damaged ego. I could not allow him to do such a thing.'

'He is dead,' she said, almost mechanically.

'He is,' Alex confirmed, taking one last step towards her to close the gap between them. He reached for her hands, yet she pulled away as she stared at the blood on his fingers.

'I did what I had to do to protect you,' he insisted.

'I did not think you would do such a thing as this,' she admitted, her voice still trembling. 'I brought him to you in order that he should walk away from us and I be freed,' she said, almost monotonously.

'You *are* free, my love,' he confirmed.

There was something deep inside her that made

Nadia doubt those words. 'I did not wish him dead.'

'I did not wish it thus,' he pressed, uncertain in that moment of the truth of his own words. 'He insulted you. I could not allow such a thing in your own home.'

Alex did his best to wipe his hands on his breeches. After what felt like an eternity, she finally looked at him, her emerald eyes still wide with shock.

'What are we to do?' she asked, her voice an octave higher than usual. 'Pray tell me, Brother Mine, what are we to do? Look at him,' she said, her eyes darting back to the body on the grass, both the throat and heart discarded.

Alex followed her gaze, realising he felt no emotion over what he had done to his rival; if anything, he felt invigorated, a sense of power flowing through his body, the like of which he had never experienced.

Nadia's voice broke their silence. 'He is a noble of another country, Alex. I was promised to him, and now he is dead. Such things start wars,' she said, her voice trembling with fear.

Alex took her face in his bloodied hands, forcing her to look at him, his own gaze firm and severe. 'Do not heed such thoughts, my love,' he said. 'You were within your right to reject his betrothal and he showed you abject disrespect in return. He was no gentleman.'

'But—'

'You are a Demeter, Nadia,' he said forcefully. 'Do you forget such a fact? Your very name holds sway across all of Europe. It may not be spoken, but we are feared, and you know what I speak is true.'

He watched as her face became placid, and he knew his words were finally making sense to her.

'We are *feared*, Nadia,' he emphasised, his gaze intense as she stared into his eyes. 'He died at my hand as I defended your honour, and I will allow no man to question my intentions.'

They both knew it was a power they had never sought to exploit, as it had never seemed necessary; they were a rarity among their kind, with powers even beyond those centuries older than themselves, and for that alone they were feared, albeit with respect. Together, they held a supremacy over those who knew them and their family name, and Alex was starting to accept that in order to be truly free, they needed to embrace such influence.

'What are you saying, Brother?' she asked carefully, her voice and expression softening.

Alex offered the smallest of smiles. 'We will of course deal with such a tragedy as is seen fit, and help our families come to terms with events. But once we have done so, I do not wish to see you in mourning, my dearest love,' he said firmly. 'We will leave Romania, and travel as we discussed earlier. We will leave our elders to mourn if they so wish and continue their customs, but we will travel and experience life. We have eternity before us, Sister, and I do not wish to spend it trapped in our homeland, playing our dutiful parts because that is what society expects of us. Who is to say what changes the world will see over the next century or two... would you not prefer to be in the thick of it?'

'But what would the family say?' she asked quietly, unsure. 'What would they think?'

Alex shrugged. 'To hell with that,' he spat. 'We both know they are suspicious of our closeness, yet not one of them would dare to question us thus.'

'They will know for certain once we leave, my love,' she pointed out.

'Then let all be forgiven, for even if they know they will not seek to distract us. Their fear will prevent them from confronting us. Our will is our own, my love, to do as we wish. That is our freedom.'

Alex smiled down at her, holding her close. 'We no longer need to steal moments together, my love,' he whispered gently. 'You no longer have to feel despair at your predicament.'

She studied his face for a moment, and slowly a smile formed on her rouged lips. 'You truly would do anything to protect me, wouldn't you?' she asked.

He smiled at her warmly, placing a tender kiss against her forehead. 'My promise to you is set in stone, my love,' he assured. 'I will be by your side for always, no matter what.'

Nadia kissed his lips gently, staring up at him, the body of her former fiancé and lover callously forgotten.

Alex smiled.

'No matter what,' he whispered.

1908

'I do so love your dress, Nadia,' Csilla beamed across the large table in the great banqueting hall of Vallakia.

Nadia smiled sweetly at her cousin. 'Thank you, my dear,' she said cheerfully. 'It is the current fashion in Paris. Katarina had it sent as a gift.' She shifted in her chair, surreptitiously glancing around her. The room was filled with laughter and chatter, the large banqueting table a bustle of activity as servants came and went, attending to the political guests as well as family. Human politicians were not to Nadia's tastes, but she tolerated them for no other reason than enjoying a party.

The great banqueting hall of Vallakia was one of the rooms Nadia loved the most. The main feature of the room, other than the extensive table, was the enormous stone fireplace, ornately carved with the crests and emblems of the family. The pure white of the stone contrasted against the richness of the oak panelling, all of which was also carved with ornate patterns. A large fire burned in the grate, bathing the room in a soft inviting glow. Wrought iron sconces lined the walls, as they did in the great hall.

At the far end of the room, a large stain-glass window loomed over the guests, the bright reds and yellows contributing to the ambience of the room, along with the large crystal candelabra situated along the table, the candles offering their glow to the diners.

The opposite wall to the fireplace was home to several tapestries, collected by the family over the years, depicting various points of history and family occasions.

Csilla envied her cousin's dress; it was of the latest style of empire-line, deep crimson with black lace overlay. It was daringly low-cut, with a red beaded neckline. It made her feel suddenly self-conscious in her own light blue gown, which paled in comparison.

'You are lucky to have seen so much of the world,' she offered in her cheery voice; Csilla was treasured in the family for being such an optimistic happy soul, and she almost seemed to light up a room upon entering it.

Nadia shrugged with a smile. 'Paris is not that far,' she pointed out, glancing up at Alex who was seated two seats away on the opposite side; he looked her way and winked with a smile.

'That is true,' Csilla agreed with a laugh. 'Yet I have never been further than the borders of Hungary and Romania.'

Nadia studied her cousin for the moment, hiding

her distaste. Csilla wasn't a direct cousin, but related through several marriages; in a family of immortals it was often difficult to keep track of lineage, and it was easier to acknowledge members by the simplest titles.

Csilla was one of the youngest members of the family. She had matured in her late twenties, and was now no older than eighty, and although she was so young, she had met and married István only a year ago; it was a decision that Nadia thought far too serious for such a young woman.

After the tragedy of Freiderick's death, Nadia and Alex had left Romania to travel the world. The family had been shocked by the events, and yet, just as Alex had said, were unable to do anything against the will of the twins. Although the truth of their intimacy was still unknown, they knew the elders suspected their relationship involved more than what was deemed moral.

For one hundred and eighteen years, the twins had travelled the world, leaving the family to deal with the scandal of Freiderick's death. Nadia's honour had been preserved, as the truth of her indiscretion had died along with Freiderick, and the family were able to use their power, as well as that of the twins, to explain his death as the result of a serious attack against the twins. The shame was therefore passed onto Freiderick's family, and the Demeter's supremacy was not to be questioned again among polite society.

Alex and Nadia had spent time travelling across

RETRITBUTION DARKENED

Europe, staying in Paris for several years, where they cheerfully witnessed the execution of Robert François Damiens, who had tried and failed to assassinate King Louis XV. In 1762, they moved across the Channel to England, where they spent time in London, exploring both the richness of the upper classes and the bawdy back streets, where those whom society shunned lived their lives in squalor. From there, they travelled to America in 1767, witnessing much of what would come to be known as the American Revolution, and then moved onto South America in 1789. After several years, they moved on to the young country of Australia in 1798, where they enjoyed the bloods of the colonies, before crossing China, and finally Russia in 1836, when the country invaded Wallachia in Romania.

In all the time they were away, the pair became truly devoted to one another, able to spend every moment by each other's side. They shared each other's blood without fear of discovery, and tasted blood from every continent.

Nadia continued her playful teasing of her victims, her favourite scenario being enticing various men at parties before luring them to their inevitable fate. Slowly, Alex became part of her endeavours, the pair finding a deviant amusement in playing with their prey, the maliciousness of their actions growing as time passed; high society, and the debauched habits it harboured, became the ultimate hunting ground.

The pair finally returned home in 1868, the

world having changed dramatically; they had witnessed the arrival of locomotives, automobiles and photography. Wars had changed alliances, and some remained uneasy.

Their parents naturally made a fuss over their return, their mother tearfully happy they were safe and well, the truth of their travels remaining undisclosed.

To their parent's delight, the pair remained in Romania, the next forty years passing without thought.

'So which was your favourite place on your travels?' Csilla queried, her voice pulling Nadia back from her reverie.

Nadia smiled at her cousin, glancing briefly at Alex before answering the question. 'It is difficult to pick just one place,' she admitted. 'The world is so full of wonder, my dear. You really must see it one day, then you will be able to make your own decision on *your* favourite place.'

Csilla laughed, the sound melodic. 'I do hope to do so one day,' she confessed, her cheeks blushing slightly. 'Both myself and István wish to travel, but Mother believes I am too young.'

Nadia suppressed a grimace. 'Yet your mother was happy for you to get married so young?' she asked, glancing further up the table to where her aunt sat talking with another guest; Nadia had never liked the woman, who was married into the family, not a true blood relation. Nadia looked back to the young lady opposite her.

Csilla blushed once more. 'It was an advantageous marriage,' she said quietly, her face brightened by a smile. 'Yet one with a happy ending. István is a wonderful man, so kind and caring. By the time we were married, I was in love with him, and he with me. We are very happy,' she beamed.

Once more, Nadia resisted a sneer; Csilla really was a little princess in her own fairy tale world. She had been protected all her short life, and knew nothing of the world outside of the walls her family had built around her.

Nadia smiled sweetly, glancing across the table at Alex who was grinning at her.

Can this girl be any more pathetic? she asked mentally.

Now, now, my love, play nicely, he teased, a chuckle filling his mental thoughts.

'Was it advantageous for *you*?' Nadia asked flatly, watching the young girl's face flush.

Csilla tried to shrug off the comment. 'I'm sure I don't know what you mean?' she said, innocence in her tone.

Nadia stared at her. 'Was it advantageous for *you*, or for your mother?' she said, more plainly. 'I am surprised she did not introduce you to my brother,' she admitted. 'He is, after all, one of the country's most eligible bachelors.'

Csilla glanced down at her hands, clearly uncomfortable. The girl seemed unable to answer.

Nadia smiled. 'You are blushing, my dear,' she teased. 'I suspect you find my brother attractive?'

Csilla glanced up the table towards her mother, who was too busy with her own conversation to notice her daughter. She glanced back at Nadia, her words failing her as her cheeks continued to flame.

Nadia chuckled. 'Forgive me,' she said softly. 'I did not mean to offend you or cause you distress. I only meant that you are so young. There is much of the world to see and explore, and you should do so.'

Csilla relaxed, a smile brightening her gentle face. 'I should very much love to hear about your travels,' she said with excitement.

Nadia forced a smile. 'Then perhaps we can recount them together after dinner,' she offered, noting the girl's enthusiasm.

Nadia picked up her napkin, dabbing at her mouth as she glanced along the table to Alex, aware of him smiling at her.

'You are amused, Brother dear?' she asked mentally, her words filled with her own amusement.

'Simply glad to see you making friends, my love,' he chuckled, teasing her.

There was a glint in her emerald eyes that only her twin could understand.

'Why are we even here?' she asked.

'It's not like you to dislike a party, my love,' he teased mentally, laughter in his words.

'I cannot think of a time when I was more bored,' she grumbled.

RETRIBUTION DARKENED

'*Dear little Csilla is not proving very interesting company?*' he queried, his words full of amusement.

She glared at him, though her thoughts betrayed her amusement at his playful teasing. '*I could not have asked to share conversation with anyone more dull,*' she said. '*The creature is a poor sheltered wretch. I almost feel sympathy for her.*'

'*Almost?*' Alex tested with a grin.

'*She is nothing more than a child, allowing herself to be manipulated by those around her into a marriage that no doubt benefits our dearest aunt more than it does her daughter. It is pitiful.*'

Alex's chuckle sounded in her mind. '*Believe me, the dutiful husband is not much better company,*' he said, nodding his head in the direction of István, who sat on Alex's left, chatting to the guest next to him.

Nadia studied Csilla's husband for a moment. She had been introduced to him only hours before, aware of the attentions he lavished on his wife like a lovesick adolescent.

She watched as he chatted with another guest, his light-brown hair short, as was the fashion these days; by her own admission, Nadia did not miss the powdered wigs.

His brown eyes were soft and full of affection, his face handsome in its softness. He was not much older than Csilla herself, barely a century old, and his youth was evident in his look and manner.

A smile tickled the corners of Nadia's lips as she thought on the things he still had not learnt of life, and all the things she would be willing to teach him.

Nadia turned her attentions back to Csilla, who had been talking away to her about her wedding and the honeymoon, which had taken the couple no further than Budapest.

It was a subject Nadia was keen to dismiss.

'I simply must know where you got your dress, my dear,' she purred, with a gentle smile. 'It makes you positively radiant.'

Csilla blushed and smiled. 'I am afraid it pales in comparison to your own,' she said quietly.

Nadia dismissed her comment with a swipe of her hand. 'Nonsense, my dear. It is the perfect shade for you.' She glanced at Alex. *'Pale and inconspicuous,'* she added mentally.

Alex grinned. *'You are wicked, my love,'* he teased.

She ignored him, smiling kindly once more at Csilla. 'I am so glad you are staying at Vallakia for the next week. It will give us plenty of time to spend together.'

Csilla grinned at her cousin, her face brightening with the prospect. 'I would truly enjoy that, Nadia. Thank you.'

'I look forward to it, my dear,' Nadia said, glancing at Alex.

He smiled at her. *'What are you up to, dearest?'* he asked.

Her words purred in his head, her eyes gleaming with mischief.

'All in good time, my love. All in good time.'

RETRIBUTION DARKENED

* * *

'I do so love your family home, Nadia,' Csilla commented cheerily, pulling gently on the reins of her chestnut mare with her gloved hands as the two women enjoyed their afternoon ride; the day was extremely overcast and a thick frost had blanketed the surrounding countryside throughout the day.

Nadia smiled warmly, running her gloved fingers through her own ebony stallion's mane. 'You really are too kind, my dear, truly' she said gently. 'You have had nothing but favourable things to say about your visit here. We will be sad to see you leave.'

Csilla's smile dimmed slightly, all too aware that her stay at Vallakia was drawing to an end.

Nadia observed the girl, forcing a smile. 'I insist you must return as soon as you are able, my dear,' she said cheerfully, withholding a sneer.

Both Nadia and Alex had spent almost every day with the girl and her husband during their weeks stay at Vallakia. It had been an eventful few days that had seen the small group spending their time divided between Vallakia and the Demeter family home.

As the days had passed, Csilla had become almost devoted to Nadia, spending as much of her time with her cousin as she could.

In return, Nadia had offered her cousin every attention, pandering to her every whim.

In her usual, cheerful manner, Csilla had

constantly mentioned her love of everything she saw and did at Nadia's side, and in turn it fed Alex's teasing of his sister, which he enjoyed once they were both away from the attentions of the young married couple.

His teasing sought only to encourage her mischievousness, which grew with each passing day.

Csilla brightened at Nadia's words. 'Oh, I do hope so,' she said, excitement filling her tone. 'I have so loved my time here.'

Nadia suspected Csilla had enjoyed the time spent away from her controlling and somewhat overbearing mother; it definitely seemed that the girl's life was extremely restricted at home. Nadia almost felt sorry for the poor creature.

Almost.

She smiled. 'I dare say the time you have been able to spend with István while here has been a treasure,' she said softly. 'No doubt privacy is in short supply at home,' she added with a wink, insinuating her meaning.

Csilla blushed, a short giggle escaping her lips. 'I'm sure I do not know what you mean, dearest cousin,' she said, unable to meet Nadia's gaze or prevent her shy smile.

Nadia laughed. 'I am sure you do, my dear,' she teased. 'You can confide in me,' she pushed gently.

Csilla swallowed her embarrassment, finally meeting Nadia's gaze. 'It has been nice to have the time together,' she said finally.

Nadia once more held back a sneer. The child's innocence was sickening; Nadia doubted the girl was a very effective wife in practice.

'Only nice?' she probed softly. 'I would imagine a young couple such as yourselves would be rampant,' she teased.

Again, Csilla's face turned red.

Nadia smiled to hide her disdain. 'Forgive me, my dear, I am only teasing you.'

Csilla laughed gently. 'I do not take offence.'

'I am glad to hear it,' Nadia chuckled.

'Do you regret not marrying?' Csilla asked innocently.

Nadia seethed internally, though she smiled graciously. 'Regrets are not worthy of time,' she purred. 'Herr Walser dishonoured me and my kin. He was not worthy of entry into our family.'

Csilla looked across at Nadia as she gently steered her horse. 'I'm sorry,' she said sadly. 'I am sure you will find someone worthy of you one day,' she assured cheerfully.

Nadia looked at her. 'You are a true champion for love, aren't you, my dear?' she asked with a smile.

Csilla blushed. 'So I've been told,' she admitted coyly. 'Though I suppose I am lucky to have found it so completely.'

Nadia scrutinised her. 'You put much faith in a marriage so young,' she stated. 'Forever is a long time.'

Csilla smiled. 'And yet not long enough with a

husband as loving as mine.'

Nadia withheld a sneer. 'I envy your conviction, my dear,' she said with a smile, aware of Csilla's smile faltering.

Nadia supressed a grin; it was not the first time she had touched on the subject over the last few days, and despite Csilla's cheerful dismissal of Nadia's concerns, it was clear the young woman was troubled by Nadia's words.

The two women continued their ride in comfortable silence around the grounds of the Demeter family home.

They steered the horses through the main gate, gently trotting through the stone archway and into the main courtyard.

As they passed the large stone steps of the front entrance, Nadia spotted Alex walking with István.

She smiled at her brother.

Excellent timing, my love, she told him mentally, amused by his knowing smile.

She steered her horse closer to the steps, Csilla dutifully following.

'Good afternoon, gentleman,' Nadia purred as they approached her on the steps.

Alex smiled at his sister, both men bowing to the women. 'Good afternoon, Sister. How was your ride?'

'Exhilarating,' she answered, looking down at him. Her gaze caught that of István and she offered him the smallest of mischievous smiles. She was amused when he could not maintain her gaze for very long, shifting his attentions to his wife.

Alex nodded. 'Quite so,' he grinned. He smiled at Csilla, approaching her horse.

Nadia watched her brother and Csilla, aware of the young woman's nervousness around Alex. Nadia smiled. She knew Csilla found Alex attractive, another point she had tested frequently over the last few days, and he had willingly helped, lavishing attention on the young woman whenever he could.

István bowed to Nadia, taking a step in his wife's direction.

With a gentle smile, Nadia used her mental agility to spook her horse, the animal rearing in terror at the images and sounds she sent directly to its mind.

She gasped in feigned surprise, a shriek escaping her lips as István turned her way, instinctively holding up his arms to the rearing animal as it whinnied and snorted.

'Easy, boy,' he soothed, grabbing hold of the reins as they flapped about the beast's neck. 'Easy,' he whispered, slowly coaxing the horse back to its normal, placid state. Its eyes were wide, full of panic, yet under István's gentle touch and soothing voice, it calmed.

After another minute to ensure the horse was completely placid once more, István held out his hand to Nadia, offering to help her down.

'Are you okay, my lady?' he asked gently.

Nadia slid out of her side-saddle, her expression

full of gratitude. With her feet on the ground, she withdrew her hand from István's slowly, maintaining his gaze.

'I am indeed, kind sir, thank you.' She looked around at her horse, taking the reins in one gloved hand whilst rubbing his nose with the other.

She glanced back to István. "I don't know what got into him. He is such a beauty, yet I do declare the hum of a bee would startle him so. Thank you kindly for coming to my aid.'

'I'm glad to have been of assistance, my lady.'

'You were indeed, sir. Csilla is most blessed to have such a hero by her side,' she said, aware she was pandering to his ego; perhaps something his wife failed to do, considering the glint in his brown eyes.

Nadia glanced towards Alex, who was helping Csilla from her saddle as they spoke.

She turned her attentions back to István.

'You have such a charming wife, sir,' she said, her smile full of warmth. 'I do declare you must be the sweetest couple I have ever met.'

István blushed slightly, glancing across to his wife who stood talking to Alex. 'You are too kind, my lady,' he said. 'We have truly enjoyed our stay here. You and your family have been so kind and welcoming.'

Nadia swiped a gloved hand through the air. 'It is our pleasure, and you are both welcome here anytime,' she smiled.

'You are very generous, my lady,' he offered.

She held his gaze for a moment, her smile widening. 'Indeed, I am.' Then, threading her arm through his, she led the way towards the house.

'Come now,' she said cheerfully. 'We must discuss plans for your next stay.'

* * *

Csilla played the piano beautifully, there could be no doubt of that. Her thin fingers glided over the keys effortlessly and her voice carried lightly across the room as she sang.

Nadia smiled at her as she leaned against the side of the black grand piano in the drawing room, listening intently.

Her parents, Alex, and István were all sat together in the room, chatting amongst themselves quietly so as to not interrupt Csilla's singing.

Nadia glanced across the room at her brother and smiled, mischief in her eyes.

He returned her smile, knowing her plan.

'Did you accomplish what you wished for this afternoon, dearest?' he asked mentally, teasing in his tone.

Her gaze shifted from her brother to István as he sat speaking to her father. Her smile widened.

'Let's just say the seed was finally sown. The rest will play out later, as we agreed,' she purred.

István looked up towards his wife as she continued to play; his gaze momentarily caught

Nadia's.

She smiled sweetly at him, yet her eyes were filled with suggestion.

He looked away quickly and she grinned to herself. He had been far too easy to reel in over the last few days, and over the course of the afternoon she had continued to pamper his ego gently, never making it obvious, and yet stroking it just enough to have him warming to her even more as the day had progressed.

Csilla finished her song and Nadia was the first to applaud her, along with the rest of the company in the room.

Csilla blushed with the attention. 'Thank you,' she said cheerfully, her face alight with happiness.

Nadia smiled at her. 'That was beautiful,' she offered. 'You are a very accomplished player.'

'You certainly are,' Alex agreed as he approached the piano.

Csilla smiled coyly under Alex's attentions. 'Thank you, my lord,' she said bashfully.

Alex leaned against the side of the piano, his gaze maintaining hers for a moment before she looked away. He smiled at her. 'Will you play something else for me?' he asked eagerly.

Csilla nodded, a blush forming on her cheeks. 'It would be my pleasure,' she said. She seemed to think for a moment before clearly settling on another song.

As she began to sing, Nadia excused herself from

the side of the piano, smiling at István as she stepped away, allowing Alex to keep Csilla's attentions during her song, which was every bit as tuneful as the first.

As Nadia crossed the room, heading for the door, she maintained István's gaze. There was uncertainty in his eyes and perhaps a small amount of fear.

Nadia smiled, her eyes gleaming.

She didn't say a word as she left the room, knowing that he would soon follow.

* * *

István stood by the stable door, staring at her.

Delicate shadows danced across Nadia's face from the oil lamp hanging from the wall, her emerald green eyes glowing with mischief. Her raven-black hair fell loosely about her shoulders, her body enveloped in a purple satin kimono.

The smallest of smiles danced on her red lips.

'Good evening, sir,' Nadia said softly, her voice warm and inviting.

István was nervous, she could tell; no doubt he had never felt the intensities of the passion he was now experiencing, not even on his wedding night.

Tentatively, he stepped into the darkness of the stable, his gaze never leaving hers.

'I shouldn't be here,' he said eventually, his voice rough and unsure; there was no conviction in his words.

'Yes, you should,' she answered simply. 'You

would not have come otherwise.'

He took another step towards her, proving her words to be true.

Without speaking another word, Nadia untied the belt of her kimono, maintaining István's gaze. Then, with a gentle movement, she shrugged out of it, the delicate material falling to the floor of the stable, exposing her naked body.

István finally broke her gaze, his own wandering down over her perfect skin, illuminated by the glowing light of the lamp. He stared at every inch of her body as if it were the first time he had ever set eyes on a woman.

The silence between them growing, his gaze finally met hers once more.

She smiled at him, her eyes full of seduction. 'No one need ever know,' she whispered gently. She bit her lip.

Her words seemed to cement his decision and he closed the gap between them, taking her naked body in his arms, kissing her hard. His tongue sought hers hungrily, his hands grasping her naked buttocks, pulling her body against him harder.

She groaned as she felt his erection and his desperate need for her, her hands tugging at his clothes, ripping open his shirt.

He pushed her back against the hay bales, a gasp escaping her lips as the sharpness of the grain pricked her skin.

She fumbled blindly with his trousers, freeing

him easily as he lowered his head to kiss her breasts and nipples, making her groan louder.

She combed her fingers through his brown hair, forcing his head up, kissing him once more ferociously. He grasped her thighs, lifting her so that she buttressed his hips.

He entered her sharply and she cried out with pleasure.

* * *

'I will be truly saddened to leave this place,' Csilla said sombrely, walking slowly by Alex's side along the terrace.

He looked down at her and smiled. 'If Nadia has her way then you will be back here in no time at all,' he soothed. 'It has been a joy having you stay with us.'

'Thank you,' she said softly, not quite meeting his gaze; Alex was unsure if she was intimidated by his presence or attracted to it. It amused him.

'You have both made us feel so at home,' she added.

Alex continued to smile at her, disguising his amusement. 'As it should be,' he said gently. 'You are family, after all.'

They stood in silence for a moment, Csilla constantly gazing around her as if she were intending to memorize every brick of the buildings around her, the darkness broken by the light emanating from the many windows, the warmth of the home within too inviting to resist.

Alex glanced at her. 'Will you walk with me?' he asked quietly, offering her his arm.

Csilla looked at him and then over her shoulder towards the house, her expression uncertain. 'István will wonder where I've got to,' she said, unsure.

'I'm sure we will not be missed for a few minutes,' Alex coaxed smoothly. 'And you can enjoy the grounds once more before you leave in the morning.'

He knew the notion would appeal to her, and he struggled to hide his amusement when she beamed at him.

'I should like that,' she said. 'I dare say a few minutes would not hurt. You are most kind.'

She took his arm with a smile, her hold tentative.

They walked together in silence for several minutes, leaving the light of the terrace and heading into the shadows, strolling along the path that led across the lawns of the Demeter family home. They walked past the lake, which glittered in the moonlight, the surface disturbed occasionally by the fish beneath.

The moonlight barely disturbed the shadows that danced across the paths and buildings as they made their way past the orchards. The cool air around them was crisp and filled with the scent of the trees and flowers that decorated the grounds.

'It is a beautiful evening,' Alex said gently, his steps slowing slightly as they headed towards the stable blocks.

Csilla glanced at him. 'Indeed it is,' she agreed.

Alex sighed to himself, the sound melancholy. 'I shall miss you when you leave,' he admitted. 'You have made my recent days so joyful.'

Csilla blushed and he smiled. She didn't answer him.

Alex stopped in his tracks, standing in front of her. She paused and looked up at him, uncertain.

He smiled down at her softly. 'You are very quiet, my dear. I hope I have not spoken out of turn?' he asked carefully.

She looked down at the ground beneath her feet. 'Indeed not, my lord. Your words are very kind.'

He hooked a finger under her chin, feeling her stiffen at his touch. He forced her head up so that she looked at him. He studied her for a moment, amused at how she did not push him away.

'Have you enjoyed your time here with me?' he asked, his tone hopeful.

She was unable to meet his gaze, her cheeks still flushed red. 'Indeed, my lord,' she said, her voice weak.

'You are very beautiful,' he whispered, trying hard to hide his amusement at her discomfort.

She blushed once more. 'Thank you, my lord,' she said, unable to quite meet his gaze.

Alex brushed her jaw with his thumb, feeling her shiver beneath his touch. 'István is a very lucky man,' he murmured, moving ever-so-slightly closer to her.

She met his gaze, unable to speak.

'I hope he knows how lucky he is,' he said, his thumb brushing past the edge of her lips.

Csilla stood there, staring at him in silence, her eyes full of uncertainty.

Alex took another step closer until he could feel the heat of her body. 'I should treasure such a beauty as yours if you were my own,' he whispered.

She drew a ragged breath of anticipation, her gaze now transfixed by his own. She trembled as he drew her into his arms.

'My lord, I...' Her voice trailed off as he brushed his lips against hers, his kiss fleeting as he breathed against her skin

Alex withheld his smile as she failed to object to his advances, aware that she was too intimidated to move.

He trailed gentle kisses along her jaw, her breath shuddering as he pulled her tighter into his arms.

He ran his tongue along her neck, her body shivering in his illicit embrace.

'I wonder,' he breathed against her skin, 'whether you taste as delectable as you look?' he asked, smiling to himself as she still refused to answer him.

Tentatively, he bit into her throat, hearing her gasp as he broke the skin. Her hands gripped his shoulders as he drank from her, her blood sweet and innocent, just like her; it had nothing of the devastating seduction and ecstasy of Nadia's blood.

He licked at the wound, kissing the area gently, his fingers teasing the bodice of her dress, her hands shaking as they continued to rest on his shoulders. Her breathing was erratic.

He continued to kiss her throat, trailing kisses down to the top of her cleavage, her gasps of restrictive pleasure humouring him as he ran his tongue along the top of her breasts.

His hands pushed against her skirts as she stood before him, feeling for the shape of her legs.

Csilla released a gentle moan and Alex stood to look at her, brushing another fleeting kiss past her lips.

'You taste simply divine, my lady,' he lied. 'I should like to sample more,' he said with a smile, knowing she knew what he was suggesting.

She looked up at him, a strange fear in her eyes; the fear of her own arousal.

She opened her mouth to speak but Alex kissed her, hard, his tongue seeking hers in a soft and seductive kiss, until he felt all the fight leave her body.

She leaned into him, welcoming his kiss and his touch, her heartbeat pounding.

Alex licked her lips as he grinned down at her. He took her hands in his. 'Come with me, my love,' he soothed, his voice tempting, promising her release.

Nervously, she followed him as he led her along the path towards the stable, the smell of the horses filling the air around them.

As they approached the stone building, Alex pulled her to him once more, kissing her feverishly. He backed her against the stone wall, his hands caressing her breasts through her dress.

She groaned into his mouth and breathed a ragged breath as he moved his mouth to her neck once more, licking at the blood that still slowly seeped from her wound; she was nowhere near as powerful as the twins who could heal in an instant.

She pushed her body against his and he looked up at her, brushing another kiss past her lips, promising her more.

Without a word, he took her hand and led her to the door of the stable block.

He pushed gently on the wooden door, allowing it to swing open slowly.

Inside it was dim, the light from the lamps barely chasing away the shadows.

Yet it was not too dark to see the two people who already occupied the stable.

Csilla moved to Alex's side, a gasp escaping her lips as her gaze fell upon her husband, his trousers around his ankles and his shirt cast onto the floor.

A woman's legs straddled his waist, her cries of excitement and pleasure filling the air as her identity remained hidden behind István's thrusting body.

Alex glanced to Csilla by his side, her cheeks stained with tears as she watched her husband making love to the mystery woman. Her mouth moved as she tried to find the words to speak, yet no sound emerged.

Alex did not move or make a sound; he simply remained a spectator to the whole debauched scenario.

'How... how could... you?' Csilla finally said, her words raspy as they left her mouth.

István froze in his movements and drew a shuddered breath.

Alex instantly saw him trembling.

Slowly, István glanced round, his face paling as his gaze met that of his wife.

Csilla sobbed as she stared at him, yet her face whitened and her whole body convulsed as she finally saw the woman who had ensnared her husband.

Nadia glanced around, her face flushed and her breathing unsteady. She was naked, sweat glistening on her porcelain skin.

Csilla collapsed to the ground at Alex's feet in shock.

Her husband quickly pulled up his trousers and took several hurried steps towards her, yet she withdrew from him as if he carried some disease, her body shaking.

'How could you?' she asked once more.

'I am so sorry, my love. Please forgive me,' he begged, standing in the middle of the room.

Nadia straightened herself as Alex crossed the room to stand by her side, helping her back into her robe. He slid the material over her body tenderly and stood behind her, placing his hands on her shoulders as the pair of them watched the sorry couple before them.

'Forgive you?' Csilla asked, staring at István. 'You ask for forgiveness after what I have just witnessed?'

'I was not myself,' he reasoned. 'I lost control of my senses.'

Nadia laughed. 'You seemed to be in full control, sir,' she said firmly.

Csilla looked up at the woman who she had considered to be a friend. 'You would lay with my husband?' she asked. 'Why would you do such a thing? I confided in you.'

'So you did,' Nadia said simply. 'I believe I tried to warn you of such... instances.' Her smile was as hard as her glare. 'You were far too naive to believe in my words.'

'You did this because I would not listen?' Csilla asked incredulously, her tears flowing freely as she sat crumpled on the ground.

Nadia offered no apology in her words. 'You are but a child and you put too much faith in what you do not have the capacity to understand. You are not without sin yourself this night, I believe?' she accused harshly.

Csilla shivered as she continued to cry on the floor, her wide gaze focussing on Alex, shame marring her innocent face.

Nadia sneered. 'You find my brother to be most agreeable, it seems,' she taunted cruelly.

Csilla sobbed brokenly. 'Stop it, I beg you,' she pleaded.

István stared at his wife, disbelief on his face. 'Is this true?' he asked.

He stepped towards his wife, ignoring the way she pulled away from him. He turned her head to one side, choking on a sob of his own as he saw the bloodied wound on her neck.

She looked up at him, her eyes filled with a deep shame and sorrow.

István turned from her and stared at the twins. 'How could you do this to her?' he asked, glaring at Alex.

Alex laughed, unable to help himself. 'You dare ask me such a thing?' he asked, his tone cold. 'I find you defiling my sister like some damn ram in rut and you dare question me?'

Alex took a step towards István, amused when he saw the man flinch. 'I sampled your wife, yes.' He grinned at the man before him. 'Though I can appreciate why you would prefer my sister,' he said cruelly.

Tears filled István's eyes as he stared between the twins, beaten.

Nadia glared at the crying woman on the floor. 'We attempted to open your eyes, my dear,' she called across the room. 'If it were not this night, then you still would have been betrayed. Do you know how easily he came to me?' she asked coldly, eyeing the husband with contempt. 'And how easily did you give yourself to my brother? You put too much faith into marriage so young, my child. So simply he betrayed your trust, with no thought for you.'

Csilla sobbed. 'I believed you to be my friend,' she said brokenly.

Nadia stared at her, no emotion in her eyes. 'Then your belief was misplaced, my dear,' she said coldly. 'As was your belief in him, it would seem,' she said, pointing at István as he stood in the middle of the room, a beaten and pathetic excuse for a man.

'Your ego did this, sir,' Nadia taunted harshly. 'So desperate were you to know that you were still desired as a man that you betrayed your eternal partner without thought. Your lack of devotion is nauseating, to say the least. You should be ashamed of yourself.'

István looked up at her. 'You enticed me,' he argued. 'I forgot myself.'

Nadia laughed and Alex grinned at him.

'Do you hear yourself, sir?' she asked. 'You would dare to lay all the blame at my feet? As you would my brother for his sampling of your wife? She gave herself to him, and you came to me willingly, with no coercion. Your conscience did not sway you otherwise, which says much about your character.'

She looked at Csilla as she lay crying on the floor. 'You should have heeded my warning, child,' she hissed. 'A ring on your finger does not guarantee loyalty and a man's ego will always come high above your needs.'

RETRIBUTION DARKENED

With a heavy sob, Csilla pushed herself to her feet and ran off into the night.

Nadia and Alex began to laugh.

István turned on them. 'You did this on purpose, yet to what end I do not know.'

She glared at him, malice in her eyes. 'Because we could,' she said simply. 'She put up no fight against a man she barely knew, and she needed teaching of your flaws. She had you on such a pedestal and I only sought to test your worthiness of such a place. Needless to say you failed,' she smiled, the action devoid of any warmth.

In a flash, she crossed the room, grabbing his arm, her sharp nails piercing his still bare flesh.

She glared at him, hatred in her eyes. 'You are *worthless*. You'd betray everyone if it suited your needs.'

Alex watched her carefully, her words stirring memories within him and he could no longer be sure if this game had not in some way been about Nadia proving all men would betray, just as Freiderick had betrayed her confidence and honour.

'You make me sick,' she continued. 'You are vile and deserving of no one's devotion.' She pushed his arm away as if his very touch would taint her.

Without another word, he grabbed his shirt from the floor and ran out of the stable.

Nadia watched him go, a smile on her face.

'Did you enjoy yourself, my love?' Alex asked, sliding his hands around her waist, feeling her naked body beneath the thin fabric.

She turned in the circle of his arms, looking up at him, her emerald eyes gleaming with mischief.

'Were you jealous, dearest?' she teased, stroking his cheek with her finger.

He could not deny her words. 'It is never easy seeing you in the arms of another,' he admitted.

She laughed playfully. 'Then next time perhaps our roles should be reversed. I think you are due a little fun.'

He chuckled along with her, kissing her softly. 'I intend to hold you to that.'

'Do come on, Nadia,' Alex sighed with a smile. He steadied his horse as it grew restless with him sat in the saddle.

Nadia rolled her eyes. She pulled on her riding gloves as she stood next to her horse, the stable boy holding onto the reins.

'You are very impatient, do you know that, Brother?' she teased with a smile.

He laughed. 'I have been patient all morning, dearest,' he pointed out.

She shrugged. 'I could not find my riding boots,' she said simply.

Alex shook his head, knowing it was fruitless trying to argue with his sister; he would never win.

'There,' she said, playfully holding up her

gloved hands. 'I am ready.'

'Finally,' he chuckled.

Nadia stepped towards her horse.

'You did this,' István bellowed at her from across the courtyard, his loud and public outburst attracting the gaze of every servant walking the grounds. 'This is *your* fault.'

Nadia paused by her horse, glancing at up at Alex as he sat atop his own stallion. She rolled her eyes as he smiled at her, his gaze unsure as he looked across the yard at István.

As he approached the pair, Nadia turned to him.

She sneered, disliking what she saw. The man was an emotional wreck, tears staining his cheeks. His clothes were dishevelled as if he had slept in them, and his very demeanour was of a broken man.

István pointed at her as he approached, his tearful gaze accusing. '*You* did it,' he repeated, his voice shaking. 'It's *your* fault.'

Nadia sighed. 'What is, my dear sir?' she asked nonchalantly. 'Speak clearly.'

He glared at her, sobs escaping his lips. 'She's... why did I do it...?' He mumbled something incoherent, staring at the ground.

When he looked back up at her, he began crying again. 'You have done this.'

Nadia leaned in closer, amused at the way he recoiled from her. 'I do not remember having to coerce you, dear sir,' she pointed out, her words and tone venomous. 'You came willingly, with the very slightest amount of temptation. You would have tasted that most forbidden of fruit, whether with me or another, at another time and place. Your betrayal is on your own head, and I will not be bothered by it any longer.'

She turned to face her horse once more, prepared to step up to the saddle, when István grabbed her arm harshly.

She turned back to him, her gaze cold. 'Unhand me, sir,' she hissed.

Alex, who had been watching the scene carefully, now glared at István, his teeth bared in a snarl.

'Do as the lady says,' he warned.

István chuckled sadly, releasing her arm; he had no fight left.

'I do not see any lady, my lord,' he reprimanded, ignoring the hiss that emanated from Nadia's lips. 'My darling wife was a lady, the greatest there was.' He stared at nothing in particular, his voice empty of emotion. 'She was...' His voice trailed off as he crumpled again into sobs.

He looked at Nadia sadly. 'How will I ever gain her forgiveness now?' he asked, falling to the floor in a heap.

She moved her feet away from him, staring at the pathetic creature on the floor beside her. 'Of what do you speak?' she asked him.

When he didn't answer, she turned to Alex. 'Am I supposed to know the answer to such riddles?'

He shrugged. 'They are but the rantings of a

madman in the throes of his own guilt. Let us ride as we have planned, Sister.'

Nadia made ready to mount her horse.

Her foot in the stirrup, she paused at the calling of her name from the entrance of their home. She recognised her mother's voice.

Nadia sighed with frustration, glancing at Alex. 'Are we not intended to ride this morning, Brother?' she asked, gritting her teeth.

He smiled at her, glancing towards the house. His smile vanished as he saw his mother standing in the doorway across the courtyard, her beautiful face marred by sadness. She beckoned him towards her.

He frowned, confused by her behaviour.

Nadia stepped back down from the stirrup, seeking her brother's reassurance.

'What is wrong, Alex?' she asked carefully.

'I do not know, dearest,' he said softly, dismounting his horse.

He took Nadia's gloved hand in his own, holding it firmly; there was something in his mother's gaze that unsettled him.

Together, the pair crossed the courtyard, hand in hand; they had become more comfortable with outward gestures of affection, and no longer cared that the servants stared or whispered.

Their joined hands did not escape Aurelia's attention as they approached, yet she withheld any vocal judgement.

Alex tried to read the expression on his mother's

face, yet failed. There were tears in her emerald eyes, frightening him.

'What is it, Mother?' he asked carefully.

'What has you so distressed?' Nadia added, concerned for her mother's paleness.

Aurelia looked between them, finally finding her voice. 'Something has happened,' she said sadly, her voice breaking with emotion. 'It is Csilla... something has befallen...' She trailed off, unable to continue.

Alex released Nadia's hand to embrace his mother and comfort her.

Nadia stared past her mother towards the staircase, where one of the maids sat on the stairs in tears. Nadia took a step towards the young girl.

Alex watched her carefully.

Nadia approached the staircase and proceeded to place her foot on the bottom step. The maid looked up at her.

'Please, Miss, do not go up there. It is not a sight for a lady,' the young woman implored through her sobs.

Nadia ignored her. According to a growing number of people she was no lady; perhaps they were right. She climbed another few steps.

Alex continued to watch her.

'Go to your sister,' Aurelia whispered, squeezing his hand. 'Shoulder this burden together.'

Her words confused him and she was unable to look him in the eye, he realised.

He stepped back from her, not uttering a word.

Heading for the staircase, he followed his sister.

At the top of the stairs, the pair found their father, instructing the steward of the household to contact Csilla's family.

His gaze caught that of his son and daughter, yet it remained impassive as he continued with his conversation.

Outside a door, there stood two maids, both in tears. It was the door to the room Csilla had shared with her husband.

Alex glanced at Nadia, taking her hand.

Without speaking a word, the pair pushed past the maids, neither of the girls meeting the gaze of the twins.

Nadia was the first to enter the room, the curtains at the windows pulled as they always were when grief was upon a family.

A brief gasp escaped her lips as she realised she had stepped into something viscous on the wooden floor, her riding boots stained with the glistening blood.

Alex placed his hands on her shoulders as he approached behind her, supporting her as he stared over her shoulder at the body on the floor.

His blood ran cold, the air around him feeling too close and suffocating; the anger, grief and pain were almost too palpable in the air.

Csilla's body was still, lifeless on the floor. Her hair was fanned around her face, the lengths covered in her own blood. Her eyes had been closed by someone – their father maybe – yet Alex instinctively knew they would have been open when her body had been discovered.

He released Nadia's shoulders; she didn't make a sound or move at all. She simply stood there, staring. There was no emotion on her face.

He took a step forward, taking care not to slip as his boots disturbed the coagulating blood on the floor.

As he approached Csilla's body, he could plainly see the hilt of a dagger protruding from her chest. It was the same hunting dagger she had told the twins she had given István as a wedding present; the one with their initials engraved on it.

Alex swallowed past the lump of emotion that formed in his throat; she had used it to pierce her own heart, her suicide an act of pure heartbreak.

He glanced back at Nadia, her face still set like stone as she stared at the dead woman on the floor. Her gaze flickered to his, something unreadable in her eyes.

For a moment, he found himself unable to hold her gaze and he looked away, unsure of the emotions that flooded through him; regret, guilt maybe?

He stared back down at Csilla. In all their travels and the games they had enjoyed at other people's expense – some of which had been pretty depraved – never had he felt guilty or as ghastly as he did now. Before, they had only ever really played with humans, the inevitable death something to enjoy rather than regret.

Now, someone innocent had died as a result of their games; a member of the family had killed themselves, heartbroken and shattered by the dreadful deeds they had performed.

His mind was too full of images of her death to fully comprehend what that meant.

He tore his gaze away from the body on the floor, looking around the rest of the room. The curtains had been closed as a mark of respect for the dead, but other than that the rest of the room had not been touched.

From the overturned chairs and the smashed mirror on the dresser, Alex assumed she had had an angry outburst, no doubt in tears, destroying the room around her; the smashing of the mirror the only way she could destroy the vision of herself in such a tormented state. She could clearly no longer bear to look at herself, no doubt as a result of his seduction and Nadia's vicious words.

Bottles and other glass trinkets women use were smashed across the dresser and over the floor. Even the bedding had been slashed with the dagger before she had turned it on herself, goose feathers covering the sheets and pillows, some having fallen on the floor, covered in her blood.

It was then he noticed the piece of paper on the bed. He took another few tentative steps towards it, retrieving the paper.

He turned to Nadia, her gaze fixed on the body

still on the floor. She didn't look upset, or hurt, or even repentant. There was no expression or emotion in either her face or her eyes. There was nothing. It was if the body wasn't there at all.

'There is a note,' he said, surprised at how rough his voice was. He cleared his throat, watching as Nadia slowly looked up at him.

'Should I read it?' he asked, unsure.

Nadia's face remained impassive. 'Words will do her no good now, Brother,' she said, her words void of any emotion.

He glared at her. 'Do you feel nothing for what has occurred here?' he asked, incredulous.

She stared at him, a darkness entering her gaze. 'What is done is done, Alex,' she said, her words harsh. 'Do you wish me to fall on my knees and grieve uncontrollably? Would that suit you?' she asked, almost with a sneer.

'*We* did this, Nadia,' he hissed.

She shrugged. 'She stabbed herself. We played no part in that.'

His gaze narrowed. He had never known his sister to be heartless, but he could find no other word for her behaviour.

'We played our part in the actions that drove her to such a demise,' he said. 'Are you proud of that?'

Her gaze narrowed. 'I am no monster, Brother,' she warned. 'She learnt a hard truth about life, but she chose to end her it this way. That was not my doing.'

'You seduced her husband,' he pointed out.

'And you drank from her and led her to the very spot where I was doing so,' she spat back. 'You did not have to do such a thing, Alex, so I refuse to allow the blame to fall entirely at my feet.'

'We destroyed her life, such as it was,' he argued. 'She was devoted to him. Who were we to question that?'

'Not devoted enough that she would think twice about allowing you to seduce her. And he was not devoted to *her*. It took me but hours to turn his head. He was willing to give up everything for a quick fumble. We did her a favour.'

He couldn't listen to her words anymore; they taunted him of the truth. He had indeed willingly played his part in the game and could not be a hypocrite and place all the blame on his sister.

He turned his attentions back to the note.

'Read it if you will, Brother,' she said, still standing in the same spot. 'Her words will not give either of us absolution.'

He knew she was right, yet he needed to know the thoughts that had gone through Csilla's head before her death; he owed her that much.

With a deep breath, he allowed his gaze to roam over the perfectly formed handwriting:

My gratitude to you, Lord Victor and Lady Aurelia Demeter, for your hospitality. You have shown me every care, and I am truly thankful to you for showing me such kindness. I envy you so, for you have found each other's light in such a world of darkness. I pray you endure.

Alas, my heart is broken and I fear it will not be mended again. There is no light to be had in the darkness in which I find myself. It is a disease, spreading its wickedness as it disguises itself with the face of kindness. It corrupts and manipulates, and I fear there is no sanctuary to be had from such an unrelenting monster. I see its mockery still, in every reflection of myself. It has made me wretched.

There is a darkness within, evil to its core. No warmth is there within its cold heart, nor shall there ever be, I fear.

Alex glanced up at his sister.

She continued to glare at him, that same emptiness in her green eyes. It was cold and somehow unrelenting.

He continued to read the note, the final words chilling him to the bone:

For those who find such joy in the destruction of others there can be only sorrow, and a misery so deep it can never be eroded. The darkness has destroyed me, but in time it will destroy itself, for no happiness can be had from such evil hatred.

1912

Alex sat at the window, looking out at the Parisian streets below, the rain interrupting his view as it streaked down the glass pane. He stared at the letter in his hand, unsure of the words he had read.

He turned the paper over in his hands several times, unable to fathom the chaos of thoughts going through his mind.

It had been three years since he had last seen his sister, and he had ignored every one of her letters.

His guilt had forced him to flee the family home in Romania. The devastation caused by their games and Csilla's death had been too much to endure. The tragic loss of such a rare, happy soul such as Csilla had plummeted the family into a severe mourning, such was the heartbreak of her passing. Her family had vented their anger at the twins, accusing them of murdering their precious daughter, and the rest of the family, including the elders, had given both himself and Nadia space, barely speaking to them. The coldness of their rejection had hurt terribly.

He had distanced himself from his sister, her eyes still containing that same empty coldness he had seen the day they had discovered Csilla's body.

Unable to bear the guilt and sorrow any longer, he had fled Romania less than two weeks after the tragic event, without warning and without telling his sister where he was going.

He had wandered for a while, allowing himself to come to terms with his own guilt by himself.

After many months, he had written a letter home, to his parents only, informing them of his safety and wellbeing, yet not divulging where he was, which at that time had been Italy.

He had spent a number of months in Venice, and then Milan, before travelling to Switzerland, where he resided for almost a year.

Eventually, via Norway and England, he found himself in Paris, where he took refuge with his cousin, Katarina de Seraucourt. At least fifty years older than himself and Nadia, Katarina was welcoming and kind, her open-minded approach to life ensuring Alex found sanctuary from judgement and reproach.

His time in Paris seemed to fly by, as Katarina made him ever part of the high society she so enjoyed, her parties valued amongst the rich and powerful of the city.

Alex softened somewhat while staying with his cousin, and he finally sent another letter home, addressed to both his parents and Nadia, informing them of where he was and that he intended to stay for as long as Katarina would have him, which, of course, she was open to.

It was not long after this letter home that tragedy struck the family once more, surfacing Alex's guilt over Csilla's death all over again; István, driven mad by the loss of his wife and the reasons behind her death, had killed himself by putting a pistol in his mouth.

As if to compound Alex's guilt, he soon received a letter from his sister, her words begging him to speak to her directly, telling him she could no longer bear the separation.

He had not answered.

Several weeks later he had received another letter, and then another, and so it had been for the past few months, every letter growing more and more desperate, shorter and shorter, all of them with one core wish: *forgive me*.

His gaze fell to the latest letter he had received only two days ago, the words having been read too many times to count:

Dearest Alex,

My letters will not cease to arrive. I am wretched without you, or of any word from you. I have to know that you do not hate me, and your silence only continues to feed my anxiety of such fears.

I pray you can forgive me for what has

passed, for if you cannot I do not see how I should go on. It was not my intention to drive you away and I know now that this is what my actions have done.

Please, dearest brother, forgive me and return to our home once more, so that we can be twins, as we always have been. I miss you and cannot exist in this cold emptiness without you here. You have been by my side since before our birth and this is a separation I can no longer abide.

I pray to hear from you soon.
All my love, always
Your sister, Nadia.

Alex swallowed past the lump that had formed in his throat, as it did every time he read one of her letters.

He stared at the paper in his hands, unable to form coherent thoughts.

'That letter should be made of solid gold, you seem to treasure it so,' said a voice behind him, soft teasing in the words.

Alex turned to look at Katarina as she stood in the doorway to the parlour, her navy and white empire dress striking against her pale complexion and light brown hair, which was pinned up on the crown of her head.

He offered her a small smile, yet did not answer.

She chuckled, stepping into the room quietly.

'You needn't be coy, Alex,' she said gently. 'Do you think I do not know that you keep all her letters?'

He glanced at the floor, embarrassed she had seen through him so easily. 'I do not have the heart to destroy them,' he admitted.

She looked at him cynically. 'And yet still you will not answer her,' she said gently, a statement rather than a question.

He looked up at her. Katarina was too shrewd for her own good, just like Gabriella.

He shrugged. 'I would not know what to say,' he admitted.

Katarina took another step towards him, placing a supportive hand on his shoulder. 'Perhaps you could try saying sorry for allowing her to suffer so in silence for so long?' she suggested.

He nodded, admitting she was right. 'I know I am wrong to do so. I am as much to blame as she.'

'Then is it Nadia you are running from, or your own guilt?' she posed, no severity in her gaze.

His own gaze dropped to the floor, knowing that she was right on both counts.

Katarina removed her hand from Alex's shoulder and took a seat next to him by the window. She sighed gently.

'I have had my own correspondence,' she said gently. 'Gabriella wrote to me a number of days ago. Nadia has gone to stay at Vallakia for a while, on the suggestion of the elders. It was felt she needed the sanctuary of its walls,' she added. 'She has been there these last two years.'

Alex didn't answer.

Katarina looked grave. 'Gabriella mentioned that Nadia spends all her time alone, every minute of every day. She speaks to no one, and will see no one but you. She lives in seclusion and silence. The family are worried for her wellbeing,' she said, quoting Gabriella's letter.

Alex stared at her, her words hurting him. 'I did not realise,' he said, shocked. 'I knew from her letters to me that Nadia sought forgiveness, but I did not realise she had isolated herself so.'

She watched him carefully. 'It is such a pleasure to have you here, Alex, truly it is, but do you not feel that perhaps you should return home? Perhaps both of you have learnt a valuable lesson through this tragedy. No good will come from this enforced separation, and you are only hurting yourselves. None of this will bring Csilla back,' she said sadly. 'What is done is done, and you must both learn to live with that burden. Perhaps you will find it easier to shoulder it together.'

Her words brought tears to his eyes. 'I'm not sure if I can,' he admitted.

'You must forgive her, Alex, as she must forgive you. It is the only way you will forgive yourselves.'

Her words were true, he knew, yet the thought of going back and facing his sister scared him more than anything.

Katarina studied him for a moment. 'I do not

pretend to understand your bond, Alex. No one in the family can. You are both unique, and I know of your relationship,' she admitted to him, no expression on her face.

He stared at her, wide-eyed. 'I did not realise...' he began.

She shrugged, interrupting him. 'I do not judge what I cannot understand, mon cher,' she said with a smile. 'If I was of a judgemental disposition, I would not live in Paris,' she teased.

He smiled at her, though his words were serious. 'I wish I understood it myself,' he admitted. 'It scares me often.'

She smiled softly, taking his hand supportively. 'Unfortunately, that is a burden the two of you must share alone, for not many will understand it, and few will support it. I will only warn you to be careful, Alex,' she said seriously.

'Perhaps in that respect it is best I do not return home,' he sighed.

She chuckled. 'Yet you know, deep down, that you must,' she advised. 'You cannot run forever. It will drive you mad.'

She studied him for a moment, before laughing to lighten the sombre mood their conversation had caused. 'Of course, you will be missed. Your handsome presence has not gone unnoticed,' she teased. 'You certainly caught the eye of a couple of young ladies who were at my last party. I'm sure they would appreciate your attention.'

Alex smiled at her. 'I will consider it,' he said sadly.

Katarina sighed, releasing his hand and standing from her seat. 'You torment yourself so, mon cher,' she whispered. 'If I did not know any better, I would say the bond you share with your sister means you feel her despair also, which cannot be any good for you.'

She stepped towards the door, glancing over her shoulder at him as he still clutched the letter in his hand.

'Write to your sister, Alex,' she advised solemnly. 'I fear you will not feel at peace until you do.'

1914

It had been a journey of mixed emotions, unsure of his feelings regarding his home and his sister. Alex felt uneasy returning to the scene of Csilla's death, and was equally worried in regards to his sister's reception of him on his return.

His journey through Europe was wary, due to the growing threat of war; he sensed the world was to change indescribably.

Once home, he had been welcomed by his parents, and they had confirmed Nadia's condition to him, his unease growing.

He had then travelled up to Vallakia, preparing himself to set eyes on his twin once more.

Vlad and Gabriella had welcomed him warmly and had tried to prepare him for his first meeting with Nadia after so long.

Now, standing in front of the door to her room, he found his hands trembling.

He stared at the wood before him, his mind a myriad of thoughts.

He had written to her eventually, on Katarina's advice, though it had taken him several weeks of procrastination to do so.

He had spent hours writing and rewriting, unsure of his words.

He had assured her he was to return home, though gave no indication as to a timeframe.

He knew he was a coward, yet his guilt was still too raw, even after years away from home.

Taking a deep breath, he finally knocked on the door.

Quietly, she admitted him entrance to her room, the place she had barely left since he had been away, except to hunt.

He pushed open the door, unprepared for the sight of his sister before him.

To see his sister so bereft shocked him to his core. She looked untidy and her clothes were dull and lifeless; unlike the glamour of her appearance he was used to. Her long raven hair was plaited and fell down her back, no styling evident. Her emerald eyes seemed devoid of any emotion.

She sat on a chair by the dresser, a garment of some sort draped over the mirror, hiding her reflection.

She stared down at her hands that were clasped in her lap.

She did not look up as he entered the room.

He closed the door softly behind him, unable to look away from the pitiful creature before him. His guilt in that moment amplified, knowing it had been his absence and silence that had driven her to such a state of isolation.

'You blame me,' she said simply, her voice hoarse from lack of use. 'You hate me for what I did.' There was no emotion in her voice. It was as if she were speaking to her own shadow.

Alex was unsure if she were addressing him or not.

He went to her side regardless, dropping to his knees beside her so that he was able to look up into her face.

She still refused to look at him, her body remaining as still as a statue.

'I do not blame you and I certainly do not hate you,' he said, hoping she would believe him. 'I needed time to accept what had happened. It was a shock. I did not anticipate the outcome of our actions.'

'Nor I,' she said quietly, 'though I am punished for it by silence and abandonment.'

'I did not do what I did to punish you,' he assured her. 'I thought the space would help us both with our grief. I was misguided,' he admitted.

'You have come back to me then?' she asked. 'You are not only in my dreams? I have had so many of your return, only to be cruelly awakened and informed that it is no more than fantasy.'

Alex felt devastated in that moment, knowing he had caused her such suffering; he had promised to never leave her side and he had broken that promise in her hour of need.

'I am here,' he said firmly. 'I am here for you, Sister. But our games have ruined lives when they had no right to do so. *We* had no right. I cannot condone to myself what we have done.'

With his words, she wept, deep-felt sobs that shook her entire being.

He hated seeing her in such a state and knew that image would haunt him forever. She looked so wretched, and without further thought he took her in his arms.

She clung to him tightly.

'I am sorry, dearest,' he said gently. 'I am sorry for leaving you, and hold true to my promise to never leave your side again, unless you yourself send me away. I forgive you, as you were not alone in your duplicity.'

She continued to weep and he continued to hold her.

'I promise we will deal with our grief together,' he affirmed, though unsure how easy it would be; images of Csilla dead on the floor still haunted his dreams occasionally, as did the empty look in his sister's eyes.

'I hope so,' she managed to say through her sobs.

He soothed his hand over her hair.

'I have missed you, Brother,' she said quietly.

'And I you, dearest,' he assured her, placing a tender kiss against her forehead.

She turned her head against his shoulder, her mouth brushing against his collarbone, her breath hot against his skin.

He pulled away from her, unable to meet her gaze.

She looked at him, hurt and rejection shining in her eyes. 'Will you not share blood with me, Brother, now that you have returned to me?' she asked.

Alex stared at her. 'I fear I cannot,' he admitted quietly, feeling as though he was betraying her somehow; Katarina's words still resonated with him. 'It was our blood indulgence while travelling that twisted our games into something more sinister,' he explained, aware of the emptiness returning to her eyes.

'You are my sister and I love you,' he assured. 'But I fear I cannot continue with you after such a tragedy as that which has befallen us.'

Nadia stared at him for a moment, no emotion on her pale face.

Without a word, she turned away from him, facing the covered vanity mirror once more.

'Please leave me be, Brother,' she said quietly, her voice void of emotion.

Alex felt the sting of her dismissal, but pushed himself to his feet. 'As you wish,' he said, heading slowly for the door.

As he grasped the door handle, he turned to look at her.

'Will you be returning home with me, Sister?'

he asked.

    She refused to look at him.
    'I wish to stay, my lord,' she said, her words flat. She stared down at her hands.
    'There is nothing there for me now.'

1916

The flames in the hearth crackled loudly as the wood split and burnt, the warmth filling the large room.

Alex stared into the dancing flames as he stood by the mantle, his forearm resting against the polished mahogany. The room of the inn in which he stood was surprisingly quiet, given the bustle of the bar down below.

Outside, the sky grew dark as thick, rolling clouds blew in from the mountains and small drops of rain began to appear on the window pane.

The room itself was warm and inviting, the majority of it dominated by the large four-poster bed along one wall. The rest of the furniture consisted of a dresser with a large mirror, a table and two chairs, and a small chaise longue. There were many pictures on the walls of Carpathian scenery, as well as oil lamps.

The clock on the mantle chimed six o'clock.

He stared at it for a moment.

Time had passed too slowly these past two

years and the world around him was changing as war raged on. Only recently, his own homeland had been drawn into the conflict, with Transylvania playing host to battles over its ownership.

As the months passed, Nadia's absence had been a separation Alex had endured with difficulty, the absence of his twin – his other half – disturbing him on a much deeper level than he had anticipated. It had been different when she had gone travelling all those years ago, for they had been young and untainted by the harsher realities of life outside the walls of their own little realm.

Now, after so many years of being together and sharing blood, it made the separation hard to suffer, a deep need and craving eating away at him with every passing hour of every empty day.

Their separation was a hard sacrifice and his need for his sister's blood never left him; the remembered taste of it woke him during his sleep and he thirsted for it while hunting. Yet somewhere within him he found the strength to resist it, though he was never sure how he found such resistance.

Yet the refusal of her blood seemed to dampen his need for her in any way other than that of a sister, and he felt content with his feelings; his dreams often resurfaced lost needs, yet he struggled through, trying to ignore them. It was not always easy, but he managed.

She had punished him with silence at first. After six months she had finally sent him a letter, admitting her understanding of his decision.

They had written to each other often over the last eighteen months, yet had not seen one another; the elders had felt this was best given past events.

Alex was grateful to his elders for helping Nadia overcome her demons; her letters had begun to portray a woman happy with her situation, her attitude much calmed.

Her words had told him of her time at Vallakia, spending her time with Vlad and Gabriella, as well as many other family members as they came and went, including Monika, and her letters were always filled with enjoyment and kind words.

Then, after several months, the tone to her letters had changed. His parents had not seemed to notice a change in their own letters, and he was unsure whether he imagined the slight anger to her words. Her letters mentioned the elders less and less and on occasion, when they did feature in her writing, her attitude against them was easy to see.

Knowing Nadia the way he did, he assumed she had simply grown restless and bored. Her mischievous nature had reared its head once more and she had resumed her rather vicious ways of killing; seducing men and boys to their deaths and detailing her movements in her letters. He found most of it amusing, imagining her actions all too clearly; it had made him miss her all the more, wishing he could be by her side during the hunt.

He was lonely for his sister, for her

companionship and her presence; the house had felt so empty without her.

As he had so many times over the last few years – and more so since his return – he looked to his wrist, absently tracing the vein under his pale skin where his sister had so many times feasted from him.

After all this time he still craved her blood, the sweetness and tantalising taste of it; it was a taste that created so much ecstasy within him, no human blood had ever satisfied him quite the same.

Looking at the clock on the mantle once more, he reached into his pocket and took out a folded piece of paper. He unfolded it with a smile.

It was a note from Nadia.

My Darling,

Time moves too slowly as I wait in earnest to see you once more, and I accept your invitation willingly.
I will meet you as requested at the inn in the village of Orlat, on the eve of Wednesday.
I miss you greatly, my love, and look forward to seeing you once more.

All my love
Nadia.

Alex grinned as he looked at the clock, placing the note back into his pocket. He could not wait until this evening, when he would get to see his sister once again.

Over the last month, unable to bear the separation any longer, the pair had agreed to meet, in secret, in Rășinari at night to share the hunt.

It had been a joyful reunion, one where they had both shed tears of happiness to once again be able to embrace and talk, and laugh and joke. Most of all, it had been an immense joy to have her by his side as they had hunted.

They had then agreed to continue meeting in secret, every few days in various locations, sending additional notes to each other as well as the letters so that no one grew suspicious. It was the very clandestine nature of their meetings which made them fun, and brought the childish joy of playing games back into their lives.

Alex felt alive once more.

He sucked in a sharp, ragged breath.

Two nights ago, on their last meeting, Alex had helped Nadia entice a gentleman and his wife to their deaths, the kill coming after several hours of chatting and laughter with the victims at their own party in a very stylish home on the outskirts of Saliste.

At the end of the evening, as the guests had left, Alex and Nadia had turned on their hosts, killing them viciously in front of one another.

It was a thrill Alex had not felt in a long time, and although deep down he knew he should feel ashamed of his actions, all he really felt was exhilaration and power. The pair had laughed together in the blood-soaked room, the adrenaline fuelling them both.

They had embraced, and as he had wiped a strand of hair from her face, Nadia had grasped his wrist and bit into his flesh, shocking him.

She had given no indication of her desire for his blood, and had not mentioned it once in all her letters and notes.

Yet the joy of her feeding from him once more engulfed him in a need so great it had made him weak. He remembered their times together while travelling so long ago, and all the nights spent indulging in each other's blood like some depraved dessert after feasting on a human.

She had allowed him to take a small taste from her own wrist, her cheerful teasing almost too much to abide.

They had separated then, she returning to Vallakia and he back to their family home, the taste of her blood on his lips and tongue.

His need for her had overwhelmed him and he had almost immediately written her a note, inviting her to meet him in Orlat, in the inn, where they could be alone.

Her answer had arrived yesterday and he had read her note over and over again, the excitement of her acceptance building until he was sure he could no longer contain it.

Now he stood here in the inn, awaiting her arrival, and he could no longer tolerate the desire that flared within him.

The clock on the mantle chimed half past six.

As the final chime sounded, a light knock came at the door.

Alex did not have time to answer as it opened and Nadia stepped into the room, the lace veil from her black hat covering her face.

She closed the door behind her without a word and turned to face her brother, pulling back the veil so that she could smile at him. She wore a long, fur-trimmed bottle-green coat, which she removed along with her hat, not uttering a word to him.

Alex took a sharp breath; she looked stunning.

Beneath her coat, she wore an evening gown of the deepest blue satin and velvet with lace sleeves, the empire-line dress daringly low cut. Her sleek raven hair was pinned away from her face.

He looked her up and down, trying to take in every detail.

She smiled at him, mischief in her emerald green eyes, dropping her coat and hat to the floor. Then, in a flash of movement, she ran to him, crossing the room and jumping into his arms, wrapping her own around his neck to embrace him.

He held onto her, the scent of her perfume intoxicating. He held her as if she would be taken from him at any moment; too long had he suffered without her embrace and warmth, and now he had it back he was determined to make the most of every sweet second.

Nadia drew back from him, still in the circle of his arms.

Alex smiled down at her. 'I have missed you so much,' he breathed against her lips. 'Two days has been far too long.'

She smiled. 'Any separation is now too much to endure,' she admitted, her finger stroking his cheek.

Without another word, she met his lips, harshly at first, the kiss softening until they were like lovers once more, the warmth of their kiss melting away the coldness in both of their hearts.

Here, in this room, they could be who they knew they were to each other, with no one to tell them that their bond was wrong or inappropriate. Here, they were away from prying eyes, rules, and expectations.

They were free.

Nadia slowly kissed a trail from his lips, moving across his cheek and down to his throat, teasing him.

He shuddered at her touch and she smiled against his skin.

His hands gripped her body, his need for her becoming too much.

Gently, Nadia bit into the delicate skin on his neck, spilling his blood.

Alex gasped at the instant pain that mingled with pleasure as her lips met with his skin, her tongue licking at the blood, drinking it. Her fingers gripped his shoulders, her need for him evident.

She teased him by only licking at the wound to his neck, the bleeding stopping as quickly as it started.

She stepped back and stared at him for a moment, her gaze intense and full of need. She gripped his arms, pulling him across the room towards the bed, her smile seductive.

She sat down on the soft mattress, her gaze not leaving his once.

Alex stared down at her, his need for her overwhelming. He bent down and kissed her once more, the taste of his own blood on her lips so intense and forbidden he knew he would find it hard to ever leave this room.

He wanted all of her. Forever.

He unbuttoned his shirt as he pulled away from her kiss, her gaze still watching his every move, a smile on her seductive lips.

Leaning over her once more, he kissed her neck, biting into her soft flesh, making her gasp, the sound so sexual it had him breathing faster as he drank her blood properly for the first time in years.

The flavour was far richer and sweeter than he had ever remembered. The thickness coated his tongue and throat as he drank, the warmth inviting; his entire body felt alive and on fire as her blood fed his soul, a feeling so full of ecstasy he was sure he would go mad from the sheer pleasure.

Nadia groaned beneath his touch as his hands ran over the satin of her dress, feeling her stunning body beneath.

He had not known how much he had wanted

this, needed it. He had missed her. He had missed her blood; especially her blood.

She was his twin and they had shared blood since the womb. They were part of each other, now and forever. She sustained him as he sustained her, and no one could ever deny them that. Theirs was a darkness wholly shared.

With her here, on the bed, beneath him, offering her all to him, he felt invincible.

Nadia was his and his alone.

She was his other half, the other part of him that he could not exist without.

He would never allow anyone to deny him what was his.

1963

'It truly is so good to have you stay with us for Christmas,' Alex said, grasping Katarina's hand warmly as they stood in the parlour of the Demeter family home.

She placed her hand onto his with a smile. 'So it is,' she said cheerfully. 'What's the fun in travelling if you cannot visit family on the way home?' she asked with a laugh.

Nadia smiled warmly as she faced her cousin. 'You simply must tell me all about Egypt,' she insisted.

Katarina released Alex's hand and linked her arm through Nadia's, smiling widely. 'I must, dearest,' she said. 'I have plenty of stories, I can tell you.' She winked. 'Though some may be best discussed in private, away from your mother's delicate ears,' she laughed playfully.

The two women crossed the room to sit together on the chesterfield, chatting away.

Alex watched them, a wide smile on his face as their laughter rang out. It was good to see Katarina once again; he had not seen her since his stay in Paris, although he wrote to her often.

He took a deep breath, glancing out of the window. The snow continued to fall gently. His gaze briefly fell on his sister as she laughed with their cousin.

After they had continued with their clandestine meetings, they had finally admitted to the family that they had been seeing each other in secret, unable to tolerate only seeing each other every few days; they needed to be together every moment.

Nadia returned home days later, the family aware of the level of the twins' involvement, yet at a loss to stop it or control it.

As a result, Alex and Nadia had spent the next forty-seven years together openly, no longer apologising for their bond or the power it brought them. Their blood sharing dominated their lives and they fed on the intimidation and fear their bond raised, even the elders no longer willing to interfere; the twins were left to their own devices for the sake of peace and harmony.

The family knew that the will of the twins could not be argued against; it was futile to try.

Their wishes were to be respected and obeyed.

Alex had fed on the new power, Nadia even more so; her attitude towards the elders had changed during her stay in Vallakia and she viewed them as weak and not worthy of her time, something Alex did not agree with – they were still his elders and he gave them every respect – but he supported her nonetheless.

Time had passed far too quickly and the world had changed dramatically around them all. Global war had come and gone twice over, though war still raged in Vietnam and segregation in the US was a huge issue; one with which Alex did not agree at all.

Humanity was now sky borne, and space was to be the next frontier of exploration.

Music had taken a completely different direction, as had the fashions, and only last month the president of the US, John F Kennedy, had been assassinated.

It was a new and exciting world that could be explored all over again.

Alex looked at the two women who sat laughing together. Nadia shone in her bright-green duster dress, and Katarina looked sophisticated in her two-piece.

His cousin had been travelling for over a year when she had sent the family a letter, telling them she was passing through Romania on her way home. His parents had then invited her to stay for a few weeks over Christmas, which she had happily accepted.

He was looking forward to spending time with her again, just as he had in Paris. Katarina was a soothing soul, her open-minded attitude welcome in his otherwise judged life.

He was also glad that Nadia would have some company, as her days were spent entirely with Alex, and he knew it would be good for her to have some female company.

'Alex,' Nadia called across the room, waving at him.

He smiled at her.

'Come here and listen to what happened in Cairo,' she smiled.

With a laugh, he crossed the room towards the two women.

He was going to enjoy the next few months.

* * *

Nadia looked out of her bedroom window in the south tower of Vallakia, the leaded frames shimmering with ice and snow. Outside the sky was heavily overcast, more snowfall expected before the evening.

She stared down into the large main courtyard, watching as Alex and Katarina strolled together arm in arm, laughing at some unheard joke.

Nadia sneered at them, her hands clenching against the windowsill.

Christmas had come and gone, as had the New Year where the family had travelled to Vallakia to spend time with the elders, and throughout that time she had watched Alex spend more and more of his time with their cousin, laughing and joking about their time in Paris.

At first it had been fun to listen to all their stories of parties and adventures in such a grand city. Yet as

Katarina's stay had continued, Nadia had felt more and more excluded from their conversations; after all, she had not been privy to their parties at which Alex was clearly the centre of attention.

You abandoned me at home, she thought angrily, *while you played the field in Paris.*

The thought of him and other women angered her and, despite her best efforts, jealousy engulfed her as she thought of him giving his affection to others.

As she watched Alex spend his time with Katarina, she grew more and more resentful of the time they had shared without her, and even more resentful of the way they seemed to constantly raise the subject during conversations, something always seeming to link back to Paris.

Naturally, everyone else was thrilled to discuss such times with the pair, and Nadia felt pushed aside, her jealousy over Katarina's presence growing.

Nadia watched the pair out in the courtyard, unable to prevent the images of the two of them together in Paris dominating her thoughts. She imagined Alex touching and kissing Katarina and it made her stomach twist, her nails biting into the flesh of her palms as she gripped her fists tighter together.

How dare this other woman try and come between them, reminding Alex of a time when he was clearly happy without his twin beside him, having callously abandoned her at home with no word for years.

With an angry hiss, she unlocked the window

and pushed it open, the ice-cold air from outside hitting her in the face.

'Alex,' she called, interrupting their conversation as she had done so many times over the last few weeks. Often it worked, though there had been other times when he had pushed her to one side in order to continue with their conversations.

Alex and Katarina looked up at her.

Katarina smiled up at her cousin, yet Alex looked a little put out by the interruption.

'What is it?' he asked flatly.

'I needed to see you for a moment,' Nadia called down, her voice as sweet as she could make it.

Katarina smiled. 'We were just about to go riding. Won't you join us?' she asked kindly.

Nadia resisted a sneer. *So I wouldn't have been asked had I not interrupted you*, she thought angrily.

She forced a smile. 'Maybe later,' she said, looking at her brother. 'Alex?'

She saw the frustration pass across his face. Without answering, he turned to look at Katarina and clearly apologised. She shook her head, her smile still firmly in place.

With a stern glance up at his sister, Alex walked away, heading back towards the entrance.

Without another glance at Katarina, Nadia slammed the window closed, turning to face the room and awaiting Alex's knock at the door.

It came quicker than she expected.

'Come in,' she said cheerfully, watching as he

stepped inside the room. He didn't bother to close the door, she noticed.

'You're keen,' she said playfully.

He looked at her expectantly. 'Well?' he asked flatly. 'What was so urgent that it couldn't wait?'

She stepped up to him, placing her hands against his chest. 'I would have thought that was obvious,' she purred, suggestion in her emerald eyes. 'A lady has needs, dearest.'

He shook his head, no smile on his face. 'As have I, my love, but I was about to go riding. We can meet later.'

'But you're here now,' she teased, brushing her lips against his. 'Katarina can wait, I'm sure.'

'That is not the point,' he said firmly. He took hold of her hands and pulled them from his chest, holding them lightly in his own. 'I will be all yours later, but I cannot just abandon our cousin when I have promised to go riding with her.'

Like you could abandon me, despite your promise, she thought angrily, her face remaining untainted by her rage

'I miss you,' she said, pouting.

Alex sighed. 'Like you did yesterday before we went hunting, or the day before when you stopped us going into the town?' he asked, giving her a pointed look. 'I know what you are up to, Nadia,' he said sadly.

She looked at him innocently. 'What do you mean?' she asked.

'I am not stupid, dearest. I apologise if you have felt left out, but continuously interrupting conversations and excursions is not the way to deal with it. I am here now because you did not want me to go riding, isn't that true?'

Nadia remained silent, sulking as she had done as a child when she had not gotten her own way.

Alex kissed her fingers on both hands before staring at her. 'It is the attention you crave and not I, my love,' he said sadly.

She glared at him then, angry at his words. 'How can you say such a thing?' she hissed. 'I *miss* you, my love,' she said. 'Though perhaps your affections now lie elsewhere,' she accused, pushing away from him, her gaze darkening.

'You speak nonsense,' he said simply, unable to meet her gaze.

'Do I?' she queried. 'You spend all your time with *her*,' she spat. 'Spending time with me no longer appeals to you. When was the last time you came to me without a request? You no longer want me. She has stolen you from me, no doubt her plan all along.'

Alex stared at her. 'You do not know what it is you say, Sister,' he said angrily. 'Katarina has done nothing wrong.'

'Of course, you would defend her,' she snapped.

'I will defend her because I will not have her accused of actions she is not guilty of. She would be extremely saddened to hear you accusing her of such acts. She loves you,' he said firmly, standing his ground. 'Yes, I have been happy to have her staying with us, but only because she is family.'

Nadia sneered at him then. 'As am I, Brother Dearest, yet that has not stopped you in your desires, has it?' Her words were cold and she regretted them the instant she spoke them, yet she refused to back down; she would not have him stolen from her side.

Alex stared at her, his eyes wide. 'I cannot believe this conversation,' he said, exasperated. 'Katarina helped me when I stayed with her, and whether you believe it or not, it was she who helped me see sense and return to your side. I am extremely thankful for that, for had she not then we would not have had all these years together as one.'

He turned from her then, heading for the door.

'Where are you going?' she asked angrily.

He did not answer her.

'Alex,' she screamed at him, her outburst making him stop in his tracks.

He turned to look at her, wariness in his eyes. 'I will not listen to another word of this lunacy, Nadia,' he said firmly. 'Believe what you will. I have stated my case, but if you will not trust me enough to listen then I can do no more.'

'She is trying to take you away from me, Alex,' she said desperately, images of his time in Paris filling her head once more. 'You are forsaking me and it is all her doing.'

He shook his head. 'This is all in your head,' he accused. 'Take a long look in the mirror, Sister, and see who is forsaking you.'

Without another word, he turned and left the room, slamming the door behind him.

'Traitor,' she screamed, anger, rage and a deep loss flowing through her, beyond anything she had experienced before.

Turning on her heels, she began pacing the room, her mind a cacophony of thoughts and images.

Her gaze caught her reflection in the mirror on her dresser. With Alex's words running through her mind, mocking her, she angrily kicked off her shoe and threw it at the mirror, smashing the glass.

She ran her hands over and over each other, trying to think. She could not allow Katarina to steal Alex from her; he was her everything and she would not give him up.

If Katarina wasn't here, then Alex would come back to me, she thought simply, knowing that it was the other woman's presence that had caused such a rift between herself and her brother.

'She needs to go,' she said aloud to the room around her. 'She needs to go, now.'

Taking several deep breaths to compose herself, she crossed the room to retrieve her shoe from the shattered vanity, replacing it on her foot.

Stepping over the broken glass, she headed for the far wall to where the golden rope hung to call for the servants, her head held high as it always was.

Outwardly, she was composed and calm; inwardly she was seething, full of rage and hatred.

She pulled on the rope several times, continuing to pace the room as she waited for the inevitable knock on the door.

A few minutes later, the knock sounded, and Nadia opened the door.

Ramona, the young maid, stood on the other side.

'You called, Miss,' she said quietly, curtseying.

Nadia rolled her eyes. Ramona was fairly new to Vallakia and was far too quiet for Nadia's tastes.

'I did,' she said flatly. 'I need you to bring Mademoiselle de Seraucourt to me, here,' she instructed.

'What shall I tell her, Miss?'

'Does it matter?' Nadia hissed. 'Tell her I need to speak to her on a matter of some importance. Now go,' she said, dismissing the young girl.

She watched the maid disappear down the stairs and then closed the door.

Nadia continued to pace the room, her agitation growing with each passing moment, the silence amplified around her.

She did not know how long it was before she finally heard the knock at her door.

She crossed the room quickly and opened the door, smiling warmly at Katarina who stood on the other side.

The maid hovered behind her.

Nadia glared at her. 'Thank you, Ramona,' she said, dismissing the girl.

Nadia grabbed Katarina's arm and pulled her into the room.

Katarina laughed at Nadia's secrecy. 'Are you okay, my dear?' she asked. 'This is all very clandestine, isn't it?'

Nadia smiled at her once she had closed the door. 'I needed to speak to you in private. I hope you don't mind?'

'Not at all,' Katarina said with a smile. 'We have not had a good chat in a while, have we?' She noticed the broken mirror on the vanity. 'Oh, dear, what happened?' she asked.

Nadia laughed. 'I am so clumsy,' she offered. 'I dropped something and it bounced right into the mirror.'

Katarina joined her laughter. 'We shall have to go shopping for a new one,' she offered kindly.

'Indeed, we shall,' said Nadia, her cheerful tone wavering.

'So,' Katarina said with a smile. 'What did you wish to discuss?' She stepped further into the room, looking around her. She turned back to Nadia and offered her a warm smile.

Nadia stared at her, the smile disappearing from her face. 'I wish to discuss how you are trying to turn Alex against me and take him for your own,' she hissed.

Katarina's smile vanished and she stared at her cousin, dumbfounded. 'Excuse me?' she asked. 'I do not know what it is you speak of,' she assured.

Nadia snarled, making her cousin flinch. 'Yes, you do. You have been trying to take him away from me ever since you arrived, taking up all his time so that he has none to spend with me.'

'Nadia, this is ridiculous. I have not tried to do any such thing and it is hurtful that you would think so.' Katarina moved towards the door of the bedroom. 'I can see that you are upset,' she said. 'So I think it best we forget this conversation. You need to calm down.'

'You are not going anywhere,' Nadia hissed. 'Not until you say you will leave him alone.'

'Nadia, I am not interested in Alex in any romantic way, I can assure you. He is a dear friend, and—'

Nadia did not give her time to finish. She flew across the room, grabbing her cousin by the hair, her strength unrelenting.

Katarina cried out in pain, yet Nadia ignored her.

'Liar,' she screamed at her. 'You think I do not know of what the two of you got up to in Paris?'

Tears fell down Katarina's face as she struggled against Nadia, her efforts in vain. Some of her hair fell to the floor as Nadia pulled it from the roots.

'I swear to you, Nadia, that nothing happened between us. I do not know why you would think such things. He is devoted to you,' she gasped, as Nadia pulled her across the room by her hair.

'He *was*,' she corrected. 'Now he only wants to

spend time with *you*, and I will suffer it no longer.' Viciously, Nadia pushed Katarina against the dresser hard, slamming her head against the wood.

Concussed, Katarina fell to the floor.

Nadia released her hair, turning towards the large chest that stood at the foot of the large four-poster bed.

With a callous smile, she lifted the heavy lid and threw out all of the clothing that was inside, casting it across the floor without another thought.

Then, turning back to the stunned Katarina, she grabbed the woman once more by the hair, pulling her easily across the floor; her strength had far surpassed anyone's expectations for someone of her age and both she and Alex had marvelled at their abilities, using them often to their own amusement.

Lifting the woman with ease, Nadia dropped her pitilessly into the chest, moans of pain escaping from Katarina's lips as she slowly regained her senses.

The chest was not very accommodating and Nadia had to push Katarina's legs and head down, making the woman groan further.

'Please, Nadia,' she managed to say eventually, her voice wavering. 'I have not wronged you and neither has Alex.'

'Do not speak his name to me,' Nadia hissed at her, grabbing a pair of tights from the floor and using them to tie Katarina's hands behind her back, pulling the material tight so it bit into the woman's flesh. She then grabbed a pair of knickers and screwed the material into a ball, forcing it into Katarina's mouth to ensure her silence.

Satisfied, Nadia gave her one last violent shove before slamming the lid of the chest closed.

Nadia closed the clasp to lock the chest, then stood and watched as if the woman inside it would somehow climb out.

Smiling at her handiwork, she turned on her heels and headed for the door to her room, the appearance of tranquillity restored to her porcelain features.

As she left her room, she was aware of the young maid standing further along the landing, rearranging roses in one of Gabriella's ancient vases.

The young girl caught Nadia's gaze but instantly looked away again.

Nadia approached her slowly, leaning closer to the girl so that she could whisper.

'You will say nothing of this, girl, do you understand?' she hissed, menace in her voice. 'Your very life depends on your silence.'

Without another word, Nadia stormed off, leaving the young maid trembling.

* * *

'Where can she be?' Alex pondered, looking out of the window of the drawing room into the falling snow; the sky was growing dark and night would soon be upon them.

Victor approached his son. 'I am sure Katarina will turn up, Son,' he said. 'She cannot have vanished into thin air.'

'Father's right,' Nadia added.

Alex turned to look at her, along with his father. His sister sat on the chesterfield, casually flicking through a magazine, seemingly oblivious to what was going on around her.

'Have you even bothered to look for her?' he asked incredulously.

She looked up at him then. 'I did my part,' she said flatly. 'Vallakia is a large place. Would you have me upturning furniture and peeking in cupboards?' she asked, sarcasm filling her words. 'She has probably just gone off by herself for a while, and I do not blame her if this is how you fuss over her.'

Alex stared at her for a moment, yet when he opened his mouth to answer, his father placed a hand on his shoulder.

'Leave it be, Alex,' Victor soothed. 'Arguing with your sister will not help, though she may indeed have a point in that Katarina may have simply gone off by herself,' he pointed out.

Alex frowned as he looked at his father. 'But we were supposed to go out riding earlier and after I came back from talking to Nadia she had simply vanished. No one's seen her.'

Victor shrugged. 'Then maybe she went out riding alone?' he suggested.

Alex shook his head. 'There is no horse missing

from the stables,' he said.

Nadia laughed. 'Sounds like we have our very own Sherlock Holmes,' she taunted.

Alex glared at her; he still had not forgotten the way she had acted earlier and was finding it hard simply being in the same room as her.

She rolled her eyes, dropping the magazine onto the chesterfield next to her. 'Well, not that all of this isn't *fabulously* entertaining, but I think I will leave you to your needless worrying.' She stood from her seat and headed for the door. 'I will be in my room if anyone needs me,' she added, looking at Alex with a smile.

He ignored her, turning away as she left the room. Yet his efforts to remain angry at his twin were in vain, for he found it increasingly difficult to be annoyed with her for any given length of time; she knew how to get back into his good books every time, and he even found it strangely fun. She would tempt him eventually; the promise of her blood was always too much to ignore.

He knew that lately she had been offering it more and more because of Katarina's presence, and he admitted to himself that he had perhaps slightly pushed her aside over the last few weeks, fuelling her doubts and insecurities. He did not excuse them, but would admit his part in causing them; he decided to apologise to her once he had solved the riddle of Katarina's disappearance.

He looked up as Gabriella entered the room

quietly, her face marred by concern. By her side, there followed a young maid, one Alex recognised as new to the household.

He frowned. 'What is wrong?' he asked.

Gabriella's eyes were filled with what Alex could only define as shame. 'I have been informed of something which might help you in your search, my child,' she said softly.

She glanced at the maid next to her. 'You must tell him, my dear,' she said firmly.

Alex stared at the maid, uneasy. 'What do you have to say?' he asked carefully.

The maid looked at everyone in the room, wariness in her eyes. 'Earlier this afternoon, I was instructed to take Mademoiselle de Seraucourt to Lady Nadia's room.'

Victor glanced at his son before looking back at the maid. 'And what then?' he asked.

The maid shifted on her feet, uneasy. 'Lady Nadia emerged a little later, but there was no sign of Mademoiselle de Seraucourt. She did not reappear from the room.'

Alex stepped forward. 'Why did you not inform us of this earlier?' he demanded.

The maid looked at the floor. 'I was in fear of my life, my lord,' she said quietly.

Alex's eyes narrowed. 'You mean Lady Nadia threatened you?'

The maid nodded slowly.

Alex sighed. 'You will not be harmed for

offering this information, you have my word,' he said, glancing between his ancient grandmother and his father before heading for the door.

Gabriella and Victor both followed him.

Out in the main hall, the three of them climbed the stairs.

A sense of dread crept over Alex's skin as he ascended the staircase, icy tendrils snaking up his spine as his mind filled with reasons why Katarina would not emerge from Nadia's room.

He hurried along the landing until he reached the stairs to the south tower. He took the steps two at a time and jogged along the corridor, pausing at the door to Nadia's bedroom.

He glanced around at his elders, unsure he wanted to know the answer to the questions in his head.

They both looked equally worried.

With a deep breath, Alex turned back to the door and opened it.

Nadia looked up at them as they all entered. 'You really should knock before entering a lady's room, you know,' she said with a grin.

Alex stared at her as she lay on her bed, flicking through another magazine. She looked so calm and he tried to convince himself that the maid was wrong; Katarina had simply left the room when the maid's attentions had been elsewhere.

He glanced around the room, noting the broken vanity mirror. 'What happened?' he asked.

She shrugged. 'I lost my temper with you earlier, remember?' she said, not looking up from the magazine. 'I took it out on the mirror.'

Alex continued to look around the room, unsure of what he was looking for.

'Where is she?' he asked firmly, staring at his sister.

She looked up at him, innocence in her eyes. 'Where's who?'

A growl rumbled in his chest. 'You know damn well who,' he pressed. 'What have you done?'

When Nadia refused to answer, Alex turned his attentions to the room, rushing to her wardrobe and pulling the doors wide, brushing her clothes aside roughly in his search.

'Do you mind?' Nadia hissed, turning her attentions to her elders. 'Are you just going to stand there and let him do this?' she asked.

Victor sighed. 'We know Katarina was in your room, child,' he said, his words weary.

Nadia's gaze darkened. 'Good for you,' she sneered. 'Clearly she's not here now.'

Alex ignored his sister's objections as he knelt to look under the bed, finding nothing but a pile of Nadia's clothes. He frowned as he stood; Nadia was never untidy and always ensured her clothes were properly stored.

With a claw of fear clutching at his stomach, Alex's gaze fell to the large chest at the foot of her bed.

He took a step towards it. 'I would not have thought you capable of such atrocity,' he said quietly, aware of his sister looking up at him.

He took another step towards the chest.

'Alex, leave it be,' Nadia warned, sitting up on her bed.

Yet the glare her brother gave her had her staying put.

'Why would you do this?' he asked.

'She needed to be taught a lesson,' she said simply. 'She wouldn't listen to my warnings.'

Without another thought, Alex made a grab for the chest, releasing the clasp and throwing back the lid.

Inside the chest, huddled and shaking was Katarina. There was dried blood on her forehead from a cut, her mouth was filled with material and her hands were bound behind her back, her wrists cut and bleeding.

She looked terrified.

Without thought, Alex grabbed Katarina's arms and ripped through the fabric, her cries of pain making him wince as he pulled the material out of the bleeding wounds.

He pulled her free of the chest in which Nadia had trapped her, watching as Katarina pulled the ball of material from her mouth, retching loudly. Her breathing was rapid, her panic and fear all too evident.

Alex helped her to her feet, steadying her as she

wobbled, unable to stand straight.

'I am so sorry,' he whispered, unable to comprehend what had just happened.

'How could she do this to me?' Katarina screeched, finally finding her voice, every word wobbling.

Alex glanced at his elders, their shock evident in their faces. Then he glanced at his sister.

There was no expression on her face and he was reminded of the day they had found Csilla's body; just like that day, his sister showed no remorse for her actions.

As he helped Katarina towards the door, Nadia's words echoed in his head.

'She should have listened and left you alone. It's her own fault.'

An involuntary shiver ran the length of his spine.

He was instantly terrified of what his sister was truly capable of.

1964

'What are you doing?' Nadia asked cautiously as she hovered in the doorway.

Alex didn't turn to face her. He sat at the walnut desk in the large library of Vallakia, the candle on the desk flickering shadows across the paper in front of him. The sky outside was filled with dark foreboding clouds, which afforded little in the way of brightness into the room. Instead, light from oil lamps on the walls filled the room with a soft glow, although the library always seemed dark to him; he assumed it had to be the deep-red of the carpet that ran throughout the room, paired with the rosewood bookcases that lined the walls. A fire burned in the small fireplace, in front of which were situated two large chairs and a walnut table, which was inlaid with ebony, ivory and boxwood.

Alex gripped the quill tighter, hoping she would take the hint and leave him be.

His hope was in vain.

'Earth to Alex,' she said, sarcasm filling her

words. 'You've been in here for ages. I'm bored.'

He sighed heavily. 'Then go and find something to do,' he said simply. 'Surely I am not your only source of amusement,' he added, no emotion in his voice.

'You are in this dreary place,' she moaned. 'You know I hate it here.'

He dipped the quill into the inkwell beside him; he found it a novelty that Vallakia still only used quills instead of pens. 'Oh?' he asked, surprised. 'I thought you loved it here.'

'Once, maybe,' she answered, something detached in her voice.

Still he refused to look at her as he continued to write. 'What changed?'

'Nothing of importance,' she said simply, clearly dismissing the conversation.

He dipped the quill in the ink once more, aware of her footsteps on the wooden floor as she crossed the room.

'What *are* you doing, Brother?' she asked with another sigh.

She approached him from behind, leaning against the back of his chair to glance over his shoulder; her proximity made him shiver.

After finding Katarina in Nadia's chest, his cousin had practically fled Vallakia, returning home to France that very night. She had been terrified and badly shaken.

Nadia had shown no remorse for her actions and

her indifference had frightened him. Yet Alex was not prepared to let the episode simply be forgotten and he made that abundantly clear to her; he wanted her to apologise for her actions, which she never did.

In her eyes, she had done nothing wrong and sought no forgiveness; she was still adamant that Katarina had been trying to steal Alex from her side.

Nadia firmly believed her actions were justified and was pleased with herself that they had worked; after all, Katarina had left, which is what Nadia had wanted.

Because of this, Nadia's mood instantly changed and she was back to her usual cheerful and playful self. She was perfectly nice and attentive to Alex once more.

Yet her change of mood only unnerved him further as he realised how fickle her temper could be, knowing her niceness was only down to thinking her tactics had worked, and he was not prepared to indulge her.

When she had played up to him, only a day after Katarina had left, he refused to partake of her game and denied her offer of blood, however tempting it was.

However, this refusal angered Nadia, raising the accusations once more that it was Katarina who had turned Alex against her. The more he tried to refute those accusations, the worse she became, believing him to be defending their cousin because of his affection for her.

As the next week had passed, Nadia had descended deeper into her delusions, her fury growing until everyone around her was an enemy.

Alex grew scared of his sister's rage and what she was truly capable of.

He had hoped that remaining in Vallakia with the elders would help dissipate her irrational thoughts and behaviour, even after their parents had returned home. But Nadia's attitude towards her ancient elders, Vlad especially, left something to be desired, and Alex knew their elder was not impressed by Nadia's disrespect, warning her on several occasions.

Alex was mystified by her attitude, uncertain of the reasons behind Nadia's insolence; she had once loved them so.

'Who are you writing to?' Nadia asked, leaning over him.

'It does not concern you,' he said, uneasy.

'Then why the secrecy?' she asked, snatching up the piece of paper.

He twisted in his chair, trying to grab it back, yet his sister was too quick.

He watched her eyes grow dark as she read the words, her lips quivering with the threat of a snarl.

'You're writing to *her*?' she asked, her voice rising in volume.

Alex sighed, dropping the quill into the ink well. 'I was simply enquiring about her health,' he said flatly, unwilling to engage in another argument. 'It is the least I can do after what you put her through.' He stood from his seat.

'Then why not tell me?' she asked, her voice rising with hysteria as it had so many times over the last few days. 'Why hide it from me?'

Alex tried to take the letter back, yet still she held it out of his reach. 'Because I knew you would react like this,' he said, tired of fighting with her.

'Liar,' she spat, her green eyes blazing with anger. 'You hid it from me because you did not wish me to know of your sordid attentions. You did not want me to know because you are guilty of what I have accused you of.'

'I will not enter into another argument with you about this, Nadia,' he said firmly.

'Because you know I'm right,' she shouted.

A gentle knock sounded at the door and Alex glanced across the room as Gabriella stood in the doorway.

'Is all well in here, my children?' she asked carefully, concern etched on her ancient face.

'It's none of your business,' Nadia snapped, glaring at their elder before turning her attentions back to Alex.

He looked to Gabriella with apology. 'I'm sorry,' he said quietly. 'We were simply having a disagreement,' he ventured.

Nadia laughed. 'Is that what it is?' she asked venomously. She turned to Gabriella. 'Alex is a liar and a traitor,' she hissed. 'He sends letters to a lady whom he claims not to have any intimacies with,' she added, waving the letter in the air.

She turned back to Alex. 'Well, to hell with your lies,' she screamed again, ripping the letter in two and discarding the pieces. 'I will rip every piece of paper in this place if it prevents you from sending any more letters.'

Gabriella stepped further into the room, her hands clasped in front of her. 'My dear, I am sure Alex did not mean to distress you so,' she said calmly. 'He is merely keeping in contact.'

Nadia glared at her with a look that sent a chill down Alex's spine. 'So you knew of his duplicity?' she asked, snarling.

Gabriella stood her ground. 'There is no duplicity in Alex's actions, my child. You imagine such betrayal where there is none.'

Nadia laughed once more. 'Do I indeed,' she sneered, her gaze intent on her elder. 'Or perhaps I see betrayal and all its filth where others dare not.'

Alex caught the darkness in his sister's eyes as she glared at their ancient grandmother, puzzled by her words that seemed very much like an accusation.

'That's enough,' he warned. 'Apologise, Sister.'

Gabriella held up her hand and shook her head gently. 'Do not trouble yourself so, Alex,' she murmured.

Nadia stamped her foot like a petulant child. 'See, why is *he* the golden child who can do no wrong?' she screamed, pushing her brother.

Alex stumbled backwards, yet steadied himself

against the chair. His gaze was wary as he appraised his sister.

'You need to calm down,' he warned.

'Why?' she screeched. 'Because you tell me to? Am I to do what you tell me, Alex, like a child?'

Alex glanced at Gabriella, who shook her head sadly.

With a deep breath, he pushed his sister aside and headed for the door.

'Where are you going?' she shouted.

'Away from your mania,' he stated flatly, exiting the room with Gabriella who took his arm and linked her own through it, quietly leading him away from the room.

Nadia wasn't too far behind. 'You leave because you know I speak the truth,' she called.

Alex unravelled his arm from Gabriella's and turned to look at his sister. 'You do not know of what you speak,' he said. 'You do not know what the truth is any more, Sister. Your delusions have grown more powerful than you, I fear.'

He turned from her, finished with the conversation.

Yet before he could take a step, Nadia grabbed him by his hair, pulling him backwards.

'Traitor,' she screamed, scratching at his face with her claw-like nails.

'Nadia, you must cease this behaviour,' Gabriella commanded, her usually gentle voice full of authority as Vlad rushed from the drawing room, calling loudly for Demitri, the steward.

'You do not get to tell me what to do,' she hissed, as Alex struggled against her; Nadia's delusion made her a much more powerful foe as she pulled him to the floor and kicked him hard.

He tried to shield himself from her onslaught yet she repeatedly called him a traitor as she kicked and punched him without restraint. Her foot connected with his ribs, winding him.

An angry cry escaped Nadia's lips as he tried to catch his breath, finding himself instantly free from her onslaught. Gabriella helped him slowly to his feet.

Looking up, Alex saw Nadia being held by Demitri and two other servants who had rushed from their duties to assist their masters. Vlad stood beside them, his expression full of concern as he watched them struggle against Nadia's rage.

Alex stared at them all as they maintained their hold on his sister, her grey dress crumpled in their hands.

Nadia glared at him. 'Alex, stop them,' she cried, anger blazing in her eyes. 'Tell them to unhand me.'

He found himself unable to move. 'What are you doing to her?' he asked, every part of his body clouded by a strange numbness.

Gabriella wrapped her arm about his shoulders. 'What I fear must be done, my child,' she murmured, sadness in her voice. 'You need to let us help her now.'

Alex stared at his sister, unable to make sense of

what he was witnessing.

Nadia's eyes blazed with anger and hatred as she glared between Alex and Gabriella. 'You can't do this,' she snarled.

Alex felt tears sting his eyes as he watched her struggle. 'Do not fight it, Nadia,' he pleaded, finally finding his voice. 'They are trying to help you.'

'I don't need their help,' she screamed, her hair falling about her face.

Unable to watch the scene before him, he turned to Gabriella, his tears falling over his cheeks. 'Please, there has to be another way,' he begged.

Gabriella's eyes were filled with regret. 'I wish there were, my child,' she soothed. 'But her behaviour of late has gone too far. Now she is willing to attack you, I fear this is the only way.'

Alex glanced at Vlad, silently begging him to intervene.

His elder only shook his head. 'This will help her, I promise,' he assured, his tone severe. 'You both may not see that now, but you will in time. It is not something we consider lightly, but we have witnessed her descent into madness and can no longer ignore the danger she poses to others or to you.'

Vlad's words confirmed Alex's worst fears; he knew what happened to those who needed time in order to recover from a trauma or upset. It was a treatment that had been used for millennia, sometimes voluntarily, but most often as a last resort.

Nadia would be taken deep into the dungeons

and crypts beneath Vallakia and placed into a casket, where she would be locked away and left for however long it took for her mania and delusions to pass. There was no knowing how long that would take. Over the course of time, the starvation of blood allowed the body to truly rest; this in turn allowed the mind to let go of all the issues it was battling with, as the person lay in absolute silence.

It was a confinement Alex found terrifying.

'Alex, stop them,' Nadia screamed, her gaze seeking his. 'Tell them to leave me be.'

Ashamed, he glanced down at the floor, cursing himself for being such a coward. He couldn't bear to think of her being taken away, yet was at a loss to know what alternative he had.

'Alex,' she screamed. 'Don't let them do this, please.'

He glanced up and watched as Vlad stepped in front of his sister. He attempted to take her face in his hands but she snarled at him like a wild animal, her green eyes glaring at him from beneath her matted hair.

Vlad sighed. 'It is for your own good,' he said quietly. 'Your anger will dissipate in time, my child, and you will be yourself once more.'

He looked at Alex as if seeking permission.

Alex was unsure whether anything he said now would make a difference to Vlad's opinion; Nadia had shown herself to be uncontrollable whilst staying at Vallakia, her outbursts erratic and often frightening.

Now she was growing violent and the elders would not tolerate such behaviour in a building meant for solace.

He remained silent.

Vlad nodded at him, understanding in his ancient eyes. He then turned to the servants and nodded by way of instruction.

Without a word, they began to drag Nadia away, struggling with her every step.

'Alex,' she cried out, hysteria filling every word she spoke. 'Don't let them do this to me. I'm supposed to be at your side. Don't let them take me away from you.'

Gabriella held onto him tightly in support as he continued to focus on the floor, Nadia's words not growing any quieter as they dragged her away.

'Alex, don't you dare ignore me,' she screamed, every word chilling him to the bone. 'Please, I beg of you. Please don't let them take me away from you. My place is at your side. Help me, please. You promised me, my lord. You promised...'

Her begging continued constantly, her words growing quieter as she was dragged further away.

Yet despite the quieting of her cries, still her words echoed loudly in his head as if she were standing next to him. A shiver ran the length of his spine as her cries filled his mind.

He doubted he would ever forget the sound of her screams for as long as he lived.

1971

Alex took a deep, unsteady breath as he waited nervously.

He buried his hands deep into his trouser pockets to hide the fact that they were shaking.

He cast surreptitious glances at his parents as they wandered around the large drawing room in Vallakia, both of them equally anxious.

He tried to push aside the thoughts of his sister and her incarceration. His efforts were in vain, for he had not been able to ignore such images in the six years since she had been dragged away by the Others and locked away in the depths of the crypt below Vallakia.

The memories of that day still haunted him. He heard her screams in his dreams, disturbing his rest many a night since that day.

He was not so sure he would ever forget it.

He had attempted to distract himself so many times over the last few years. He had tried to stay in Romania after she had been taken away, yet he found himself unwilling to travel to Vallakia and socialise when he knew his sister was locked away below his feet. Even his family home seemed too desolate without Nadia by his side, and so, to get away from the suffocating silence of the house, he left to travel as he had once before.

In 1967, he had begun travelling, visiting first Italy, then Spain, and then onto France in 1968, visiting Katarina to check on her after Nadia's ordeal. She had recovered, though she still politely declined to visit the Demeter family in Romania anytime soon; she could not forget what Nadia had done to her, though she admitted she felt pity for her cousin and her predicament.

Alex spent several months with Katarina, using her parties and social occasions as a way to try and distract himself. Yet in the cold light of day, he knew his efforts were fruitless, and Katarina would often talk to him, listening to his stories of what had transpired between himself and Nadia over the years, without judgement or reprimand.

The following year he had travelled across Europe and onto Russia, visiting his other cousin, Monika, who had only recently moved onto Moscow after many years in Norway.

She had not been to Romania in a long time, not since Nadia had stayed there during his absence after Csilla's death, and Monika's distance puzzled Alex; she had so loved Vallakia as a child, yet she would not disclose any issue that had kept her from the place. She simply insisted she was enjoying life and the world, though Alex doubted her words.

It was early in 1970 that he had received a letter from home, asking him to return to Romania; the elders felt it was time to release his sister.

Alex had discussed the situation with Monika, who offered her cousin as much support as she could, though could not go as far as offering to travel with him; she simply would not entertain the idea, which again left Alex perplexed.

He had been extremely nervous and unsettled on his return home, the unknown of what he would see disturbing him.

Yet for six years he had been lonely for his sister, knowing that what had befallen her was his own fault for indulging her insecurities and then dismissing them.

Now, he stood in the drawing room, awaiting Vlad and Gabriella who had gone to the crypt to release his twin.

His parents looked as nervous as he felt.

The monotonous ticking of the clock on the mantle was making his anxiety worse.

His heart seemed to stop and his stomach twisted as the door handle moved, and he stared at the door, along with his parents.

The door opened.

The world around him seemed to stop.

Vlad and Gabriella stepped carefully into the room, as if the floor below their feet would break should they tread any harder.

Between them, supported by their hands, was Nadia.

His mother let out a saddened sob, and Alex could understand her anguish.

After six years of starvation, Nadia was frighteningly thin. Her pale skin was almost translucent, having none of the radiant glow she was famed for. Her lips were shrivelled and pulled back to reveal her sharp canine teeth. Her dress was like a rag, hanging from her body so loosely that Gabriella had to keep hold of the material to maintain Nadia's dignity. Her hair was thin and wispy, strands of it straggled across her face; it was in a tangled mess.

Her green eyes, usually so full of life and seduction, were pale and empty as she stared at the floor. She would not look at anyone.

She did not make a sound.

It was like staring at a ghost.

Aurelia sobbed once more, crossing the room and taking her daughter in her arms.

If Nadia noticed the embrace, she did not show it, for she remained still as a statue within the circle of their mother's arms, her gaze still fixed to the floor.

Alex glanced at both Vlad and Gabriella; both their faces were expressionless, though Gabriella's eyes were soft.

As Aurelia released her daughter, Gabriella spoke:

'We need to get her cleaned and changed,' she

said gently. 'Then she will need to feed.'

Aurelia continued to sob, seeking solace in her husband's arms. 'Will she be all right?' she asked, desperation in her voice.

Vlad nodded. 'In time. Her body and mind have been cleansed. Now, she needs to be refreshed and fed, and she will come back to you renewed,' he said, glancing at Alex. 'Time is a great healer.'

Alex found he couldn't speak; the pitiful sight of his sister in such a state had shocked him to his core.

As Vlad and Gabriella led his sister away, he could only form two words in his mind, and he communicated them to his sister in the only way he was able.

'I'm sorry,' he said mentally, hoping her mind wasn't too weary to hear him.

He received only silence in reply.

1972

Alex leant against the window frame in his room, staring out at the mountains in the far distance.

He had spent many a day standing at this window over the last year, staring out and watching the trees change as spring made way for summer, then autumn, and the snows of winter. Now the blossoms were back once more.

He had lived a relatively pitiful existence over the last year.

After Nadia was released, he had hoped she would slowly return to normal. His optimism had been wasted.

For the last year she had refused to speak to anyone, and the silence had been deafening. She had not so much even looked at anyone, always keeping her eyes fixed to the floor.

Alex had stayed out of her way and she had stayed out of his. They hunted separately; Nadia would only feed on the rats and other creatures she found in the dense forests surrounding their home.

She would disappear into those forests for hours at a time, and when she returned she would be as silent as before.

As the days passed, they barely acknowledged each other's presence.

It hurt Alex to live such a life; he did not know whether it hurt his sister also, as her eyes remained as blank as they had been the day the elders had released her.

He ran his fingers through his black hair, weary with his guilt; he had suffered another restless night, haunted by her screams.

A gentle knock sounded at his door.

With a weary sigh, he turned away from the window and bid whomever it was to enter.

Slowly, the door opened.

Alex's breath caught in his throat as he stared at his sister.

She stared at the floor, as always.

Over the last year, her appearance had been the only thing to return to normal, though it had taken longer due to her restricted diet. Her raven-black hair had regained its silky smoothness, her body its voluptuousness, though she kept it covered with long flowing dresses. Her eyes had returned to their deep emerald green, though it was hard to notice when they were constantly downcast.

Alex watched her as she stood in the doorway, her hands clasped in front of her.

A tear slowly fell down her cheek.

Once more, he found himself unable to speak; he had not witnessed his sister cry in a very long time.

Very slowly, her head lifted, her gaze finally falling on him.

There was so much sorrow in her eyes, Alex felt his own tears fall.

Her pink lips parted and she spoke the first words she had uttered in over seven years:

'Forgive me, Brother.'

1988

'Are you ready yet, Nadia?' Alex called through her bedroom door, his impatience growing.

'I will be with you in a moment,' she called back, no hurry in her tone.

Alex sighed and leant against the wall. He wanted to go hunting and Nadia's delay was doing nothing to soothe his craving for blood. His sharp canines tingled and his body tensed in readiness for the hunt and kill to come.

'We are going hunting, Sister, not attending a grand ball. How long does it take to get ready?' he asked, irritated.

'Good things are worth waiting for,' she sang out, amusement in her tone.

He tried to suppress the smile that spread across his lips, but failed miserably; she always knew how to break through his anger, just as she knew which buttons to press in order to arouse it in the first place.

He listened to his sister as she sang a tune he remembered hearing on the radio some time ago, the music of the past century having changed greatly in such a short space of time.

His smile dimmed; many things had changed over the last seventeen years since his sister had been released from her incarceration by the Others.

After she had finally spoken to him after her year of silence, Alex had spent his time ensuring her full recovery, promising her that he did indeed forgive her.

Slowly, she had returned to some semblance of normality, hunting humans once more instead of animals and interacting with the family again.

There had still remained a distance, however, which both of them sensed, yet neither of them voiced.

Despite Nadia's open desire to share Alex's blood, he had not been willing to offer his nor partake of hers; he knew, deep down, it was this bond that corrupted them, changing the way they saw the world, feeding their arrogance and power, which ultimately resulted in them hurting those around them, including themselves.

It was a break in their bond that had all but shattered their relationship, and over the next sixteen years they had lived a rather pitiful existence, never hunting together, barely spending time with one another or talking as they once had; any conversations they had were mainly made of small talk, rather than anything meaningful.

Alex sighed as the memories came flooding back, unwanted yet nonetheless potent.

He knocked on his sister's door once more.

'Nadia, it will be morning before you emerge from that room,' he chastised. 'Can you please hurry up?'

The door opened as he stared at it, and Nadia smiled brightly as if he hadn't said a word.

'Finally,' he said, unable to hold back his smile. He glanced over her attire. 'A little overdressed for hunting, aren't we?' he asked, admiring her short, black satin cocktail dress, paired with black stilettos. Her ink-black hair was pulled back in a tight ponytail.

She shrugged. 'If it serves the purpose...' She allowed her words to trail off as she stepped ahead of her brother and strolled along the landing.

With a chuckle, he followed her.

He watched as she descended the stairs, her head held high as if she didn't have a care in the world. Anyone could be fooled into thinking she didn't; only Alex knew otherwise.

At the start of 1987, Nadia had disappeared, without a word to anyone.

After spending so long living like virtual strangers, Alex blamed himself. He searched everywhere for her, asking everyone he could think of. He spent night after night searching bars and clubs, towns and cities trying to find her.

For months he refused to give up, torturing himself that he was the reason for her disappearance because he'd been too cold towards her.

Then, one cold November afternoon, she

returned home, just as suddenly as she had left. She refused to disclose where she had been or why she had vanished.

It was as if the whole thing had never happened.

Alex had been so relieved to see her again, he hadn't cared about her reasons for leaving; he doted on her every moment of every day, ensuring she never felt the need to leave ever again.

Nadia warmed to her brother once more and the pair became as they had once been, before their blood bond had interfered. They hunted together, spent their time together laughing and talking, growing ever closer, and Alex felt content that he finally had his sister back.

Yet as time passed, Nadia's hunting became more violent and she took up her old habit of teasing her victims once more, often meeting men in the bars and clubs of the towns and luring them to their deaths after having her fun with them.

Alex didn't interfere; it was the way she had always hunted, though he dutifully kept his eye on her, knowing she was aware of his scrutiny.

Slowly, he found himself exchanging furtive glances with her occasionally, often during the hunt when she would look his way as she seduced her next conquest.

The glances had continued and Alex had found himself increasingly unable to resist his sister's teasing.

He shook the thoughts away as he neared the

bottom of the stairs, watching as his sister shrugged into her favourite mink fur jacket.

She turned to him and smiled, a gleam in her emerald eyes. 'The night awaits us, Brother,' she purred, amusement in her tone.

Alex smiled. 'That it does.'

* * *

The night air was mild as they made their way through the streets of Sibiu, the clear spring evening inviting small gatherings outside the local bars and restaurants.

The twins walked side by side, Alex aware of the attention Nadia's attire provoked; every man glanced at her as she passed by and he found himself fighting his own jealousy, telling himself he was being ridiculous.

They continued walking through the streets, crossing the Grand Square with its Baroque buildings and houses that Alex always found nostalgic.

Most of the local shops were closed for the day, their windows dark and uninviting.

Nadia hummed as she walked by his side, a happy bounce to her step.

He smiled at her. 'You are incredibly cheerful this evening,' he pointed out.

She shrugged with a grin. 'Can't a lady be happy?' she asked.

Alex nodded. 'Indeed. It is nice to see you so,'

he admitted, unwilling to think of the many reasons why she hadn't been in the past.

'Good,' she said firmly.

She stopped in her tracks and turned to him, forcing him to a stop in front of her.

'Wait here,' she grinned.

Alex stared at her, confusion on his face. 'Why?' he asked, glancing around. They were stood outside a small bakery, the darkness within offering no welcome.

She rolled her eyes playfully. 'You are full of questions this evening,' she laughed, mimicking his tone.

He chuckled.

'Just wait here for a moment. I will be back.'

With that, she turned from him and approached the door to the bakery.

Alex watched as she pulled a small key from her clutch bag and used it to unlock the door to the shop.

Confused, he opened his mouth to question her actions just as Nadia disappeared into the shadows within. He remained where he was, just as she'd asked.

He stood in the gloom of the evening as the minutes ticked by, his impatience growing.

Nadia finally reappeared in the shadowy doorway of the small bakery, a large, self-satisfied grin on her face.

She grabbed his hands. 'Come with me,' she said, her gaze holding his.

There was something in her eyes that he couldn't read, yet it sent waves of anticipation through his body. He took a step forward.

'What is all this about?' he asked with a smile as he crossed the threshold.

'You'll see,' she teased, locking the door behind him before leading him into the darkness of the shop that smelt of a combination of fresh and stale bread. He caught the undertones of milk and walnuts in the air, as well as the sweetness of fruit.

He shook his head. 'How did you get the key to this place?' he asked, cautious of her answer.

She grinned, mischief in her eyes. 'You'll see,' she repeated, exaggerating her words. 'Close your eyes,' she whispered.

He did as he was told, her clandestine behaviour stirring unforgotten memories, his excitement building.

As she slowly led him onwards through the shop, Alex caught another scent in the air, one that had his hunger writhing and the thrill of the hunt burning in his veins. He could hear whimpering as Nadia led him further still through the shop into what he guessed was a back room.

Finally, she placed her hands on his chest to stop him walking any further. Her giggle was nervous.

'You can open your eyes now,' she said, her words full of excitement.

Alex did as he was told.

He stood in the doorway of a small rear room to

the shop, beyond which was the kitchen. In the gloom he could see a small table with a discarded newspaper and magazine, along with an ashtray containing several squashed cigarette butts. A dirty white apron had been dropped to the black tiled floor.

Alex's breath caught in his throat as he stared at the young human woman, tied to a wooden chair in the middle of the room.

Her eyes were wide with fear, a cloth in her mouth to prevent her from screaming. Tears flowed over her cheeks as she wept silently. Her dark hair was plaited and pinned to her crown, showing off a slender neck.

Alex felt his hunger flare. He forced his gaze away from the woman and looked at his sister, who stood to one side, her hands clasped in front of her like a child who was pleased with their behaviour.

'What is this?' he asked gently.

Nadia beamed at him. 'It is your Maturity Day present,' she declared.

Alex smiled at her, amazed. 'But you never remember it,' he chuckled.

She shrugged, her grin still firmly in place. 'Well, this year I did,' she stated simply. 'And to make up for all the years I have forgotten, I decided to make your gift extra special.'

She stepped up behind the woman, who tried to shy away from her despite the restraints.

Nadia placed her hands on the woman's shoulders, making the human weep harder.

'She is all for you, Alex,' she purred, warmth in her emerald eyes as she stared at him. 'To feed on and use however you deem fit,' she added, her smile instantly full of amusement.

Alex took another ragged breath. 'I don't know what to say,' he said, aware of what she was suggesting.

He studied the woman as she wept, from her slender neck down to the pale skin of her chest where it was barely visible above the neckline of her blue knitted jumper. A long striped skirt covered her legs.

His smile widened as he considered the possibilities Nadia had provided.

'You do not need to say anything,' Nadia breathed, her gaze holding his with intensity.

He swallowed past the lump in his throat, lost in her eyes.

Nadia leaned forward, her gaze still holding Alex's, until her mouth was level with the woman's ear. 'Shhh,' she soothed gently, her sharp teeth bared. 'If you make a sound, you'll die. Do you understand me?' she asked.

Alex watched the woman who visibly shook with terror.

Her eyes still wide, she slowly nodded.

With a victorious grin, Nadia removed the gag roughly from the woman's mouth.

Her gasps of panic aroused Alex even further.

'Please, Strigoi,' she begged in their native tongue, tears flowing faster down her face. 'Please, let me go.' Her voice trembled with fear as she stared at Alex; she knew all too well what he was.

He maintained her gaze, enjoying the sensations that ran through his body as he considered all he could do in the hours Nadia had given him.

He glanced at his sister who still stood behind the woman, her gaze intense.

Her smile was all too tempting.

Alex looked back at the woman. 'You wish to be released from your bonds?' he asked softly.

She sobbed as she nodded, broken.

Alex smiled. 'Then I am happy to grant such a request,' he assured her, glancing at Nadia.

With a cruel laugh, Nadia immediately loosened the rope that had the woman restrained to the chair. But as she attempted to stand from her seat, Nadia grabbed her arms, forcing her back down onto the chair.

'He agreed to release you from your bonds,' she hissed against the woman's ear. 'He didn't agree to let you go.'

With wide eyes, the woman glanced between the pair, her terrified sobs shaking her entire being.

Nadia laughed, caressing the woman's arms as she licked at the skin of her throat.

Alex's hunger raged once more as he watched, realising Nadia's intention earlier; she had purposefully taken her time leaving the house, making sure his hunger was at its tipping point.

The woman stared at him, fresh tears falling

down her face. 'Please,' she begged, her voice barely audible through her sobs. 'Please, don't do this.'

Ignoring her pleas, Alex took a step forward.

She shrunk back against the chair, her body shaking uncontrollably with fear as Nadia released her hold and stepped back.

Instantly he was by the woman's side, grasping her shoulders and biting into her throat, unable to contain his hunger any longer. Her hot blood filled his mouth, coating his tongue as he drank the hot liquid.

The woman's cries of pain were feeble as Alex lowered her to the floor as he drank slowly, his hand travelling from her shoulder down to her breast, his lust fuelled by the taste of her blood. He felt it awaken every fibre of his being, as if he had never fed before.

Holding the woman close, he glanced up at Nadia, who stood in the corner of the room, fixated on the scene before her. She was leaning against the wall, one foot placed flat against the brickwork behind her so that her dress slid up her thigh, her stockings visible.

She bit into her bottom lip as she watched him.

He stopped drinking, the weakened woman unable to fight against him.

Maintaining Nadia's gaze, Alex slowly moved his hand over the woman's body, down to her pelvis, his fingers teasing the material of her skirt against her body. Her mumbled cries of resistance were ignored.

Nadia's fingers slowly stroked across the skin

of her cleavage, her intense green gaze never leaving that of her twin. She licked her lips.

'She'll keep for now, my love,' she whispered. 'We have all night to enjoy her.'

All reason left his head and Alex released the woman's body. He got to his feet, crossing the room in a flash of movement.

He took his Nadia's face in his hands, kissing her lips hard.

She moaned as she returned his kiss, her hands grasping his shoulders, pulling him closer.

He trailed kisses down her jaw to her throat, biting down hard as he stared at the weeping woman on the floor.

Nadia cried out, hissing in pain before biting into his shoulder.

He had avoided this for so long and yet knew he no longer had the power to do so. He needed her blood, no matter how much he had tried to convince himself otherwise over the last few years. He had forgotten how sweet and intoxicating her blood was, the taste eradicating any memory of the human blood he had just imbibed. It filled him with ecstasy and a feeling so overwhelmingly powerful he was at a loss to give it a name.

He gave himself freely to Nadia, knowing that no matter how hard he tried, he would never be able to relinquish the temptation of her blood and body.

He had tried too many times, and failed.

He no longer had the desire to care.

1992

'Thank God she's leaving in a couple of hours,' Nadia sighed, frustrated. She sat herself down heavily on the Chesterfield, her arms crossed. She stared at the clock on the mantle in Vallakia's drawing room.

Alex smiled at her. 'Sulking does not suit you, my love,' he stated, moving away from the mantle to sit at her side.

'It's her fault I'm in this mood,' she sneered, staring at the fire in the grate.

Alex wrapped his arm around her shoulders. 'Come now, my love. She does not mean to offend,' he soothed. 'She is our ancient grandmother, after all. She deserves our respect.'

He watched his sister roll her eyes; the reunion had not gone as smoothly as everyone had perhaps hoped.

His ancient grandmother, Străbunică, had come to stay at his family home for a few days as she passed through Europe on her way to the Himalayas.

Alex had not seen his ancient grandmother for

centuries; he and Nadia had visited her during their long travels back in the eighteenth century, when she had been residing in Scotland.

For the last century and a half, she had resided in Alaska, the openness and solitude suiting her perfectly; she was over three thousand years of age and had seen the world change vastly over that time into something she barely recognised.

At first, Nadia had been pleased to see her relative, yet once Străbunică arrived at the Demeter family home, their ancient grandmother had clashed with Nadia as they disagreed on every topic, from politics to marriage; Nadia's evident disrespect of the elders seemed to extend to Străbunică for reasons Alex was unsure of, and Nadia had been especially annoyed at Străbunică's insistence that she should have been married off after her failed betrothal to Freiderick.

Alex had felt uncomfortable with the direction of those conversations; Străbunică was not aware of the truth behind Nadia's failed marriage or the extent of the relationship between the twins. Most of their antics had been kept secret from their ancient grandmother, which had been made easier by her reclusive life over the last few centuries.

After an uncomfortable few days, both himself and Nadia, along with their parents had then escorted Străbunică to Vallakia in the early hours for a final goodbye with the elders before she left at sunset.

It struck Alex as odd that she would not want

to spend more time in Vallakia; Străbunică seemed to see it as a necessity of duty rather than a warm family reunion.

He put his concerns to the back of his mind and rested his head against his sister's tenderly. 'Do not fret, my love,' he whispered.

Nadia sighed. 'I just want everything to go back to normal,' she said. 'I'm fed up of treading on eggshells and holding my tongue. I have to constantly put up with her talk of marriage and suitors, as if we were still living in the eighteenth century. It bored me then and it still bores me now,' she huffed.

Alex chuckled gently. 'All will be as it was,' he sighed. 'Come sunset she will be on her way for another century or two. Then it will just be the two of us once more.'

It had been hard to be together as they wished when there was a visitor in the house; they missed their freedom. Alex had secretly been counting down the hours all day to when Străbunică would leave Vallakia on her travels.

'I miss you,' Nadia pouted, uncrossing her arms and turning to him.

He took her face in his hands and placed a tender kiss against her forehead. 'And I you, my love,' he whispered against her lips. 'Let us go hunting once we have bid her goodbye,' he said with a grin. 'We can reclaim our freedom as our own.'

She smiled up at him. 'I would like that,' she said, hugging him.

He held her close.

The door to the room opened and the two released each other quickly.

Their ancient grandmother entered the room with a smile. 'There you two are,' she said kindly. 'You two must be glued together, as I dare say I never see you apart,' she said lightly.

Nadia withheld a sneer, turning back to the fire.

Alex stood from his seat with a courteous smile as Străbunică sat herself down in the large armchair by the fire.

He returned to his seat next to Nadia.

The light of the fire played across Străbunică's ancient face, her features unchanged for centuries; her porcelain skin was completely free of flaw, her eyes still a vivid deep green. Her long hair was a rich chestnut brown, something Alex had always noticed considering those of the direct Demeter bloodline inherited the ink-black hair of their ancestors.

She looked at the pair of them. 'Did I interrupt something?' she asked carefully.

Nadia turned to her. 'Actually—'

'We were just discussing how sad it is that you are leaving us so soon, Străbunică,' Alex interrupted, offering his sister a quick glance of warning.

She glared at him before returning her gaze to the fire.

Străbunică smiled. 'It has been very nice to be amongst family once more,' she sighed, her delicate voice almost melodic. 'It has been far too long. But of course, you must come and visit,' she said, by way of instruction rather than an offer.

Nadia sighed, fixing her ancient grandmother with her most sarcastic smile. 'That would be most agreeable,' she said forcefully.

Alex stared at her. *'Please be nice, my love,'* he pleaded mentally.

Străbunică ignored Nadia's sarcasm. 'Good,' she said with a smile, looking between the two of them once more. 'I really cannot believe how fine you two have grown,' she appraised.

Nadia nodded. 'So you have said,' she pointed out. 'We are not children any longer.'

Străbunică shrugged. 'Indeed you are not,' she said thoughtfully.

Nadia glanced at Alex. *'Wait for it...'* she sneered in his mind.

'I am still surprised that after all this time neither of you have settled down,' she said, looking at each of them in turn suggestively.

'And here we go again.' Nadia's words dripped with sarcasm in Alex's mind.

He looked at the floor. *'Let it go, Sister,'* he pleaded with her silently. *'She is old fashioned. You know from experience that is all women had to talk about back then.'*

'She has spent too much time alone,' Nadia sneered. *'It's sent her mad. She thinks we all still wear corsets and pantaloons.'*

She forced another smile. 'Well, as I said the

other day when we had this conversation, perhaps we just haven't found the right people. You can't rush these things.'

The ancient woman chuckled. 'You are quite right,' she agreed. 'Herr Walser was clearly not the correct choice. I'm glad that was called off.'

Nadia grinned. 'So was I,' she said, vindictiveness in her voice.

Alex stared at her, uncomfortable with the direction of the conversation.

He stood from his seat. 'Should we go and find the Others, Străbunică?' he asked, trying to disguise his discomfort. 'Time is too short to not spend these last hours together.'

Nadia stood to stand by his side. 'I'll come with you,' she offered.

Străbunică laughed. 'Good gracious, young lady,' she said cheerfully. 'Do you have to go everywhere your brother does? You two spend far too much time together,' she added.

Nadia frowned. 'What do you mean by that?' she asked, incredulous.

Alex glanced at his sister. *'Leave it, my love,'* he begged mentally.

She ignored him.

Străbunică shrugged. 'You two are so close, but you spend far too much time together. It is quite unnatural. I dare say young men are scared to approach you, my dear,' she laughed light-heartedly.

Nadia did not see the funny side. 'Then they are

not worth the trouble, are they? I do not waste my time on those unworthy of my presence.'

Alex released a slow breath, his gaze holding his sister's for a moment. 'I'm sure, in time, there will be someone worthy of my sister's hand,' he said, his voice rough. He cleared his throat.

Nadia glared at him. 'And maybe there will *not*,' she added, her tone sharp.

Străbunică laughed. 'Of course there will,' she insisted.

Nadia frowned. 'Why should there?' she asked, frustrated. 'You have raised this subject every day since the moment you arrived at our door and you refuse to listen. Why should I need to depend on someone else? I am happy as I am,' she protested.

The ancient woman waved her hand through the air in dismissal. 'With only your brother for company? Nonsense. Everyone needs someone,' she insisted. 'You both just need more time.'

Nadia's gaze darkened as she glared at the woman before her.

Alex watched his sister, trying to warn her off; he knew what she was like when she lost her temper.

'I do not need *time*,' she argued. 'I do not need someone else in my life, telling me what I should do or how I should behave. I had enough of that with Herr Walser.'

Străbunică stared at her. 'I do not appreciate raised voices, my dear,' she cautioned. 'I am only giving my advice.'

RETRIBUTION DARKENED

Alex did not like the atmosphere that had instantly gathered in the room. 'Ladies, I believe we should perhaps leave this conversation to another time,' he soothed.

Nadia ignored him. 'No, you're not, you're interfering. What right have you to do so? Where have you been for the past few centuries?' she chastised. 'Was I not *advised* that the marriage would be good for me in the first place?' she stated. 'Yet I do believe that was very misguided advice, in the end. He was a man with no honour or respectability, and certainly showed me no benevolence.'

Străbunică frowned. 'From what I understand, he was not amenable to your closeness to your brother,' she stated sternly. 'Which, I believe, is my point exactly.'

Alex stared at his sister hard. *'Let this go, my love,'* he cautioned mentally. *'Let her believe what she will.'*

Nadia did not answer him. She continued to glare at the ancient woman in front of her.

'Alex is my twin,' she insisted. 'I do not need to apologise to you, or anyone else, for being close to him and spending my days with him. Who do you think you are, coming here after so long and believing you can dictate to me?'

Străbunică glared at Nadia. 'How dare you speak to me in such a manner,' she hissed.

Nadia lifted her chin. 'I will speak to you however I see fit,' she snarled. 'No one tells me what to do. Herr Walser tried, and he paid for it.'

Alex stared at her wide-eyed, not believing what she had just divulged.

Străbunică looked at him, confused. 'What does she mean by that?' she asked.

Nadia growled. '*She* means that Herr Walser tried to dishonour his fiancée in the most vilest of ways. He tried to control and dictate, and for that he paid with his life.'

Realisation crossed the ancient woman's face as she stared between the twins. 'I was told the marriage was called off on account of his disrespect of the family.'

Nadia smiled maliciously. 'You were misled,' she said sharply.

Străbunică turned to Alex, yet he refused to meet her gaze; he didn't need reminding of his actions that day, or the reasons behind them.

'This is folly,' she declared. 'I don't believe it.'

Nadia hissed. 'Then you are a fool,' she scathed.

'Why would you do such a thing?' Străbunică asked.

'He tried to take me away from Alex's side and I was not prepared to allow that,' Nadia said. 'He was too egotistical to accept my affection for my twin. He was threatened by it. He was weak.'

'You destroyed one of our own?' she asked, shocked. 'How could you do such a thing? This is what results from your bond,' she stated. 'It is too restrictive on your lives,' Străbunică stressed, still shocked at the revelations.

'Our bond *is* our lives,' Nadia pointed out. 'Your ancient age reflects in your ignorance,' she said scathingly.

Silence fell on the room for a moment.

Alex stared at the floor, knowing that any attempt to sooth the conversation was now lost.

Nadia glared at her ancient grandmother, a darkness in her green eyes.

Străbunică stared into the fire, the shock of Nadia's revelations etched on her face.

Nadia's grin was vindictive. 'It would seem this family hides a great many secrets,' she sneered.

The ancient woman finally looked round at Alex. 'Is what she tells me the truth, my child?' she asked numbly.

'You dare call me a liar?' Nadia asked, her words filled with malice.

Alex looked to his sister before returning his gaze back to Străbunică; there was no point in lying any longer.

He nodded. 'We share blood, yes. We have done so for a long time.'

'There,' Nadia spat. 'So now you have the truth, despite it having nothing to do with you.'

Străbunică sat staring at Alex for a moment, ignoring Nadia completely. She stood from her seat, pacing the room.

Alex glanced at his sister; she smiled as if pleased with herself.

Străbunică suddenly turned to him. 'You have touched your sister?' she asked, disgust filling her tone. Her expression was pained. 'You take her blood and touch her? You live as lovers?'

Alex suddenly found he could not answer; her reaction was not a surprise, yet the way he was feeling was. For so long, no one had dared to condemn the relationship he shared with Nadia. Now, someone was openly voicing their revulsion and disgust; a deep-seated shame washed over him.

Nadia laughed as he remained silent.

'Yes, he does,' she answered for him, no repentance or apology in her tone. 'And do you know what?' she asked, sneering. 'He *enjoys* it.'

Străbunică stared at the floor, her gaze thoughtful as if she were trying to organise her thoughts. 'Then the vileness has spread far more than I feared,' she murmured to herself. 'It contaminated everything.'

Alex watched her, mystified; something about her very words chilled him to the bone.

Nadia's eyes narrowed. 'And who's fault is that?' she asked.

Străbunică looked up and glared at Nadia. 'I despair of you, child,' she said.

'Excuse me?' Nadia asked fiercely.

'You seduced your own brother,' she accused, 'and used him to dispose of your fiancé.'

Nadia snarled. 'How dare you,' she seethed.

Străbunică took no notice. 'You corrupt your own flesh and blood and use him for your own ends.'

Nadia's gaze grew darker. 'You dare blame me for it all?' She glanced at Alex.

'That is unfair,' he protested.

Străbunică shook her head. 'I say not,' she stated. 'You mean to tell me that you would have committed such acts were it not for this debauched bond you share?'

Alex could not answer.

The ancient woman turned to Nadia. 'You are evil, my child,' she stated. 'There is something dark and corrupt within you. You destroyed your own brother, the one piece of goodness in your life.'

Nadia snarled with a viciousness Alex had never seen her use before; it severely unnerved him.

'You dare place all the blame on my shoulders?' she shouted, her voice filled with rage.

'I judge as I see fit,' Străbunică snapped back.

'You do not have the right to judge me,' Nadia screamed. 'No one does. My life is my own and I live it as *I* see fit. You dare come here and dictate to us what we can and cannot do? You think you hold sway because you are our elder? You are *nothing*. Weak, just like the rest of them. Vile, decrepit husks with an inflated illusion of control. I damn you all. I damn you to Hell!'

Alex stared as his sister stormed out of the room, slamming the door behind her.

Străbunică turned to look at him, her expression stony and accusing.

Once more, he found himself lost for words.

* * *

'Will you not come hunting with me, Brother?' Nadia asked, leaning against the doorframe of Alex's bedroom.

He looked up at her from where he sat on the bed, noting her short dress and thigh-high boots.

'I'm not too hungry right now,' he answered, hoping she wouldn't see through his lie.

He had hidden himself away in his room after the argument in the drawing room, hoping to wait out the next hour until Străbunică left Vallakia. Yet despite the silence of the room around him, the memory of that confrontation relived itself over and over in his mind, taunting him with the truth of the shame he'd felt.

Nadia continued to stare at him as she entered the room. 'Is something wrong?' she asked carefully.

She stood at the foot of his bed, staring at him.

He felt uncomfortable under her scrutiny. 'No,' he lied. 'I am just not very hungry right now. Perhaps I will hunt later, after Străbunică has departed and we have said our farewells.'

Nadia rolled her eyes. 'I thought we could forgo that little inconvenience and seek our freedom as we had planned,' she stated.

Alex watched his sister carefully. 'We only have to say goodbye,' he pressed.

'*You* can if you like,' she sneered. 'But I will do

no such thing. I am not a hypocrite,' she pointed out. 'I refuse to be nice to that woman to satisfy everyone else's sense of duty.'

Alex sighed and stared down at the floor. Străbunică had stormed out of the drawing room soon after Nadia, continuing to voice her disgust as she sought out his parents to confront them for allowing "incestuous activity". He doubted Vlad and Gabriella had escaped rebuke, either.

His ancient grandmother's words still played in his head: *"You mean to tell me that you would have committed such acts were it not for this debauched bond you share?"*

He could not forget them, or answer the question. He knew it was their blood sharing that corrupted them; it was the very reason why he had refused to partake of Nadia's blood for so long. Yet since they had started once again, she had become his life; he could not envisage an existence without her in it, nor did he want to.

Still the shame washed over him.

'Come hunting with me, Alex,' Nadia pouted, her tone full of impatience.

'You go,' he said softly. 'I will feast later.'

She glared at him. 'You're avoiding me,' she said, her words a statement, not a question.

He found he could not quite meet her gaze as he tried to hide his discomfort. 'Don't be silly,' he said, his voice wavering under her dark glare.

'I am not stupid, Alex,' she warned. 'You wanted

us to hunt together until *she* interfered. Now you wish me to go without you.'

He shook his head, still unable to look at her. 'You are being ridiculous,' he said.

'Am I?' she asked, incredulous. 'Your distance tells me otherwise. If that witch hadn't—'

'Don't call her that,' he retaliated, staring at her for the first time; the glare in her eyes unnerved him.

'Why not? It is what she is.' Nadia sighed, her words softening. 'She does not understand what we have, my love, and for that she condemns it. Her words were untrue. You know how you feel when we are together and she would have you doubt that. She questions our power and you have heeded her words.'

'I haven't,' he lied once more.

'Liar,' she spat. 'You dare sit there and lie to me? She has turned you against me.'

'No, she hasn't,' he argued.

She snarled at him. 'You listened to what she said and she has made you ashamed of me.'

'No, Nadia, she—'

'Liar,' she screamed. 'Stop lying to me. You have taken her side. You listen to her wicked words and reject me. She has turned you against me,' she repeated.

Alex stood from his seat on the bed. He reached out for his sister, but she pushed his hands away.

'Do not pretend you care,' she snarled. 'You hate me. She has turned you against me and made you hate me for the bond we share. She has made you ashamed of it.'

'Nadia, listen to me,' he said, struggling to grasp her arms.

She lashed out, slicing his cheek with her sharp nails.

He recoiled from her, pressing his hand to his cheek.

She glared at him. 'She won't get away with this,' she warned, a calmness to her voice that seemed more threatening that her hysteria.

Alex stared at her, dread seizing his body. 'What do you mean?' he asked tentatively.

She didn't answer him.

Nadia smiled sweetly, only the darkness in her eyes betraying the madness within.

Alex felt a chill settle deep within him as he watched his sister leave the room.

* * *

He had not seen Nadia since their argument nearly an hour ago and he had not been able to get rid of the feeling of dread that seemed to have taken root deep within him; there had been something terrifying within her eyes.

Alex found himself unable to stand still as he paced the drawing room, watching the clock tick down the minutes until his ancient grandmother would leave Vallakia and the uncertainty of his sister's actions far behind.

His parents sat together on the Chesterfield, talking quietly. Alex was aware of their furtive glances every so often, which only served to make his melancholy mood worse.

The events of the afternoon ran through his mind, haunting him; for once, he felt very alone.

Alex sighed and stared out of the window, the peace of the mountains around him feeling out of his reach; there was nothing peaceful about the life he had fashioned for himself.

He closed his eyes as the carriage clock continued to count down the minutes, the rhythmic ticking almost therapeutic.

He took a deep breath and exhaled slowly, repeating the process several times; trying in vain to embrace some semblance of calm.

A distant scream pierced the air outside from somewhere in the grounds.

An icy coldness filled his entire being as Alex opened his eyes.

'What was that?' he asked, looking at his parents.

Victor stood from his seat, his expression filled with concern. 'I have no idea,' he murmured, holding on to Aurelia's hand.

The door to the drawing room burst open and Alex turned to see Gabriella standing in the doorway, her eyes filled with terror as tears fell down her cheeks.

'What's happened?' Alex asked, dread seizing

every inch of his body as the scream sounded again; his stomach twisted with fear.

Gabriella met his gaze as she struggled to find her voice. 'Your sister...' she wept, sending Aurelia to her side.

Gabriella held onto Aurelia with desperation as she sobbed. 'Străbunică... she's...'

The air suddenly felt too thick to breathe and Alex forced his legs to move as he crossed the room towards his elder.

'Where?' he asked simply; any other words failed him.

Gabriella looked up at him, the fear in her eyes chilling him to his core.

'The clearing... in the orchard,' she breathed.

Without another word, Alex pushed past his elder and rushed through Vallakia's main hall, out through the main entrance and into the courtyard, the ice-cold air filled with a sickening smell of burning smoke.

His feet instantly felt too heavy to move as he forced himself forward with each step towards the gardens, the smoke growing thicker as the unmistakable glow of a fire raged above the treeline.

He could hear Gabriella's sobbing, now matched by his mother's, as they followed somewhere behind, the sound somehow feeling detached as he pushed himself on, the smoke beginning to sting his eyes and lungs. He could feel the heat from the flames now as the mountain air became thick with rancid smoke that made him heave with every breath.

The unmistakable screams of agony were growing louder; he found himself stopping in his tracks, terrified to go any further.

Other sounds mingled with the screams ahead of him and sobs at his back; those of shouts and arguing, though he was unable to make sense of the words.

Cursing himself for being such a coward, he pushed himself forward into the clearing on the edge of the castle orchards.

Alex felt nausea well up in the pit of his stomach at the sight in front of him.

Nadia stood to the side, held by Vlad and several of Vallakia's staff as she struggled in their arms, her eyes burning with the reflection of the flames that burned on the ground. She looked pleased with herself, a maniacal grin on her lips as she stared, transfixed, by the fire in front of her. Her hand was covered in blood as she grasped something tightly in her fist. At her feet, on the grass, was a wrought iron sconce, no doubt taken from the walls of Vallakia's great hall.

She had started the fire.

Alex heard his elders behind him as they sobbed collectively, seeking shelter in each other from the grotesque scene before them.

Alex tried to swallow past the nausea as the ringing in his ears subsided.

Screams filled the air around him, the unholy

sound tearing what was left of his resolve to pieces. His blood ran cold as he forced himself to stare at the flames before him, the smell of burning flesh making him retch.

The silhouette of a woman writhed within the flames as she lay on the ground, a long metal spike pinning her to the ground where it had been driven through her stomach, fixing her in place before her clothing had been set alight..

Alex knew it was Străbunică.

He found himself grotesquely unable to look away from the burning figure, the flames licking at the tragic woman's skin that blistered and burned as she continued to scream with unimaginable agony.

The overwhelming intensity of the hatred needed to commit such an act had him trembling and the smell of his ancient grandmother's burning flesh had his stomach heaving as he fell to his knees, nothing but bile forced from his stomach.

He turned his attentions to his sister, who stood there as if mesmerised by the flames.

The smile remained on her face as Vlad and the others maintained their hold on her.

'*How could you do this?*' Alex asked her mentally, unable to find the words to speak aloud.

She didn't look at him. '*I told you she was a witch,*' she said, the words echoing in his head; there was amusement in her tone. '*You remember what they used to do to witches, Alex,*' she jeered.

He glared between his sister and the fire, unable

to make sense of the cacophony of thoughts in his mind.

Nadia looked at him.

There was no remorse on her face. She laughed, the sound terrifying.

A shiver ran the length of his spine as he stared at her, his hands shaking by his sides, tears filling his eyes.

She continued to laugh, her hysteria and madness plain for all to see.

Finally, he managed to find his voice. 'How could you do this?' he shouted at her, his voice breaking with emotion.

She glared at him. 'Because I can,' she screamed at him, her voice echoing around the clearing. 'She deserved it. She tried to turn you against me with her judgement.'

She opened her blood-stained fist and threw something onto the grass at her feet.

Alex felt the bile rise once again as he stared at the tongue his sister had sliced from their elder's mouth.

Nadia grinned. 'We call them our elders, but they're weak and pathetic. They're nothing. *Nothing*,' she screamed.

Alex remained on his knees as he watched Vlad and the staff struggle with his sister, her eyes filled with a sadistic victory as she glared at him.

As his parents and Gabriella sobbed behind him, he watched as Vlad and the staff grappled with

Nadia as she continued to scream at them, her words no longer registering; all he could hear were those terrifying screams emerging from the flames.

She snarled and hissed at her captors as they started to drag her away towards Vallakia.

He didn't try to stop them; there was nothing he could do for her now.

Nadia glared at Alex across the clearing. *'Do not let them take me, Brother,'* she screamed in his head, the force of the words making him wince. *'I did this for you, for us. You cannot let them take me again.'*

He looked to the floor, trying to keep her out of his head.

He failed.

'Alex, please,' she screeched. *'You promised.'*

She screamed as they dragged her away, the sound filled with defiance as it echoed around the clearing.

'No matter what.'

2003

Alex sat up in bed, his head thumping.

He had tried so hard to escape the despondency he'd felt constantly since Nadia had been taken away, yet nothing he tried seemed to ease the helplessness that encased him; every minute of every day was spent mourning the loss of his twin as if she were dead. His dreams were filled with visions of her, her whispers both seductive and equally destructive.

Death may be the greatest of all human blessings. He thought on the words he had learnt many years ago; Socrates, as he recalled. How true those words seemed to him now, though at the time he had thought little of them; he had been young and full of anticipation of the eternity before him.

Four centuries of tragedy and loss had made those words all too true.

Time could be a dangerous curse, he mused.

The darkness engulfed him, the silence of the early hours overwhelming to his ears.

With a sigh, he glanced at the woman beside

him, the misery within him growing.

She was a beauty, there was no doubt of that. He'd spotted her straight away at the party his parents had held; the pointless one that he knew was only to get him socialising again after mourning his sister for so long.

After his sister had been locked away, he'd decided to travel with his parents across Europe. They had visited numerous members of the family, no doubt in the vain hope of distracting him from his despair and guilt.

It hadn't worked.

On his return to Romania, his parents had deemed it necessary to fill the family home with parties and other social events, clearly trying to give him something to focus on rather than his loneliness.

He shook his head with despair as he continued to look at the woman beside him.

Not even her gentle breathing as she slept broke through the wall of stillness that surrounded them.

She had been charming company, though too young for his tastes; she hadn't experienced enough of life to understand the hardships, tragedies and heartbreaks it could yield.

Even her skills as a lover had left much to be desired.

He stared at the mark on her throat where he'd taken her blood. It had barely started to heal; another sign of her vampiric youth.

Her head rested against the pillow, her black

hair framing her pale face as it fanned across the pillow.

He closed his eyes, reprimanding himself for being such a vile bastard; he couldn't even remember her name.

During the party, he'd simply gravitated towards her due to her looks; ink-black hair, pale face, voluptuous body – not that she knew how to utilise it properly.

The woman had reminded him of *Her*.

He'd tried so hard to pretend throughout the party and the subsequent intimacy they had shared. Yet his efforts had been in vain, for no matter how hard he tried, the beauty's eyes were not *her* eyes; they weren't green like emeralds, nor did they shine with life and seduction. The woman's face hadn't been the same one that haunted his dreams night after night.

When she'd bitten into him during their lovemaking, her bite had been tentative and in no way matched the kiss he craved; the one that made him shiver with excitement and commanded his upmost attentions.

Her blood had tasted like so many others he had sampled over the centuries; it was bland and pointless, lacking the sultry taste that he desired above anything else. The one that filled him with ecstasy and longing. The blood that possessed him.

He ran his hands over his face, trying to wipe away the disgust he felt at himself. This young woman wasn't to blame for his own inadequacy; it wasn't her fault he was unable to leave his past desires where they belonged.

He was weary with trying to pretend for the sake of everyone around him. He needed to see his sister once more; he could no longer abide the separation.

He could imagine her still so clearly, her beauty statuesque and not marred by time at all. She was as perfect now, four centuries after she had matured, as she had been that very day.

The desolation filled him once more as he remembered that today had indeed been their Maturity Day.

He could live with the pain no longer.

He'd tried to live without her, God knew he had tried. He didn't want to think of the reason he was without her now; the memory was far too painful to bear.

He'd forgiven her so much over the centuries, even though deep down he knew she didn't deserve it. She'd shown no remorse for her actions that had caused unspeakable suffering to others.

He'd been wholly complicit in many of her games, the dark thrill of their power too enticing to resist; shame washed over him as he thought on the innocent lives they'd destroyed for their own amusement.

If he could go back and undo such acts, he'd gladly do so if he knew it would spare the pain he'd helped to inflict.

It was all his fault. His need for his sister's blood

had drawn him back to her side time and time again and he'd been too weak to resist. For four centuries, she had been his sister, his twin, his lover, and his life. He was bound to her, always, as she was to him.

There was nothing either of them could do to change that harsh truth.

Closing his eyes, his thoughts tormented him.

He could still hear her defiant screams as the Others had dragged her away, their punishment for her actions severe and relentless; just as her own conduct had been.

Her intense green gaze, so filled with hate and rage, had been fixed on him as he had stood by and let them take her.

The memories haunted him still, just as he feared they always would.

He was unsure if she would ever truly forgive him for accepting her fate so willingly.

He was equally unsure if he deserved it.

* * *

Alex avoided his mother's gaze as he wandered into the drawing room; he was grateful for his father's absence as he was unsure if he could face them both.

Aurelia smiled at her son. 'I had thought you were avoiding me, my child,' she said softly, no accusation in her words. She stood by the window, her stylish skirt and blouse accenting her features.

He stopped in his tracks, not quite able to meet

her gaze. 'Not at all, Mother,' he said, the tremble in his voice betraying his lie.

Her smile widened. 'Did your guest find everything to her agreement?' she asked gently.

Alex felt his cheeks flush, his gaze settling on the floor at his feet. He cleared his throat.

'She did indeed,' he answered, his words feeble.

Aurelia stared at her son for a moment, then crossed the room towards the chesterfield. She sat herself down, patting the seat next to her.

'Come and sit with me, Alex,' she said, her voice full of cheer as if there was nothing wrong; he admired his mother's strength so much in that instant.

Looking up, he took a deep breath before crossing the room, sitting himself next to his mother.

She took one of his hands in hers, giving it a small squeeze. 'I miss our little chats,' she said sadly. 'You distance yourself so, it is painful for me to watch,' she admitted.

Alex placed his other hand on top of her own, his gaze finding hers. 'It was not my intention to cause you distress, Mother,' he assured her, hating himself for upsetting her so.

'I know it was not your intention, my child,' she said gently. 'I do not accuse you of such. I only know of your solitude and angst, and cannot sit by and watch my son torment himself so. When we returned home I thought that filling the house with laughter and light once more would help you away from the darkness you find yourself enshrouded in.'

He smiled at her. 'I know you were only doing what you thought was best,' he said softly. 'And I thank you for it, truly.' He shrugged. 'Maybe in time...'

Aurelia stared at him. 'It has been eleven years, my child,' she said, concern clouding her beautiful features. 'I am unsure how much longer you can punish yourself and allow your life to go on without living it.'

Alex couldn't answer her; everything she said was true, yet he couldn't let go of the past. Despite everything, he needed his twin back.

She sighed. 'I am not a fool, my child,' she said softly. 'Nor am I blind. It did not escape my notice that the only woman you seemed interested in last night, your lady friend, was one who resembled your sister, albeit vaguely.'

He stared at her, wide-eyed. He knew his mother was incredibly perceptive – it was her gift, in a way – yet he had not realised how obvious he had been; his judgement was lapsing, as was everything else.

He opened his mouth to speak, yet found the words would not come.

Aurelia squeezed his hands in hers once more. 'You are so lost, my child, and I fear for you,' she said, emotion filling her voice.

Alex closed his eyes, fighting back his tears. 'I do not know what to do, Mother,' he admitted. 'I have tried, so hard, to carry on without her here. I cannot explain it to you, no more than I am able to explain it to myself.'

'You must try,' she insisted. 'You must, for your own sanity and peace of mind. You cannot continue to live with this alone.'

He sighed. 'I miss her,' he admitted finally.

Aurelia smiled. 'She is your twin, Alex. Whatever else has befallen the pair of you over your lives, there is no shame to be had in admitting such loss.'

A tear escaped his eye as he glanced at his mother. 'I've tried to carry on without her, but it feels that every day my efforts grow more and more futile. She's my twin. She's part of me, as I am of her. We share the same blood. Her pain is my pain. I cannot explain it when no one truly understands it, but I am lost without her. Her absence is as if part of me is missing and I can no longer abide it. I want her back by my side.'

Finally saying such things to someone other than himself felt as if a weight had been lifted.

He wiped the tear from his cheek and looked at his mother.

Aurelia smiled at him tenderly. 'I know you do, my child. There is no wrong in wishing to have your sister by your side. You are right when you say no one understands. We truly never will, and for that I am sorry,' she said sadly. 'I am sorry that you have to shoulder such burdens alone because no one can truly understand and help you, but you must not continue to hold your fears and worries within, as it will not do to continue torturing yourself.'

Alex nodded, knowing she was right, as she always was.

'However,' she said, her tone serious. 'That does not mean that I condone any of your actions, my child,' she warned. 'The pair of you have committed some atrocities over the years that cannot ever be forgotten, or forgiven.' A tear appeared in her eye and she quickly wiped it away.

'Your actions and deeds have been unspeakably horrific,' she said, her emotion breaking into her voice. 'And as for the intimacy you share...' She trailed off, taking a deep breath to compose herself. '...That in itself has been the evil that has fuelled all of it. You and your sister have destroyed all decency with your... I cannot find a suitable word for it, my child,' she said.

Alex stared down at her hands holding his, the familiar sting of shame washing over him. 'I cannot explain the bond I share with Nadia, nor can I seem to fight it. However,' he said quietly, 'I feel you have perhaps misunderstood it.'

He looked up at her.

Her gaze was clouded with confusion. 'How so?' she asked carefully.

'I'm well aware what everyone thinks. No doubt I'll never be able to rectify that, no matter what I tell you here in this room. Yes, I confess to sharing blood with my sister, which in itself is wrong. Even more so when the way in which we share it is as lovers would.'

He was aware of his mother shifting

uncomfortably in her seat, yet she still maintained her hold on his hands in support.

'I confess to drinking my sister's blood whilst holding her as a lover, and yes my thoughts alone have been vile and indecent as the need for her blood has grown more and more over the centuries. I cannot explain it, but her blood holds a power over me like no other ever has. No other taste compares, no matter how much I wish it would. It's a desire that's consumed us both.'

Alex held his mother's hands firmly, staring into her eyes and hoping with every fibre of his being that she believed what he had to say. 'Yet I swear to you now, Mother, that nothing in any physical form has ever happened between us. I'm aware that this is what people have concluded and that many will not believe me. But to you, Mother, I swear with my being that I tell the truth. My relationship with my sister is beyond that of family, yet it is not so far as incestuous. My thoughts may have been anything but pure, and for that I take my punishment, yet I have never defiled my own sister.'

Aurelia stared at him for a moment, words seemingly lost.

Alex took a deep breath, his heart pounding in his chest. Confessing the truth to his mother was a relief after so many years living with the darkness of his own thoughts and desires. He didn't care what others thought of his relationship with his sister; they would make their own judgements regardless. But he could no longer see his mother torment herself with thoughts and images that weren't true.

He owed her the truth.

She cupped his cheek with her hand tenderly. 'You are braver than I perhaps gave you credit for, my son,' she said gently. 'I am proud of you for confessing such hard facts to me.'

She wiped a tear from her cheek and grasped his hands. 'There is hope still,' she said quietly.

Alex glanced down at her hand holding his. 'I fear I am beyond hope, Mother,' he admitted sadly.

'Those with true remorse are never beyond hope,' she advised, pulling him to her in a tender embrace. 'The light is always there, so long as you do not close your eyes to it.'

For the first time in many years, he felt warmth within.

'All I ever wanted for my two children was happiness,' she admitted. 'You will find it, one day,' she said, certainty in her voice.

'Yes, Mother,' he said, tears falling unchecked down his cheeks as he pulled away from her embrace to look at her; he wasn't sure he believed her words.

She reached out and wiped away his tears. 'You will,' she insisted. 'You will find it in the most unlikely place and at the most unlikely time, as is the way with these things,' she smiled.

'And Nadia?' he asked, hope in his voice.

Aurelia sighed. 'You are both powerful beyond words, my child,' she said. 'With each other you are stronger, and I cannot question that. However, it is your blood bond that makes you dangerous. It separates you from those around you and corrupts you. If you are to find a way through this and both of you are to find happiness, then your blood sharing must cease. If it does not, then I am unsure what your future will be, for either of you,' she admitted sadly.

Alex knew she spoke the truth. He'd known for far too long that it was their blood sharing that had caused so many of the atrocities they had committed. It corrupted them into shameless monsters who glorified in their own twisted sense of power.

To be without that bond was a torment he found near impossible to endure, yet endure it he would if it meant saving his sister from the terrifying ordeal she'd suffered these past eleven years. He'd sensed her pain and agony on many occasions as she'd starved and reflected on her actions, her own screams her only company in the darkness.

He owed it to Nadia to secure her freedom, even if she never wished to see him again.

Maybe then he wouldn't feel so lost.

'Would you speak to the Others about Nadia's release?' he asked, hopeful. 'I cannot truly rest until she is freed from that atrocious place. I cannot live my life while I know she suffers so.'

Aurelia stared at her son, unable to find the words to answer him.

Alex waited, yet still his mother remained silent.

There was no answer to be had.

Now...

Chapter 48

Alex shifted in his chair as something tickled his ear, like someone blowing gently against his skin.

'Wakey, wakey.' Nadia's voice was full of sarcasm and hostility.

He stirred slowly, unwilling to be part of whatever game she had in mind to play.

She flicked his earlobe.

He opened his eyes, glaring at her with scorn.

'Can't you let me rest for one moment?' he asked, agitated by her very presence.

Nadia fell back on the sofa, her short black skirt riding up her thighs. 'No,' she said shortly, a smug smile on her face. 'Where would be the fun in that?'

Alex snorted in disgust, standing from his chair. He crossed the room to stand over the mantle, the pain of his memories still too raw.

Nadia had finally been released thirteen years after being locked away. Alex recalled there had still been a great deal of hurt within the family and many vowed never to forgive her. Some swore to never forgive the Others for releasing her.

Once released, she'd refused to speak to anyone. She would only hunt animals and it had been pitiful to see her in such a state.

Alex grasped a small log from the side of the mantle and placed it onto the open fire, the wood cracking and spitting as the flames encased it. He stared into the fire, too many thoughts racing through his mind.

He'd decided to take Nadia away from all the judgement and memories of the past. He'd spent hours arguing his decision, and eventually Vlad had seen sense in Alex's reasoning and gave his permission.

Leaving Romania, he'd travelled with his sister for the next three years. At first, Nadia still wouldn't speak to him. She continued hunting only animals and avoided all human contact.

Eventually she'd turned to him, desolate and tormented.

To prove to her he didn't hate her, he'd promised never to mention the past again. They would continue as if all the bad had never happened. It was a new start.

Alex listened to the crackle of the flames in the grate as he closed his eyes; it was a promise he'd failed to keep after confessing everything to Catrina.

As their travels continued, Nadia had become his life once more, and when he finally tasted her blood again after so long, everything started to unravel.

Alex knew he should have known better, but his needs had overcome his common sense, just like they always had.

He wasn't proud of himself. Once more, his mistakes had cost lives and ruined many more.

Nadia sighed behind him. 'I take it your little princess is on her way to fairy tale land?' she asked, a sneer evident in her voice. She chuckled. 'Though I suppose she's now more a beast than a beauty.'

Alex growled. 'You're sick,' he grunted, turning to stare at her.

She shrugged, studying her nails in her usual careless manner. 'So you've said, too many times to recall,' she sneered, glancing up at him from under dark lashes. 'Though you're not exactly purity incarnate, are you?' Her lips curved into an insidious grin. 'How was our lovely Catrina this morning before she left?' she asked callously. 'I do hope she's feeling better.'

Alex felt his anger rise at the forced concern in her words. 'Don't act the little innocent with me, Nadia.'

She laughed, the sound filled with bitterness. 'Why, dearest Brother? Because you know I'm not?' she asked, challenge in her voice.

He turned from her, staring back into the fire. 'You haven't been innocent in a very long time,' he stated bluntly.

'As you know all too well, brother dear,' she hissed.

Alex ignored her.

Nadia sighed. 'Innocence is a boring burden to bear, dearest,' she purred. 'Life is so much more interesting without it.'

'You would know,' he snorted, refusing to look at her.

'Ouch,' she conceded with a smile.

She watched him for a moment, amused at the way he tried to ignore her. When he didn't turn around, she shrugged and pulled out her cell phone, typing in her unlock code.

Alex glanced at her surreptitiously as he remained at the mantle, watching as she checked her phone, the unmistakable look of disappointment in her eyes.

He smiled.

'No word from lover boy?' he questioned, still not turning to face her.

Nadia shifted on the sofa, her gaze dark. 'Not that it's any of your business...' she sneered.

He chuckled, finally turning to face her. 'Now that's where you're wrong,' he said, almost cheerfully. 'You see, Matt and I had a rather lengthy chat after you left his place last night.'

Nadia's expression darkened as she glared at her brother. 'Oh?'

Alex paced slowly across the room, finally perching himself on the arm of the chair opposite his sister. 'I don't think you'll be hearing from him again.'

He stared at his sister, making sure she was

listening to every word. 'Oh, Matt and I had a really "in-depth" chat.'

She glared at him. 'You influenced him, didn't you?' she asked calmly, though her eyes betrayed her anger.

Alex shrugged with a grin. 'What can I say? You taught me how to enjoy it again after your little scene with the police.' He laughed, knowing he was goading her and enjoying it for the first time in a long while; too long had he let his sister rule his life, and he finally had a chance to turn it against her.

Her games were over.

'So, yes,' he confirmed, 'I did indeed influence him. By the end of our chat, he hardly acknowledged who you were. You're simply my sister who went on a date with Jason, but whom he knows hardly anything about. You've never met for a drink or really had a chat. He certainly never kissed you or nearly betrayed Lola with you. He's not even been having relationship issues with Lola. I spoke to her as well, of course. I helped her get some real sleep, without your interfering, and after a good rest she was much more relaxed. Again, she barely knows who you are.'

He grinned at his sister. 'I do believe they're going out for dinner later tonight for some *quality* time together.'

Nadia glowered at him, her face hard like stone. 'Well done you,' she hissed sarcastically.

'Thank you,' he accepted, almost proudly.

She tossed her phone onto the coffee table and

sat forward, resting her elbows on her knees as she watched him closely. 'So I suppose you think you've won,' she said, by way of a statement rather than a question.

He snorted at her words. 'It isn't about winning, Nadia,' he said, exasperated. 'The games are over, finished. We've already done too much damage.'

He sighed heavily, sadness overwhelming him as he remembered too many unwelcome thoughts. 'Too many times in the past I've had to pick up the pieces after the unspeakable things you've done.'

Nadia smiled as she glared at him. 'And here you are, doing it again, dear brother,' she said softly, her gaze still pinned on him. 'What a knight you are, my lord,' she sneered.

'Don't call me that,' he snapped, the old unwelcome memory flooding back. 'I'm no longer that person,' he growled, avoiding her gaze.

'You'll *always* be that person,' she purred, her words sounding like a warning. 'You can't change who you are,' she said, standing slowly from her seat. 'You can't change what you've *done*.'

'I can try,' he said, his words filled with sadness.

She gently shook her head. 'You've tried for too long, Alex, and failed.' She took a step forward. 'You cannot atone for the things you've done.'

There was something sinister about her words and he stared at her, unnerved; he was aware she was taking his interfering with her games far too calmly.

'Then neither can you,' he challenged.

Her smile widened as she took another step closer. 'Maybe I don't want to,' she countered. 'You're the one who enjoyed being a shoulder to cry on, always there when things turned bad.' She studied the vacant look in his eyes.

He knew her words were true.

'You were my sister. It was what I was supposed to do,' he said slowly, glaring into her deep green eyes that mocked his own.

She shook her head. 'Oh, but it always meant so much more than that, didn't it, Alex?' she said softly, taking another step until she was close enough to reach out to him had she wished. 'It has always meant a *lot* more.'

'You were my sister, my twin,' he countered, staring into those eyes of hers that suddenly seemed too soothing. 'You were everything to me.' His words were filled with sadness as if he were speaking of someone he'd lost a long time ago, which in truth he had; the creature before him now was only the shell, but his sister, the girl he'd grown up with, had long since disintegrated.

'As you are to me,' she whispered gently, her words filled with tenderness. 'We did everything together once. We hunted together, fed together. Do you think I've forgotten the way you used to look at me as you fed?'

Alex looked away; he didn't want to remember. 'Our blood sharing corrupted what we had. It corrupted *us*. We were never supposed to—'

She placed a finger on his lips, her touch gentle. 'It's nothing to be ashamed of, dearest. We are of one blood, as we were within our mother. Our power was born to be shared with one another. It maintained our bond.' She caressed his cheek softly, aware he didn't pull away.

He felt lost in his grief as every memory came flooding back from over four centuries of corruption and betrayal.

'It was wrong,' he managed to say eventually, his voice breaking as he found himself unable to look at her. '*I* was wrong.'

She stared at him as her hand remained cupping his cheek, almost supportively. 'Alex,' she said, so softly it was barely audible. 'My poor, lost Alex.' She tipped his head up so that he was forced to look at her. 'You punish yourself still,' she whispered.

'I was wrong,' he repeated sadly.

She smiled gently, her green eyes soft. 'You were not wrong,' she said tenderly.

As he watched, she raised her hand to her mouth, running her thumb across her lips slowly, before placing it in her mouth and biting through the skin delicately, her blood beading on the surface.

As he sat there, motionless, she reached out to him, running the same thumb across his lips so softly her touch had him shivering. She coated his lips with her blood.

'See, my love,' she whispered. 'My blood sustains you, as yours sustains me. It always has.'

'It was not meant to,' he said quietly, unable to find the strength to move.

'But it does regardless,' she soothed. 'And it forever will.'

He knew he should have wiped her blood from his lips. He knew it with every fibre of his being, and yet he didn't. Her words, although hurtful, were full of truth, and he could no longer deny it.

She did indeed sustain him, as he did her; four centuries of blood sharing had all but corrupted them both, and he only had himself to blame for it all.

His reasoning lost, he instinctively licked his lips. The sweet viscous liquid invigorated him, just as it always had, and seemed to wash away all the sadness and regret with just that one small taste.

Alex lost all sense of time and space as he stared into her soft green eyes, and for a moment he thought he saw the innocent girl he'd once known all those centuries ago. His eyes filled with tears as he lost his resolve.

With a warm smile, Nadia pulled him close to her, embracing him as she had once done as his innocent sister. She held him tightly and with affection as he sobbed against her, her fingers combing through his hair to soothe him.

'Hush, my love,' she whispered, as she rested her cheek against the top of his head. 'Do not weep for what cannot be undone.'

Slowly, his tears subsided as she continued to pacify him, her gentle and tender caresses easing his pain.

She took his head in her hands and placed a kiss against his ink-black hair, continuing to soothe him.

'I'm sorry,' he managed to say, his words trembling. He held onto her tightly, needing her support; needing her forgiveness.

She nuzzled her face against his, her embrace tender. She placed another kiss against his wet cheek.

He slowly lifted his head, her hands still holding his face, and looked into those green eyes that reflected him right back. Tears still fell over his cheeks as he stared at her.

She stroked a finger down his face as she smiled at him, her gaze holding his.

'Do not cry, my love,' she whispered, brushing another kiss past his lips. 'I'm here,' she soothed, combing his hair with her fingers.

His lips were so close to hers; he found himself lost in her eyes.

Nadia brushed another kiss against his cheek, her breath hot against his lips.

He lost all sense of reason as he brought his mouth to hers in the gentlest of kisses, her intoxicating breath overriding his thoughts and needs until all he could see was her.

She returned his kiss, her tongue seeking his as her fingers pushed further into his hair, bringing him closer.

Her gentle sigh had Alex panicking and he quickly pushed her away, his breathing heavy as he stared at her.

She stood back from him, her gaze intense. She licked her lips, the movement slow and sensual.

He watched her run her fingers through her raven-black hair. She trailed her fingers down her throat and over the blue vein beneath her skin, promising to spill the blood beneath.

Nadia slowly ran a finger lower, past the base of her throat and down to where her cleavage was visible above her top.

Alex's gaze stopped with her finger.

He didn't want to think about what she was promising, yet the taste of her blood was still on his tongue and he simply found it too enticing to ignore.

He gazed back into her eyes.

She grinned at him, a seductive glint to her eyes.

He watched as she broke the skin above her breast with her sharp nail, spilling her blood for him.

His resolve snapped.

Pushing himself to his feet, he crossed the room, pushing Nadia back until she was pinned against the wall, steadying herself with her hands.

She glared at him, her breathing unsteady.

Without a word, he kissed her hard, grasping both her arms tightly. She didn't show any sign of a fight.

She surrendered to his kiss as he deepened it. He moved his mouth to the top of her breast where her blood trickled down her skin, biting down with a violent passion, her agonised cries exciting him all the more. His hand travelled down her body, grasping her thigh as she lifted her leg to buttress his hip, her short skirt rising high on her thigh.

He heard her moan.

She glanced over to the mantle as she combed her fingers aggressively through Alex's hair. A small picture of Catrina sat in a silver frame, and she smiled wickedly to herself.

She always won.

Nadia's excitement heightened and she moaned as Alex trailed kisses along her throat, his hand squeezing her thigh. He wasn't just taking her blood; that wasn't good enough for him this time.

'I knew you always wanted this, my love,' she breathed against his ear, feeling his sharp teeth pricking against the delicate skin of her throat, taking her pleasure higher. 'We're power incarnate. Your blood is my blood.'

She shuddered as he bit into her throat, his hand travelling up her skirt. 'You have always belonged to me, my lord.'

Alex's eyes snapped open.

Her words dragged him back to reality. He pushed himself away from her so fast she nearly fell to the floor.

He ran his hands over his face, his fingers trembling. 'What the hell am I doing?' he asked, his voice unsteady as the reality of his actions hit him with full force.

'What you should have done so very long ago,

to end your thirst for what your heart truly desires.'

'No.' He stared at her, his eyes full of hurt. This hadn't been simple blood sharing; this was incest. The thought screamed at him, making his guilt flare and his body tremble with regret. How could he justify feeling the way he did after all these centuries? How could he ever hope to justify feeling a deep passion for his own sister?

'No,' he repeated. 'You're wrong. *This* is wrong, as it always has been.'

She laughed, the sound chilling him to the core. She straightened her clothes as she glared at him.

'That never stopped you,' she hissed at him, withheld anger in her emerald eyes. 'That never stopped your need for my blood... or my body.'

'No,' he screamed at her, knowing that every word she spoke was the truth. 'I tried... so hard,' he said, knowing his voice lacked the conviction he so needed it to possess.

Nadia growled, her eyes narrowed.

'Not hard enough, my love,' she seethed.

Chapter 49

Alex took a step back and lowered himself onto the arm of the chair as before, his mind a cacophony of thoughts and memories as he stared at Nadia, unable to decipher the darkness in her eyes.

He ran his hands over his face, trying to eradicate the images flashing through his mind; despite the passing of the centuries, the memories had lost none of their vividness.

Nadia took a step towards him, her gaze unfaltering. 'You promised me,' she hissed, her anger barely contained. 'You promised me we would never be apart, that you would be there for me and love me forever, no matter what.'

'That was so long ago,' he choked. 'I was blinded by what we shared.'

'You promised,' she screamed, her resolve lost.

He stared at her, unable to form the words to argue against her reasoning.

'You promised me, and I gave up *everything* for you,' she snarled.

'But the things you did...' he said, his argument trailing away.

'No matter what,' she reminded him, her gaze dark. 'I did those things for *you*,' she seethed, taking a step closer. 'To remind you of your promise. They were all trying to take you away from me.'

'They didn't deserve what you did to them,' he said, fresh tears entering his eyes. 'Csilla, Străbunică, Catrina... they didn't deserve it.'

Nadia snarled, her sharp teeth bared. 'Deserve?' she spat. 'Did *I* deserve what you did to *me*? You betrayed me over and over again. You took away my one real chance to be happy in this miserable existence, and you enjoyed it.'

He stared at her, dumbfounded by her outburst. 'What?' he asked numbly, his hands trembling.

'You enjoyed destroying Freiderick.'

'I didn't enjoy it,' he argued.

'Liar,' she shouted. 'You revelled in his death because I was to marry him. You were jealous and convinced me my feelings for him were false. I delivered him to you because you *promised* me, and I watched you take his life, believing you.'

Alex's heart was breaking inside him as he stared at her, seeing the hurt in her eyes; something he hadn't seen in a very long time.

She took another step until she stood in front of him, her eyes burning with vengeance. 'You betrayed me, again and again. You betrayed *us*. You left my side too many times and pushed me aside for another, when you would never have me do the same.'

She leaned in closer until her face was inches from his, her breath hot against his face. 'So tell me, Brother Dearest, why I should *ever* let *you* be happy without me?'

He stared at her, momentarily unable to process what she'd said. 'This was all a game to you?' he asked finally, his voice trembling with shock and disbelief.

'You left me after Csilla's death, ignored me and punished me for an act you were more than compliant in. You let the Others lock me away,' she hissed against his face. 'You let the Others take me away when you could have stopped them. I begged you to, and you ignored me. They didn't lock you away for killing Freiderick, did they? I wouldn't let them. I fought for you, because you promised me we would never be apart.'

Nausea overwhelmed him as he stared into those eyes that blazed with hatred. He found himself unable to speak.

'Our blood made us power incarnate, Alex,' she said, her words harsh. 'Not even the Others would ever dare argue against us. You told me that yourself. You relished in the power we had. One word from you and they would never have punished me the way they did. But you said *nothing*,' she snarled. 'They locked me away like an animal, leaving me to scream and scream in the darkness, terrified and alone, starved of blood for years until I wasted away into nothing more than a shell. They made me suffer.'

'I was not without suffering,' he whispered, remembering all too clearly the look in her eyes as the Others had dragged her away; her screams haunted him still.

She laughed then. 'Why? Because you had to live without my blood? That was *your* choice, Alex, and you chose to betray me. Did you think I could *ever* let you forget that?'

'So all of this was about your retribution?' he asked incredulously.

'I gave you one more chance after they released me,' she gritted. 'While we travelled, I almost believed I had you back, but then we came here and your interest in that pathetic excuse for a woman once more diverted your attentions.'

'Catrina was innocent,' he argued.

'So was I once,' she snarled, her eyes filled with contempt. 'I even relinquished that in order to protect you. From that very first meeting, you were quite taken with pretty little Catrina. So it amused me to twist the situation into a challenge. One that you were more than eager to take me up on. The prize was me, after all.'

The air suddenly felt too thick to breathe. 'No,' he murmured, too many memories and conversations flooding his mind.

Desperate to get away, Alex pushed Nadia aside and stood from his seat.

She snatched hold of his arm, her sharp nails gripping the skin. 'Where are you going?' she snapped.

'I need some air,' he protested, trying to pull his arm away.

'You're weak, Alex Demeter,' she hissed, pushing him hard and making him stagger backwards. 'Pathetic and weak,' she sneered. 'You won't even take my body and blood when I surrender them to you.'

Tears filled his eyes, his stomach knotting inside him with the pain of her words and actions. 'You're my sister, for God's sake.'

'No, I'm not, Alex. I'm your *equal*, the other half of you.' Her words were harsh and her vindictive gaze still bore through him, watching the tears roll down his face. 'We are one, you and I, no matter how you argue against it. My blood is your blood. I belong to you, as you do to me, for *all* time.'

She stepped forward, her lips twisting into a smile when he backed away from her.

'That's why the Others fear us,' she continued. 'They fear the power we have, because we have each other. They know what we're capable of.' She sneered at the memories. 'Why do you think old granny dearest tried to turn you against me? She tried to take you away from me,' she screamed. 'Can't you see that?'

Alex wretched at the memory, his tears falling faster. 'You didn't have to do what you did, Nadia. She didn't deserve that.' He stared at his sister, still seeing the mania behind her green gaze that had been there that night; he could still hear those agonised screams as the flames had burnt his elder's skin.

'What you did to her was wicked, it was—'

'It was necessary,' she said cruelly, no feeling to her voice. 'I did it for you, for *us*,' she said sarcastically. 'Because you belong to me,' she screamed, making him flinch. 'You always have, you always will. You're my twin, my brother, my lover. You have been mine since the moment we were conceived and will forever be so.'

She crossed the room towards him, amused at how he shied away from her. 'And when I want you, I take you,' she purred, her eyes glowing with hate. 'And you have never tried to stop me, because you are *weak*.'

Without warning, she grasped his arms and threw him towards the sofa violently. He toppled back against it, unsteady.

In a flash of movement, she climbed on top of him, pinning him to the spot.

He struggled against her, but she was too powerful, driven by her hate and anger.

'Nadia, please don't do this,' he pleaded.

She tore at her wrist, ripping the delicate skin. Blood beaded along the wound and she pressed it to his lips, which he held firmly closed.

'Drink it,' she screamed. 'It's the only thing you have ever truly wanted, even above me. Take it all and be done with it.'

He struggled against her, yet her strength and

delirium made her too strong.

'Drink it,' she snarled. 'Give in to it, Alex, and end your thirst.' She pushed her wrist harder against his closed lips.

He tried to fight her, but her power was too great and he was unable to stop her as she twisted her wrist against his mouth, forcing his lips open. Against his will, he felt her blood trickle onto his tongue, the sweet liquid raising that old flame within him.

She pulled her wrist away only once she was satisfied that enough of her blood had been imbibed. She lowered her mouth to his throat, biting down hard.

He cried out, trying to stop her, yet she clawed at his arms and hands with her sharp nails.

He froze as her lips softened against his skin and he realised she was kissing his neck.

Her hands caressed his body as he tried to push her away, but his efforts were futile against her strength, made more indomitable by her delusion.

'You love me, Alex, I know you do,' she cried, as she grabbed his hands and forced him to touch her breasts.

He struggled still, but she wouldn't let him go as she kissed his mouth hard.

'I know you love me,' she added, continuing to make him caress her breasts. 'This body... my blood is all you've ever wanted. Take it. Promise me we will never be apart again. Promise me you will never leave me. Promise me,' she screamed.

'No, Nadia, I won't,' he cried out, tears breaking through.

Her eyes burned with anger. She snarled and gripped his hair tightly in her hand, pulling it at the roots and forcing his head to one side.

With a vicious snarl, she bit hard into his throat, ignoring his pained cries.

'You betrayed me, Alex,' she said, her voice sounding as cold and ruthless in his mind as it would have if she had spoken the words aloud. *'You promised me everything would be forgotten. That it was in the past. You promised you would never speak of it ever again.'*

Desperately, he pushed against her as she drank from him.

'You betrayed yourself, Nadia,' he answered out loud, not willing to give in and play her games. 'I wanted to believe my sister was still in there somewhere. I believed I could bring you back. I didn't want this. These games... too many people have been hurt. You've killed innocent people.'

He needed to be honest with himself for once in his immortal life, no matter how much it hurt; his beloved sister was beyond help. He'd known it for a very long time, he just hadn't wanted to face the horrid truth. She was a monster of his own making, a tainted soul driven mad by the corruption of their own forbidden bloodlust.

Nadia sat back and laughed, that haunting maniacal laugh he'd heard so many times that chilled him to the core. His blood glistened on her lips and teeth.

'And you had no part in all this whatsoever, did you, Brother Dearest?' she sneered, staring down at him.

'I know the wrongs I've committed,' he said sadly, knowing he could never put right the damage he and his sister had caused.

'But I begged you to stop,' he added, desperation in his voice. 'I begged you to leave Jason alone. He didn't need to die.'

'He wanted me,' she hissed, no remorse in her voice. She fixed him with a withering glare as she climbed off of him. 'We both know what happens to men who want me, Alex, don't we?' she mocked, her dark stare vindictive as she looked down at him.

He sat up on the sofa, holding the wound on his neck until he was certain the bleeding had stopped. 'You've held that against me all this time,' he said, hurt by her revelations.

'You killed him,' she screamed, making him flinch.

'For you, damn it,' he shouted back, angry that she would dare to pin everything on him. 'Freiderick was willing to disgrace you, or have you forgotten that? You brought him to me that night. You facilitated the entire situation for your own ends.'

'Because you swore you and I would never be apart,' she screeched angrily, the betrayal evident in her voice. 'You promised you would never leave my side, but you did. After Csilla's death you left me and ignored me for years, punishing me for an act you were wholly complicit in,' she screamed.

'I was wrong, I admit that,' he conceded, knowing that had he never taken his sister's blood or made that promise, they would not be where they were now. 'I never intended to betray you.'

'But you did,' she spat. 'The first opportunity you got, you fled.'

She glared at him, her eyes blazing with hate. 'Your promises are not worth shit. You destroyed Freiderick for your own gain, not mine.'

Alex shook his head. 'I only wanted you to be happy and I knew you wouldn't be with him. You knew it in the end when he so easily revealed your transgressions. He would have seen your place in polite society destroyed, just to satisfy his own ego. He was no gentleman and not fit to marry you.'

Nadia snarled. 'And no other ever was, either. I was my brother's whore as far as anyone else was concerned, whether they voiced their opinions or not.'

'I never meant to hurt you,' he soothed.

'How gallant of you,' she sneered. 'Surprising how that gallantry can hide so many sins. All men betray eventually. You betrayed me over and over again, and then you deserted me,' she hissed. 'For a human, of all things,' she added, disgust in her voice.

Alex stood from the sofa, his anger building. 'Catrina has nothing to do with this,' he warned.

Nadia laughed, the sound hollow. 'She took

you away from me,' she accused.

Alex sighed. 'She's innocent in all this. This was *your* game, Nadia. *You* set it in motion, and for once you lost. What you did to her was unforgivable.'

Nadia smiled, her sharp incisors glistening. 'She was in the way,' she hissed. 'I should have done more to destroy that face. You would have forgotten her in time. You know that as well as I do. A couple of hundred years and you wouldn't have remembered her name.'

He shook his head. 'You're wrong,' he said adamantly. 'I love her.'

'You loved *me* once,' she screamed. 'And yet here we are. Your promises and pledges mean nothing. You're a traitor, nothing more. You'll get bored, you know you will. You always did. Forever is a long time, my love. She can't captivate you or excite you like I can,' she purred. 'She simply isn't enough for you. Even when you knew you were falling for her you kept coming back to *me*.' Her voice mocked him. It made fun of his feelings.

Alex fought back. 'Say what you will, Nadia, but she has a part of me you will never have.'

'I have *all* of you,' she seethed.

'You only think you do,' he countered. 'But you relinquished your right to my heart a long time ago. You'd willingly hurt me every chance you had in order to get your own way, to exact your twisted sense of retribution. You only care for yourself and your deluded fantasies. You corrupt people for your own amusement, to fill the empty void your hate and jealousy have left behind. Catrina is the most selfless person I have ever known, the most caring and beautiful person, both inside *and* out. Even your twisted punishments couldn't take that away from her. She doesn't enjoy destroying people like you do.'

If he'd known any better he would have thought he saw Nadia flinch. But he knew his sister better than that; she didn't bow down to anyone. They bowed down to her.

Her top lip quivered with the threat of another snarl.

Alex glared back, unwilling to back down. 'I tried so hard to help you,' he said sadly. 'I'll admit my faults and my hand in creating what you have become. But too often I tried to help you and failed.'

'Liar,' she screamed. 'You merely wallowed in your own self-pity at losing what you craved the most.' Her gaze darkened once more. 'Surprising what you miss when your brother has you locked away like a wild animal.'

'I did what I felt was right,' he confessed.

'You did what was best for *you*,' she sneered. 'Poor tragic Alex, having to do such a thing to his vile and evil sister.'

She leaned closer towards him, her gaze full of hatred. 'Did you enjoy being the centre of attention while I rotted in that hole? How did it feel to have the family pander to your grief and sadness? Boo hoo, poor little Alex, how tormented he is,' she growled, slapping him hard across the face.

His cheek stinging, his anger surged and Alex retaliated, pushing Nadia hard, sending her crashing into the coffee table.

She sat herself up, brushing her black hair from her face as she glared up at him.

'You're a pathetic excuse of a man, Alex Demeter. You're nothing without me and you know it. You can deny it to yourself as much as you like, but without me at your side you're a mess. You need my blood, you always did, and without it you will not remain good and noble for long. You'll become the monster you fear in me.'

Chapter 50

Slowly, Nadia got to her feet.

'Truth hurts, does it?' she hissed, each word filled with malice.

'Enough, sister,' Alex demanded.

She glared at him, no compassion in her eyes. 'You don't get to tell me what to do,' she spat. 'You relinquished that right when you betrayed me.'

'You're wrong,' he said firmly. 'You betrayed yourself. I'm not faultless, but I was willing to admit my wrongdoings, whereas you have spent a lifetime manipulating and betraying everyone you ever loved or held dear, even yourself. You became a monster, Nadia, one of my own making, I do not deny that. But everything you did, every wicked deed you committed, you committed out of spite and malice, trying to hurt me in any way you could, no matter who got in the way. You say it was because you loved me, but you don't know the true meaning of the word. You corrupt and destroy everything you touch. You blame me for everything, yet it was *you* who committed every indiscretion and malicious act. You did it all because you *enjoyed* it.'

His words hit her hard; the darkness vanished from her gaze for a brief second.

She sneered. 'You always were good at playing the innocent one, weren't you?' she snarled, her words filled with malice. 'Always the one with the right words to talk himself out of whatever situation he found himself in.'

'I'm not innocent, Nadia, nor do I pretend to be. I admit to my sins and repent them as much as I am able.'

'Even me?' she asked gently. 'Would you repent me?'

Alex stared at her, instantly unsure of the change in her tone.

'I'm your sister, your twin,' she soothed. 'I'm the only one who truly understands you and you know it. You admit yourself that you have tried to live without me, yet never could. You are nothing without me.'

'You destroy everything, Nadia, you always have. What we shared was an illusion, nothing more.'

'No, it wasn't,' she purred, her words soft and enticing. 'You know it wasn't. What we shared was the most real thing in the world. No one understood it, no one could stop it, not even you. We're one, you and I.'

She raised her fingers to his cheek. 'You cannot destroy what we are, Alex,' she whispered. 'No one can.'

He stared into her emerald eyes, her gaze shattering any courage he had. Something inside him told him her words were true, no matter how much he tried to deny it.

She stepped closer, her breath hot against his lips. 'You're mine, as I'm yours, my love. Forever.'

She placed her hands on his chest and he instantly felt powerless as he stared into her haunting green gaze that mimicked his own. All the feelings from the past returned to him in an instant; every thought, every memory, every need and desire returned to haunt him all at once, leaving him weak with pain and guilt.

Nadia smiled against his lips.

He let his guard fall too easily.

She pushed him violently and he fell back onto the floor.

'I'll take you any time I damn well need to, Alex,' she screamed. 'You can't stop me. You never have and you never will. You are *mine*, for *all* time.'

He snarled at her, angry at himself for falling for her sultry seduction once more. He refused to allow her words to be true; he was no longer willing to allow her free reign over his life.

He got to his feet and lunged at her, grabbing hold of her arms. She struggled against him, trying violently to free herself from his grip.

He tried to maintain his hold on her to keep her still, yet she refused to let him.

Nadia tore at Alex with her nails, slashing him across the face and neck, yet still he refused to let her go.

In retaliation, she pulled him to her and bit him hard on the shoulder.

Hissing in pain, he pushed her away, holding the wound as it healed.

She snarled, striking out at him again.

He grabbed her wrists firmly.

'Let me go,' she screamed, the hysteria in her voice confirming to him that she was beyond his help now; she could never go back to the girl Alex had grown up with, ever.

'Stop this madness, sister,' he pleaded with her, trying hard to keep his hold on her as she fought against him.

She hissed, her eyes blazing with madness. 'You're *mine*,' she screeched, not listening to his words. 'Mine!'

Repulsed by this creature who had once been his sister, Alex pushed her away, instantly unable to bear touching her.

She stumbled backwards against the mantle, her gaze never leaving his.

Straightening herself, she took a step back towards him, her eyes filled with insanity.

Alex leapt at her, knocking her to the floor.

Nadia snarled, struggling against him as he straddled her, pinning her to the floor.

Without thinking, he grabbed the iron poker

from the hearth, holding it before her as a threat.

She glared at him, intense hatred and anger raging in her emerald eyes. 'You think you're any better than I am, my lord?' she hissed, her words cold and chilling. 'You're no more innocent than I am. My blood runs through your veins, as yours does through mine. I sustain you, Alex Demeter. I'll never let you have any real peace. You're mine, for *all* time.'

Her words destroyed every ounce of guilt he had left. They stirred his anger, hate, love, and dignity. They stirred in him all the memories of what she had put him through over the centuries.

He raised the poker above his head.

It would end, now.

With a loud cry of anger and remorse, Alex drove the poker into Nadia's chest, his knuckles white as they gripped the iron rod tightly.

She screamed as the blood sprayed across his face and hands, her cries leaving his body trembling; almost as if he could feel her pain.

Alex watched the colour drain from her face. He saw the darkness fade from her green eyes. He witnessed her skin become almost translucent as the blood poured from her wound.

His sister clawed at him with her nails, her blood gurgling in her throat as she tried to speak to him, but no words left her lips; at least nothing coherent.

The blood seeped from her chest, staining the carpet beneath her.

Her skin colour faded completely until it was as

white as paper. Her face grew thin until the cheekbones protruded through the skin, her lips pulling back to expose her sharp teeth. Her once glossy hair became wispy and grey.

Nadia's scream was piercing, the sound growing louder until Alex was forced to cover his ears.

It was an unholy sound of contempt.

It was an eternal scream of defiance.

Her body became that of a skeletal corpse, the skin thinning over the bone.

Her body went limp.

Nadia was dead.

Chapter 51

The room fell silent, only the crackling of the flames in the grate disturbing the silence.

Alex cowered on the floor, his hands still over his ears.

He stared down.

Guilt tugged at his soul as he stared at Nadia's body. He glared at the blood that stained the carpet.

His sister's blood.

The smell made him nauseous.

He slowly picked himself up from the floor, every movement feeling somehow surreal.

He took hold of the poker. With a deep breath, he pulled it effortlessly from his sister's chest, dropping it on the floor by his feet.

Alex's stomach tightened painfully as he held on to his own grief, swallowing the lump of emotion that lodged itself in his throat, staring down at his bloodied hands.

He'd killed his own sister.

The sense of loss hit him hard. She was dead,

by his own hands; he'd never be with her ever again.

Guilt surged through him relentlessly, making him weak. He'd done this to her; he'd made her into the monster she'd become. He was to blame for it all, and she had suffered for it.

He could never hope to forgive himself for that. Ever.

Alex sat down in the armchair and stared at his bloodied hands. He closed his eyes, allowing every thought and memory to attack his mind; he didn't deserve peace.

The reality of his actions suddenly overwhelmed him, and he wretched as he let go of his grief, his tears flowing as he sobbed, broken, wrapping his arms around himself, mourning the loss of his sister.

The grief was crushing, his heart aching for his twin whom he would never see again.

He'd watched the life drain from her body, making her suffer. He felt sick with his guilt.

Fuelled by a morbid desperation to look upon his sister's face, he glanced over towards her body.

He shivered as he looked at her pale and skeletal face; it was a sight he knew would haunt him forever.

He said a silent prayer for his sister. He prayed for her immortal soul.

He prayed she would finally find peace.

Chapter 52

Alex heaved the suitcase onto the Demeter's doorstep and leant against the doorframe.

The darkness of the night was eerily silent. He shivered, though he suspected it had nothing to do with the icy air.

He stared down at his hands; he'd scrubbed them clean though he was certain he could still see his sister's blood glistening on his skin.

He doubted he'd ever be free of that image.

Every part of him ached; the shock and pain of the night's events weighed heavy, like a nightmare he could never wake from.

Less than four hours ago, his sister had been alive. Now, she lay dead in the house behind him; destroyed by him for the second time. He'd created the monster she'd become; he'd made promises he couldn't keep, betrayed her and turned his back on her when she'd needed him the most.

He wiped the tears from his eyes. The phone call to his parents had been the hardest thing of all;

the sound of his mother's agonised cries had torn his resolve to pieces, her heartbroken sobs at the loss of her child chilling him to the bone.

He knew he deserved to be haunted by that sound for the rest of his immortal life.

He didn't deserve their forgiveness any more than he had deserved his sister's.

Yes, Nadia had been beyond help. It was doubtful that even the Others could have helped her.

His father's last tearful words to him had assured Alex that no one blamed him for what had taken place.

Alex wished he could stop blaming himself.

With a sigh, he picked up the suitcase and carried it to his car. He added the case to the boot with all his other cases and belongings before glancing up at the ancient house before him.

He wouldn't miss the place. To much had transpired within its walls over the last few weeks to be remembered with fondness; two friends had been left to rot in the basement, while his sister had tortured and mutilated the woman he loved. Plots had been devised and innocent lives had been destroyed.

He'd relived his darkest moments.

Taking a deep breath, he closed the boot, glancing around him. A cat ran across the empty street at the sudden disturbance to the silence; the remainder of the world around him remained shrouded in hushed darkness.

Alex stared across the street at Lola's house.

RETRIBUTION DARKENED

All the lights were out and he sincerely hoped they would remain that way until morning, allowing the poor woman some much-needed rest after her mental torture at the hands of his sister. It had taken a lot of mental strength to influence Lola's mind back to where it had been before Nadia had interfered with her thoughts and dreams; he was unsure how successful he would be in the long run.

Only time would tell.

Alex turned back to the house and approached the front door.

He stared at it for a long moment before finally grasping the handle and pulling it closed for the last time; he'd never return to this place. It was his sister's tomb.

He'd only grabbed his clothing and a few other things; the rest of the house would remain as it was. His sister's things remained untouched; he couldn't bring himself to even look at them. Everything from her clothes to her tiniest trinkets would remain in the house.

Alex sighed. There would be much to organise over the next few hours. His parents would arrange the transport of Nadia's body back to Romania so she could be put to rest in the family crypt in Vallakia.

He'd also need to organise the removal of the bodies from the cellar, which would take a much more detailed approach; he was thankful to those of his kind who could arrange such things without question.

There was nothing he could do for those who he did not know, but for Jason and Camilla, Alex would ensure they could be found, in time, allowing their families some form of closure; as much as he could offer them anyway.

Once more he glanced at Lola's home, saddened that she'd be the recipient of such devastating news at some point in the future; Jason had been like a brother to her and his loss was something he wished he could spare her from.

With a heavy sigh, he turned back to the car, taking one more look at the house before him. He'd felt so suffocated within its walls over the last few weeks, he should have been relieved to be walking away.

Instead, all he felt was empty.

Alex opened the door to the car and climbed in, starting the engine.

The headlights illuminated the low fence that bordered the drive; he stared at the large crow that sat on the weathered wood, its presence in the dead of night unsettling.

The ink-black bird glared at him, the light from the car reflected in its beady eyes.

With a low growl, Alex stared at the bird, mentally ordering it to leave him be.

The creature ignored him.

Bemused, Alex tried again; he'd never known the creatures to resist his mental coercion before.

The crow remained resolute on the fence, lifting

its head and cawing loudly.

Alex flinched, the sound unnerving; it was almost as if the bird were laughing at him.

With a mumbled curse, he put the car in gear and pulled away from the house, glaring at the bird as he passed.

As he drove slowly along the street, he dared a glance in the rear-view mirror.

The crow was still staring at him.

Darkness Falls...

Lightning flooded the grand hall with an eerie glow, before darkness engulfed it once more, the only reprieve from the suffocating shadows being the soft light of the sconces on the walls. No fire burnt in the great stone fireplace.

The figure moved in the darkness, her form lithe as she entered the ancient building from the onslaught of rain outside.

She paused in the doorway, her thin dress soaking wet. Water pooled around her bare feet as it dripped from her wretched form.

The hall was illuminated momentarily by the storm outside as the thunder roared through the ancient walls.

She brushed her long wet hair away from her face, strands clinging to her wet skin like tendrils of black ink.

She stared at the familiar stone crow that stood upon its pedestal, watching over all with its eyes set with deep-red rubies that glowed as the lightning flashed once again.

She reached out to the inanimate creature. Her long thin fingers stroked the solid head, feeling every engraved feather as if they were real.

Her green eyes gleamed in the darkness of Vallakia's walls as she bit her lip with anticipation, blood beading on the broken skin.

She gazed into the deep-red glow of the stone crow's eyes, smiling as if something she saw amused her.

The lightning flashed as she laughed, the sound lost to the crash of thunder...

The story concludes in

DARK CHILD

Where to begin...

'Don't you dare walk away from me, Alex.'

Alex Demeter stopped sharply on the corner of the street, turning to face the young woman as she caught up with him. Her dark hair blew out behind her like an inky veil, her fists clenched at her sides in anger.

She'd had to push herself to keep up with him as he walked, that much was obvious. Her breathing was laboured, her cheeks flushed; it was unnatural.

He glared at her intently, his deep-green gaze holding hers.

'I cannot do what you ask of me, Kia,' he said, putting emphasis on every word. 'I'm sorry,' he added, looking away.

The night air was cold and fresh around him and he stared across the street at the old bakery in Wiltham Village, its shop front unchanged in the three years he'd been gone from the small London borough.

Kia stared at him hard, a dark shadow in her

eyes.

'Why not?' she demanded childishly. 'Why do you deny me a privilege you know to be mine? You've already taken my blood. You desired it in that instant and I know you still do.'

Alex took a deep breath and closed his eyes, pained by memories that returned to him as clear as the day each event had happened.

There was that word again: desire. That one word didn't help his anger or his pain.

He didn't want to think about what that word had driven him to do in the past.

Kia grasped his arm, forcing him to face her. 'If I never ask another thing of you, I ask you this. Please do this one thing for me. *Please.*'

Tears filled her eyes. 'Please,' she sniffed. 'Don't make me beg.' Desperation filled her voice as she tugged at his shirt.

He stared at her for moment, knowing that what she was asking was impossible.

After a long minute, he shook his head. 'I cannot do it to you,' he breathed.

'But you wanted to,' she screamed at him, pushing him away.

'I wanted no such thing,' he retaliated angrily, grabbing her by the wrists and holding them firmly with an inhuman strength.

He glared at her until she could no longer stare into his ancient eyes.

'Were you not crying as I explained the death to

you?' he asked. 'You were crying for your mortality. You were scared of *dying*, Kia.'

'No, I was not,' she protested, tears falling over her cheeks.

'What about as I fed from you?' he asked sadly. 'You were in agony and shock. You felt death as close as I am to you now. You were scared and closed up on that instinct. A *human* instinct.'

'It was not,' she shouted, her voice breaking with her tears.

'Kia, that experience frightened me.' He took her face in his hands, staring into those eyes that mocked his own. 'Your blood is far more precious to you than it is to me. You must forget what has happened,' he pressed. 'You *must*, because I cannot and will not do it.'

Kia pulled away from him angrily, only her eyes betraying her sorrow.

She wiped the tears from her cheeks. With one last withering glare, she pushed past him and ran along the street, disappearing into the shadows.

Alex sighed heavily, running his fingers through his black hair.

Why was this happening to him? The question rewound itself constantly in his head, as it had since the first day he'd set eyes on her.

How long ago that seemed now, yet in reality had been no more than a few days. He knew he should go after her; she was a stranger here and would no doubt get herself lost. But she'd tried his patience enough already and he wasn't in the mood for another confrontation.

Stuffing his hands into the pockets of his jeans, he strolled along the street, remembering his way easily through the dark old town.

In the stillness of the night, Wiltham Village felt like was it frozen in time, with its ancient houses, cobbled streets and foreboding church that towered above its cold and desolate graveyard. The frost glistened on those old stones tonight, the moonlight picking out the delicate crystals.

It all seemed as if he had never left.

Turning another corner, Alex found himself facing his family home, tendrils of dread clawing at him, the sensation almost painful.

There were far too many memories here and very few of them were welcome.

He'd been crazy to return.

Forcing his gaze away from the ancient building, he stared across the street at the familiar house, thinking on its occupant who had been at the very centre of Nadia's malicious games.

He stood there, staring at the Victorian mid-terrace. The house looked just the same as it had when he'd left, a gentle light obvious from within.

Taking a deep breath, Alex crossed the street, wanting to be away from the desolate facade of his family home.

He approached the front door of the familiar house, noting the rubbish bags piled in the far corner of the small concrete front yard.

Without another thought, he rang the doorbell and waited.

A silhouette soon appeared behind the frosted glass in the door.

The door opened slowly.

Alex smiled. 'Hello, Matt.'